A Knife Ill-Used

Cynthia Faudin was an eminent and well-known scholar at Oxford. Her married life was happy, her husband rich and her twin children grown-up. But one morning in Oxford she met an old acquaintance which led to a series of unexpected and dramatic incidents, culminating in two suspicious deaths.

Detective Chief Inspector Tansey of the Thames Valley Police investigates. A breakthrough leads Tansey to suspect that the roots of the matter lie deep in Mrs Faudin's past.

Death's Long Shadow

A relatively unknown but prestigious college in the centre of Oxford is bombed, but there are no indications that terrorists are involved. Chief Inspector Tansey and Sergeant Abbott of the Thames Valley Police Force investigate.

Tansey, with his usual acumen integrates himself into college life and interviews undergraduates and dons. But the investigation is fraught with danger as the unexpected conclusion turns dramatic.

JOHN PENN

A Knife Ill-Used

Death's Long Shadow

Diamond Books

An Imprint of HarperCollins*Publishers*

77–85 Fulham Palace Road

Hammersmith, London W6 8JB

This Diamond Crime Two-In-One edition
published 1994

A Knife Ill-Used © John Penn 1991

Death's Long Shadow © John Penn 1991

The Author asserts the moral right to
be identified as the author of this work

ISBN 0261 66459-X

Cover photography by Monique Le Luhandre

Printed in Great Britain

A Knife Ill-Used

This book is fiction. All the characters and incidents in it are entirely imaginary.

Part One

CHAPTER 1

It was a blustery spring day and, although it was during the Easter vacation, Oxford seemed more crowded than ever, obviously because of an early influx of tourists. Cynthia Faudin, battling her way through a group of earnest Japanese who were occupying the entire pavement as they stared in seeming awe through the wrought-iron gates of Trinity College, thought that the City hadn't improved since she had been an undergraduate.

She was glad that the College of which she was now Principal was some distance from the centre of the town and, being red-brick and modern, did not attract many sightseers. It might be pleasant to have been elected Dean of Christ Church, for example, but such an appointment would have its disadvantages. And her own College had an excellent and growing reputation for its academic achievements, and for the Shakespearean play that was produced in its own gardens each Trinity Term. That had been one of her many ideas, and she was proud of the results.

In spite of all this, it would be wrong to suggest that Cynthia Faudin was a contented woman. She was happy enough with what she had achieved so far, but there were still several goals she had not yet attained, though she had every intention of doing so. As she passed Balliol lodge and turned right towards St Giles', she thought with some irritation of the meeting, just over, that had brought her from Longacres, her home in the Cotswolds, into Oxford.

The Vice-Chancellor of the University, who in Cynthia's opinion was prejudiced against her because she was a woman, had not given her a fair hearing. When she had said that her College was no different from any other, and that she was certain that there was little, if any, abuse of hard drugs among her undergraduates—or her senior members, for that matter—he had made light of her conviction. He hadn't quite called her a liar but, airing his knowledge—he had recently visited the University of California—he had stated categorically that the use of heroin and crack was on the increase among all Members of the University. He wanted to know what the Heads of Colleges intended to do about it. Stupid old fool, Cynthia thought.

The next moment she had walked straight into a woman who had suddenly stopped in front of her, nearly knocking her over. 'I'm so sorry,' she said automatically, though the collision had not been her fault.

'Cynthia—my dear! It *is* Cynthia Courtland, isn't it?'

Cynthia Faudin stepped back in surprise, and smiled feebly. To her knowledge she had never before seen the woman who was addressing her by her maiden name, but obviously it was someone who had known her a long time ago. She had been Cynthia Faudin now for thirty-odd years.

'You don't recognize me, do you, Cynthia?'

'I'm terribly sorry.' Again Cynthia apologized.

'I'm Pauline Brune. You must remember me.'

Cynthia bit her tongue to block the surprised exclamation she had nearly uttered. 'Pauline! But of course I remember you,' she said, trying to sound pleased and even affectionate, 'but it's been such ages. I hate to think how long.'

'Well, time's been kind to you, Cynthia. You look wonderful! I'd have known you anywhere. You haven't changed in the least—not like me.'

For once Cynthia Faudin, who prided herself on her ability to cope with any situation, could think of no reply. Considering that she had been twelve and Pauline seventeen when they had last met, it was absurd to suggest that they hadn't changed—though in her case, Cynthia thought, it had been mostly for the better. Her hideous school uniform and the inferior clothes that she had been forced to wear in the holidays until she grew out of them were just memories of the past, as was her then straggly hair. Now she wore designer garments, and was always perfectly groomed. Few realized that she was over fifty.

The same could not be said for Pauline. Pauline Brune—she had said her name was still Brune, so she probably hadn't been married—looked her sixty years, or more. Her face was lined and bare of make-up. She wore a thin, unfashionable suit and a nylon sweater that didn't match it. She shivered as the wind whipped around the Martyrs' Memorial, sending a flurry of leaves along the pavement.

'Let's go and have a coffee,' Pauline said.

Cynthia hesitated. In fact, she had no genuine excuse with which to refuse. Derek was in London at some directors' meeting; even at seventy-three he still sat on several boards. She would be alone at Longacres, apart from the staff, and had no reason to hurry home, except that she had been looking forward to a peaceful lunch, a discussion with Mrs May, her most efficient housekeeper, and then a long afternoon working on her current book. But, even so, she still had time to have coffee with Pauline.

'All right,' she said a little reluctantly, hoping that she didn't sound ungracious. 'Where shall we go?'

'There's a little place in Ship Street. I have lunch there sometimes on my day off.'

'Your day off?'

'I'm the housekeeper-companion to an elderly lady—or that's the theory. In fact, I'm a dogsbody. It's fetch this and fetch that, do this and do that. She spends most of the day lying on the sofa with her legs up though there's nothing wrong with her, and she's very little older than I am. The difference between us is that she's got pots of money and I haven't.'

Dodging a young girl pushing a pram, Cynthia murmured something incoherent and vague. What was there to say? She remembered Pauline as one of those individuals who always believed they were hard done by, and clearly she hadn't had the guts to try to change her situation in the intervening years. Suddenly, and for no reason, it was

Cynthia's turn to shiver, and she was glad when they reached the café.

It was a chintzy place that Cynthia wouldn't ordinarily have patronized, though Pauline seemed at home there. She greeted by name a woman in slacks and a brightly-coloured smock whom Cynthia assumed was the owner, and led the way to a table in the window. The café was only half full.

'We'll have coffee—a pot, please—and cakes,' Pauline said to the woman, who had followed them to their seats, and she added to Cynthia, 'The cakes are superb here. All homemade, of course, and the cream is generous. They're very seductive.'

Pauline smiled in a proprietorial manner, as if she were personally responsible for the establishment and its food. 'And now you must tell me about yourself, my dear,' she continued as they settled themselves. 'You're married, I see from your rings. That's a beautiful diamond. He must be a rich man.'

Cynthia restrained a temptation to put her hands under the table. She told herself that she was being stupid to resent Pauline's probing. It was natural that she should be curious and there was no harm in it.

'Yes, I'm married,' she said, 'to someone called Derek Faudin, and I have been for some long time. Our two children are grown-up by now.'

'Two children? Not twins, like—?'

'Yes. A boy and a girl.'

'Just like you and poor Colin. I suppose it runs in your family. How fascinating! Do you have grandchildren?'

'No. Neither of ours is married yet.'

'That's for the future then, but I must admit, Cynthia—'

The arrival of the coffee and cakes interrupted Pauline. With a gesture she indicated that the pot should be put in front of her, as hostess. Cynthia found herself wondering if her companion would be as eager to seize the bill.

The coffee poured and the cakes chosen, Pauline returned to her theme. 'I must admit, Cynthia, I'm surprised you should have become a contented housewife. You were such a bright child, far brighter than poor Colin, though of course your dear father would never have admitted that. But he was one of the old school, wasn't he? Your papa, I mean. He thought that males were superior mortals—vastly superior to females—and should be educated accordingly.'

Cynthia put down her coffee cup. Her hand was shaking, and she couldn't drink without spilling the liquid. She steadied herself and managed to smile.

'Oh yes, my father was a man of his generation, as you say, Pauline. By present standards, his ideas about women were prehistoric.'

'A pity!' Pauline nodded sympathetically. 'More coffee?' She lifted the pot.

'No, thanks.'

'You know, I always visualized you as the headmistress of one of our famous girls' schools—Cheltenham, perhaps, or Benenden.'

'You were wrong. I never wanted to be a schoolmistress. Actually, I became a don.' Cynthia hesitated. She didn't want to boast, but she was proud of her career and a little surprised that the name Cynthia Faudin apparently meant nothing to Pauline. She said, 'I'm the Principal of St Saviour's College now.'

'My dear, how wonderful! But I'm not really surprised. You were always so clever and—and capable, even as a child, and of course you were fortunate to get such an excellent education, in spite of everything. One can't get anywhere these days without qualifications, but I don't need to tell *you* that.'

'They're certainly essential in the academic world,' Cynthia agreed, and covertly glanced at her watch.

She wanted to leave. The irritation caused by her earlier meeting with the Vice-Chancellor was being exacerbated by Pauline's chatter, and she was beginning to get a headache. She decided to plead another engagement. Then Pauline helped herself to a second cream cake, so that it became impossible to stand up without seeming churlish.

'And for any worthwhile job,' Pauline said. 'I've found

that out to my cost. I've absolutely no training, and look what's become of me. I'm a servant, Cynthia, badly paid and treated like dirt, not only by my mistress but also by her friends. It's—it's degrading. After all, as you know, my father was a clergyman and if he hadn't died so soon . . . But, well, there you are. I really am pleased that you've become such a success.'

And Pauline did sound genuinely pleased. Cynthia, who was not easily moved, felt sorry for her. Allowing for the fact that Pauline had always been inclined to whine, she didn't doubt that the older woman led a dreadful life in comparison with her own. But there was nothing she could do about it. She could scarcely offer Pauline money.

'Won't you be able to retire soon?' Cynthia asked.

'On my pension?' Pauline laughed. 'My dear, the State pension's a pittance, and I've never had a chance to increase it. What little I did manage to save once upon a time disappeared when I had a nervous breakdown and couldn't work for ages.'

'I—I'm sorry,' said Cynthia.

But by now she had had enough. Her head was aching badly, and it had become unexpectedly hot in the café. She opened her handbag, took out a five-pound note and slipped it under the cake dish. She pushed back her chair.

'Pauline, forgive me, but I have to go. I have a luncheon date,' Cynthia lied. She held out her hand. 'It has been nice meeting you again. All best wishes.'

'Thank you.' Pauline shook the hand being offered to her, but didn't get up. 'Goodbye, Cynthia. The best to you too.'

With a feeling of relief Cynthia Faudin closed the door of the café behind her. It had begun to drizzle and soon her face was damp, and a spider's web of moisture glistened in her hair as she walked into the wind. She could have lowered her head, but chose to hold it upright and take deep breaths of the fresh moist air. Her headache was clearing already.

She felt absurdly elated—almost as if she had escaped from some menace, and indeed she had feared briefly that Pauline Brune's sudden reappearance in her life might prove something of a hazard. But she had been wrong. Pauline had made no attempt to detain her, or to suggest another meeting. She hadn't asked for help or tried to borrow money. All she had done was take up an hour of time that could have been better spent. But in itself that was not important.

Cynthia reached the car park and unlocked her BMW. She got in, fastened her seat-belt, started the engine and waited for the windscreen to clear. Suddenly conscious of how wet she had become, she did her best to dry her face and hair on a handkerchief that was much too small for the purpose. She thought with a spurt of anger that if she hadn't met Pauline she would have reached the car before the rain began, and been almost home by now.

She sighed. She must forget Pauline Brune. There was so much else to consider. Derek's birthday was fast approaching, and that would mean a house full of family and friends for the weekend. She must discuss the food with Mrs May, and the wine with Derek. She still hadn't bought him a present; it was difficult to know what to give a seventy-three-year-old man who could buy whatever he wanted for himself. And she must not neglect her book.

She drove out of Oxford, heading north towards Longacres, her mind divided between the road ahead and the politician whose biography she was writing. But, in spite of her resolution, the occasional thought of Pauline insisted on intruding. This annoyed her. After all, with any luck she would never see or hear from Pauline again. She hadn't asked, and Pauline hadn't said, where she was living, but it was clearly by chance that they had met in Oxford.

An angry hoot from a car which she had overtaken too fast on a curve warned her that she was driving carelessly, so Cynthia slowed and continued more circumspectly, but the BMW ate up the miles. She was soon home, and by then her meeting with Pauline Brune, if not forgotten, no longer troubled her.

Pauline was still in the café. She had decided to have an early lunch before catching the bus to Charlbury. Mrs Kent

would not be pleased at her having been away from the
house for so long, but she didn't care. She would say that
the dentist had been running late with his appointments,
and had kept her waiting. Anyway, it didn't matter;
she would be bidding the old hag goodbye in the near
future.

She smiled to herself as she recalled the events of the
morning. Everything had gone according to plan, and very
satisfactorily. Cynthia had never suspected that their encounter had been other than accidental, or that the answers
to most of the questions put to her were already known, and
she had swallowed all the flattery she had been offered. It
was strange, Pauline thought, that a woman as clever as
Cynthia Faudin, née Courtland, should be such a fool as
not to sense danger.

CHAPTER 2

That evening Cynthia Faudin stood at the french windows
and stared into the sunlit garden of Longacres. Yet again
she admired the smooth lawns, the oak tree more than a
hundred years old, the archway leading to the rose garden,
the distant woods. For as far as she could see the land
around belonged to the Faudins. One day it would belong
to her.

She had come to Longacres over thirty years ago as a
prospective bride. She had been slightly overawed by her
first sight of the manor house, a long sprawling building of
Cotswold stone, with its stabling, its extensive grounds, its
tennis court and swimming pool—and the staff, large
enough to maintain the whole place in ideal order. But she
had been determined not to show her uncertainty, not to
give any sign that she was unaccustomed to such a style of
living. And after her marriage she had soon grown used to
it, first learning to accept Longacres as her home, and then
to love it.

Turning from the windows, Cynthia Faudin went through the beautifully-appointed drawing-room to a smaller sitting-room beyond, which she and Derek normally used when they were alone. Dear Derek, she thought. He was a good and kind husband, if less than wildly exciting, and she had never regretted her decision to marry him.

Her own background had been very different. True, her father's family had been reasonably wealthy and her father had been at Eton before going into business, but somehow over the years the money had slipped away and finally, just before the Second World War in which her father served with some distinction, he and her mother, her brother and Cynthia herself found themselves living in relatively modest circumstances on the Isle of Wight.

Cynthia knew that she had been a most intelligent—and ambitious—child, but in view of her father's determination to make every sacrifice to send her twin brother, Colin, to Eton, there had seemed no prospect that she would be able to complete her higher education. But fate had stepped in, Cynthia reflected, and at the age of twenty-four she had been a young don at St Anne's College, Oxford, though without much money or any influential friends. She had grown up to become moderately attractive, with a good figure and lovely blonde hair. She had had one or two lovers, but she seemed to frighten men of her own age, and nothing had come of these affairs.

But she had been content to wait. She had a precise idea of what she wanted and Derek Faudin, eighteen years older than herself, whom she had met at an Oxford party, had provided the answer. That he was no longer young and was considering marriage to a widow nearer his own age didn't worry her, especially after tactful inquiries had shown that he was rich. He had a splendid home near enough to Oxford to make commuting simple and, though he had no need for a career, he was in fact an able and successful businessman, and a director of several companies. What was more, he had been, and still was, fully prepared to indulge his wife and help to satisfy her own ambitions.

For her part she had fulfilled all her husband's expectations. She had always been affectionate and faithful, seemingly happy with the love he offered her. She had guessed
that Derek, basically modest, had been surprised when she
had agreed to become his wife, and that he had never
realized that the concepts of love and sex played very little
part in her scheme of things.

In any case, she had proved herself to be an excellent
hostess, and Derek could afford efficient staff, so that she
was not burdened with the running of Longacres, and could
pursue her own career. And, above all, he loved her—
though it was always hard for him to show his feelings—
and was clearly proud of her academic achievements, proud
that she should have become the youngest head of an Oxford
College.

But especially she knew that he was proud that she had
given him two children. She smiled a little sourly at the
thought. She had known before the marriage that he had
wanted a family, and she hadn't cheated. She had done her
duty by her husband, and had become pregnant almost at
once; the twins had been born within a year, and she had
made sure that the pregnancy had scarcely interfered with
her work.

But still, Derek had been delighted. He adored the twins.
Her own attitude towards the children was somewhat more
ambivalent. She was certainly no doting mother, but Derek
had not expected her to be so; a well-trained Norland nurse
had been employed as a matter of course to care for them.

Twins they may have been, but Clare and Peter could not
have developed more differently. In principle, remembering
the favouritism that had been shown to her own brother,
Cynthia was inclined to prefer Clare, though Peter was
everything that Clare was not—brilliantly clever, attractive
and ambitious. He had read law and been called to the Bar,
but made no secret of the fact that he soon intended to go
into politics. Cynthia could readily think of him as Foreign
Secretary or even—someday—Prime Minister. He was so
busy, and by now had so little in common with his parents—

especially his mother—that he visited Longacres only on special occasions. One such occasion would be his father's forthcoming birthday party.

Irritably Cynthia went to a corner cabinet. It was early for a drink but, dear God! she needed one. She poured herself a large whisky and added a splash of soda. Bad for the figure, she thought, though at fifty-five she was still a handsome woman. Her hair had retained its natural colour, and her sharp, rather foxy features had changed little with the passing years. But she had to watch her weight. She despised individuals of either sex who let themselves drift into a spreading middle age.

And, she thought, that included daughter Clare, a pretty girl but already growing fat. Clare, unfortunately, seemed to possess no particular talents and, after a number of trivial jobs, had started to work in a friend's antique shop in Buckingham, where she had acquired a small flat.

Cynthia sighed, though it was not in her nature to allow herself to be depressed for long. She dismissed her children from her mind and, surprised to find that her glass was empty, went to the cabinet and poured herself a second whisky. She had much to look forward to, apart from her ultimate ambition: a new term at Oxford in a few weeks' time, the publication of her latest book—a political biography on which she had already received encouraging comment from fellow contemporary historians—the acceptance of an honorary degree from Edinburgh University and, best of all, the fact—known only to herself—that she had received the usual preliminary approach inquiring if she would accept an Honour. She had agreed, naturally, and it was almost certain that after the publication of the next Honours List she would become Dame Cynthia. Nothing could be more pleasing, and it would help towards the eventual crowning of her career—to become the first woman Vice-Chancellor of Oxford University.

Cynthia shrugged. Apart from the staff she was alone in the house and she decided to go to bed early and ask Mrs May to send a tray up to her room later. She was not feeling hungry—merely tired, and still somewhat frustrated by her meeting with Pauline Brune.

A few days later Cynthia and Derek Faudin were dressing in preparation for a dinner-party at a friend's house, when Derek called, 'Telephone for you, darling.'

Cynthia hurried out of the bathroom, wrapped in a huge pink towelling robe and wearing a matching shower cap at a rakish angle. Her face was bereft of make-up, and Derek thought that she looked young and very vulnerable. As always, he wondered at his luck in marrying her.

Some people, including Derek's brother Simon and Simon's wife, Valerie, who had both wanted him to marry Valerie's widowed friend, thought that it had been Cynthia who had been fortunate—and shrewd, but no one could deny that the marriage appeared to be among the happiest. Certainly Derek had always seemed more than content with it. He was a man of medium height, only an inch or two taller than his wife, and invariably well-groomed. His hair was thick, if grey by now, and his figure had remained trim. In addition, he carried with him the assurance of wealth, both inherited and created, so that he was able to take pride in Cynthia's successful career without envy.

'Who is it?' Cynthia asked.

'I don't know. I thought she said her name was Brown. She sounds upset, as if she were crying.'

'Brown?' Cynthia frowned and held out her hand for the receiver. 'Hello. Cynthia Faudin here,' she said crisply.

'Oh, Cynthia!' There was an unmistakable sob on the line. 'This is Pauline. Oh, my dear, I'm sorry to bother you, but I'm in such trouble and I've nowhere to turn.'

'What's happened?'

Cynthia sat down heavily on the bed. It was only three days since she had had coffee with Pauline Brune in Oxford, and she had hoped never to see her again. If the wretched woman was in trouble, it was no concern of hers.

'Please help me, Cynthia. Please!'

'What is it?' Derek was asking anxiously; even from a

distance he had been able to sense the distress coming over the line. 'Is it anything to do with the children? Has there been an accident or is one of them ill?'

'No!' In her confusion Cynthia almost shouted at him.

'You can't mean that, Cyn. You just can't refuse me. I'm desperate.'

'For God's sake!' With an effort Cynthia regained control of her temper; no one but her brother Colin had ever called her Cyn. 'Hang on for a minute, Pauline. I'm talking to my husband.' She put her hand over the mouthpiece. 'Derek, put that dress down,' she ordered. 'You look absurd.'

'Sorry.' Derek, who had whisked Cynthia's dress from the bed to prevent her sitting on it, was vaguely holding it in front of him. He arranged it carefully over the back of a chair, and repeated, 'What is it?'

'An—an old friend of mine. I'll tell you later.' Cynthia returned her attention to the phone. 'Now, Pauline, what's the matter? We're going out to dinner, so please be quick.'

'Of course if you don't care what becomes of me—'

'Pauline! What on earth has happened? I can't help you unless I know.' The answer was a loud sob. 'Is it money?' Cynthia asked tentatively.

'I—I've been sacked like—like a common servant, told to leave first thing in the morning and not to expect a reference. She—she was furious.'

'But what had you done?'

'I broke a vase. It was an accident. I'd been cutting her toenails and—'

'What? You'd been what?'

'Oh yes, it was one of my duties to cut her toenails. And as I was standing up I knocked over an occasional table and broke her precious vase. You might have thought I'd done it on purpose, she was so angry. She called me all sorts of names. She said I was lazy and a slut and—and not to be trusted. I asked her right out if I was as bad as that why she had employed me for six years, and she told me I could pack my bags and get out of the house in the morning because she wouldn't put up with my insolence any longer.'

'I see.' Cynthia paused.

She didn't altogether trust Pauline's story. She suspected that Pauline had been at least partially to blame, but the idea of having to cut someone else's toenails, when one was not a professional chiropodist, revolted her. For a moment, she was at a loss, not knowing how to reply. To make matters worse, Derek was tapping his watch to indicate that time was passing, and they would be late for their dinner-party if she didn't hurry.

Pauline forestalled her. 'Cynthia, could you possibly give me a bed for a night or two? I know it's asking a lot, but I'm desperate. I might be able to find a room, I suppose, but money's short. Foolishly I've bought a new winter coat—I hadn't dreamt anything like this would happen so suddenly, not after six years—and I've got to pay for the precious vase I broke. Cynthia, if you could I'd be extremely grateful.'

Cynthia Faudin was not given to vacillation, but now she couldn't decide what action to take. She didn't want Pauline's gratitude. She didn't want Pauline at Longacres. She didn't want Pauline to meet Derek. But it wasn't asking much to provide a bed for a night or two and a few meals— if that was all Pauline was asking. She told herself that she was being foolish. If it had been anyone but Pauline Brune she wouldn't be hesitating; she would have agreed at once, or produced a reasonable excuse for refusing.

Conscious of Derek's growing impatience, Cynthia made up her mind. 'All right, Pauline. When would you like to come? Tomorrow?' She heard the reluctance in her voice, and tried not to sound so unwelcoming. 'Will you get yourself here, or do you want to be collected?'

Pauline's thanks were mingled with tears. Cynthia steeled herself to listen but at last, when Derek threw up his hands in a gesture of despair, said she must go. She agreed to pick Pauline up outside Colombury station, about five miles away, the next morning at eleven o'clock and, cutting short a renewed flood of thanks, put down the receiver.

'Who the hell was that?' Derek demanded.

'Someone called Pauline Brune.'

'And who's Pauline Brune? I don't remember you ever mentioning anyone by that name.'

Cynthia didn't answer immediately. She had dropped the bath robe to the floor and was getting into her underclothes. She never minded Derek seeing her naked; apart from a slight thickening of the waist, she was proud of her figure. When she was in her slip she went across to the dressing-table and began to do her hair and make up her face.

'Pauline's an old friend,' she said at last, thinking that 'friend' was not a word she would normally apply to Pauline. 'Her father was our clergyman when I was a child in the Isle of Wight. He died suddenly when I was about twelve, leaving no money, and she came to live with us as a sort of home help. She was meant to do light housework and take care of my brother and myself when we weren't at school.'

'She's not a young woman then?'

'No.' Cynthia carefully painted her mouth. 'She's five years older than me, though to judge from her appearance you'd think the difference was a good deal more.'

'So you've seen her recently?'

'Yes. I bumped into her by chance in Oxford a few days ago, and we had coffee together. I must say I didn't recognize her.' Cynthia stood up. 'Pass me my dress, Derek, there's a dear.'

Derek brought the dress, which was of velvet and the colour of rubies. It had long sleeves and a high neckline, and was very simple. It had cost a lot of money, Cynthia reflected as she stepped into it and drew it up over her body. Derek pulled up the zip for her and then kissed the nape of her neck.

'As always, you look wonderful,' he said, 'and much younger than your age. No wonder this Pauline looks old beside you.'

'From what I gathered she seems to have had a hard life. She hasn't had someone like you to spoil her, Derek.' Cynthia took a moment to fix her diamond earrings.

'Anyway, you'll be seeing her tomorrow. She's coming to stay for a couple of days. I hope you don't mind.'

'Mind? Of course not, darling. Why on earth should I mind if it gives you pleasure.' Derek was adjusting his bow tie in the mirror, and he didn't see the sudden sour expression that flickered across his wife's face. 'But it's a bit unexpected, isn't it? Is she in some kind of trouble?'

Cynthia relayed a brief and expurgated version of what Pauline had told her, and Derek nodded his understanding. If he was a little surprised that Cynthia should be so considerate towards someone she hadn't seen or heard from for years he didn't comment.

'Well, she's welcome here,' he said, 'and for as long as you care to have her, providing she's gone before my birthday. We're going to be a full house that weekend, what with the family and Chris Winter.' Winter was a very old friend of Derek's. 'It should be great fun. I'm looking forward to it.'

'So am I,' said Cynthia with sudden warmth. 'And Pauline will be gone long before then. I promise.'

She hoped it was a promise she would be able to keep.

The next morning Cynthia arrived early at Colombury station, but Pauline was already there. Cynthia had refused Derek's offer of the Rolls and chauffeur, thinking it would look too ostentatious. But when she saw the pile of suitcases around Pauline she wondered if she had made a mistake.

'I'm sorry there's so much luggage,' Pauline said, as together they heaved the cases into the boot of the BMW. 'These are all my worldly goods. I couldn't leave anything behind.'

'No, I suppose not,' said Cynthia shortly, picking up the last bag.

Pauline took it from her. 'I'll have that one inside the car. It's got my camera in it. You remember how keen I used to be on photography when I was young? I even had an old ciné camera, which was quite unusual at that time. I'm still interested in it, but I don't do much these days. It's an expensive hobby, and of course I can't spare the money.'

'Derek has a ciné machine, too,' Cynthia said. 'He took lots of film of the children when they were small, but he doesn't use it much now. He's thinking of getting one of those video camera things, I believe.'

'How fascinating! Photographs and film always make a wonderful record, don't they?'

'Yes.'

It was a bare monosyllable, but Cynthia couldn't think of anything to add to it. She told herself that she was becoming paranoid, reading double meanings into almost every remark that Pauline made. It was absurd that she should let the woman get to her like this. She was no longer the little girl, and Pauline the near-adult. If anything their positions were reversed; she herself was the more responsible of the two—the one in a position to give rather than receive orders.

To change the subject, she said, 'Is that your new coat?'

She had noticed the coat as soon as she saw Pauline at the station. It was an expensive garment of fine wool, and beautifully tailored. Somehow it spoilt the picture of Pauline as a homeless woman surrounded by her few poor possessions. But, seen at close quarters, the coat did not appear absolutely brand new, though it was difficult to say why this was so. Besides, with its mink collar and cuffs, it was a winter coat, much too thick for this comparatively mild day.

As if she had read Cynthia's thoughts, Pauline said, 'Do you like it? As a matter of fact I'm rather proud of it, even if it is second-hand. Believe it or not, I bought it in Chipping Norton at one of those shops where rich ladies sell perfectly good clothes when they grow tired of them. All the same, by my standards it was far from cheap and more than I should have afforded.' She shook her head sadly, as if in self-reproach.

'It's a lovely coat,' Cynthia said. She had no reason to disbelieve Pauline's story, but somehow she felt quite certain that it was untrue. Still, it was none of her business. 'But isn't it rather warm for today?'

'Indeed it is, yes, but I had nowhere to pack it.' Suddenly Pauline laughed. 'Your husband will think I've come to stay for good when he sees all my bags,' she said.

Derek Faudin was disturbed. He was a level-headed man, but not normally especially sensitive, though over the years he had learnt to assess his wife's moods with fair accuracy, and he had known for a few days that something had been worrying her. She had been distracted and on edge— 'uptight' was the modern word, he supposed. And all this had culminated at dinner the previous evening when she had alternatively been distant almost to the point of rudeness, or inclined to gush, which was totally unlike her. She was usually—at least in his view—not only the perfect hostess, but also the perfect guest, able to cope equally well with some self-opinionated celebrity and with a dull, but often more important, character. It was an attribute of hers that he had always admired. Clearly something was wrong.

After giving the matter some consideration, Derek thought that he was now able to pinpoint the reason for Cynthia's worry. It must have started when she met this Pauline Brune in Oxford, and been exacerbated by the impending visit. But he still couldn't understand why. It would be no trouble to Cynthia to put up Miss Brune for a few days. Such nominal extra work that a visitor, who was also a stranger, could cause would fall on the shoulders of Mrs May and, in the circumstances that Cynthia had described, the offer of hospitality was merely an act of charity. Besides, surely if Cynthia hadn't wanted to ask the woman to stay, she had been under no compulsion to do so.

Irritated with his wife—and with himself, because he felt inexplicably restless and unable to settle to anything, Derek waited for Cynthia's return from Colombury station with Pauline Brune. Watching from the library window, he was glad when at last he saw Cynthia's BMW coming up the drive, and he hastened down to the hall to welcome them.

Mrs May had forestalled him. The front door was already open and Vernon, the houseman, was standing by to deal with the bags.

If Pauline was surprised by this welcome she didn't show it. She shook Derek warmly by the hand, and said, 'It's awfully good of you to offer me a home, Mr Faudin—' she paused—'and what is obviously such a beautiful home, too. I'm most grateful.'

'Derek, please,' he demurred, and thought that she had phrased her gratitude rather oddly.

He commented on this to Cynthia when she had shown Pauline to her room and left her to unpack before lunch. Cynthia shrugged. 'She's an odd woman, Derek. She's apt to make peculiar remarks. Don't pay any attention.'

'She seems pleasant enough.'

'Yes,' replied Cynthia somewhat hesitantly. 'She—she's fine.'

Derek thought this might be the moment to ask Cynthia why she had invited Pauline to stay if she really didn't like her, but he guessed that his curiosity would not be welcomed. Cynthia rarely reacted well to queries about her motives. Anyway, the chance had gone. Pauline had come into the sitting-room.

'Do you dress for dinner?' she asked conversationally as she sat down on a sofa.

Derek avoided catching his wife's eye. He wanted to laugh. It was an unexpected question at this particular moment. 'Not as a rule,' he said, 'if you mean into a black tie. Only if it's a special occasion, or we have guests. We usually change, though.'

'Even if you're just *en famille*?' Pauline's gesture embraced the three of them.

'Yes.' Derek rose to his feet.

'Good. I like to have a bath and put on something fresh in the evenings.' Pauline smiled across to Cynthia, who made no effort to respond.

'Time for a drink before lunch,' Derek said hastily. 'What will you have, Miss—Pauline?'

'Gin and tonic, please, Derek. With a twist of lemon if
you have it.'

'Right.'

Derek Faudin hid his surprise. He had expected Pauline
to ask for a soft drink or perhaps a small sherry, and he
hadn't expected her to speak with such assurance. She was,
he thought with amusement, an unusual woman. The next
few days might prove to be full of surprises, and not unpleasant, at least if Cynthia recovered her normal good
temper.

CHAPTER 3

'Cynthia, how much longer is Pauline going to stay with
us? I had the impression she would be here for two or three
days, but it's already turned into nearly three weeks. What's
more, there seems no likelihood of an end to it unless we do
something, and the house will be full at the end of the week.'

'I know, Derek.' Cynthia didn't answer the question but
smiled placatingly. 'But it *is* difficult, isn't it? She hasn't got
anywhere to go, and I can't ask her to leave just like that.'

'Why not? As far as I can see, she doesn't seem to be
making much of an effort to find anywhere to go.'

Again Cynthia didn't answer. Instead, she said, 'You
know that she's been making herself useful in the house,
helping Mrs May with small jobs and—'

'Mrs May is well paid, and she has enough help,' said
Derek sharply.

Cynthia changed tactics. 'Derek, what's the matter with
you?' she asked. 'What's Pauline done to annoy you so
much? I thought you were getting on with her quite well.'

The Faudins were having breakfast. They were by themselves for once. Pauline had breakfasted earlier. She had
complained of toothache the evening before, and Cynthia
had hastily arranged for her to be driven into Oxford to
visit the Faudins' own dentist, Charles Parker.

'I'm just tired of having her around the place all the time.' Derek was aware that he was sounding irrational, even peevish, but he added, 'Isn't it nice to be alone this morning, for instance?'

'Yes, of course, but—Surely Pauline doesn't bother you that much. You'll be in London a couple of days this week and—'

'And she'll have to be gone before I get back, by the weekend. It's my birthday, remember, Cynthia. The house will be filling up from Friday on.'

'I've not forgotten, Derek! I'll speak to Pauline, but I do think you're being a little unreasonable.' Cynthia watched her husband push his scrambled eggs around his plate. 'What really *is* the matter? Are you sure Pauline hasn't annoyed you in some way? She can be very tactless at times, I admit.'

'Well, if you must know, I found her in my study yesterday,' Derek burst out finally. 'I'd left some papers on my desk while I went to the loo, and when I came back she was leafing through them. Perhaps it was careless of me, but Nature's call was sudden and I couldn't ignore it. Anyway, it's my house, damn it! I ought to be able to leave my study for a few minutes without this Pauline Brune going through my papers.'

Coming from Derek, who was on the whole a calm, un-aggressive character, this explosion constituted a positive tirade. Cynthia appreciated that he must have been extremely angry about the incident, but his lengthy speech had given her time to think. She managed to smile at him.

'Were the papers important?'

'They were private and personal.'

'Connected with finance?'

'Yes.' There was the faintest hesitation.

'Then Pauline wouldn't have made head or tail of them. She doesn't know the difference between a share and a bond. I expect she just saw the door open, and went in to look around out of mere curiosity.'

'I dare say, but—'

Derek didn't want to continue the argument. In some ways he blamed himself for what had happened. He should at least have thrust the documents into a desk drawer instead of leaving them spread out on top. But he had shut the door; of that he was positive. There was no question of Pauline walking along the corridor and, seeing a room she hadn't previously entered, going to inspect it.

'Anyway,' he added with renewed firmness, 'quite apart from that, I'll be glad when she's gone. Perhaps you could find out what she wants to do, Cynthia. We might be able to help her get another job. We've got to be practical. She's had a good holiday here, but she can't stay for ever.'

'No, of course not,' Cynthia agreed at once.

The subject was shelved as Vernon, the houseman, knocked and came in, carrying the day's post on a silver tray. He was young—in his late twenties, but tall and thin and he took his duties seriously. Derek, especially, had come to appreciate his quiet competence. 'There's a lot this morning, sir,' he said, dividing the envelopes neatly between Derek and Cynthia, and leaving magazines on the table between them.

'Thanks, Vernon.'

The Faudins took their post seriously. They threw out obvious junk mail, and put to one side bills, receipts, bank statements and requests from the charities they patronized; all these could be dealt with at leisure. This still left what could be classed as personal or semi-personal correspondence—letters or postcards from family and friends, and invitations, for example—and these they would often interchange, with comments.

On this particular morning a sudden pleased exclamation from Cynthia made Derek look up. 'Good news, darling?'

'Very pleasing.' She passed him the letter. 'I'm terribly sorry, but I never told you about it when they first approached me informally, in case it never happened. But this is the official confirmation. I'm to become a Dame! My name will be in the Queen's Birthday Honours List.'

'Congratulations! Oh, that's splendid!' Derek's pleasure

was heartfelt, untinged by envy. 'Dame Cynthia Faudin! That really is something. The children will be proud of you. We all will.'

'Peter will probably say it sounds like a character in a Christmas pantomime.'

'Nonsense. Cynthia, it's wonderful news.'

'I'm so happy you think so.'

'We must celebrate. Champagne for dinner tonight, and what would you like to do? Go up to town and—'

'No!' Cynthia interrupted sharply. 'Not while Pauline's here. She'd want to know why, and we mustn't tell her— nor anyone else, Derek, not even the family—till after the List appears. That's important. Even at this stage Honours have been withdrawn because someone boasted in advance.'

'Oh dear! But you're right, of course. We'll postpone the celebrations, but it's only a postponement, so think what you'd like to do. A weekend in Paris, perhaps?'

'That sounds marvellous,' Cynthia said. But her thoughts were not on Paris.

At Longacres Cynthia usually worked in the library, where the reference books she needed were at hand, and she had a large desk, especially made for her, which housed her papers and files. Out of term she tried to work for three or four hours a day, but it wasn't always possible. This week, for example, Derek's brother Simon and his wife would be arriving on Friday, and from then until Monday the house would be full of guests for the birthday-party. Opportunities to get on with the current book would be lacking.

Admittedly the coming weekend was exceptional, but there had been too many interruptions lately, and even when she had had every chance to work, she had found it difficult to concentrate. Repeatedly, she had caught herself sitting and staring at the almost blank screen of her word processor, thinking about Pauline Brune.

She had hoped that after a week or two at most Pauline would have suggested leaving Longacres of her own accord, but this had been a foolish expectation. Pauline had shown no inclination to take her leave. Now Derek had demanded that Pauline should go, and it was clear that she would have to take action of some kind.

Recalling how angry Derek had been that Pauline should invade his study and look at his papers, an idea occurred to Cynthia. While Pauline was at the dentist she had an excellent opportunity to turn the tables and inspect Pauline's room. Probably this would yield nothing, but . . .

With a sense of purpose—at least she was doing something—rather than with any feeling of guilt, Cynthia left the library and went along to the small suite that Pauline was occupying. It was known as the Rose Room because the predominant colour in bedroom and bathroom was a deep pink and, as the bed was three-quarter size, was intended to sleep two if necessary. The decoration was not entirely to Cynthia's taste and she had been planning to make changes, but for one occupant it was very comfortable, if not luxurious.

Cynthia ignored the bathroom and concentrated on the bedroom. It held few surprises. Pauline had unpacked all her possessions, and had put them neatly away—as if to prepare herself for a long visit. Her clothes were varied, mostly inexpensive, though there were some unexpected items: a Chanel suit—a copy, but a good copy—a velvet evening skirt, a beautiful silk blouse and a couple of long-sleeved pullovers, not even lambswool but cashmere. Pauline had worn none of these garments during her stay at Longacres. In addition, there was a crocodile handbag that Cynthia herself would have been happy to own.

She frowned over these finds, knowing that they must all have been well beyond Pauline's means to buy. She could only assume that they and the coat Pauline had worn on her arrival had been gifts—say from her former employer, Mrs Kent. But this idea didn't jibe with the picture of the elderly harridan that Pauline had been at such pains to draw.

Sighing, Cynthia was about to abandon her search. She had discovered no letters, no papers, nothing personal—

not even a bank book or statement of any kind. Nor, she suddenly remembered, had she seen the camera Pauline had mentioned while they were loading her bags into the BMW in Colombury.

On impulse she bent down and glanced under the bed. There was a suitcase, more readily available than the ones that had been piled in the high cupboards above the fitted wardrobe. The suitcase was unlocked, and inside were not one but two cameras, the first a standard 35 mm single-lens reflex instrument, and the second a much smaller and expensive miniature model that could be hidden in the palm of a hand. Cynthia wondered what use Pauline made of this.

There was also a metal box, long and narrow, and some rolls of film for both cameras. The box was locked. It could, Cynthia thought, have contained transparencies or negatives. She gave it a gentle shake, but this told her nothing, and she returned it to the suitcase. The search had been a waste of time.

It was also to prove slightly embarrassing, for Cynthia was still on her knees beside the bed when the door of the room opened. For one awful moment she was sure it was Pauline, but it was only Mrs May with an armful of clean towels.

'Why, Mrs Faudin, what are you doing?' the housekeeper asked at once.

Cynthia scrambled to her feet to confront the small, neat figure of the housekeeper. Mrs May, a widow in her fifties, had been a mainstay of Longacres for many years and a major source of support for Cynthia from the time of the latter's arrival in the house. 'I—I was trying to catch a spider,' Cynthia said. It was the first explanation that occurred to her. 'I seem to have lost it.'

'A spider?' Mrs May sounded somewhat affronted. 'In here, Mrs Faudin? Are you sure?'

'Yes,' said Cynthia positively. 'I came in here to—to see if Miss Brune had put out an old photograph she promised to show me, and I saw the spider scuttle across the carpet.'

Mrs May regarded her mistress silently for a moment, but she was too well-trained to question the story, however feeble she might have thought it. 'The room should have been cleaned this morning, Mrs Faudin, but I'll get Beryl to vacuum under the bed to make sure there are no creepy-crawlies around.'

'Thank you,' Cynthia said, and made her escape while Mrs May took the towels into the bathroom.

What on earth would I have done if it had been Pauline, she asked herself as she reached what now seemed to be the sanctuary of the library. She sat in front of her word processor, but found it impossible to type; her hands were shaking as she wondered how she was going to solve her problem. Derek had been adamant that Pauline must leave, and she couldn't blame him. But it meant that she would have to face Pauline and attempt to fix a firm date for her departure. And she was far from confident that she would succeed.

Pauline Brune arrived back at Longacres shortly before noon. The chauffeur helped her into the house, and left her on a chair in the hall. She was very pale and she clutched a bloodstained handkerchief to her mouth. The chauffeur fetched Mrs May, who went in search of Cynthia.

Cynthia had abandoned her work in the library and was in the sitting-room with Derek. They were reading when Mrs May came quickly into the room.

'It's Miss Brune, Mrs Faudin. She seems to be unwell.'

The Faudins hurried into the hall, where Pauline made an effort to smile at them. 'I'm sorry,' she mumbled through her handkerchief. 'It's my tooth.'

'Oh dear!' Cynthia looked at Derek.

'You'd better go to bed, Pauline,' Derek said at once.

'I'm afraid I shall have to,' Pauline agreed. She glanced about her helplessly until her eyes lighted on the chauffeur who was standing by, unsure where his services would be required. 'My parcel?' she said.

'I'll get it, Miss Brune.'

'You managed to do some shopping?' Cynthia knew that her voice sounded vaguely accusatory.

'Luckily the tooth didn't hurt too badly until the anaesthetic started to wear off on the drive back home. I expect I'd done too much, and that's why it started to bleed.' Pauline continued to speak with difficulty. 'But while I was in Oxford I had to seize my chance to get Derek a birthday present. It's not much, I'm afraid, but I couldn't be the only one not to have a little something to give him on the great day, could I?'

Derek hesitated. To Cynthia his dilemma was obvious. At length he said evenly, 'There was absolutely no need.'

In fact, Derek was angry. He felt that somehow he had been consciously tricked into a most embarrassing situation. The woman was a guest in his house, though she had outstayed her welcome as far as he was concerned. Now, by making an effort to buy him a birthday present when she was in some pain, she had put him under an obligation. Even worse, the purchase made it clear that she was taking it for granted she would be part of his birthday celebrations, so that the difficulty of asking her to leave before the weekend had been doubled or redoubled.

Cynthia intervened. 'Come along, Pauline. I'll help you upstairs. If your tooth doesn't stop bleeding soon, I'll phone Mr Parker.'

'Thank you.' Pauline stood up. She swayed slightly, but refused the arm that Mrs May offered her. 'I'm sorry to be such a nuisance. I'll be all right soon.'

She moved towards the stairs, followed by Cynthia and Mrs May, who was carrying the parcel the chauffeur had brought in. Derek retreated to the sitting-room, where he poured himself a stiff, neat whisky.

'Damn the woman!' he said when Cynthia rejoined him. 'I don't want her wretched present. And why does she choose this particular moment to have trouble with her teeth?'

'Oh come, Derek, that's a bit unfair,' said Cynthia. 'But it is unfortunate.' She flung herself into an armchair. 'Pour me a sherry, there's a darling.'

Derek brought her the sherry and gave himself another whisky. 'Did you phone Parker?' he asked.

'Yes. She didn't want me to, but I thought I'd better. He said he couldn't understand it. It was a back tooth, but not a difficult filling, and there shouldn't have been any bleeding. However, he suggested cold compresses, and paracetomol for the pain, and she's to let him know if the trouble continues.'

'What the hell are we going to do about her, Cynthia?'

'There's really nothing we can do. She says she'll be fine in the morning, and I expect she's right.' Purposely Cynthia misunderstood her husband's question.

'I mean about asking her to leave.'

'Derek, it's not possible at the moment, is it?'

'You said she'll probably be all right in the morning.'

'We'll have to see.'

'I want her gone before the weekend, birthday present or no birthday present.'

'You know you're being unreasonable, Derek. I can't turn her out of the house if she's unwell,' Cynthia replied decisively. 'So please don't let's quarrel over the matter.'

'I've no desire to quarrel—' Derek began and stopped. He simply didn't understand his wife; at least, he couldn't interpret her attitude towards this Pauline Brune. She didn't seem to like the woman and yet—

'Well, we'll have to hope she recovers quickly,' he said, 'for all our sakes.' He had no idea why he added his last four words.

Pauline's hopes were quite different. She had deliberately brought on the pain and the blood by biting the inside of her mouth and her lower lip while she was being driven back to Longacres, and stabbing a nailfile into a finger to stain her handkerchief, and now she proposed to make the most of her 'indisposition'. She went to bed, and stayed there for the rest of the day.

By the next morning her face was satisfactorily swollen. When Cynthia came to inquire after her, she was able to report that the bleeding had stopped, though the pain continued. She enjoyed a second day in bed. Cynthia had brought her some reading matter, and Mrs May arranged for trays of easy-to-eat food to be sent up.

At noon the following day, looking suitably wan, she went downstairs. Derek, she knew, would have already left for London, and wouldn't be back until Friday, when Simon and Valerie Faudin were to arrive. And after that he would be busy with his guests.

She was pleased with herself. She had achieved her primary purpose—to avoid a direct confrontation with Cynthia's husband. She had been surprised by the strength of his suppressed anger when he had caught her in his study, and had been afraid that he would ask her to leave the house there and then. But now there was no fear of that, at least for a while.

That the confrontation would come she was well aware—indeed, she would want it to come, but not yet, not until it suited her.

CHAPTER 4

On the Friday, the weekend that was to end so disastrously at Longacres did not begin well for Cynthia.

A series of telephone calls precipitated a corresponding number of minor crises. The first was from Derek, to say that he had been a witness to an accident and had to make a statement to the police; he would almost certainly be late for dinner. This meant unexpected complications, especially as Derek seemed to have forgotten that Simon and Valerie planned to arrive in time for tea. When Cynthia reminded him of this, he assured her that they wouldn't mind waiting dinner for him.

Cynthia was not so sure. Derek's brother and his wife were in their middle-sixties. They had no children and though Simon, who had been a lawyer, was less well-off than Derek, the couple had always managed to indulge their tastes and whims. To call them selfish would have been unfair, but over the years they had become set in their ways, and preferred their lives to follow an even path—an organized path, with no unforeseen variations. They visited Longacres frequently, and were usually not disappointed with the arrangements, but when some unanticipated event or change did occur, Cynthia felt that she invariably received the blame—even if this was indicated by no more than an irritated shake of the head. Over the years, Cynthia had come to disregard the unstated fact that Simon and Valerie tended to dislike her; even when things were going well, they always appeared to exude a faint aura of disapproval.

In particular, they liked their meals to be punctual, and they were careful about what they ate. This Friday it seemed they were likely to be unlucky, for no sooner had Derek said goodbye and Cynthia replaced her receiver when the phone rang again. This time it was the butcher, full of apologies, for the Faudins were good customers of his. But he couldn't perform miracles and the veal he had promised to deliver that morning to make a delicious *blanquette de veau* for dinner was just not available. Cursing silently, Cynthia consulted Mrs May, who said she had seen some beautiful turbot in the fishmonger's in Colombury, and it wouldn't take Vernon long to fetch it. But Simon and Valerie didn't eat fish, and Cynthia finally decided on readily-available steaks from the deep freezer.

The next call was from Derek's old friend, Christopher Winter. He was at Colombury railway station which he complained was cold and draughty, and he wanted to know when someone was coming to pick him up. He had told Derek when his train was due, and for once it had been on time—but there was no hide nor hair of anyone to greet him. He sounded aggrieved, and went so far as to remark that he had no wish to spend the weekend in bed with bronchitis.

Cynthia was horrified. Christopher Winter at seventy-six

was three years older than Derek and, since catching a virus
the previous spring, he had become somewhat frail. Derek
was devoted to him, and would never forgive her if she
allowed his aged friend to catch a chill by hanging around
the station. That Christopher had made a mistake in the
date and was in fact not expected until the following day
made no difference. She must do something at once.

'I'm terribly sorry,' she said. 'Derek's been delayed in
London, and stupidly I forgot the time. I'll send a car for
you right away, but it will take a little while to get there.
Why don't you go along to the Windrush Arms? It's an
excellent hotel, and you can have some coffee to warm you
up while you're waiting.'

Reassured of his welcome, Christopher Winter readily
agreed to go to the Windrush Arms and wait to be fetched.
Meanwhile Cynthia was thinking quickly. Who was to do
the fetching? Derek had taken the Rolls to London with the
chauffeur. Vernon, the houseman, was busy cleaning silver.
She didn't want to send a gardener. Fleetingly she considered Pauline, but dismissed the idea; she had no wish to
ask the woman a favour, and in any case didn't even know
if Pauline could drive. There was no alternative; she would
have to make the trip herself.

Hurrying upstairs to get a coat and find Mrs May,
Cynthia glanced through the open door of the library, and
saw Pauline sitting comfortably in an armchair, reading a
newspaper. Facing her own problems, Cynthia experienced
a surge of almost uncontrollable rage at this domestic scene.
For a moment she felt faint, and had to lean against the
wall of the passage. But Beryl, the housemaid, a chubby
girl in her late teens, came out of a bedroom pushing a
vacuum cleaner before her, and Cynthia forced herself to
stand upright.

'You all right, madam?' Beryl asked anxiously in her soft
Oxfordshire burr.

'Yes, I'm fine, Beryl. I must have run upstairs more
quickly than I should.' Cynthia smiled at her excuse, to
show that it wasn't to be taken too seriously, and added,

'Beryl, Mr Winter is coming today instead of tomorrow, so
will you check his room and make sure his bed's aired?'

'Yes, Mrs Faudin.'

'Good. Do you know where Mrs May is?'

'I think she's in the kitchen.'

Cynthia nodded her thanks. She collected her coat and
ran down the back stairs to the servants' quarters, where
she found Mrs May giving instructions to the cook.

'I'm sorry,' she said, 'but there are more changes. Mr
Winter is arriving today instead of tomorrow. In fact, I'm
going into Colombury to fetch him now. It means there'll
be one extra for dinner and, I regret to say we'll need a
more substantial lunch than the salad Miss Brune and I
planned to have.'

'That'll be fine, Mrs Faudin,' Mrs May said immediately.
'Mr Winter's always welcome at Longacres. He's very popular with all the staff. He's very generous,' she added with a
laugh.

Cynthia shared in her amusement, thanked her and cook,
and gratefully left it to them to provide for Christopher
Winter's needs. Once she had got him safely home, Christopher, she was sure, would have no further cause to complain. In a better temper now, and forgetting Pauline, she
set off for Colombury.

Thereafter Cynthia's day continued smoothly. Simon and
Valerie arrived in the afternoon in good time for tea and
Derek, contrary to his expectation, returned shortly before
seven, so that dinner was not delayed. They spent a pleasant
evening, chatting about family and friends. Pauline stayed
in the background, and said little, but she gave the appearance of being politely interested. Old Christopher Winter
was the first to make a move. He said that he was tired after
his journey and would like to retire. Pauline soon followed,
and the Faudins were left to themselves. To Cynthia it was
an ideal opportunity to relax; she knew that tomorrow
was Derek's birthday, when she would certainly be fully
occupied.

But the day wasn't over yet. As soon as the four of them had decided to go to bed and Derek and Cynthia had reached their bedroom, Derek said, 'Cynthia, I've not had a chance this evening to ask you about Pauline. Obviously she's still with us, and will be here over the weekend. Why on earth –'

'She's been ill, Derek,' Cynthia interrupted. 'Maybe she's allergic to anaesthetics, but that tooth business really upset her. She was in bed for two days and—'

It was Derek's turn to interrupt. 'But you have spoken to her and made it clear that we expect her to leave very soon?'

Cynthia hesitated. Then, 'Not yet,' she admitted as she started to undress.

'But, Cynthia, you promised. It's bad enough having her here this weekend. She doesn't fit in with our family or our friends. You must see that.'

'I thought she was getting on rather well with Christopher over dinner.'

'It's not Christopher—' Derek stopped abruptly.

'I'm sorry about this weekend, truly I am,' Cynthia said. 'It's just unfortunate that she's been ill.'

'She's not been all that ill! By now you could have spoken to her and made some arrangement.'

Derek heaved a sigh. He had passed a hard couple of days in the City, attending long drawn-out meetings, and with another birthday looming had been feeling his age. But he had been looking forward to the weekend, and the continued presence of Pauline Brune had spoilt everything. For he didn't trust her. He was sure that she had read the papers he had so foolishly left on his desk, and he was fearful she might disclose what she had learnt from them, either involuntarily or even out of sheer malice. He had caught her regarding Simon speculatively during dinner. He would have to warn Simon . . .

'What?' he said. 'Sorry, my thoughts were elsewhere.'

'I said that I consider you're being unreasonable about Pauline, Derek.'

'You do? Well, I don't! And if you won't ask her to leave, Cynthia, I shall.'

'As you wish.'

Cynthia spoke calmly. Wrapping her robe around her as if she were cold she went into the adjoining bathroom. She shut the door and leant against it, mouth set in a bitter grimace. It was, she thought, a miserable irony that just when everything was going so well for her Pauline should have reappeared. For the first time she wondered if their meeting had really been accidental, though that scarcely mattered now.

There was a tap at the bathroom door. 'Are you all right, darling?' Derek asked.

Cynthia blinked back unexpected tears. Knowing Derek, she recognized his unnecessary question as an apology for his brief show of anger and the curtness with which he had spoken to her. 'Yes, I'm fine,' she said. 'Won't be a minute.'

And, 'Don't be weak,' she told herself. 'You haven't got where you are by lack of strength. You've got to make Pauline leave—somehow.'

Both Cynthia and Derek lay awake, worried. Their worries centred on Pauline, of course, but they were unrelated to each other and could not be shared. Derek's concern was for his brother Simon, and in part for Valerie, of whom he was very fond. Cynthia, on the other hand, cared only for herself. That Pauline might also be the cause of distress to Derek, and even to Peter and Clare, seemed to her peripheral, if not irrelevant. She was determined to take action, and eventually, with that decision in mind, she fell asleep.

Derek took longer. He remained wakeful, listening to Cynthia's regular breathing and puzzling over her attitude to this Pauline Brune. He knew his wife better than she suspected, and was aware that it was unlike her to be so considerate of someone else, unless she had something to gain by it. But ultimately he too slept.

At three o'clock in the morning there was a loud bump in the corridor outside their room, the crash of breaking china and a muffled curse. Derek and Cynthia sat up in their respective beds, startled awake. Derek switched on his bedside lamp.

'What the hell was that?' Cynthia demanded.

'Better go and see.'

Derek was already out of bed and reaching for a dressing-gown. Quickly Cynthia joined him. The silence which had redescended on the house was broken again by the sound of unrestrained sobs. Cynthia didn't bother with a robe, but went straight to the door, turning on the top light which shone out into the corridor.

'Clare!' she exclaimed. 'Clare! Dear God, what on earth! Are you all right?'

There was no response. Clare Faudin lay on the carpet and sobbed. Near her was an occasional table on its side, and the shattered pieces of what had once been a large Chinese vase. On the wallpaper was an ugly scar where the table had been knocked forcibly into it.

It was obvious what had happened. Clare, fumbling her way along the corridor in the dark, had forgotten the table and stumbled into it. She was a heavy girl and her weight had been enough to bring it down, with the vase. What was not obvious was what Clare was doing at Longacres in the middle of the night, when she was meant to be at her flat in Buckingham until the next day.

Derek didn't bother with such a question, which may not have occurred to him as quickly as it did to Cynthia. 'Poor dear girl,' he said. 'Come along, let's get you on your feet.'

While Derek was helping Clare to stand, Cynthia had picked up their daughter's shoes. They were covered in mud, and had made dirty marks on the carpet. She held them out with distaste.

'Here, take these,' she said.

Derek took the shoes though Cynthia had intended them for Clare. 'Can't you see she's upset?' he said.

'Something the matter? Has there been an accident?' Simon, disturbed by the noise and the loud whispering, had emerged into the corridor.

'No. Clare broke a vase. That's all,' Cynthia answered immediately. 'Go back to bed, Simon. We're sorry to have disturbed you.'

'Clare, is it? Hello, my dear. See you in the morning.'

Simon retreated. Derek set the table upright and began to kick the pieces of vase underneath it, so as to minimize the mess. He dropped one of the shoes, making yet another mark. Cynthia took Clare by the arm.

'How did you get in such a state?' she inquired more gently, leading Clare towards the bedroom that was always ready for her at Longacres. 'You're horribly bedraggled.'

'The car broke down,' Clare said. She had stopped crying, but seemed wary. 'I started to walk but it was raining and I got lost taking a short cut.'

'Where did you leave your car?'

'I wasn't using mine. I got a lift from—from a friend.'

'So when this friend's car broke down, you abandoned her—him—and set off across the fields?'

'Yes—no! Oh, stop asking questions, Mother! You treat me like a child and I'm not, not any more. I'll be thirty this year.'

'Yes, and by now you should be a responsible adult, though sometimes you certainly don't behave like one, Clare.' Cynthia could not conceal her irritation.

By this time they were at the bedroom door, and she released Clare's arm.

'You'd better have a hot bath and get to bed,' she said shortly. 'There's no one in the room next to you. Peter doesn't arrive until tomorrow. But be as quiet as you can. You've caused enough disturbance for one night.'

'All right. Good night.'

For a big girl, who at school had earned the nickname of 'Jumbo' because of her constant clumsiness, Clare moved with surprising agility. She was in her room and shutting the door before her mother had a chance to follow her. Cynthia found herself saying good night automatically in response, but to a door panel.

She shook her head in exasperation. 'Little bitch,' she

murmured, and thought that at the present time, with so much else to worry her, she had neither the ability nor the inclination to cope with Clare and whatever difficulty the girl might have managed to get herself into.

She returned to her bedroom. Derek was sitting disconsolately on the side of his bed. He looked tired and old, and she went to him and kissed him on the brow.

'Not a good beginning to your birthday, darling,' she said gently.

Derek was touched. He patted her hand. 'I'm fine,' he said. 'What about our Clare?'

'She'll be fine, too—after a bath and some sleep. Which reminds me that we could do with some more sleep ourselves.'

'Indeed we could,' Derek Faudin agreed, and thought that, whatever else developed, his birthday was likely to prove a taxing exercise.

CHAPTER 5

Anniversaries of birthdays or weddings or any major events tend to become routine rituals or banal formalities if they are celebrated regularly over a lengthy period of years. Few of the participants enjoy such occasions, whatever faces they feel compelled to wear. For some inexplicable reason—probably felicitous planning—Derek Faudin's birthday was a considerable exception; over the years it had become an institution with its own traditions, and a milestone to be anticipated with pleasure. Like the celebration of Easter, it was a movable feast, always taking place during the weekend nearest to Derek's actual birth date. This year, as it happened, the birth date actually fell on a Saturday, which (somewhat illogically) seemed especially tidy and convenient.

Guests who were actually staying at Longacres were expected to arrive by Saturday lunch-time, when drinks would be served and a buffet laid out in the sitting-room. On this occasion, by the middle of Saturday morning only three houseguests were still awaited—Peter, who was driving down from London, and some American cousins of Derek's, called Smithson.

The Smithsons, Andrew and Janet, would be at Long-acres for just the one night. They were touring England and were on their way to Stratford. Cynthia, who had never met them, had been less than ecstatic when Derek invited them to the birthday ceremonies, but she need not have worried. The Smithsons, when they appeared, turned out to be a delightful couple in their mid-fifties who would obviously adapt easily to the other guests and to the standardized format of the party.

Sipping a glass of white wine and eating a smoked salmon sandwich, Cynthia looked around the sitting-room contentedly, though her pleasurable feelings were somewhat marred by the sight of Pauline who, in a tatty jumper and skirt, seemed determined to play the part of a poor relation. In spite of Pauline, the day was going very smoothly, Cynthia thought. Derek, although his night's sleep had been broken, was clearly enjoying himself, and Clare, though red-eyed, had made an effort over her appearance and was doing her best to be sociable. But where was Peter?

In fact, Peter failed to arrive until the buffet lunch was over, and coffee was being served in the drawing-room. Christopher Winter had already retired for his afternoon nap, and the Smithsons, who didn't drink coffee, were happily contemplating a long country walk to clear their heads before the evening's festivities, as they said. The rest of the party were seemingly prepared to do nothing more active than sit around and chat.

'Hello, Dad! Many happy returns to you! Hello, Mother—everyone.'

Peter breezed into the room with all the assurance that youth, good looks, personal success and affluence bring with them. He was of moderate height, but appeared taller because he was slim and moved with a casual ease. He smiled around the assembly. And each of the others returned his smile, except for Cynthia who was staring inquiringly at the girl behind Peter.

'You're late, Peter,' she said.

'I know, but we had to drop off Napoleon en route.'

'Napoleon?' Cynthia knew that Peter was deliberately being perverse.

'Julia's dog. He's a bull mastiff, and knowing how much you dislike animals, Mother—Oh, by the way, this is Julia who I've brought along for the weekend. Julia, my mother, as if you hadn't guessed.'

Julia, who had followed Peter into the drawing-room, held out a long, thin hand which she allowed to stay in Cynthia's grasp for the briefest moment. She was a tall girl, very slender and beautifully dressed for a country weekend. Everything about her was long and thin and narrow, including her face, Cynthia thought. Nevertheless, it was hard to deny that the total effect was both admirable and sophisticated.

'I do hope I'm not intruding on what is so clearly a family occasion, Mrs Faudin,' she said. She had one of those high-pitched, clear-cut English voices that not even the most expensive schooling and the best elocution lessons can reproduce exactly. 'But Peter assured me it would be all right.' Her grey eyes slid sideways to give Peter an apparently reproachful glance.

'Of course it's OK.' Peter didn't give Cynthia a chance to speak. 'But first things first. We're starving, Mother, so we'll go and scrounge some food in the kitchen. I'll introduce Julia around later.'

Peter and the unexpected additional guest had caught Cynthia off-balance, but not for long. She knew at once that she wasn't having the kitchen invaded, not while preparations for tonight's dinner were getting under way. 'No!' she said. 'Come along to the sitting-room. You can have a drink and I'll arrange sandwiches and whatever else Mrs May can provide.'

She led the way from the drawing-room, her temper not

improved by the broad wink she saw Peter give his father as she turned to say to Julia, 'You're very welcome, but Peter should really have warned us. This isn't a big house, and we're overflowing with guests at the moment, though I'm sure we can find a comfortable room for you. But it'll mean a little juggling.'

'I'm so sorry to cause you extra—' the girl began, when Peter interrupted her. 'Have you put someone in my old room then, Mother?' he inquired.

'No, but—'

'So that's fine. Julia and I will be quite happy there. It's a single bed, but it's large enough.'

'That won't be necessary,' Cynthia said crisply. 'We can provide better accommodation than that for Miss—er—'

'Vere-Poole,' the girl volunteered. 'But, please call me Julia. And I'll be perfectly happy to share Peter's room.'

Cynthia did not miss her son's rather malicious grin. She knew exactly what he was thinking, that whatever her feelings might be towards the unforeseen guest he had wished on her, she would have to make her more than welcome. Sir Richard Vere-Poole, Bart, was not only an extremely rich man—hence the girl's fashionable clothes and expensive accessories—but also extremely influential in many spheres, not excluding the academic world.

'Here we are,' she said, and opened the sitting-room door. Glancing in, she blessed Mrs May; the remains of the buffet had already been cleared away and the room looked tidy and pleasant. 'Peter will give you whatever you like to drink, and I'll see about some food and the sleeping arrangements.'

She went first to the kitchen, where her request was met with resignation. So luncheon could not be said to be over, after all, and the dining-room table, already laid for dinner and, because of Pauline, adapted for nineteen places instead of eighteen, would now have to undergo a further transformation and seat twenty.

'What about bedrooms?' Mrs May inquired.

'I'll let you know,' Cynthia said hurriedly.

She returned to the drawing-room and, standing in the

doorway, called to Pauline, who was talking to Valerie Faudin, 'Pauline, can you spare me a minute?'

'Yes. What is it?' Pauline asked, getting to her feet and coming to join Cynthia.

Cynthia leant forward and shut the drawing-room door behind Pauline, so that their conversation could not be overheard. 'As you gathered,' she said, 'Peter's unexpectedly brought his girlfriend down for the weekend, so I'm having to rearrange bedrooms. I want you to move into the sewing-room, Pauline. I know it's small, but—'

'No!'

'What?'

'I said no, Cynthia. I've no intention of moving from my present room to a poky little place with no bathroom. Why can't Peter's girl have the sewing-room?'

'Because—' Cynthia hesitated. She knew she couldn't explain to Pauline why it was impossible—or at least inadvisable—to put Julia Vere-Poole in such an uncomfortable room, but she didn't know what to say. Pauline's blank refusal to cooperate had taken her by surprise.

'If the sewing-room's not good enough for her, give her Clare's room, or Peter's.'

'But Clare and Peter have always had those rooms, even since they were small children,' Cynthia protested angrily. 'You can't expect them—'

Pauline shrugged. 'And you can't expect *me* to move from *my* room, Cynthia. I think it would be best if we forgot that you ever suggested such a thing, don't you?'

Cynthia was stung into action by Pauline's casual insolence. 'Do you intend to occupy that room for ever?' she demanded.

'Oh no.' Pauline shook her head, smiling. 'Merely for as long as it suits me. I'm sure you wouldn't dream of turning out an old family friend, would you?'

She didn't wait for an answer, but turned and walked away, either unaware of the angry glance that Cynthia directed at her retreating back, or heedless of it.

*

The day passed. Ironically, the problem of the bedroom was solved by adopting Pauline's suggestion. To Cynthia's relief Clare proved quite amenable to the idea of moving for a night or two, and by the time Cynthia had bathed and was dressed for dinner, she was in a more relaxed and composed frame of mind. If she had made a practice of prayer, she would have prayed that the evening would go well. And, after that, she promised herself, she would decide what must be done about Pauline. Meanwhile, for Derek's sake, she must try to forget the problem.

This, however, proved impossible.

It was part of the ritual of Derek's birthday celebrations—and perhaps its most important element—that all the guests invited for dinner should assemble in the drawing-room about seven-thirty where, while enjoying his champagne, they watched him open his presents. On this particular night, excluding Cynthia and, of course, Derek himself, they were eighteen in number, half of them staying in the house and half coming by car from their respective homes to Longacres for the evening.

The latter group included the local doctor, a Dr Gouray, and the local vicar, the Reverend Michael Bronson, with their wives; all four were personal friends of the Faudins, as was the Gourays' son, Roger, now qualified and a member of his father's practice. Some years ago, Roger had proposed to Clare Faudin and, to Cynthia's regret, been refused; as far as Cynthia knew, he hadn't asked her again, and nor had anyone else. The other guests were the Lord Lieutenant of the County and his lady, and Sir William and Lady Frost, who were the Faudins' nearest neighbours. They almost all knew each other, and the only introductions necessary were those of Derek's American cousins, Julia Vere-Poole, and Pauline Brune.

Although Pauline had chosen to make the best of her appearance, she was completely overshadowed, not only by Julia, but by the vivacious Americans; minutes after the introductions were completed it was doubtful if any of the newcomers remembered her name.

But she didn't expect to stay in the background for long. Smiling thoughtfully she watched Derek unwrap his birthday presents, which had been neatly arranged in a corner of the room. This year they varied from a fur hat to two coveted seats for the latest musical, said to be sold out for the next year. These were from Julia, whose father happened to own a part of the show, and the clever gift met with warm applause.

Pauline was content to wait. She knew that her turn would come. In fact, hers was almost the last gift-wrapped parcel in what had begun as a large pile. It was a small flat package, and when Derek read the inscription he frowned. Whatever the contents, he didn't want it; over the days Pauline had been staying as an unwanted guest at Longacres he had developed almost an obsessive dislike of her presence, and there was certainly no acceptable gift that she could devise for him, except news of her early departure.

'Come on, Derek,' someone said. 'Open it up.'

Derek tore off the paper and let it drop to the floor. He stared at the object he held in his hands. He couldn't interpret its meaning, if any. Why should Pauline—

'What is it, Derek?' Cynthia asked, her voice sharp; she had guessed that this was Pauline's present.

'A photograph,' Derek said slowly. 'But I'm not sure—Is it—is it of you, Pauline, as a small girl?'

'Good heavens, no!' Pauline laughed. 'I wouldn't flatter myself that you'd want a photograph of me at any age. It's Cynthia, of course. I took it when we were all on holiday in Jersey—Cynthia's parents, Cynthia and her brother and myself. It came out rather well, I think.'

Derek pulled himself together. 'Yes, yes, indeed,' he said. 'Thank you, Pauline. It's charming.'

'I knew you'd like it,' Pauline said with satisfaction. 'As Cynthia knows, I was very keen on photography at the time.'

'Pass it around, Dad,' Peter said. 'We're all yearning to know what Mother looked like at a tender age.'

The photograph, in its narrow leather frame, was passed around from hand to hand amid murmurs of approval. It was said to be 'adorable', 'fine', 'sweet', 'great', and 'just like you, Cynthia'. The one comment with which Cynthia agreed was the last. The small girl in the photograph had grown unmistakably and undeniably into Cynthia Faudin, in spite of Derek's pretence of not recognizing his wife.

Cynthia had gone white when Derek had first produced a photograph, but by the time it reached her she was in full control of herself. She was able to smile at Pauline, and add her praise to the rest.

'I have a few others. I must show them to you and Derek some time,' Pauline said. 'They'll bring back old memories. There are one or two of Colin, Cynthia.'

'Who's Colin?' Janet Smithson asked.

'My twin brother,' Cynthia replied, her voice level.

'You and your brother were twins, just like Peter and Clare? My, that's great!' Janet sounded genuinely pleased.

'Indeed it was great when we were children,' Cynthia lied, daring Pauline to challenge her. 'But unfortunately Colin's dead.'

'He died of pneumonia,' Pauline added. 'It was so very sad. He was only a child. The doctors at the hospital did everything they could to save him, but of course they didn't have the drugs or facilities they've got nowadays.'

Derek, who had been watching Cynthia closely, said, 'Tragic maybe, but it happened a great many years ago and today we're meant to be celebrating. I'm going to open my penultimate present.' This proved to be a beautiful silk tie from Janet Smithson, who admitted that her husband had helped her to choose it. The atmosphere lightened quickly. Young Colin's death, if not forgotten, was relegated to the back of the guests' minds, and the final present, the gift of Simon and Valerie Faudin, which was large and heavy and proved to be a case of Derek's favourite whisky, produced a burst of laughter.

Shortly afterwards Vernon announced that dinner was served. Drinks were finished, and everyone began to troop into the dining-room. Derek seized his chance to move close to Cynthia for a moment.

'Are you all right, darling?' he murmured anxiously. 'You went awfully white a short while ago.'

'I'm fine,' Cynthia reassured him. 'Just a twinge of indigestion, but it's passed off now.'

'Good,' he said. 'I can't enjoy my birthday if you don't.'

He smiled at her lovingly, and Cynthia thought yet again what a good, kind man he was. She hoped against hope that Pauline Brune was not going to spoil their relationship and ruin what promised to be the most successful and rewarding years of her life, and the culmination of her career.

Cynthia had taken considerable care over the seating plan, though it had had to be hastily rearranged twice to take account of Pauline's and, later, of Julia's presence. But twenty, she reflected, looking round the table, was a nice round number. And, what was more, in spite of all the adjustments, the table was now properly balanced—just ten men and ten women. The table itself was perfect: a floral centrepiece of appropriate size, gleaming silver and glasses, and now the guests—the men in black or white dinner jackets, Derek sporting the scarlet cummerbund he always wore at his birthday parties, and the women in their long dresses of varied hues.

But as soon as Michael Bronson had said grace and they settled into their places, Cynthia noticed that something was amiss. The seating had been changed. The place names must have been altered. By Pauline? For she had put Pauline between the parson and the doctor, but saw that she was sitting between Simon Faudin and old Christopher Winter. She could see no point in the move. Perhaps it was not Pauline's fault. Maybe Mrs May or Vernon had disarranged the cards by accident, and replaced them in a different order. Whatever the explanation Cynthia was worried by the alteration, though it was obviously impossible to take any action.

The dinner continued. As always at Longacres, the food and wines were excellent, and everyone seemed to be enjoy-

ing themselves. Cynthia abandoned a fruitless effort to keep
a covert watch on Pauline, and concentrated her attention
on her nearest neighbours. At the far end of the two long
tables that had been put together for the occasion Derek
lifted his glass to her for a moment and, telling herself that
there was no need for anxiety, she felt content, and settled
herself to enjoy the rest of the evening.

It was to be but a brief respite. The birthday cake had
been brought in, and Derek was cutting the first slice. The
port and the Madeira were circulating. By tradition there
were never any speeches but, once all the glasses were filled,
Christopher Winter, as Derek's oldest friend, would propose
a toast to him, and would lead the guests in a couple of
choruses of 'Happy Birthday'. This year, however, the
pleasing little ceremony was to be ruined.

As Christopher pushed back his chair and rose slowly to
his feet, there came a crash of breaking glass, followed by a
smothered oath. Simon, who was normally a neat and
careful man, not given to clumsy gestures, had somehow
knocked a full glass of port across the table. David Gouray
was sitting opposite him, and by chance Simon's glass had
caught Gouray's at an angle, sending the doctor's port into
Clare's lap, to ruin her yellow silk dress.

Clare gave a cry of surprise. Both Simon and the doctor
rose hurriedly to their feet. There was port all over that part
of the table, and some on the carpet. Christopher was still
standing, but was clearly unable to continue with his toast.

'Oh God!' Simon said, turning to stare at Pauline. 'I'm
sorry! I'm sorry!'

His dramatic reaction seemed a little overdone—after all,
the incident only amounted to the spilling of a couple of
glasses of wine, not an unusual event at even the best
regulated dinners—and the general confusion lasted only a
few minutes. Mrs May, who was supervising the service—
extra staff had been brought in for the evening—acted
quickly, summoning Vernon to help her. Between them
they prevented the damage from spreading, and rapidly
restored order. Clare, who had suffered most, retreated from

the room. Others, who had merely been splashed, made light of the episode, whatever their private thoughts. At last Christopher was able to propose his toast, and 'Happy Birthday' was sung.

But somehow the joy had gone from the occasion for everyone except perhaps Pauline Brune. Yet it was difficult to identify a reason.

CHAPTER 6

Cynthia was the first inhabitant of Longacres to appear at the breakfast table the next morning. Knowing that Derek had slept badly, she had left him snoring gently. Three or four times during the night she had been awakened by his tossing and turning in the bed next to hers, or found him missing and seen a light under the bathroom door. When he returned she had pretended to be asleep.

They had not discussed the birthday dinner at any length, she reflected as she helped herself to orange juice. Derek's only comment had been, 'A pretty disastrous evening, wasn't it? Perhaps we shouldn't bother to do it again.' And she had replied, 'Nonsense! What does spilling some wine matter? Your party's a tradition. Of course we'll repeat it.' But even as she spoke she was not certain that she believed her words.

Neither of them, she recalled, had mentioned Pauline, or Pauline's present to Derek—that photograph of herself as a child. Yet they were both aware that in some enigmatic fashion it was Pauline who was the cause of the strains and stresses which underlay the party's failure—if it could really be called a failure. For her part, she'd had enough of Pauline. Pauline would ruin—

Vernon's arrival with toast and a pot of coffee interrupted Cynthia's dark thoughts. She reminded him to take a tray up to Christopher Winter, and he assured her that this had already been done. Then Clare came in.

'I'd like some tea,' she said at once without any prior greeting, 'and toast, please, Vernon.'

'That's all?' Cynthia queried. 'You're not starting a diet, are you?'

'No, I'm not!' Clare flung herself into a chair. 'If you want to know, I'm not feeling well. I slept badly,' she announced.

Cynthia regarded her daughter more closely, with some concern and a certain distaste. Clare looked dreadful. Her face was a dirty yellow, her eyes bloodshot, her hair dank with sweat. Thankfully, Cynthia realized that Vernon had disappeared.

'Was it because you drank too much last night?'

'No! I got more wine on my lap from that damned Pauline than—'

'But, my dear girl, it was Simon, your Uncle Simon, who spilt the port, and—'

'Yes, but he spilt it because Pauline—'

She hesitated, and Cynthia prompted her anxiously. 'Pauline what?'

'I don't know, Mother, but she made some remark to Simon that seemed to infuriate him. For a moment he looked quite savage—and he flung out an arm almost involuntarily, I thought—and my dress is ruined,' she finished weakly.

'Don't worry, Clare. We'll get you a new one.'

'I don't want a new dress, damn it!' Clare managed not to shout. 'I just want— Oh, hell!' She stopped abruptly as Vernon came in with her tea and toast, closely followed by Peter and Julia.

'We'll talk about it later,' Cynthia said quickly, as the usual morning pleasantries were exchanged but, as soon as Vernon had departed to get more coffee and toast and eggs and bacon for both Peter and Julia, Peter surprised her by asking who on earth this Pauline Brune was.

'What—what an odd question, dear,' Cynthia said. Calmly she poured herself another cup of coffee. 'Pauline's an old friend of mine. I used to know her as a child.'

'I've never heard you speak of her.'

'We lost touch with each other for many years. Then I happened to meet her in Oxford, and asked her to stay. There's nothing curious about that, is there?'

'No, I suppose not, but—Well, she seems to be pretty well established here, Mother. And Dad doesn't like her.'

'Why do you say that?'

'Isn't it obvious?'

'No! You're imagining things, Peter.'

'Simon Faudin doesn't like her either.' Julia's cut-glass voice had intervened.

Cynthia turned her head to regard the girl, who was beginning to annoy her. 'Really?' she said shortly.

'As a matter of fact, the two of them—Simon and Pauline—are having a hell of a row in the library right now. I don't imagine he meant it, but Simon—'

Julia's words faded away as Peter gave a quick shake of his head. Cynthia would have given a lot to know what Julia had been about to say, but the Smithsons had just come into the room, and she had no wish to continue the conversation in front of them. As she greeted Andrew and Janet, and inquired if they would like to stay for lunch before driving on to Stratford, she saw Peter lean towards Julia and whisper something to her.

'What about church?' Andrew Smithson asked. 'That was a nice guy we met at dinner last night. The Reverend Bronson, wasn't it? I wouldn't mind hearing him preach if you'd be good enough to give us a light lunch afterwards, Cynthia.'

'Yes, of course,' Cynthia said. 'St Matthew's is a fine old church, much too big for its present congregation, needless to say, but Michael Bronson serves quite a large parish. And there's a charming walk to the church through the woods; Derek and I often take it when the weather's good.'

'That sounds great!' Smithson said. 'Who else will join us?'

He had addressed the question to the younger Faudins and Julia, who shook their heads in unison. But Simon

Faudin came into the dining-room at that moment with
Valerie and Derek. There was as yet no sign of Pauline.

'Join you at what?' Simon asked.

'We were talking about going to church,' said Cynthia.

'Oh,' was Simon's only response.

Breakfast continued. Vernon brought in coffee, tea and
toast and a fresh jug of orange juice. The Smithsons joined
Peter and Julia in what Andrew called a real English breakfast—fried eggs and bacon. Otherwise, no one seemed to
have much appetite. Vernon said that Miss Brune had a
slight headache, and was taking a tray up to her room; only
Janet Smithson expressed any regret. Conversation became
sporadic and general and, just as they had drifted into the
dining-room, the breakfast party drifted away.

At ten-thirty the Smithsons were joined in the hall of Longacres by Cynthia and her sister-in-law, Valerie. Derek appeared briefly to say that he had to make a long-distance
phone call, but would catch them up before they reached
St Matthew's. Andrew Smithson was clearly disappointed.

'No one else coming?' he asked. 'You can understand the
young, I suppose, but—'

'I'm afraid Simon's not much of a churchgoer,' Valerie
apologized.

'And Christopher Winter's still in bed,' Cynthia said.
'He's beginning to feel his years, poor old dear.'

'What about Miss Brune—Pauline?' Janet asked.

'I haven't seen her this morning.' Cynthia didn't elaborate. 'Let's go, shall we?'

It was a beautiful day, crisp but not cold, the clouds
driving slowly across a pale sky. Cynthia set a rapid pace,
and they walked first through the grounds of Longacres,
then across a lane, and along a path beside a hedge bordered
on one side by a field and on the other by the edge of some
woodlands. Here Cynthia paused, causing the others to stop
too.

'I don't know what's happened to Derek,' she said. 'I
hope he's all right.'

'Why shouldn't he be?' Valerie asked in some surprise.

Cynthia ignored the question. 'Look,' she said, 'you three go on ahead and I'll go back to see what's detaining him.'

Janet suggested they should wait, but Cynthia dismissed the suggestion on the grounds that it wasn't warm enough to stand around. Nevertheless, the three of them didn't move on immediately, but watched Cynthia hurrying along the field until a curve of the hedge hid her from view.

'Cynthia's devoted to Cousin Derek, isn't she?' said Janet. 'He's a lucky man.'

'You could say that. You could also say that she's a lucky woman.' Valerie spoke more sharply than she intended. Privately she shared her husband's opinion that Cynthia had had the best of the marriage. 'He's devoted to her, too,' she added.

The Smithsons exchanged glances, but made no comment. Valerie changed the subject by asking them which plays they hoped to see in Stratford, and they set off again, but more slowly. They had just reached the far end of the wood when they heard running footsteps behind them. They stopped at once, and turned.

'Cynthia?' Valerie frowned. 'She's been very quick.'

'I hope nothing's wrong.' Janet was anxious.

'Of course not,' her husband reassured her. 'Anyway, that's not Cynthia. She's not so heavy-footed.'

Andrew had scarcely finished speaking when a young man appeared around a bend and came running towards them. He was about thirty years of age, they agreed later, with fair shoulder-length hair and a slim but muscular body. He wore jeans and a heavy woollen sweater. The moment he saw them, he stopped dead. He looked from side to side as if terrified of a trap, and then dived off the path. They heard him pounding between the trees, his footsteps gradually receding.

'Who on earth was that fellow?' Andrew Smithson demanded.

'I haven't the faintest idea,' Valerie said. 'I've never seen him before, but Simon and I live some miles away, and anyway he may not be a local.'

'Does it matter?' Janet asked. 'He's probably just getting some exercise, and he's obviously nothing to do with us.'

'You're quite right,' Valerie agreed, though for some reason she was unable to identify she felt uneasy. 'I wonder where Cynthia is,' she said. 'And Derek. Everyone seems to be disappearing.'

'Well, if the Reverend Bronson's going to have any contribution to his congregation from Longacres this morning, we'd better not disappear,' Janet said. 'I make it five minutes of eleven, and unless we hurry we're going to be late for the service.'

'And there's nothing that our Pastor at home hates more than folks who arrive late or leave early,' said Andrew. 'He wonders why they bother to come at all if their time's more precious to them than doing their Christian duty.'

'I expect Michael Bronson would echo that,' Valerie said. 'And you're right. There's no point in waiting for the others. We'd better get on.' But she spoke absently. Left to herself, she would have preferred to return to Longacres. She was sure that something was awry.

Mrs May enjoyed her job as housekeeper to the Faudins at Longacres, and had no desire to change it. She had comfortable accommodation, the same food as was served in the dining-room, the use of a small car and an excellent salary. In return she ran the house with the greatest of efficiency.

This efficiency was especially apparent on such occasions as Derek Faudin's birthday weekend, when the house was full and there were innumerable beds to be made, baths cleaned and meals prepared. She could rely on Vernon and the resident staff, but she didn't altogether trust the girls who came in from the village and she liked to check everything for herself.

So on this Sunday morning, once breakfast was over and

the bedrooms were being done, she went on her usual rounds. She saw Simon Faudin in the library, but his head was buried in his hands as if he was in some distress and she hesitated to disturb him. Silently she removed a vase of tired flowers and went downstairs.

The drawing-room was empty. Peter and Julia were chatting in the smaller sitting-room, surrounded by the Sunday newspapers, sections of which were strewn on the floor. Mrs May wondered if they intended to pick them up and put the papers together again, but she didn't comment. She went on into the hall.

Here she found Christopher Winter, leaning against a wall. He was breathing heavily and seemed to be making a feeble attempt to loosen his collar. Mrs May hastened across to him and helped him into a chair.

'Mr Winter, are you all right?' She knew it was a stupid question but felt compelled to ask it. 'Can I get you anything? Water? Brandy?'

He did his best to smile at her. 'A glass of water. Yes, please.'

The nearest source was the dining-room, where there were glasses and a supply of bottled water. Mrs May hurried. She had the door open and was over the threshold when she thought she heard a muffled cry behind her, though afterwards she could not be sure that she hadn't imagined it. Then she stood, a hand clapped to her mouth to suppress the scream that rose involuntarily to her lips as she stared in horror at the scene before her.

Derek Faudin lay sprawled on his back on the floor. His shirt-front was stained red and there was blood on the carpet beside him. Pauline Brune's body was a few feet away. She had been wearing a white blouse and that too was covered with blood.

Nausea rose in Mrs May's throat, but she forced herself to remain calm. She backed slowly from the room, and shut the door behind her as Vernon came into the hall. Christopher Winter was sitting where she had left him, apparently dazed and oblivious.

Mrs May grabbed at Vernon's arm. 'There's been a—a ghastly accident,' she said. 'It's Mr Faudin and Miss Brune. They're in there.' She pointed. 'I don't know if they're dead or not!'

CHAPTER 7

The next hour at Longacres saw frantic activity. Simon, alerted by Vernon, took charge of events. Telling the house-man to telephone Dr Gouray, he dashed downstairs to the dining-room. Though aghast at the scene, to his immense relief he found that his brother was still breathing, though unconscious. One glance at Pauline Brune's body was sufficient, though he did put a hand on her heart and throat.

On her own initiative Mrs May had helped Christopher Winter along to join Peter and Julia in the sitting-room, and found him some water from the kitchen. She then went upstairs to find bath towels and blankets, and met Cynthia coming out of the bedroom suite she shared with Derek.

'Mrs Faudin!' she exclaimed. 'We thought—You're not in church?'

'What on earth do you mean?' Cynthia said. 'No, of course I'm not in church. I'm looking for my husband. And what are you doing with those things?'

Simon had heard Cynthia's raised voice, and came out of the dining-room as she came downstairs with Mrs May. 'My dear,' he said, 'I'm sorry, but Derek's had an accident.'

'What sort of accident? Where is he?'

Simon was saved from answering immediately by the houseman who came hurrying across the hall. He stopped short when he caught sight of Cynthia.

'Well, man, did you get Dr Gouray?' Simon demanded.

'Yes, sir.' Vernon glanced doubtfully at Cynthia. 'He says we're not to move them, but try to stop any obvious bleeding and do our best to keep them warm. He wanted to know what had happened, but of course I couldn't tell him. Anyhow, he'll be here as quickly as he can.'

'Bleeding!' exclaimed Cynthia. 'What on earth—'

Simon took no notice of her. 'Good,' he said. 'Vernon, take those blankets and towels from Mrs May and come and help me.' He blocked Cynthia's way as she turned to follow them into the dining-room. 'You'd better not go in there, Cynthia.'

'Why ever not? Derek's in there, isn't he? And bleeding?' Cynthia was indignant. 'Simon, he may be your brother, but he's my husband and this is my house.'

'Nevertheless—'

'And who else is in there? Vernon said "them".'

'Pauline Brune, Cynthia—your old friend.'

Cynthia stared at him, uncomprehending. 'Simon, I don't understand.'

'No, but you're wasting time. Derek's still alive, and you heard what Vernon said—he must be kept warm.'

'What about Pauline?'

'I'm pretty certain she's dead. Come on Vernon.'

The houseman, his arms now full, followed Simon into the dining-room. Cynthia pressed behind him, but stopped abruptly in the doorway at her first glimpse of Derek and Pauline lying with blood around them. She leaned against the doorpost for a moment, and Mrs May thought she might be about to faint, but she seemed to recover and went to kneel beside Derek. His breathing was shallow, and he groaned occasionally, but he showed no sign of recognizing her.

'Please, Cynthia,' said Simon, more gently. 'There's nothing you can do here.' He signalled to Mrs May, who put an arm around Cynthia's waist and drew her back into the hall. On her way, Cynthia glanced at Pauline's body, but made no comment.

'Mr Simon's right, Mrs Faudin,' Mrs May said. 'It's no place for you in there. Come along to the sitting-room. Mr Peter and Miss Julia are looking after Mr Winter—I found him almost collapsing in the hall. None of them know anything about this yet.'

Cynthia allowed herself to be led away. 'And Clare? Where's she?' she asked.

'I haven't seen Miss Clare since first thing this morning. I imagine she's gone out, Mrs Faudin.'

Cynthia nodded. She told herself that this was no moment for weakness. With an effort she straightened her shoulders. 'I'm all right, Mrs May,' she said as they reached the sitting-room. 'You go and wait for the doctor. Thank God he lives so close. He'll be here any minute.'

Indeed, by the time the housekeeper had opened the front door she heard the sound of tyres scrunching on the gravel as David Gouray roared up the drive. The doctor was not on duty that Sunday and had been gardening when Vernon's urgent call had come. He had responded at once, and arrived wearing corduroy trousers and an old jacket. But he made no apologies for his appearance. He seized his bag and rushed into the house.

Some ten minutes later Mrs May showed him into the sitting-room, where she said the family would be. Actually only Cynthia and Peter and Christopher Winter were present; Julia had said she was cold and had gone up to her room to fetch a sweater, and there was still no sign of Clare or the churchgoers. Dr Gouray didn't keep them waiting.

'I've done all I can for Derek, but he needs hospital treatment, and the sooner the better,' he said at once. 'I've ordered an ambulance from Colombury, and it will be here shortly to take Derek into Oxford. The hospital's expecting him. He's got a bad wound and he's not a young man. There'll be the question of shock, too. But I don't think he's in any immediate danger.'

'Thank God for that,' Cynthia said.

'What do you mean by "wound?"' asked Peter. 'What happened?'

'I've no idea what happened.' The doctor was almost curt. 'But Derek has what appears to be a long knife wound stretching from his shoulder across his abdomen. Fortunately it's not very deep. Miss Brune also has a knife wound, but in her case the knife probably pierced her heart. I'm afraid I can't be more specific after a mere cursory examination, but I'm sorry to say she's dead.'

'Dead? Oh, poor Pauline!' Cynthia hid her face in her hands. 'I—I can't take it in,' she said. 'It's like a bad dream.'

'I've phoned the police station in Colombury,' Gouray went on. 'Sergeant Court is getting on to the Headquarters of the Thames Valley Police in Kidlington, and they'll be sending some officers. Meanwhile, no one should go into the dining-room except the ambulance men.' He turned as Julia and Simon came into the room. 'I'm sorry, but this is a nasty business. Where are the rest of your house party?'

'Valerie and the Smithsons are at church,' Simon said.

'And Clare's gone for a walk,' Peter added.

'Everyone will have to wait for the police. I know the Smithsons were meant to be going on to Stratford, but—'

'But that's absurd, David!' Cynthia said. 'It's nothing to do with Andrew and Janet—or any of us for that matter. Someone must have broken in. Perhaps Derek or Pauline disturbed a thief. And what about me? You're not proposing to stop me going in the ambulance with Derek, are you?'

'No, of course not, Cynthia,' said the doctor. It was the only possible reply.

'In that case, I'll go and pack an overnight bag.' Cynthia marched out of the room.

'I'm sorry. I didn't mean to upset her,' said Gouray to no one in particular. 'Was she very fond of this Pauline?'

It was Peter who answered. 'No. I gather Mother rather disliked her, but she felt compelled to be kind to her for old time's sake, as it were.'

'Peter!' Julia expostulated. 'Be careful what you say.'

Peter turned to stare at Julia, who went a delicate pink. 'Why?' he inquired.

'Julia's right,' Simon said. 'The police do have a habit of attaching unwarranted significance to casual remarks. It might be best to remember that.'

The doctor nodded his agreement. 'I must get back to

my patient. The ambulance should be here soon,' he said encouragingly. But as he went he was aware of leaving behind him an uneasy silence. Maybe it was caused by the thought of the imminent arrival of the police.

Cynthia ran upstairs and made straight for the room Pauline had occupied. This was the first reasonable opportunity she'd had, and she was certain that when the police arrived they would search the room, and afterwards probably seal it to prevent anyone from entering. And she wanted that metal box from the suitcase under the bed.

Thankful not to find a maid tidying the room, Cynthia quickly shut the door and bent down beside the bed. She pulled out the suitcase and opened it. The metal box was missing. She swore softly to herself, then began to search the room more thoroughly in the hope that Pauline had chosen a different hiding-place. But the box was nowhere to be found.

'Mrs Faudin? Are you there, Mrs Faudin?'

Cynthia hurriedly went out of the bedroom. 'I'm here, Vernon,' she said, and noted his surprise. Though she knew she had no need to attempt to explain what she was doing in Pauline's room, she couldn't help herself. 'I was looking to see if I could find the name of someone who should be told—about Miss Brune.'

'Next of kin, like.'

'Yes. But I don't know if she had any close relations. A lawyer, perhaps. Anyhow, you wanted me, Vernon?'

'Yes, madam. The ambulance is here, and Sergeant Court from Colombury Police Station, with a constable.'

'Right. I'll be down in a minute.'

In the event, it was more than five minutes before Cynthia reappeared carrying a small hold-all. She had brushed her hair, remade her face and looked both elegant and composed. Derek, lying very still on the stretcher, was being lifted into the ambulance under Dr Gouray's supervision and watched by Simon and Peter. The doctor turned to Cynthia, intending to help her up the steps of the vehicle.

'They'll know what to do in Oxford,' he said reassuringly. 'I must wait for the other police.'

'Thank you, David,' Cynthia said. She gave Peter a hurried kiss on the cheek, which he accepted but didn't reciprocate. 'I'll phone when there's any news. Tell Clare from me not to worry, and apologize to the Smithsons, will you, Peter? And Simon, ask Valerie to be hostess in my place, please. Mrs May will have everything under control.'

The two men nodded their agreement, and Cynthia climbed into the ambulance. She was thankful to be alone; neither the two ambulance men nor Derek's recumbent form counted. Here, with nothing expected of her, she could consider the situation objectively and plan for further contingencies. She closed her eyes with relief.

'As usual, Mother seems to have got everything organized,' Peter said as he and Simon watched the ambulance go down the drive; Dr Gouray was busy putting his bag back into his car. Sergeant Court and the constable were occupied in the dining-room, awaiting their superiors; the Sergeant's only comment had been to echo the doctor's instructions that no one but Cynthia was to leave the house.

'Don't be too sure,' said Simon. 'She appears to have overlooked what the police might get up to.'

'Perhaps she has, though I wouldn't put it past her to phone the Chief Constable—what's his name? Philip Midvale, of course—and demand that the whole affair be cleared up in twenty-four hours.' Peter laughed mirthlessly, 'Poor old Dad! What a damned shame this should have happened to him. At least we can be grateful he wasn't the one who was killed. And once he's fit enough he should be able to tell the police exactly what did happen. I suppose Mother must be right again. It can't have been an accident. It must have been a sneak thief who panicked when he was interrupted. Don't you think so, Doctor?' he added to Gouray who had just joined them.

'I don't know. And there's no point in guessing,' said the doctor.

Simon said, 'Whatever happened—whether it was a thief
or not—the next few days are going to be very unpleasant
for all of us. Police apart, Cynthia's a very well-known
woman, and when the media get hold of the story they'll
certainly make the most of it. You can't blame them, but—
but life may become difficult.'

Peter looked at his uncle curiously. Of course there would
be some publicity. Cynthia would enjoy playing the grief-
stricken but brave little wife, he thought cynically, and
presumably Derek would have to give evidence later at the
inquest on Pauline Brune and if the affair eventually reached
a court of law. But the other people at Longacres were surely
peripheral. Why should Simon be worried?

By now the three of them were standing in the hall, and
Simon said, 'I'm going up to my room for a minute or so.
Would you ask Mrs May to arrange a light lunch in the
sitting-room, Peter? You'll join us, Doctor, of course. Then
as soon as Valerie and the Smithsons get back from church
we'll all have a drink. I don't know about you, but I need
one before the high-powered police arrive.'

'OK. I'll also ask her to send some beer and sandwiches
to Court and his constable.'

While Simon ran upstairs, Peter showed Dr Gouray into
the sitting-room and then went in search of Mrs May in
the servants' quarters. Simon, who had searched Pauline
Brune's room earlier—unknowingly forestalling Cynthia's
attempt—had found not only the metal box hidden in the
suitcase beneath the bed, but also a leather key-tainer in
one of her handbags. He had taken both, but had not yet
examined the box's contents. This, he decided, was an ideal
opportunity.

The second key he tried fitted the lock and the box opened
easily. Quickly he inspected its contents, and retrieved some
neatly-packaged photographs, negatives and a reel of 16
millimetre ciné film. As he studied the prints, turned them
over to read the annotations—names, places, dates—on
their backs, and unreeled the film to hold it up to the light
he forgot he was at Longacres, forgot that at any moment

his wife might come into the bedroom, forgot that Derek was badly hurt and on his way to hospital. He was overwhelmed with surprise and, a moment later, shock. Then he heard the sounds of cars in the drive and guessed that the police had arrived in force.

Simon hastily rewound the film and repacked the box, locked it, pocketed the keys and put the box in his briefcase. He would have to decide what to do with this material, but that must wait. He must first find out how much Derek knew, and what story he intended to tell the authorities.

It was a thoughtful Simon Faudin who went down to the hall, where he found Sergeant Court's constable relegated to guard duty outside the dining-room door. In the sitting-room he discovered that Valerie and the Smithsons had returned from church and Clare from wherever she had been on her walk. They had been told of the morning's happenings, and were looking shocked, but he had scarcely time to greet them before, after a warning knock, Vernon announced Inspector Tyler. There was an immediate silence, and involuntarily they all rose to their feet and formed a semi-circle to face the tall, thin man who came into the room.

'Ladies and gentlemen, good morning—or perhaps it should be good afternoon. As your houseman said, I'm Detective-Inspector Tyler of the Thames Valley Police Force, and I'm sure that in the present sad circumstances I can rely on your full cooperation.' His glance travelled slowly around the group and he smiled gently.

Inspector Tyler had a high voice and a lugubrious expression. He spoke rather pompously and didn't exactly inspire confidence, though this impression had misled many an evil-doer. He was no fool. Even before he knew their names, he noticed the fact that Clare had been crying, that in spite of his arrival Simon had poured himself an outsize whisky and that Christopher Winter was very nervous.

'My men and I arrived some ten or fifteen minutes ago, as you know,' he began. 'We are now waiting for the pathologist. In the meantime my officers are photographing the scene, taking blood samples, and performing other routine duties. While this is happening, I would like to ask you some questions. Perhaps you would begin by identifying yourselves.' He took a piece of paper from his pocket. 'Sergeant Court has already given me a list of names, and explained the reason for your presence here.'

Simon took a long swallow of whisky and put down his glass. 'I'm Simon Faudin, Derek's brother,' he said, 'and I'm sure I may speak for everyone here when I say we're all deeply shocked, but of course we'll cooperate to the best of our ability. Are we right to assume that you will be in charge of any inquiries, Inspector Tyler?'

'Oh no, Mr Faudin, you would not be right in that assumption.' Tyler shook his head. 'I should have mentioned that my preliminary investigations indicate that this be treated as a case of murder. I have spoken to my Headquarters and Chief Inspector Tansey of our Serious Crime Squad will take charge.'

Part Two

CHAPTER 8

Detective Chief Inspector Tansey was already on his way to Longacres. He hadn't relished being called out on a Sunday morning, with the chicken stuffed and about to go into the oven, but he was resigned to the inconvenience. It went with the territory, as they used to say; it was part of the job—a job he enjoyed and could not conceive of changing. And, he thought, thank God for a wife who understood from personal experience the exigencies of his work, and appreciated how he felt about it.

Unwilling or unable to stand the uncertain hours, the spoiled meals, the broken engagements, Dick Tansey's first wife had walked out on him, taking their baby daughter with her. But nowadays that episode had retreated into a bad dream. He had been married, happily married, for almost two years to Hilary, whose own previous unsatisfactory marriage had ended when her husband was killed in the Falklands. A widow, she had joined the police, and as Detective-Sergeant Hilary Greenway, had assisted Tansey with several of his cases. Now, after a bad miscarriage, she had to her annoyance been relegated to a desk job at the Kidlington Headquarters of the Thames Valley Police. But still, she knew the pressures that were suffered by members of the Serious Crime Squad.

Sighing gently, Tansey wished that Hilary could have been beside him instead of his present driver, Detective-Sergeant Abbot. Not that he disliked the cheerful, extrovert Abbot. On the contrary he enjoyed working with the Oxfordshire man, whose judgement he had come to respect.

'You know where this place, Longacres, is, do you, Sergeant?' Tansey asked.

'Oh yes, sir. I know it well. It's not far from Colombury. A fine property and well looked after,' said Abbot, his voice accented by a soft burr. 'Mr Faudin has plenty of money.'

'And a brilliant wife, by all accounts.'

'Yes. An academic lady, but more than that. She's the head of her College and has the reputation of being a fine administrator.'

'Not a lady to cross, in fact?' Tansey queried.

'I've never met her, sir, but I should think you're probably right.' Abbot laughed.

'I wish I knew more about this case,' remarked Tansey. 'I've merely had three minutes' chat on the phone with Inspector Tyler, who's at Longacres with a team, acting as Scene of Crime Officer. Still, at least there's not been too much delay in getting on to us.'

Some fifteen minutes later the unmarked police car turned into the driveway of Longacres. There were two police cars there already, and a closed van with windows in the side. Inspector Tyler had completed his preliminary questioning and had left the family and their friends to the buffet that Mrs May had provided in the sitting-room, with Sergeant Court's constable to keep them company. His team, too, had completed their initial tasks, and were making the best of some sandwiches in the van while awaiting further instructions. Tyler himself was waiting for Tansey in the hall and, as soon as he heard the car, came out of the front door.

'Good afternoon, sir,' he said at once, and went on before Tansey had time to respond. 'I believe you'll agree with me that this is a somewhat unusual case, though of course when you've had a chance to question Mr Derek Faudin all may become clear.'

'Yes, let's hope so,' Tansey agreed. 'At the moment I know nothing except what you told me. Apparently we've got a dead woman, probably knifed through the heart, and a man called Derek Faudin in hospital with a great slash down his front.'

'That is correct, sir,' said Tyler and, seeing Sergeant Abbot's grin, added pointedly, 'What we don't have, however, is any sign of a weapon.'

'And that is certainly interesting,' said Tansey. Tyler had scored a point, he thought. He shook himself. 'Let's see where all this happened, shall we? And then meet the inhabitants,' he said briskly.

'It was in the dining-room, sir,' said Tyler, as he escorted them there and opened the door with a somewhat proprietorial air. Together the three officers stood just inside and regarded the scene. On the carpet there was a chalk outline of a body, where Derek Faudin had fallen. Tansey went and stood beside it. He measured with his eye the distance to the place where Pauline Brune still lay, covered by a sheet.

'As you know, Mr Derek Faudin, the owner of Longacres, has been taken to hospital, sir,' said Tyler, 'but Dr Gouray showed us exactly where and how he was lying. Reasonably enough, Mrs Cynthia Faudin, his wife, accompanied him. Mr Faudin and his wife are the only persons staying in the house this weekend who are not present now. Miss Brune, who had been staying for a week or so, hasn't been moved at all, except slightly for the examination Dr Gouray had to make to pronounce her dead. At present we are waiting for the pathologist. He should be here very soon.'

Tansey nodded his approval. 'That's fine, Inspector.' He knelt and took a long look at the round spots of blood beside the chalk outline, before peeling back the sheet to inspect Pauline Brune's body. 'And no sign of a weapon,' he said thoughtfully.

'No. And the french window was unlocked.'

Tansey went across to inspect it. 'There's a minute smear of blood on the paintwork by the window,' he said, peering at it closely. 'We'll need the woodwork fingerprinted, and the handles inside and outside.'

'The handles have already been done, sir, together with the rest of the routine,' Tyler said stiffly. 'There's a good

print on an outside one, but the inside handles look to me
as if they've been wiped.'

Tansey frowned. 'That's odd,' he said. 'Could be carelessness, I suppose, but—Ah well, we're just at the beginning,
and there's a long way to go yet. You said the dead woman
was a house guest What about the room she occupied?'

'We haven't got around to the rest of the premises yet,
sir,' replied Tyler, 'but I have locked and sealed Miss
Brune's room. Here's the key.'

'Good. Abbot and I will have a look at it as soon as
possible and we shall probably need some of your men there
later, Inspector. Now, let's get down to practicalities. I saw
you had one of our vans outside. You're using it as an
incident room?'

'Yes, sir. And Mr Simon Faudin agreed that they would
move out of what they call the sitting-room where they've
been having lunch, so that it can serve as an interview room
for you. The house is full at the moment. It was Mr Derek
Faudin's birthday yesterday and I gather they had a grand
party. I have a complete list of the guests staying here and
the staff, both resident and temporary . . .' Tyler described
the situation in detail, and explained what he understood
of the relationships of the various people concerned.

By the time he had finished Tansey, who preferred to
soak up atmosphere at his own pace, was feeling slightly
overwhelmed, but he recovered himself and said, 'That's
splendid, Inspector, and very helpful. You've accomplished
a great deal in a short time and, thanks to your work, I've
got a pretty clear picture.'

'Good of you to say so, sir.' Tyler was pleased.

Tansey nodded and said, 'Now, if only I could have a list
of these individuals with a note about each, I—'

'Of course, sir. I have just what you need.' Tyler forestalled the Chief Inspector's request by proffering a typed
sheet. 'The first person to discover the—er—incident was
Mrs May, the housekeeper. Perhaps you would—'

'Yes,' Tansey said. 'I'll begin with her, after I've had a
word with this Dr Gouray. But first I'd better introduce

myself and Sergeant Abbot. It'll give me an opportunity to put faces to these names. You say they're all gathered in the sitting-room at the moment?'

'All but the staff, sir,' replied Tyler as he led the way.

Introductions over, and the sitting-room cleared, the Chief Inspector sent for Mrs May while he glanced over the reports Inspector Tyler had produced so efficiently. The housekeeper created a good impression by arriving with a tray of coffee and sandwiches. Both Tansey and Abbot, neither of whom had eaten since breakfast, were duly grateful and the housekeeper smiled at them in approval as they began to eat. Though she was a shrewd woman it did not occur to her that the relaxed atmosphere was just what the Chief Inspector wanted to create. He hoped it might lead her into indiscretions.

'Tell us about Miss Brune, if you will, Mrs May,' said Tansey as he bit appreciatively into a smoked salmon sandwich. 'Is she a regular visitor to Longacres?'

'Oh no. She's never been here before.'

Mrs May did her best to explain Pauline Brune—or the Pauline Brune with whom she was acquainted. Involuntarily she demonstrated her own perplexity. Tansey let her talk and didn't interrupt her until, suddenly, as if she had thought of something special, she stopped speaking.

'You were saying, Mrs May,' Tansey prompted.

Mrs May looked at him. She saw a tall, lean man in his late thirties with a pleasant face and serious grey eyes. He was, she realized, almost young enough to be her son, and instinctively she felt herself in sympathy with him. But she had her duty to her employers to bear in mind. What was said between her and Vernon was one matter, what she told a strange police officer quite another. And there was this big constable sitting quietly in the background, eating away, but taking in everything that was being said or hinted.

As if he had read her thoughts Tansey said, 'Mrs May, I appreciate that in a big house like Longacres, especially over such a weekend when it's full of guests, you must see and hear a lot that normally you wouldn't dream of repeating. However, the present circumstances are exceptional. Pauline Brune has been killed, and Derek Faudin, your employer, savagely attacked. It's your duty to help us in every way you can, even if you feel you're repeating gossip or—'

'It's not gossip exactly,' said Mrs May slowly, and Tansey knew that he had won; he had succeeded in breaking into her reserve. 'It's more an impression, but Vernon—he's our houseman—will tell you the same.'

Pauline Brune, Tansey learnt, had not been a popular guest. She had been arrogant towards the staff and behaved as if she were in her own home. She arrived, Mrs May had at first understood, for a few days, but had clearly outstayed her welcome. Mr Faudin had shown his irritation at her continued presence, and had even been heard asking Mrs Faudin when her 'old friend' would be leaving.

'And I don't believe that Mrs Faudin herself liked Miss Brune all that much either,' Mrs May said. 'I think she felt that by asking her to stay at Longacres she had done her a kindness, but Miss Brune was taking advantage of it, though of course it would have been embarrassing to ask her to leave. Incidentally, Chief Inspector, I imagine you'll want to see her room. Your colleague has locked it and taken the key and—' Again, Mrs May stopped.

'I know,' said Tansey absently. Then, 'And what? Were you glad to see the room locked? Have you ever seen anyone unexpected in there?'

Mrs May stared at him in surprise. 'I—er—how—'

Tansey grinned at her. 'Not magic, Mrs May, I assure you. Merely a policeman's intuition—experience, if you like. Who was it? Mrs Faudin, perhaps?'

'She had every right to be there. It's her house. But—but—'

Reluctantly Mrs May explained how she had found her employer peering under Pauline Brune's bed, with the improbable excuse that she had seen a spider. Tansey didn't press the point. Instead he asked the housekeeper to describe how she had come to find Derek Faudin and Pauline Brune in the dining-room.

Relieved that the Chief Inspector had lighted on what she felt to be a safer topic, Mrs May was expansive. She even maintained that she had hesitated in the doorway when she thought that Christopher Winter had uttered some inarticulate sound. 'I was afraid for him,' she said. 'He looked ghastly, as if he were about to have a heart attack, and he'd asked for water.'

Tansey's interviews continued. Vernon confirmed what Mrs May had said about the discoveries in the dining-room. He had fetched Mr Simon Faudin from the library and, on Mr Faudin's instructions, had telephoned Dr Gouray who had arrived very quickly.

'And the doctor phoned for an ambulance and the local police?'

'Yes, sir. Then Mrs Faudin appeared.'

'Appeared?' Tansey queried.

'Yes, sir. We thought she'd gone to church, but she came back,' Vernon said. 'When she found out what was happening she insisted on going into the dining-room and naturally became upset. But she recovered quickly and went upstairs to pack an overnight bag so that she could go with Mr Faudin in the ambulance, and to try and find the name of someone who should be informed of Miss Brune's death. I know that because she told me when I saw her coming out of Miss Brune's room.'

'I see,' said Tansey.

'Coincidence, sir?' Abbot inquired as Vernon departed. 'That's the second time we know of that the lady's been found in the victim's room.'

Tansey gave an expressive shrug. He had asked Vernon to get Simon Tansey, who came almost at once, accompanied by his wife. He explained that he could be of little help as he had spent the morning in the library. But Valerie had gone to church with the Smithsons and Cynthia Faudin, and she was able to supply the times at which they

had left Longacres and when Cynthia had left the group to
return to look for Derek. She also knew when they had been
overtaken by the young man who had run off into the woods,
and when she and the Smithsons had left St Matthew's
Church.

Valerie Faudin's detailed account was confirmed by the
Smithsons, and Tansey finally agreed that, as long as he
were given the name of their hotel in Stratford there was no
reason why they shouldn't leave Longacres.'

'That's very good of you, Chief Inspector,' Andrew Smithson said. 'Very cooperative. I guess it's more than our police
would do at home.'

'Providing you keep in touch,' Tansey warned. 'And
you mustn't leave the country without letting us know. You
may well be needed to corroborate possibly vital times or
other evidence, or to help identify the young man you
saw.'

'We'd planned to be in England for at least another four
weeks,' said Janet Smithson, 'and we'd be keeping in touch
anyway. We'll want to know how poor cousin Derek is
faring. It's a dreadful business, this—really dreadful.'

'Nice people,' Tansey remarked when they had gone. 'I
think we can safely write them off as suspects—and Mrs
Simon Faudin. But did anything strike you about the
timings, Abbot?'

'Not really, sir—except this young man—'

'Oh yes. This young man would be a very convenient
villain, wouldn't he? But the timings, Abbot. Mrs Cynthia
Faudin seems to have been hurrying back to Longacres
pretty slowly, doesn't she? I wonder why.'

Abbot had no chance to make a suggestion before they
were interrupted by the pathologist, who briefly poked his
head into the sitting-room to say that death had probably
occurred between nine and twelve, and that he hoped to
schedule the PM for Tuesday or Wednesday. In the meantime, he'd make a point of looking at Mr Derek Faudin's
wound.

The pathologist disappeared before Tansey had a chance

to protest, and the Chief Inspector laughed in disgust. 'Tuesday or Wednesday!' he exclaimed. 'That's a big help.'

Tansey sent Sergeant Abbot to fetch Peter Faudin, and showed some surprise when Peter entered the sitting-room, to be followed by his sister Clare, and Julia. Abbot, bringing up the rear, made a gesture as if to indicate that he had had no choice in the matter, and Tansey accepted the situation, gesturing to Abbot to arrange three chairs in front of the table he was using as a desk.

'As I told your sergeant, this will save you time, Chief Inspector,' Peter Faudin said with assurance. 'You'll be able to cross us all off that little list of possible suspects I'm sure you've got somewhere.'

'Good,' said Tansey drily. 'I'm always glad of help.'

Peter Faudin had the grace to grin. 'First, none of us had ever met Pauline Brune before this weekend, and Julia had never even met Dad. Secondly, Clare and I wouldn't dream of hurting our father in any way. In any case, we'd no motive to do so. Thirdly, Julia and I were together all the morning, and Clare went for a walk immediately after breakfast.' He turned to Clare, who nodded her agreement. 'Miss Brune was certainly alive at that time.'

'How can you be sure?' asked Tansey abruptly. 'Did you see her, speak to her?'

'No, but—What do you mean? She was killed in the dining-room, wasn't she? We were all *there* at breakfast-time.'

'We heard her in the lib—' Julia began.

Tansey smiled. He hadn't meant anything by his abrupt question, but had merely wanted to rattle Peter Faudin and get control of the interview. Not only had he succeeded, but he had gained some new information into the bargain. He looked straight at Julia. 'You heard her in the library. When? Who was she talking to?' he demanded.

Julia gave Peter a sideways glance. 'We were going down to breakfast. We heard her voice as we passed the library. Perhaps the door wasn't properly shut.'

'And who was she speaking to?' Tansey repeated his question more slowly and emphatically.

'Uncle Simon,' said Peter at last. 'No reason why not, surely?'

'None. They were having an argument, yes?' It was a guess, of course, but from the expressions on the two faces Tansey knew it was a good guess.

'We didn't eavesdrop,' Peter said coldly. 'Perhaps you should ask Simon.'

'I shall.' Tansey gestured to Abbot, who left the sitting-room. 'Now, what else can you tell me?'

Julia let her narrow shoulders rise and fall in an elegant movement that wasn't quite a shrug. 'Nothing, really,' she said. 'I don't imagine it's important, but I did see Simon come out of Pauline's room. I'd gone upstairs to fetch a sweater.'

'Oh,' said Tansey. 'And when was this?'

'Well after the—the discovery. It was just before Dr Gouray came into the sitting-room to explain that he'd sent for an ambulance and—'

'This is the first time you've mentioned seeing Simon in Pauline's room,' Peter said quickly.

'I'd quite forgotten about it. Anyway, it can't be relevant, Peter.' Julia turned to Tansey. 'You only had to see Derek and Simon Faudin together to know how fond they were of each other. Simon would never have hurt Derek deliberately, and if there'd been an accident I'm perfectly sure he wouldn't have left Derek lying there if he was in any danger.'

Julia spoke with a conviction that impressed Tansey, though he reflected that her acquaintance with most of these people was very limited. But Peter and Clare were nodding their heads in agreement.

'And your walk,' Tansey said to Clare. 'Where did you go?'

The girl hesitated for a moment. Then, 'Oh, just around and about,' she said. 'I hadn't been feeling well, and I wanted some air.'

'Did you meet anyone?'

'Er—no. No.'

'I see,' said Tansey, getting to his feet to show that he had finished with the three of them. 'Many thanks for your help,' he said.

The two girls went ahead of Peter, who stopped in the doorway. 'You've not had a chance to talk to my mother yet, Chief Inspector. She believes that Dad and Pauline Brune interrupted a thief, who attacked them. You've considered that as a possibility?'

'Oh yes, indeed, Mr Faudin,' said Tansey. 'That's always a convenient explanation, isn't it? But I'm bearing it in mind.'

Abbot's return with Simon Faudin put an end to the conversation. Peter went reluctantly and, without being asked, Simon sat down opposite Tansey.

'What is it now, Chief Inspector. I've told you all I know, which admittedly wasn't much, but—'

'You didn't tell me you'd quarrelled with Miss Brune in the library earlier today.'

'We had an argument, Chief Inspector, but scarcely a quarrel.' Simon Faudin laughed. 'She wanted to take away a book I hadn't finished with, though I'd put it aside for the moment. Naturally I objected. Wouldn't you have done the same?'

'I expect so,' Tansey agreed. 'I get the impression she was a what shall I say?—a difficult guest.'

'A poor creature, really. No close relations and not many friends, I should think,' Simon said. 'I tried to find a diary or something in her room to indicate who should be told of her death, but I didn't succeed. Cynthia may know, or perhaps I didn't look in the right place.' He took out a large silk handkerchief and blew his nose. 'It's my brother I'm worried about. He's quite a few years older than me and apart from his injury this must have been a shock to him.'

'A shock to all of you, I should think,' said Tansey.

Simon Faudin nodded, but made no other response. 'If there's nothing more, Chief Inspector—'

'No, thank you, Mr Faudin,' Tansey said and, when Simon had gone, 'That's a cool customer, Sergeant.'

'And clever, sir,' said Abbot. 'We certainly didn't take him by surprise.'

'No,' Tansey said absently, studying the list of names Inspector Tyler had given him. 'We still have to see old Mr Winter, and we need another word with Clare Faudin—by herself this time. But they'll keep.' He stood up and stretched. 'I think a change of scene would do us good, Abbot. Let's have a look at the rest of this establishment, and join in the popular pastime of seeing what's to be found in Miss Brune's room.'

CHAPTER 9

'And that, Sergeant Abbot, is how the other half lives,' said Chief Inspector Tansey as Mrs May, who had been showing them around Longacres, left them in the room that had been Pauline Brune's for the last few weeks.

Abbot grinned. 'A precious small half, if you ask me, sir,' he said. 'Do you think Miss Brune belonged to it?'

'The other half? I don't know. It's hard to decide.' Tansey was staring doubtfully at the clothes in the hanging cupboard. He sensed that there were some inconsistencies in the array of garments, but couldn't have said what it was. He wished Hilary was there to help him. 'Any luck?'

'Not so far. She doesn't seem to have kept any letters or personal papers. As yet, no passport—perhaps she didn't go abroad. No cheque-book. No credit cards.'

But both men were experienced police officers and they had time on their side. Their searches were both more thorough and more methodical than those of either Cynthia or Simon Faudin, and eventually they were rewarded. Abbot was the first to make a find. Sliding his hand along the underside of a drawer in the chest of drawers he touched what proved to be a large brown envelope that had been attached to the wood with tape.

'A careful lady,' Tansey commented.

'But not careful enough to avoid getting killed,' Abbot reminded him.

Tansey took a pair of surgical gloves from his pocket and slipped them on before carefully opening the envelope. It contained two objects. The first was a cheque-book from an Oxford branch of one of the High Street clearing banks, personalized with the name of Mrs Pauline Gaul.

The second was a slip of paper on which some notes had been jotted. 'Mark. b. Sep 1965. N.Y. Antonia Merridew.' Tansey showed this slip to Abbot, shrugged his shoulders, folded it and returned it to its envelope.

'Not only a careful lady but a mysterious one,' he said. 'Gaul? And married, was she? Or was that a name she assumed for some reason or other. She must have started out as Brune, because that seems to be how Mrs Faudin knew her years ago.' He thought for a moment, then added, 'With any luck the bank will help to clear that up.'

They continued their search with renewed enthusiasm, and it was the Chief Inspector who spotted the key. It was in a cheap jewellery box among a collection of necklaces, brooches and rings, none of which seemed at first sight to have any great value. He examined the key with interest.

'This kind of key's unmistakable, Abbot, as you know. It opens a safe deposit box. Tomorrow we visit her Bank and make some inquiries about Miss or Mrs Gaul. And, if he's well enough and the doctors permit, we might be able to have a chat with Derek Faudin. When we can, a lot of things may become clear.'

'Sounds good, sir, but—' Abbot broke off as there was a tap at the door. He opened it to Vernon. 'Yes?'

'Inspector Tyler would be glad of the Chief Inspector's presence,' announced Vernon. 'I gather he believes the weapon has been found.'

'Really?' said Tansey. 'All right. That's splendid. We'll be down soon. Thank you.'

A sharp-eyed member of Tyler's team, taking part in a finger-tip search of the ground outside the french windows of the dining-room, had noticed in a flowerbed what he at first thought was a small round plant. Closer inspection had shown it to be the end of the hilt of what was almost certainly a bone-handled carving knife, and indeed a rapid glance through the drawers of the sideboard had revealed a carving fork that was clearly its mate. The Inspector had been delighted.

By the time Tansey and Abbot arrived on the scene photographs had already been taken, and the knife was being carefully drawn from the ground and placed in a plastic bag. It would be shown to the pathologist before the PM, and then forensic experts would examine it, subject it to a variety of tests and pronounce their verdicts. At least for the moment Tansey was more interested in where the knife had been located.

'It helps make a very credible scenario,' said Inspector Tyler with satisfaction.

'Entitled, "The Surprised Thief", Inspector?' Tansey suggested.

'What's wrong with that?' Tyler demanded. 'It fits, doesn't it? It makes sense.'

'It's a working hypothesis, certainly,' Tansey admitted. 'And we've even come on a possible suspect.' He described the young man whom the Smithsons and Valerie Faudin had seen on their way to church that morning.

'But, sir, that—that was probably Terry.'

The three detectives turned to stare at Sergeant Court. No one had told him that his presence was no longer required, and that if he wished he could return home, or to the police station in Colombury. So he had hovered on the outskirts of Inspector Tyler's scene of crime team, watching them curiously as they went about their work and taking care not to hinder them. Now he had suddenly become the centre of attention.

'At least it—it sounds as if it might have been Terry.' He hastened to amend his previous statement.

'And who, may we ask, is this Terry?' Tyler inquired.

'I don't know what his name is, sir,' Court said. 'But he's got one of those motorized caravans and he turned up in the neighbourhood about a month ago and asked John Stone—who farms not far from Colombury—if he might park in one of his fields for a small payment. John said yes. He buys milk and eggs from the farm, and he's been no bother. He told John that he's writing a book.'

'We'll have to talk to him,' Tansey said, 'but that can wait. We've really nothing against him at the moment.' He turned to Sergeant Court. 'You keep an eye on this caravan, Sergeant. Make sure it doesn't move on in the meantime. We'll have to pick him up if it looks as though he's about to scarper. Get some help from Kidlington, if you need it.'

'Yes, sir,' said Sergeant Court smartly.

'You don't really believe he could be our man, do you?' Tyler said after Court had left them.

'Frankly, no,' replied Tansey, 'but I admit I could be wrong. Anyway, I've a couple more preliminary interviews—with old Mr Winter and Miss Clare. Then, if nothing extraordinary turns up, I think we might as well call it a day as far as Longacres is concerned. After all, it is Sunday, and there'll still be the paperwork to do and probably the press to handle.'

While they waited in the sitting-room for Christopher Winter to appear, Abbot said rather diffidently, 'Sir, you don't go for this "surprised thief" idea, do you?'

'Not much.'

'But why not? As Inspector Tyler said, it does seem to fit.'

'I distrust it primarily because so many people in the house have been so keen that I should accept it,' Tansey said slowly. 'Now I'm beginning to wonder if it wasn't laid on for our benefit. Abbot, can you imagine a would-be thief—incidentally, we must get Mrs May to check if anything's missing—surprised in the act, opening a drawer in a sideboard, finding a knife, quite by chance of course, and then attacking two able-bodied people.'

'Well,' said Abbot, 'put like that—'

'And,' interrupted Tansey, 'think of the relative positions of the three of them, remembering that Derek Faudin had a frontal wound. Either he was facing the sideboard, and both he and the Brune-Gaul woman—let's go on calling her Pauline Brune for simplicity—could see exactly what was happening. In that case surely the woman, who was nearest to the door, would have had time to run screaming into the hall to raise the alarm.'

'You're right, sir,' said Abbot.

Tansey continued, 'And exactly the same would apply if for some unknown reason Derek Faudin had his back to this imaginary interloper. It seems to me inconceivable that both he and the woman would have been ignoring the stranger to such an extent as the "surprised thief" scenario demands—unless they knew him, of course; in that case, he would hardly have been a surprised thief, would he . . .' The Chief Inspector's voice trailed away, but finally he shook his head. 'No, Abbot,' he said at last. 'I don't believe the simple theory does fit.'

There was no time for them to discuss the problem further. Christopher Winter had come into the sitting-room. He looked frail—too frail to have killed Faudin and Brune, Tansey thought—but quite composed. Yet Tyler had noticed that earlier he had shown signs of nervousness or anxiety. Whether or not the Inspector had been right about that—and on the whole it was most likely that he had—Winter was in full control of himself now.

'We won't keep you long, Mr Winter,' Tansey said. 'Just one or two questions.'

'I'd help if I could, Chief Inspector. Derek Faudin is a very old friend. Unfortunately, however, I—'

'You were leaning against the wall in the hall this morning when Mrs May came by,' said Tansey, cutting off Winter's comments. 'Were you unwell?'

'Yes. I felt a little shaky suddenly. I'm not a young man, you know, and I'm quite accustomed to these turns, as we used to call them.'

Tansey noticed that, for all his seeming amiability, Christopher Winter hadn't relished being interrupted. 'Now, why were you in the hall at that moment? Where were you going?'

'I don't see what—But if you must know, Chief Inspector, I wasn't feeling my best after breakfast. Too much excitement last night, perhaps, though I hadn't over-indulged. And I was on my way to the dining-room. I hoped a nip of brandy would help. It often does in such circumstances.'

'Ah, I understand.' Tansey smiled apologetically. 'I see that I should have asked where you had been. You went into the dining-room.'

'No!'

There was a short silence. Tansey waited, but Christopher Winter added nothing to his abrupt denial, and the Chief Inspector was forced to continue.

'Am I to understand that you've not been in the dining-room today, Mr Winter? You had breakfast in your room?'

'No, I hadn't, and yes, I did—have breakfast in my room.'

Tansey spoke slowly, emphasizing each word. 'Then, if you hadn't been in the dining-room and didn't know that your old friend Derek Faudin, as well as Miss Brune, was lying on the floor covered in blood, why did you try to stop Mrs May from entering it?'

'I—I didn't. Why—'

The old man had gone white around the mouth, but he lifted his head and glared at Tansey. 'Chief Inspector, are you thinking I'm a liar?'

'Certainly not, Mr Winter,' said Tansey diplomatically. 'It was merely that Mrs May said that you called out to her as she went to the dining-room door to fetch you some water, but she may have been mistaken. Or perhaps, as you were unwell, you made some inarticulate sound.'

'Not that I recall.' Now Winter's voice was cold and hostile.

'In that case, Mr Winter, if you're not able to help us any further . . .' Tansey paused hopefully, but there was no response. 'Then thank you very much, sir.'

Christopher Winter got stiffly to his feet. He nodded at Tansey, ignored Abbot who opened the door for him and stumped from the room. Tansey shook his head sadly.

'The old boy's not a very good liar,' he said.

'But why should he lie, sir? And weren't you pretty brusque with him? I thought at one moment he was going to faint.'

'So did I, I must admit. But he didn't. Perhaps he's tougher than he seems. As to why should he lie, that's a good question, isn't it, Sergeant? It could be because he's trying to cover up for someone.'

'You mean he might have opened the dining-room door and seen someone leaving through the french window?'

'It's a possibility,' Tansey replied, though that was not what he had been thinking. 'Go and find Clare Faudin for us, will you?'

'Yes, sir,' said Abbot cheerfully, but five minutes later he returned alone; Clare had gone to bed with a bad headache.

There was, however, to be one extra interview that day. The Chief Inspector had decided that it would be unwise to insist on seeing Clare Faudin immediately, and was tidying up his papers in preparation for his departure when, without any knock, the door of the sitting-room opened and a smartly-dressed woman came in. There was no question but that this was the redoubtable Cynthia Faudin. She even looked vaguely familiar, and Tansey realized that he had seen her photograph in the newspapers, and had once heard her being interviewed on television.

She wasted no time with any preliminaries or pleasantries; she didn't even bother to introduce herself. 'Chief Inspector,' she said, 'I've been talking to your man downstairs. He tells me that both the dining-room and Miss Brune's room must remain sealed. The bedroom doesn't matter, but it's essential we should have the use of the dining-room as soon as possible. To start with, the carpet must be cleaned immediately.'

Tansey stared at her in surprise. Surely these were trivialities compared with—However, he recovered himself and said, 'Mrs Faudin, we may well have to remove the carpet as evidence. I'd do my best to oblige you, but surely I don't have to remind you that this is a murder inquiry. And, incidentally, how is your husband?'

'In no danger, or I shouldn't be here, Chief Inspector,' Cynthia Faudin said shortly. Then, as Tansey waited, she went on. 'His condition's perfectly stable, but they're keeping him in intensive care because of the possibility of shock later. The doctors said there was nothing I could do for him, so I decided it would be best for me to return to Longacres, and a fellow don from my College was kind enough to give me a lift. Now—' Cynthia seemed to have accepted Tansey's decision about the dining-room, for she sat down and crossed her legs. 'I expect you want to ask me some questions, Chief Inspector.'

'Yes, Mrs Faudin, a few. First, have you spoken to your husband?'

'Yes, a few words—'

'About—'

'No. Not about what happened this morning. The medical men refused to permit me to raise the subject—the chance of shock, again, I suppose.'

'I see. Well, we shall have to make our own inquiries from the hospital in the morning.'

'Naturally. But you'll have to get the doctors' permission before you may question my husband.'

'Of course, but let's leave that point, Mrs Faudin. Perhaps you'd tell us what you know of Pauline Brune.'

'Certainly, though I'm afraid it's not a great deal.'

Indeed, what Cynthia had to say added little to Tansey's

knowledge of the dead woman. Cynthia told him that she had literally bumped into Pauline in Oxford, that she hadn't seen her for years, but a few days later Pauline had phoned to say she had lost her job, was homeless and more or less penniless, and . . .

She explained her earlier relationship with Pauline Brune, and concluded, 'I have to admit that she'd rather outstayed her welcome, but no one would have wished such a dreadful death on her. I'm particularly appalled that it should have happened here, in our house, and I know that when my husband's condition permits he'll agree with me that we should offer a substantial reward to anyone who can help to bring to justice the individual guilty of this appalling crime.'

The last few sentences sounded almost as if they had been rehearsed, Tansey though cynically, but he contented himself with replying, 'That's very generous of you, Mrs Faudin, but it may not be necessary.'

'You mean you—'

Tansey had no intention of explaining what he meant; in fact, he would have found it difficult to be explicit. He had been considering Cynthia Faudin's story, and asked, 'You say Miss Brune's father died, and Pauline came to stay with your family—work for them in fact—'

'Yes.'

'What about Mrs Brune, her mother?'

'Oh, I should have mentioned that. She'd been dead for some years. Pauline and her father were living alone in the vicarage of St Michael and All Angels. I guess that in fact she was housekeeping for him, before she came to home-help for us.'

'I see. And how long exactly was she with your family?'

'With us? I can't see that it matters. Less than a year, anyway.'

'And why did she leave you?'

'I—I really don't know. She found a better job, I suppose. Remember, I was only about twelve at the time.'

'I understand, Mrs Faudin,' said Tansey. 'Thank you.

Just a few further questions. Do you know if Pauline Brune was married? Have you ever heard her mention the name Gaul?'

Cynthia stared at him in apparent astonishment. 'Married? Not as far as I know. If she had been, she certainly never mentioned it. And I've never heard of Gaul, except as a classical name for France.'

'I see,' said Tansey again, changing the subject quickly. 'Now, at ten-thirty this morning you were about to set off to church with the Smithsons and your sister-in-law, I understand. Weren't you surprised when your husband suddenly said he had to make a phone call before accompanying you?'

'No, not really. Derek's retired, but he's kept a lot of business interests and it's often easier to reach a fellow-director at home on a Sunday than at his office. If the man's a friend, he won't mind.'

'And when your husband failed to catch you up, you were worried and went back to look for him. Did you come straight back?'

Cynthia Faudin frowned. 'I don't understand.'

'You seem to have taken a long time to reach here. One might have expected you to hurry.'

'Oh, but I did hurry, Chief Inspector. You want to know why I seemed so slow. I twisted my ankle on a rut and it was most painful for a short while. Fortunately it seems to have recovered, but at the time it held me up.'

Tansey nodded. 'That explains that, then,' he said. 'I'm just tidying up loose ends, Mrs Faudin. Incidentally, do you know the address of Miss Brune's last employer?'

'No. I believe it was a Mrs Kent, and I think she lived near Gloucester, but I wouldn't swear to it. Pauline was with her for six years, I gathered,' Cynthia said. 'Is it important?'

'Perhaps.' The Chief Inspector smiled disarmingly, pushed back his chair and stood up. 'It's impossible to say what is or is not important at this stage of an inquiry, Mrs Faudin. Anyway, we can't do any more today, but we'll be back tomorrow, I assure you. And I'm sorry about your dining-room.'

Cynthia Faudin nodded, but she made no comment.

CHAPTER 10

The next morning Tansey had a brief conference with Philip Midvale, the Chief Constable, before making arrangements to obtain the court order that would enable him to gain access to the dead woman's banking account and her safe deposit box. Getting the order took a couple of hours, but luckily Midvale was acquainted with Mr Timson, the manager of the branch of the bank in question, and undertook to telephone him and explain the situation and the Chief Inspector's mission.

The manager, on whom Tansey and Abbot called at about eleven o'clock, was in his early forties, capable and efficient, though clearly anxious to avoid any scandal that might reflect on his branch and his bank. He had already made himself familiar with his deceased client's affairs, and was prepared to cooperate. Nevertheless, once he had greeted the police officers affably, he called in his assistant manager, and together they examined the court order carefully. That done, he began to relax.

'As a matter of fact,' he said, 'I've sometimes wondered about Mrs Gaul's accounts myself. I've never met the lady, although she's been dealing with this branch for fifteen years, long before my time here. One can't know all one's customers, but she might have—' He paused thoughtfully. 'And what's more, I've made a few inquiries since Philip Midvale phoned, and no one on the staff here remembers her clearly. Almost all her transactions were carried out through other branches, although she did appear very occasionally, almost always just to get at her safe-deposit box.'

'I see,' said Tansey. 'We'll come to the box in a minute. But first, she really was married, as far as you know?'

'Oh yes,' said Timson, surprised. 'Look, here's the original mandate she signed when she opened the accounts; we keep these bits of card indefinitely, together with any updates. She entered "Mrs" in the appropriate space.'

'I see,' said Tansey agin. 'And you keep mentioning accounts in the plural. There was more than one?'

'Yes, indeed,' said Timson. 'Here are details for the past eighteen months. She had a current account, in which she kept a small balance—that's the cheque-book you have. As I said, she made almost all her deposits by remittance from other branches—you know the modern banking system as well as I do, I'm sure. I've checked and recently they have usually come from one of our Gloucester branches. All the debits on this account were by cheque—for cash drawn from other branches, again recently mainly in Gloucester, or for small payments. In addition, she had a deposit account, with a present balance of over £42,000. Credits for this seem always to have come through other branches, in quite large sums and at irregular intervals. Very occasionally we would receive a letter asking us to transfer the odd thousand pounds from the deposit to the current account.'

There was a pause while Tansey tried to get used to the idea that the dead woman, who was supposed to be poverty-stricken, had in fact possessed a reasonable capital sum—a sum she was unlikely to have saved from her salary as a companion-help. He studied the papers for a few minutes in silence, and then said, 'And this address—care of Mrs B. Kent in a village just outside Gloucester—is the latest you have for Mrs Gaul; it's difference from the one on the mandate, which looks like a flat here in Oxford.'

'There have been a number of changes over the years, I'm sure,' said the manager. 'We wouldn't keep a record of them all, but the Gloucester one is certainly the latest. Not that we used it much. I see she only asked for annual statements. Most customers want current account statements every month.'

'I see,' said Tansey. 'Now, these deposits—especially the

larger ones. Would there be any record of how they were
paid in, whether in the form of cheques or as cash?'

'Not here. All we would get is the remittance slip. But
the receiving branch would know. I'll make some inquiries,
though it may take a few days.'

'That would be most kind of you, Mr Timson. I see that
almost all the credits to the deposit account were round
sums, and fairly substantial sums, as you said—£4,000 or
£5,000. If they were in cash, would the receiving branch be
likely to raise an eyebrow?'

'£5,000 in cash? Not in the least. It happens all the
time. Mind you, really large sums—£25,000 or certainly
£100,000—would be noted. We'd accept the deposit, but in
the case of very large cash sums and in the absence of a
satisfactory explanation, we might consider notifying the
police—just in case, you know.'

'I see,' Tansey repeated. 'And would it be possible to get
copies of all the cheques drawn on the current account for
the past few years?'

'The past seven years, certainly. But it will take a little
time. Shall I—?'

'Many thanks, again. And we'll have to try for a formal
identification. I have some photographs of the dead woman,
and we must be certain if any of your staff do recognize her.
Surely anyone who escorted her to her box should remember
something. These photographs show only the face and
they're not in the least distressing. May we leave it to you
to pass them round, and see what you can get from your
staff? I'm sure that would be better than having police
officers swarming all over the place.'

Timson said at once that he would be only too happy to
do what he could, and Tansey produced the safe-deposit
box key. The bank manager took a look at it and said, 'Let's
go and see.'

. They trooped to the back of the bank—Tansey and
Abbot, Timson and his assistant manager. The assistant
manager undid a stout grille behind an ordinary-looking
door, and they were confronted with an array of small safe

doors of various sizes. He produced a list from his pocket and consulted it. 'Number 61, it should be,' he said. He turned his key in the lock of door No. 61, and Tansey turned his. The door opened to reveal a slim black deed box, which the assistant manager drew from its small vault.

'Shall we take it to my office?' said the manager. 'We'll be more comfortable there. You'll all witness that we don't interfere with it on the way.'

Back in the manager's office, they watched as the manager opened the box. Before removing any items from it he said, 'I can't let you take anything away, but you can make any notes you wish, of course.'

Tansey nodded, and Mr Timson, by now as curious as the Chief Inspector to see what would come to light, named each item as he laid it on his desk for inspection by his assistant and the police officers. Abbot had his notebook open and ready.

'Birth certificate,' Timson intoned. 'Mrs Gaul was born one Pauline Brune. Marriage certificate. In 1950 she married John Stephen Gaul at the Registry Office in Marylebone, London. But I'm afraid the marriage didn't last long, for here's her husband's death certificate. He died a year later—myocardial infarction, according to the certifying doctor; in other words, a heart attack.'

'She does seem to have been a rather unlucky lady,' commented Tansey.

'If I may say so, you don't sound especially sympathetic towards her, Chief Inspector,' ventured Timson.

'Observant of you,' said Tansey, but he didn't elaborate. 'What else is there?'

The next item was a passport, which showed that Mrs Gaul had taken holidays in Malta and Morocco in the last five years. Again Tansey commented, 'It would seem she didn't suffer too deprived a life.'

There remained only two thin brown envelopes. One contained share certificates, which raised the value of Pauline Brune's estate considerably. The other held two letters.

Timson unfolded the letters and began to read them.

When he had finished he appeared to hesitate and showed them to his assistant before passing them to Tansey, who looked at him questioningly. The manager responded, 'Normally I wouldn't show private correspondence to the police at this stage—only to the executors or an administrator appointed by the Court. But these letters have no addresses, and no surnames. And I understand there's no sign of a will or a reference to any solicitor. So in the circumstances—' He shrugged.

Together, Tansey and Abbot studied the letters. They were brief but passionate declarations of love, a love that had clearly been returned. They began, 'My beloved Imogen' and ended, 'For ever, come what may, your adoring Charles.' They were dated almost five years previously.

Tansey returned them to the bank manager in silence. Then he said, 'I take it that all these items will be put back in the safe-deposit box to await further developments. We'll keep the key we hold. And we assume that all these details will remain confidential.'

'That goes without saying,' said the bank manager, and his assistant nodded solemnly.

Chief Inspector Tansey was unaware that he was speaking aloud when he added, 'And further developments may take some time. We're going to have to do an awful lot of digging into the past before this case is closed.'

From the bank Sergeant Abbot drove the Chief Inspector to the hospital. It was a short journey, though the Oxford traffic was bad. Abbot concentrated on his driving and Tansey on his thoughts. By now he felt he had in his mind a fairly clear picture of Pauline Brune and even of her killer, but it wasn't one he would have been prepared to offer to anyone, least of all the Chief Constable or the Director of Public Prosecutions. A great deal would depend on what Derek Faudin had to say.

Pushing through the glass doors of the hospital, Tansey was suddenly confronted by a bevy of reporters and a cameraman, most of them local and known to him. They

greeted him with enthusiasm, but were not disappointed
when he said he had nothing for them. In fact, they were
waiting for Cynthia Faudin who, so they informed Tansey,
was being allowed a brief visit to her husband. Derek Faudin
was no longer in intensive care and, according to a nurse
whom one of the reporters knew, was doing extremely well—
better than might be expected of a man of his age—though
he was still weak.

'You see, the press knows more than I do,' Tansey said
to them with a wave of his hand as he made for the
information desk. 'As usual,' he added to Abbot.

But, though he might exchange banter with the media,
he was determined to question Derek Faudin, weak or not.
It was essential to hear his story, and if the man was able
to talk to his wife he could damn well talk to the police. He
hoped Faudin's doctors hadn't been cautioned by Cynthia,
but would be as cooperative as the bank manager. In the
event, there was no difficulty.

Cynthia Faudin was just leaving as they arrived. She
bade them a cool good morning as, escorted by matron, she
passed them in the corridor. As usual, she was well-dressed,
immaculately groomed and apparently composed. She gave
no impression of being a worried woman, but then, Tansey
thought, with her husband out of danger perhaps she believed she had no reason to worry. She had been allowed
five minutes with the patient, and so was the Chief Inspector, though he insisted that his sergeant should also be
present.

'Please try not to upset him,' said the nurse as she stopped
outside the door of Derek Faudin's private room.

'I'll do my best,' Tansey said wryly, nodding a greeting
to the police constable on guard outside the door, who rose
from his chair at his superior's approach.

The nurse knocked and led the two men in. She smiled
at Derek Faudin, who lay on his back, grey-faced and still,
only his feverishly bright eyes showing that he was alive.
His arms were outside the bedcovers, and to one hand was
attached a plastic tube leading to what was presumably a

saline or glucose drip above his head. The nurse put the bell-push close to his other hand. 'These police officers would like to ask you a few questions, Mr Faudin,' she said. 'They won't be long but, if you feel it's becoming too much of a strain, just ring.'

'Yes. All right. Thank you.' Derek Faudin's voice was surprisingly strong.

Tansey pulled a chair up beside the bed and introduced himself and Abbot. 'Mr Faudin, you can guess what we want. Tell us in your own words what happened to you yesterday.'

'Well, it was like this. I was leaving the house to join my wife and friends. We were going to church. Going through the hall I heard a sort of cry from the dining-room and went in. Pauline was on the floor and a man was bending over her.'

Derek Faudin paused, and Tansey said, 'You had been making a telephone call, I'm told. Who to, Mr Faudin?'

It was not the question Derek Faudin had expected and there was a definite pause before he answered. Then he said, 'The call was to a friend of mine who lives in London.' He mentioned a name. 'But he must have been either out or away for the weekend. There was no answer.'

So no means of checking, Tansey thought. He said, 'When you saw this man attacking Miss Brune, I presume you went to her aid, Mr Faudin?'

Faudin shook his head doubtfully. 'I—I think I did go towards them, but the man turned immediately. He had this knife in his hand and he came at me. I remember staggering back as he slashed me—and nothing more till I came round in hospital.'

'I see. Can you describe the man, Mr Faudin?'

'Thirtyish. Fair-haired. A big nose, I seem to remember.'

'What was he wearing?'

'Jeans and—and a leather jacket, I think.'

'You'd know him again?'

Derek Faudin hesitated. 'Chief Inspector, I'd hate to swear to a man I'd seen only for a second or two—if it meant him getting a long sentence. Terrible mistakes of that kind have been made in the past, as I'm sure you're aware.'

'Indeed,' said Tansey shortly.

Faudin had obviously tired. There was a thin rim of sweat on his upper lip, and his hand was plucking nervously at the sheet. Tansey stared at him, reflecting. He was sorry for the man but he had a job to do.

'One last question, Mr Faudin,' he said. 'Does the name Antonia Merridew mean anything to you?'

If the Chief Inspector had wanted to shock Derek Faudin, he must have been gratified by the result. Faudin's eyes widened, his mouth drooped and his tongue came out to wet dry lips. Then he was fumbling for the bell-push.

'No!' he said as the nurse arrived. 'I've never heard of anyone called Merridew.'

'Thank you, Mr Faudin.'

Tansey was already on his feet, prepared to leave. He didn't need the nurse's admonition that her patient had had enough. He knew that he would get nothing more from Faudin for the moment. But he was well satisfied with the interview; lies, he thought, could often help as much as the truth.

'Whew!' said Abbot, when they got to their car. 'Did you expect that reaction, sir?'

Tansey merely nodded enigmatically, but gave no direct reply.

The media, satisfied with the interview that Cynthia had graciously granted them, and having little hope of getting any more information from Chief Inspector Tansey, had dispersed. Tansey and Abbot had made their way to the car park without causing any interest.

They sat in silence for a moment and Abbot didn't pursue his original question. Instead he asked, 'What next, sir?'

There was another pause before Tansey replied, 'That's a problem, isn't it? There are half a dozen things I'd like to do now. The question is priority.'

'This guy Terry?' Abbot queried. 'He fits Mr Faudin's

description pretty well, except for the leather jacket, and it would be easy to make a mistake about that. Do we take him in, sir?'

Again there was no immediate answer and Abbot, about to start the car, turned to look at the Chief Inspector, who seemed to be gazing into space. Abbot stared in the same direction.

'See him?' Tansey asked. 'Passing by that blue Volvo.' He pointed.

'Mr Simon Faudin,' Abbot said. 'Come to pay his brother a visit, presumably.'

'Yes. And to make sure their stories agree.' Tansey spoke so softly that Abbot barely caught what he said. 'Interesting that he and Cynthia didn't come together. I wonder if Simon knows Antonia Merridew—'

'Sir?' Abbot was puzzled.

'No matter. Forget it, Sergeant. "What next?" you were asking. The answer is food. Someone else can bring in this Mr Terry Whatshisname—'

'Terry Danforth, sir. I made inquiries.'

'Good. Get on the blower, Sergeant, and lay it on. We'll go straight to Headquarters, and take an hour off for lunch. Mr Danforth should be waiting for us by the time we've finished. And I suggest you eat well. I've got a feeling we've a long day ahead. For one thing, I'm hoping we can get over to Gloucester to see this Mrs Kent that Pauline Brune used to work for.'

CHAPTER 11

After a rapid lunch in the officers' mess at Kidlington, Tansey was at his desk studying a file when Abbot appeared. 'Danforth—Terence Danforth,' he announced. 'He's been picked up, sir. He's downstairs now.'

The Chief Inspector looked up quickly. 'Thanks, Abbot. Any trouble?'

'Apparently not, sir. The report is that he came perfectly willingly. Only—'

'Only what?'

'Miss Faudin—Miss Clare Faudin—she's with him. She was in the caravan when Inspector Tyler went to find Danforth, and insisted on accompanying him here.'

'Really?' Tansey pushed back his chair and surveyed Abbot. 'So he *has* got connections with the Faudins. That could put a whole new interpretation on what we know—or think we know, Sergeant. Anyway, put them both in the end interview room to stew for a while, with a uniformed man to keep them company. And ask Danforth if he'd mind being fingerprinted—for elimination purposes—you know the kind of approach. If he doesn't object, get his prints compared with those from the outside handle on the french windows of the dining-room at Longacres. Let me know when that's done, and we'll go along to them in ten minutes or so.'

'Very good, sir.' Sergeant Abbot turned and left the Chief Inspector's office.

About fifteen minutes later the two officers were outside the interview room. Abbot opened the door and gestured to the constable on duty inside, who emerged and reported that Danforth and Miss Faudin had sat, holding hands, in almost total silence. Tansey nodded, and he and Abbot went into the room together.

Tansey said at once, as if surprised, 'Miss Faudin, what are you doing here? Unless of course you've decided that you want to make a formal statement—'

'That's just what I do want—to make a statement,' Clare interrupted. 'I want to state as forcefully as I can that it can't possibly have been Terry who killed Pauline Brune and attacked Dad. I know that Terry was in his caravan when it must have happened, because I was there with him.'

'And that's all?' queried Tansey mildly.

'Yes. Isn't it enough?'

'We'll have to see, won't we? In the meantime, thank you, Miss Faudin. You've made your statement. The

Sergeant here has taken it down and maybe we'll have it typed for you to sign later. Now, will you please leave?'

There was a tap at the door and a police officer brought in a note which he handed to Tansey. The Chief Inspector read it with satisfaction before passing it to Abbot. A simple comparison of fingerprints had shown that Terence Danforth's left-hand thumb and fingers corresponded with the prints outside the french windows at Longacres.

Tansey said, 'Constable, will you please arrange for Miss Faudin here to be taken home in a police car?'

'I'm not going home. I'm going to wait for Terry.'

Tansey lost patience. 'Then you may have a long wait,' he snapped. 'Mr Danforth, listen carefully. I'm about to give you an official warning. As you must be aware, this case is being treated as murder and criminal assault, possibly with intent to murder. You are not obliged to say—'

'But it's absurd!' Clare burst out. 'Terry would never hurt anyone.'

'Miss Faudin!'

'Clare, please go. You're only making more trouble for me. I know and you know that I haven't done anything wrong. I'll be all right.'

It was the first time that Terry Danforth had spoken. He had a pleasant, rather gruff voice with the remains of a Yorkshire accent, and Tansey thought that he and Clare made an odd couple—hardly one of which Cynthia Faudin would approve. But Clare did as Terry asked, albeit reluctantly, and as soon as he had gone Tansey returned to his official warning.'

'Does this mean I'm being charged?' Terry asked when the formality was over.

'Not necessarily. It means that I've got reasonable grounds for suspicion. I'll charge you if I have to, but for the moment I'd rather not.'

'So I'm just "helping the police with their inquiries", is that it?'

'That's about it, yes.'

'It all comes of getting mixed up with the nobs—the

gentry.' Terry was resentful. 'But it's not fair. Why pick on me?'

'Because you were at the scene of the crime,' said Tansey, 'and later you were seen running off into some woods nearby.' He let Terry digest this for a moment, and then added gently, 'We do have proof, Mr Danforth.'

'Proof? You mean you've got the word of that old bugger Faudin. What beats me is how he could describe me, as Clare says he has, when he's never seen me in his life.' The young man shook his long fair hair. 'He's a bloody liar, that's what he is, even if he is Clare's dad.'

'Supposing you tell me your version, then,' said Tansey, 'but first let's get some information about you. You don't come from these parts, do you?'

'No, I come from Yorkshire, and at the moment I damn well wish I'd stayed there. But if you want facts and figures, Chief Inspector, here you are.'

Terence Danforth was twenty-seven. The youngest son of a miner, he had gained an English degree from Durham University. On the strength of this, he had taught for a couple of years, but hated it. At present he was unemployed. He lived in a second-, third- or fourth-hand caravan and was writing a novel.

'The great English novel!' Terry concluded wryly.

Tansey grinned; at least it seemed that Terry could find some humour in his situation. 'And how did you come to meet Clare Faudin?' he asked.

'Ah, you mean she's not in my league—or I'm not in hers, perhaps. How right you are, Chief Inspector,' said Terry scornfully. 'I met her by chance. I was living in my caravan on the outskirts of Buckingham at the time. I went into the town one day, and when it started to pour with rain I took shelter in an antique shop. I thought Clare was just a sales girl. We chatted and found we had a lot in common. One thing led to another, as they say, and when she said she had to go home to her village for a few days I moved over to be near her.'

'When did you discover that she was the only daughter

of rich parents, who would scarcely approve of you—or at least of your present prospects?'

'Last Friday. The farmer where I get milk and things said something about the Faudins and Longacres. The result was that Clare and I had a hell of a row—I was furious that she hadn't told me and she walked out.' Terry heaved a sigh. 'Anyway, by Sunday we were both prepared to pocket our pride and we made up.'

'You've left out the important part—important to me, at any rate,' said Tansey. 'You went to Longacres on Sunday morning to find Clare. You went into the dining-room. Your fingerprints are on the handle of the french windows. What happened then?'

Terry didn't answer immediately. He contemplated his fingernails, which were in need of cleaning. Finally he said, 'Chief Inspector, before we begin this jolly you gave me a warning. OK? I'm taking you up on it. You said I didn't have to say anything, and I'm not.'

'It's your right, Mr Danforth,' Tansey said amiably, 'just as it's your right to see a solicitor, if you wish—'

'No. No lawyers. Not at this stage. I don't need them.'

'Very well. Now, I don't intend to charge you at the moment, but I propose to keep you here overnight. Then in the morning we can think again.'

And, with a dismissive nod, the Chief Inspector abruptly terminated the interview and walked out of the room, leaving behind a surprised Abbot and a slightly shocked Terence Danforth.

It was about four o'clock that afternoon by the time Tansey and Abbot arrived at Longacres. They were confronted by what could only be described as a family conclave assembled in the drawing-room. Nevertheless, they were made welcome, especially by Cynthia Faudin, who seemingly desired their presence, if no one else did. Mrs Faudin was thin-lipped, her voice unusually shrill, as after greeting them she immediately pointed an accusing finger at Clare, who glared back at her.

'My daughter, Chief Inspector—my daughter has telephoned two London newspapers and the editor of the *Oxford Mail*. She has given them a story.'

'A story, Mrs Faudin?' said Tansey.

The others were seated as if to signify their attitudes to this dispute. Clare faced her mother, with Peter and Julia beside her. Simon Faudin and his wife, Valerie, sat close by on a love-seat. Christopher Winter, in a large armchair apart from the members of the family, had his head sunk on his chest and might have been asleep, though the nervous tapping of fingers on a knee betrayed him.

'Yes, Chief Inspector. She's told the press that you've arrested this young man, Terry Danforth, her fiancé, for the murder of Pauline Brune and the attack on my husband. She says she believes in his innocence and intends to marry him as soon as you realize you've made a mistake and have set him free.'

'Really?' Tansey was fascinated. 'I take it you'd disapprove of such a marriage, Mrs Faudin?'

'Of course. He's a wastrel, as far as I know. No money. No job. He's after Clare for what he can get, that's all.'

'And Mr Faudin would also disapprove?'

'Most certainly.' Cynthia ignored Clare's protest that Terry loved her.

'What you say interests me, Mrs Faudin, because it does give Terry a motive,' said Tansey. 'If he had come to Longacres yesterday morning, hoping to talk to Mr Faudin about Clare, and they quarrelled, and Miss Brune interrupted them, he might—'

'It sounds a pretty poor motive to me,' Peter said. 'Any competent barrister would make mincemeat of it.'

'Besides, it was Pauline who was killed, not Mr Faudin,' said Julia. 'Surely a casual thief makes much more sense.'

They began to argue among themselves, until Tansey said, 'Please. All this is premature. Mr Danforth is merely helping us with our inquiries. He's not been charged, though we do have proof that he was at Longacres during the relevant time.'

'What proof?'

It was Simon Faudin who asked the question, but Christopher Winter had looked up sharply at Tansey's assertion, as the Chief Inspector did not fail to notice. He didn't answer the question. Instead, he changed the subject and asked, 'Does the name Antonia Merridew mean anything to any of you?'

There was a general shaking of heads. Only Abbot, as ever watching the scene unobtrusively, noticed that Simon Faudin had almost imperceptibly stiffened at the mention of the name. Tansey would have sworn that Cynthia Faudin was quite unmoved.

'Wasn't that the name of Mark's mother?' Valerie Faudin said at last in a puzzled tone, as if she were not quite sure of the fact.

'Yes, it was,' Simon said slowly. Then obviously realizing that some further explanation was necessary, he turned to Tansey. 'Mark's my godson,' he said. 'But why on earth? Mark lives in New York. He can't possibly be involved in this business.'

Cynthia Faudin was frowning. 'Mark's not called—' she began.

Peter finished the sentence for her. 'He's Mark Carter.'

Simon laughed. 'He *was* Mark Merridew. When his parents were killed in a car crash he was adopted by his grandmother who had married for a second time, and he took her new name. So it's not a great mystery, Chief Inspector, though frankly I can't imagine what it's got to do with you or your investigation.'

'Possibly nothing, Mr Faudin,' Tansey said lightly. 'What about an Imogen and a Charles, in relation to each other?'

He was met with blank stares until Julia said, 'There was an Imogen at my Swiss finishing school, and naturally one knows lots of Charleses—'

Her obviously irrelevant interpolation broke the building tension, and there was a burst of laughter. Even Tansey and Abbot found themselves smiling. And in this sudden atmosphere of apparent good will, Peter seized his chance and asked if he and Julia could return to London.

'You've got our addresses and phone numbers, Chief Inspector, and I'll certainly be back next weekend to see Dad. I should have thought it must be obvious by now that none of us can contribute anything further to your inquiries.'

'The obvious can be deceptive,' Tansey replied cheerfully. 'However, I see no reason to keep you two here. But I would like the rest of you to stay, at least for a day or two, if Mrs Faudin doesn't mind and no one has pressing business elsewhere.'

'That will be all right, of course,' Cynthia said.

'What about Terry?' Clare demanded. 'In all these arrangements, everyone seems to have forgotten him.'

'Far from it,' Tansey assured her. 'Indeed, it's with Mr Danforth in mind that I propose to consider once again the times of your various comings and goings yesterday morning. Perhaps we could start with you, Miss Faudin, if you'd come along to the sitting-room.'

Any police officer knows that the checking and re-checking of statements is a tedious business. Naturally those with a guilty conscience will attempt to deceive, and sometimes individuals may lie or lay false trails to protect others or to hide an irrelevant secret. The innocent, the ignorant or those who just don't want to be involved can be equally mischievous, providing half-truths that can on occasion prove more misleading than an outright lie. To sift such conflicting details requires a skill that can only partially be learnt and lengthy experience, as well as a well-developed intuitive sense. It was this latter gift that Detective Chief Inspector Dick Tansey had finely honed.

Five minutes after Christopher Winter had come into the sitting-room Tansey sensed that the old man was more assured than he had been at his first interview. Nevertheless, there was something about his tale which did not ring true. His new confidence could stem from repetition, or from a decision—willed or involuntary—to distance himself from

these distasteful events. Tansey determined to take a risk
and press him hard.

'Mr Winter, so far you've been a great help. You'll be
prepared to act as a witness for the prosecution, I assume?'

'A witness? But—but to what?'

'You wouldn't mind repeating on oath what you've
already told us twice, would you? After all, there's no death
penalty these days so you wouldn't need to feel that your
evidence was helping to hang a man. Actually, he probably
won't serve more than ten or fifteen years.' Tansey ignored
a cautionary cough from Abbot.

'Who?'

'Why, Mr Danforth, of course.'

'And my evidence? How can my evidence—'

'It's a matter of timing, Mr Winter,' replied Tansey. 'The
crime can't have been committed while you were in the hall,
can it? You'd have heard something, surely?'

'Yes, but there must be more against him than that. Derek
saw him—and so did the others on their way to church.'

'Mr Faudin says he can't identify his assailant, and there's
no law against running into the woods to avoid people. It's
all the scraps of evidence taken together that form a case.
For instance, the fact that the knife was buried outside the
dining-room, and certain fingerprints on the paintwork by
the window. Incidentally, Mr Winter, you'll let us take your
fingerprints, won't you—for elimination purposes?'

Christopher Winter had gone white around the mouth
and he seemed to be having difficulty in breathing. Abbot
uttered a warning cry. 'I'll get some water,' he said.

'Yes. Quick,' said Tansey, as Abbot ran from the room.
The Chief Inspector was alarmed but not unduly surprised
at the attack he appeared to have precipitated. He went to
Winter and loosened his collar. 'It's all right,' he said
meaninglessly.

'You know, don't you,' the old man murmured as Abbot
returned with a glass of water, and Tansey knelt beside
him and helped him to sip it. He paused and then seemed
to recover a little. He said, 'I did go into the dining-room.

They were both lying there and—and the knife was near Derek's hand. I knew nothing about Clare's young man and—and I thought Derek had killed Miss Brune, because—Well, he told me that she was a bitch. She'd been reading his private papers. He didn't say precisely, but I believe she'd discovered some sort of family secret, and perhaps—

'I'm sorry Chief Inspector,' Winter continued. 'I shouldn't have done it—opened the french window, gone into the garden and buried the knife like that—but Derek's a good man, and I wasn't thinking clearly. I wanted to save him from what I thought must have been an act of madness on his part—I know he'd never hurt anyone in cold blood and—and that realizing what he'd done he'd turned the knife on himself. Anyway, I seem to have got it all wrong,' he ended sadly. 'I'm sorry, terribly sorry.'

CHAPTER 12

From Longacres it was less than fifty miles along the A40 to Gloucester, and Sergeant Abbot's police car ate up this distance at speed. He drove in silence, because Chief Inspector Tansey was slumped in the seat beside him, dozing—or pretending to doze—with his eyes shut. It was quite clear that he had no wish to talk, to discuss the events of the day, or to answer any of the questions that Abbot would have liked to ask.

In fact, the Chief Inspector was trying to plan his forthcoming interview with Mrs Kent, Pauline Brune's former employer who, according to what Pauline was said to have told Cynthia Faudin, was an 'absolute bitch'. But in spite of this preoccupation Tansey's thoughts kept returning to Christopher Winter.

He was not proud of himself. He disapproved strongly of police brutality, and in his book bullying an old man was tantamount to brutality. And he *had* bullied Winter; he was

in no doubt about that. Nor, he thought regretfully, was
Bill Abbot. Of course, it could be argued that the intimi-
dation had been necessary, and that he had extracted some
valuable information as a result. But in reality Tansey knew
that he had learnt little that he had not already guessed or
surmised.

He wondered about the knife. He would know more the
following day when he attended the post-mortem on the
Brune woman, and saw the pathologist and got the final
reports from forensic. But the evidence that Winter had
destroyed—the exact position of the knife on the carpet,
and the blood on it which might have been affected by its
plunge into the earth—could have been invaluable. Now
it seemed probable that a great deal might depend on an
old man's word, and Winter, vague and muddled, sure
that he had 'got it all wrong', would make a dreadful witness.

As Tansey continued to muse he recalled Winter's reference to a 'family secret'. It reminded him of *Jane Eyre* or a
Chekov play. But he had enough experience as a detective
officer to know that many families had intrigues of which
they were inordinately ashamed, though to an outsider they
could well appear trivial. But before now murder had been
done in the cause of concealing trivia.

He was roused by Abbot's announcement that they had
reached their destination, and the car drew up in front of
an attractive house in a country lane; they were near a
small village on the outskirts of Gloucester, and Abbot's
map-reading had been unerring. West Winds was an old
house, obviously well cared for, with a trim lawn in front.
And, Tansey thought, in all probability it had been modern-
ized within so that it was convenient to run; but it was in
a different class altogether from Longacres. He was not
surprised when the door was opened to them, not by a
white-coated houseman, but by a woman who was presumably Mrs Kent herself.

They introduced themselves on the doorstep and Mrs
Kent, warned by phone of their impending visit, responded

amiably. Barbara Kent herself was a surprise. She was in her early sixties, Tansey guessed, but still slim and with the elegant body of a dancer or a model. It was not until they saw her limp as she led the way into a comfortably-furnished sitting-room full of books and flowers that they appreciated her disability. She gestured Tansey and Abbot to chairs, and arranged herself on a sofa with a sigh.

'Forgive me,' she said, 'but my arthritis is troubling me badly today.' Brown eyes contrasted with her white hair as she smiled at them in turn. 'If it weren't for this damned complaint I wouldn't need a housekeeper-companion—I have plenty of daily help from the village. As it is, I'm more or less dependent on someone who lives in, so it was a blow when Pauline walked out without warning.'

'Pauline Brune walked out on you?' asked Tansey.

Having already formed a certain opinion of Miss Brune, and having now met Mrs Kent, the Chief Inspector had been half expecting some such statement. Clearly, Mrs Kent was no dragon. Nor did it appear that she was likely to have been the kind of slave-driver Pauline Brune had suggested; certainly Brune had not been compelled to do all the house-work without assistance. Tansey wondered in what other ways the woman had misrepresented her situation.

'Yes. A friend had kindly taken me out to lunch, and when I returned Pauline said that she'd had a phone call to say her sister had been taken ill; she had to go to look after her and she'd be leaving the next morning. It was the first I knew about a sister—she'd never mentioned one before.'

Tansey didn't comment. 'So how long was she with you?' he inquired.

'Two years and a half or so. She was very helpful to start with, but recently she'd been doing less and less and complaining more.' Mrs Kent sighed again. 'Of course, she wasn't young and everything becomes more of an effort as the years go by. Hers wasn't a job I'd want for myself. But she had a good home here. Her own bedroom, naturally, and a little sitting-room. A bathroom to herself, except when

I had someone to stay, her own television, use of a car, the same food as I have and an excellent salary.'

'And in return?'

'She did the housekeeping, shopped, got the meals, supervised the women who came in, coped with the laundry—the sort of things any wife might do. On my bad days, helped me to bathe. Chief Inspector, I'm not suggesting it was an ideal life for a woman, and I suppose she envied me—arthritis and all— which is why I took no action. But . . .' She lifted her shoulders, suddenly reminding Tansey of Julia Vere-Poole.

'Action about what?' he asked.

Mrs Kent stared at him, brown eyes wide. 'Isn't—isn't that why you're here? Not because of me. I didn't lodge a complaint, make an accusation or—'

'Please, Mrs Kent!' Tansey interrupted. 'I don't know what you're talking about.'

'I—I'm talking about Pauline,' Mrs Kent said hesitantly. 'When she left here she took some of my belongings—a coat, some other clothes and a necklace. None of any *great* value, but still . . . I twice tried to phone the number she gave me but there was no answer and I haven't bothered to write. I took the line of least resistance and decided to forget the whole thing. Then when you phoned I assumed she'd been caught stealing something more valuable and—'

'No,' said Tansey, remembering certain clothes in Pauline's room at Longacres. 'No one's accused her of theft. I'm afraid Pauline Brune is dead, Mrs Kent.'

'Dead! How?'

'She was killed. We're engaged on a murder inquiry.'

'Good God! Poor Pauline! How did it happen? Was she attacked in the street, mugged?'

'You haven't read about it in this morning's papers? Or heard of it on radio or television?'

'No. I've had an old friend to stay for the weekend, and he only left a short while ago. We were so busy talking that we had no time for radio or TV or the press.'

'I see,' said Tansey. He explained briefly the circumstances of Pauline Brune's death, saying that she had been staying with some people and had possibly surprised a thief. He didn't mention any names. Mrs Kent was shaking her head.

'Poor Pauline!' she repeated. Then she stared at the two officers. 'But I still don't understand why you've bothered to come to me.'

'You were her last employer,' Tansey said, 'and we're trying to trace her relations, if any. All we can do is work backwards. So we hoped you might be able to help.'

Mrs Kent gestured towards a handsome escritoire. 'Top right-hand drawer,' she said. 'You'll find the card she gave me with the phone number—the one that didn't answer—and an address in case I needed to forward anything. So far there's only been junk mail and I've not bothered. She didn't get many personal letters, as far as I know.'

Abbot rose and went to the escritoire. He found the card and showed it to Tansey, before noting the details in his book. Tansey thanked Mrs Kent. 'Just one more question,' he said. 'How did Pauline Brune happen to come to you?'

'She answered an advertisement in the local paper, and I interviewed her. Frankly, Chief Inspector, there wasn't much choice and she had an excellent reference from her last employer, Lady Gandoyne of Ryveley Hall.' Abbot nodded immediately, and she added, 'You know her, Sergeant?'

'*Of* her, madam. The Hall's not far from Colombury, where I was brought up and where my parents live. Young Mr Gandoyne is their MP,' Abbot said.

'Did Pauline Brune give you any reason for leaving these people?' Tansey asked.

'I gathered that one of the daughters was coming home, so Pauline wasn't needed any more. But I'm not stupid, Chief Inspector. I did phone to check on the reference, and Lady Gandoyne spoke highly of her.'

'Did you give Pauline a reference when she left you so abruptly, Mrs Kent?'

Barbara Kent laughed. 'Not a written one, no. But I did

say she could use my name, though that was before I discovered that some of my things had disappeared with her. I doubt if she'd have referred anyone to me, anyway.'

'It would seem unlikely,' Tansey agreed.

He thanked Mrs Kent for her help, apologized for having bothered her and said they would see themselves out. In the doorway of the sitting-room he hesitated as if he had suddenly remembered a point, and asked her if she knew of a couple called Imogen and Charles. But the names meant nothing to her.

'A pleasant woman,' ventured Abbot as they got into their car.

It seemed that the Chief Inspector was now prepared to talk. 'Yes, indeed,' he said thoughtfully. 'Charming. And she did her best to be helpful. I don't imagine the address and phone number Pauline Brune left will be much use, but get through to Headquarters right away and have them checked.'

'Yes, sir. And where then? Ryveley Hall?'

Tansey grinned. 'How did you guess, Sergeant? While you're on the phone get them to warn Lady Gandoyne, will you? And when you've done that, we'll get going and you can tell me all about these Gandoynes.'

'I don't really know all that much about them, sir,' Abbot said as they drove off. 'The old man—Donald Gandoyne, who died a couple of years ago—worked in America for a long time, I believe, but he inherited this baronetcy from a cousin, and he and his wife—who's also English—decided to come back and live in the UK. They're a large and close-knit crowd, I do know, and the present baronet and his family were living at the Hall when the old man died.'

'Pots of money?'

'They're not poor, sir, but they don't live like that lot at Longacres, I understand. Much simpler and more natural. "Hall's" a bit much as a name for their house, if you know what I mean.'

Indeed Tansey understood as soon as he saw the place—

considerably less stylish than Longacres—and the front door was opened to them by a woman in her thirties, businesslike in slacks and a man's shirt, long red hair tied back with what looked like a shoelace. Behind her he saw an untidy hall, where, with the assistance of a yapping dachshund, a boy of about eight was teaching a smaller child to ride a bicycle, to the detriment of the polish on the parquet floor.

'Detective Chief Inspector Tansey and Detective-Sergeant Abbot to see Lady Gandoyne,' he said. 'We did arrange for our Headquarters to warn you.'

'You certainly did, Chief Inspector, and we're all thrilled.' She gave him a wide smile. 'Come along in. We can't imagine why you'd want to see me. Unless it's—'

'See *you*?' In his surprise Tansey interrupted her.

'Yes. You said Lady Gandoyne. That's me.'

For a moment Tansey's heart sank. Either there had been a mistake or Mrs Kent had been tricked by Pauline Brune. The latter seemed to be more likely. He couldn't picture this young, lively woman needing a companion-house-keeper. Then he recalled Abbot's description of the family, and opened his mouth to explain. But before he could do so the small boy brought the bicycle and its rider and the dog to an abrupt tumbling halt at Abbot's feet.

While the Sergeant extricated himself, and Lady Gandoyne expostulated, the boy held out his hand to Tansey. 'Hello,' he said. 'I'm Jeremy. I've never met a Detective Chief Inspector before, or a Detective-Sergeant.'

'We're quite human,' Tansey said solemnly, shaking the proffered hand.

The boy, who had the same colouring as his mother, grinned broadly, showing gaps in his teeth. 'I think it's Gran you want to talk to, Chief Inspector, not Mum. Mum's only become Lady Gandoyne since Gramp died a year or so ago, and anyway Gran's more likely than Mum to have a murky past, because she's much older.'

Abbot tried to turn a snort of laughter into a bout of coughing at this remark, and Tansey bit his lip. But Jeremy's

Mum was nodding her agreement as if the boy had made a
sensible suggestion.

'I was just going to say, Chief Inspector, if it's about
Pauline Brune, by any unlikely chance, it *is* my moher-in-
law you want to see. She may be able to help you more than
I can.'

'You know about Miss Brune?' asked Tansey.

'Well, there was a small bottom-of-the-column paragraph
in *The Times* this morning. It didn't say much, but when
your office phoned we thought that perhaps—'

'You were right, Lady Gandoyne,' said Tansey. 'It does
concern Pauline Brune.'

'Horrid old Pauline!' Jeremy said. 'What's she done now?'

'Horrid old Pauline!' echoed the smaller child. 'What's
she done?'

'If they don't know, I think perhaps—' Tansey began.

'Yes, of course.' Lady Gandoyne was swift to understand.
'Jeremy, run ahead and warn Gran she's about to have
visitors and you, John, go off to the kitchen and find
Susan. Take Fritzi but leave your bike. It's time for your
tea.'

Slightly to Tansey's surprise the children obeyed at once
and without question and, when they and the dachshund
had gone, their mother said, 'Frankly, I'm sure my mother-
in-law will be glad to answer any questions, but I can't see
how Pauline's death might concern any of us. It must be
almost three years since she left here. She came as a sort of
companion-help after Gran broke her hip and was forced to
use a wheelchair and, to be honest, none of us liked her
much. But I mustn't speak ill of the dead. How did she die?
The paper only hinted—'

'That she was murdered, Lady Gandoyne? They were
right. Possibly she interrupted a potential thief who killed
her. The matter only concerns you because we're making
inquiries into her background, and she seems to have had
no family.'

Shown into a large, comfortable but slightly untidy
drawing-room, Tansey offered the same explanation to the

thin elderly woman who sat in her wheelchair, a book on her lap, a large sheepdog dozing beside her. She bowed her head in agreement as her daughter-in-law repeated that they hadn't seen or heard of Pauline Brune since she left Ryveley Hall two or three years ago.

'How did you come to employ her?' asked the Chief Inspector.

The reply was identical to Mrs Kent's—answering an advertisement in a local paper, and getting a reference from Pauline's former employer which had been checked carefully. But the lady in question had been on the point of emigrating to Australia to join a married son, and they had no idea of her present whereabouts.

'A dead end for you, I'm afraid, Chief Inspector.'

'So, if that's all—' the younger woman said. 'It's really my turn to supervise the children's' tea.'

'There are one or two more—' Tansey began, but was quickly interrupted.

'Penelope dear, off you go to the children. Hugo will be home soon and Susan has a dreadful cold. If the pups are whelped in the night—'

For a moment Dick Tansey felt himself overwhelmed by the family life of the Gandoynes. Abbot, he saw, had an identical reaction; he was sitting with the same dazed expression that the Chief Inspector feared was showing on his own face. But the elderly Lady Gandoyne was fully in charge of the situation.

'Now, Chief Inspector,' she said when she was alone with the officers. 'What are these one or two extra questions you want to ask me?'

'Well, first, I'm puzzled by the fact that you gave Miss Brune such an excellent reference when I get the impression that she wasn't entirely satisfactory.'

'It's difficult to get people these days, Chief Inspector, and useless to expect too much of them. Besides, in the beginning, she did well.'

'Did she steal anything from you when she left?'

'Steal? No. Why do you ask?'

'Because she stole from the lady to whom you recommended her, Lady Gandoyne.'

There was a brief silence. Lady Gandoyne had flushed and her mouth became set in a firm line. At last she said, 'I'm sorry. I had no idea she was a thief.'

'Or you wouldn't have recommended her?' said Tansey.

Lady Gandoyne gave him a cool glance. 'I consider that an impertinent question, Chief Inspector.'

'I'm sorry. I had no intention of being impertinent,' Tansey said, 'but I have a job to do, Lady Gandoyne, and I must remind you that this is a murder inquiry.' Quickly he continued, 'Some letters have been found among Pauline Brune's possessions—letters written by someone called Charles to one Imogen. Would these names mean anything to you?

Lady Gandoyne sighed. 'Yes,' she said reluctantly. 'Imogen is my elder daughter. Oh, Chief Inspector, it's a repeat of an old, old story. She and Charles fell madly in love. They were both married, both with young children. Charles and Richard—Imogen's husband—were in the same regiment. At the time—about five years ago—Charles was a captain and Richard was his commanding officer, a lieutenant-colonel. It was an embarrassing situation to say the least and God knows what would have happened if fate, as it were, hadn't taken a hand. Charles was killed in Northern Ireland.'

'But there were letters, that Pauline Brune found?' Tansey prompted gently.

'Yes. Imogen was a fool to have kept them. Richard's a fine man, a good husband and father, but if he'd learnt of the affaire he'd never have forgiven her. It would have been the end of their marriage and I didn't want my grandchildren to be brought up in a broken home. So when Imogen appealed to me I gave Pauline six thousand pounds—not a great sum, but it could have been better spent—and, to my shame I suppose, excellent references.'

'It didn't occur to you to go to the police?' asked Tansey.

'No. I never considered it,' Lady Gandoyne said honestly.

'In return for the money Pauline gave me a couple of photographs that she had taken—Charles had spent the weekend with us while Richard was on a course somewhere—and the letters. She was very businesslike. She admitted she had kept two letters in case I thought of making trouble for her, but she said she would return them at the end of three years, and would ask nothing more of me.'

'You believed her?'

'Oddly enough, yes. I had the impression that she'd done this sort of thing before and—I have to admit—might do it again. She seemed to know just how much to ask, so as not to push her victim too far.'

'A professional blackmailer in a small way of business?' Tansey said.

Lady Gandoyne gave him an appreciative smile. 'Yes, you could say that,' she agreed. 'Where are the letters now?' she demanded suddenly.

'They're safely in the hands of the police,' said Tansey. 'And at the moment I see no reason why they should figure in the case. I promise they'll be returned to you at the end of the inquiry.'

CHAPTER 13

In spite of working late the previous evening Detective Chief Inspector Tansey was in his office early on Tuesday morning. He read the forensic reports that had come in overnight, and checked on Terence Danforth's condition, to be told that the young man had slept well; he next had a brief meeting with the Chief Constable and gave a press conference during which he was inundated with questions about the story that Clare Faudin had given to the media. He then drank a cup of coffee and ate a scone in the officers' mess. He felt he needed a short respite before he attended the post-mortem on Pauline Gaul, née Brune.

Although he had no part to pay in such proceedings other than to observe so that, if necessary, he could be an official witness to any 'trail of evidence' that resulted, Tansey hated PMs. Over the years as a police officer he had become hardened to the sight of death, even when the body or bodies had suffered horrific injuries. But he had never lost his extreme aversion to seeing dead individuals lying in the artificial surroundings of a mortuary, and being intentionally cut up by a professional with their entrails treated rather like offal. What was more, most pathologists seemed to Tansey to take a cynical, sometimes amused, attitude to their job which grated on the Chief Inspector, though he did his best to conceal his feelings.

Today, as always, he was thankful when the PM was over, and the pathologist—in fact, an old acquaintance—suggested a drink in his office. Even here the smell of formaldehyde lingered, and he wondered if the medical man was ever entirely free from it. He waited there while the pathologist washed and changed.

'I've seen the forensic reports, and I know the specks of blood that remained on the knife matched the deceased's, so there's no doubt about the weapon. You agree, John?' began Tansey when the doctor joined him, followed by an orderly with the coffee.

'Of course I agree. There's no doubt about that, or about the cause of death, as far as I can see. But tell me, Dick, is it true what the papers say—that you've already arrested a chap? Some boyfriend of Faudin's daughter? If so, that's quick work.'

'He's helping us with our inquiries, as we always say, and that's all, though he did spend the night with us. I hoped it might rattle some of the others involved, and I think it has. I don't intend to charge him.'

'How big a man is he? I'd suggest that whoever knifed Pauline Brune was not much taller than she was, and also that either he was a powerful character or else a sudden burst of anger gave him extra strength. The angle of the knife, the penetration—and the fact that it went right through a rib—proves that. There's another point, too. I'm pretty certain it was a fluke.'

'A fluke?'

'In the sense that even I, with my knowledge of anatomy, wouldn't guarantee to plant a knife in that vital spot unless the lady promised to stand still to receive the blow. And that seems pretty unlikely as she must have been facing the chap that killed her.'

'So the villain could possibly plead manslaughter?'

'Ah, that'll be up to you and the lawyers. But look.'

The pathologist seized a ruler that was about the same length as the carving knife, and advanced on Tansey, raising it into the air. Involuntarily the Chief Inspector got to his feet and put up an arm to ward off the blow.

'See what I mean, Dick?'

'Yes,' said Tansey. 'Incidentally, you're right-handed, so I assume the killer was also right-handed.'

'Sorry, Dick! Sorry! I should have mentioned that before. There's every indication from the angle of the blow that he was. Anyway, you'll be getting my full report later in the day. All I can say is "good luck".'

Luck was always involved in solving any complex case, Tansey thought philosophically as he drove back to Kidlington. A nosy neighbour, an unwise remark that someone let slip—almost anything could help to point an investigating officer in the right direction. But there was bad luck, too. Deliberate lies, for whatever purposes, the destruction of evidence, wittingly or unwittingly, carlessness or illogicality on the officer's part at the end of a long day—again, almost anything could mislead.

Tansey parked his car and went straight to his office. His in-tray, which he had pretty well cleared earlier that morning, was once more full. Sighing, he sent for Terry Danforth.

Terry seemed to have survived his night with the police very well. He greeted the Chief Inspector cheerfully. 'You get smashing grub in this place,' he said. 'Best breakfast I've had for ages. Clare's not much of a cook.'

Tansey was not immediately responsive. 'It's not half as good at Dartmoor or Pentonville,' he remarked. Then he took a notepad and ballpoint pen and pushed them across his desk to Terry. 'Write your full name on that, please.'

'Why?'

'Because I say so!'

'You must know my name by now, and all sorts of other details about me and my past life,' Terry objected. 'Your sarge never stopped asking questions.' Nevertheless, in spite of this mild remonstration he pulled the pad towards him and wrote as he'd been told. 'OK?' he asked, turning the pad back to Tansey. 'I wouldn't win a prize for handwriting, but I hope that's what you want.'

'It's exactly what I want.' At last the Chief Inspector smiled at Terry. 'Have you always been left-handed, Mr Danforth? I hadn't really noticed when we met before.'

'Yes. Always. It's a damned nuisance sometimes.'

'I'm sure it could have advantages,' Tansey said, but offered no elaboration. 'Now, in a short while, we'll get a police car to take you to your caravan, or anywhere else you want to go, for that matter, but first –'

'You mean you're not going to charge me?'

'No. You're in the clear. There's no question of charging you. You've been a great help to us, but I'd like a little further cooperation before you go. You could be a material witness in clearing someone else.'

'I—I don't think—' Terry was wary.

'I suggest you *do* think—and think very seriously,' said Tansey. 'Mr Danforth, your fingerprints were on the outside handle of the french windows of the dining-room at Long-acres, so we know that you were there about the time the crime was committed.' This stretched the truth somewhat, the Chief Inspector realized, but in the circumstances he felt the ploy was justified. 'What I want to know is what you saw in the room. Was there anyone inside? Remember, it could have been a totally innocent individual.'

'No, no it wasn't—an innocent, I mean!' Terry swallowed

hard. 'Oh, what the hell! All right, I'll tell you, Chief Inspector. I didn't want to, because of Clare, but—'

'But?'

'Well, I saw the old boy, Clare's dad. He was standing there with this great knife in his hand and looking down at what I suppose was this woman's body. I couldn't see her. The dining table and chairs were in the way.'

This was considerably more than Tansey had expected, and he could scarcely believe it. Yet Terry Danforth had nothing to gain by accusing Derek Faudin. To gain a moment for thought, he asked, 'Can you describe exactly where Mr Faudin was standing?'

'On the far side of the table.' Terry screwed up his face as he tried to revisualize the scene. 'Fairly near to the door. With his back more or less to a large sideboard.' He stopped. 'What's wrong? You were frowning.'

'You know Derek Faudin—Clare's father?'

'No. I've never met him. In fact, come to think of it, I'd never seen him before that moment. But who else—'

It was ironic, Tansey thought, that Derek Faudin had by chance described his attacker in terms that were so applicable to Terry, and that in his turn Terry had assumed that the 'old boy' he had seen with a knife was Derek Faudin. But Terry had been quick to cotton on to his possible error.

Tansey spoke rapidly. 'The man you saw was almost certainly a house guest who found Faudin and Pauline Brune. We know about him,' he said.

'Ah, that's good, then,' said Terry, obviously relieved. He grinned at the Chief Inspector. 'So I don't have to worry about Clare.'

The phone rang, forestalling any questions that Terry might have been tempted to ask. Tansey picked up the receiver. 'Yes,' he said and repeated the word several times.

'Interesting conversation,' commented Terry.

'As a matter of fact, extremely interesting,' replied Tansey.

The caller at the other end of the line had been Sergeant Abbot, relaying a message from the hospital. Mr Derek

Faudin wished to see Chief Inspector Tansey urgently.

Tansey stood. 'I have to go out,' he said. 'I'll arrange a
car for you, as I said, Mr Danforth. You won't move your
place of abode without informing us, will you? Now, come
with me.' He took Terry into an outer office and gave
instructions to a woman police constable on duty there. He
lifted a hand in farewell to Terry. 'Thanks a lot for your
help, Mr Danforth,' he said.

He was gone before Terry had time to think of a suitable
pithy rejoinder.

Derek Faudin, supported by an array of pillows, was sitting
up in bed when Tansey and Abbot were shown into his
room. There was no longer an intravenous drip in his hand.
His cheeks had a little colour and he looked much fitter
than he had the previous day. He greeted the two officers
curtly.

'Both my son and my daughter have been to see me this
morning,' he said. 'They told me of this young man whom
you've arrested, Chief Inspector—this Terence Danforth.
To my knowledge I've never seen him, but unfortunately I
seem to have given you a fairly accurate description of him
which has led to his arrest.'

'And now you'd like to withdraw what you said, sir?'

'I did make the point that I wouldn't be prepared to give
a positive identification, Chief Inspector.'

'Indeed you did. But you needn't worry. There is some
other evidence against Danforth, so your daughter would
have no reason to blame you.'

'What evidence? If you mean this absurd idea that he
wanted to get rid of me because he thought I'd object to
him marrying Clare and cut her off with the proverbial
penny or something, that's patent nonsense, as my son says.'

'So you wouldn't object to such a marriage? Your wife
believed you would.'

'Terry doesn't sound ideal, I admit. No job. No prospects.
But I dare say we can do something about that. In any case,
Clare's old enough to marry anyone she wants.'

'I see, sir. Well, if that's all—' Tansey stood up, as if about to leave. 'Incidentally, do you still maintain that you were attacked by a young man answering Danforth's description, whom you came on seconds after he had killed Pauline Brune? You'll swear to that, sir? You don't want to withdraw that statement, or amend it in any way?'

There was a sudden stillness. Tansey looked around him with what he hoped would be taken for an air of indifference. It was a pleasant room, the walls painted the colour of ducks' eggs, the furniture white, a couple of Dufy prints adding brightness. There was a large remote-controlled television set perched on a bracket in front of the bed, vases of flowers, and on a side-table a big basket of fruit with several get-well cards. Faudin's family and friends had clearly rallied quickly to his aid, Tansey reflected.

'Why do you ask that, Chief Inspector?' Derek Faudin spoke at last.

'Because, sir, you know, and I know, that that's not what happened—at least not as you described it.'

'You're calling me a liar?'

'I'm merely suggesting that the forensic evidence contradicts what you've told me, Mr Faudin. Perhaps you should consider the consequences.'

'And now you're threatening me, Chief Inspector?'

'Certainly not, sir.'

There was a warning cough from Abbot and, Tansey thought: Here I go again, bullying an old man, and this time a sick one. He was still standing, and Abbot had also risen to his feet. Tansey knew they couldn't stay like that for long. Either they would have to leave, and the opportunity that he had created in an effort to force Faudin to tell the truth would be lost, possibly for ever, or Faudin would break.

Derek Faudin gave a long, shuddering sigh and closed his eyes. Tansey moved swiftly to ring for a nurse, but to his relief Faudin opened his eyes again.

'No!' he said sharply. 'Don't call anyone, Chief Inspector. Sit down. I'll tell you what happened—the truth. I'm afraid

I've been very stupid, though from the best of motives—
just like my dear friend, Christopher Winter. He phoned
me to say that it was he who had taken the knife and buried
it in the garden. I suppose you could call that obstructing the police but, as I'm sure he told you, he only did
it for my sake, so I hope you won't take that matter any
further.'

'I should think it fairly unlikely, sir.'

'Good.' Faudin reached for a glass of water and drank
thirstily, as if his throat were dry. 'Then please listen—'

Derek Faudin told his story in some detail. On Sunday
morning he had arranged to meet Pauline Brune in the
dining-room at ten-thirty, giving as an excuse that he had
something private and urgent to discuss with her. She hadn't
seemed surprised, and he thought that she had probably
guessed the reason. He had chosen the dining-room because
once it had been cleared after breakfast they were unlikely
to be interrupted there.

He paused at this point, and Tansey said, 'You told those
who were going to church that you had to make a phone call
and would catch them up before they got to St Matthew's?'

'Yes. That's what I planned to do. There was no phone
call, but I didn't think my business with Pauline would take
long. Anyway, she was there in the dining-room waiting for
me, and I told her bluntly that I'd like her to leave Longacres. I said that my wife had shown her great kindness by
asking her to visit us for a few days when she was in some
need, but that she had outstayed her welcome. We wanted
the house to ourselves for a while. I was firm—after all,
she'd ignored all the hints we had given her—but I wasn't
positively unpleasant.'

Again Derek Faudin took a drink of water and Tansey
saw that his hand was shaking. 'She—she laughed in my
face!' Faudin said, unable completely to suppress the anger
that he still felt. 'She threatened to tell the media that,
although she was a childhood friend of Cynthia's and was
poor and homeless, we were turning her out of our house,
and God alone knew what would become of her. It wouldn't

worry me if the story got out, but there are reasons why Cynthia might not like it at the moment.'

Derek Faudin stopped, without elaborating. Tansey didn't press this point because it was obvious that Faudin was becoming exhausted, and the Chief Inspector was worried that he might collapse before he had finished his story. But, after a minute or two, he appeared to recover his strength once more.

'I'm just coming to the worst part,' he said. 'I'd give anything for it not to have happened. I—I lost my temper—something I rarely do—and I cursed Pauline. Perhaps I even made a threatening gesture as if I were about to hit her. I've tried to remember, but I can't. Anyway, she seized the carving knife that was lying on the dining-room table—'

'On the table?' Tansey's question was involuntary.

'Why yes, Chief Inspector. There were glasses, some plates, place mats, things ready for setting the table for lunch—and the knife was among them.' Faudin dismissed the position of the knife as unimportant. 'Pauline ran at me and slashed me. I remember staggering back towards the sideboard. Then she came at me again, but this time I was prepared. I thought she meant to kill me. I seized her arm. We struggled over the knife and—and I must have—Oh God, I never meant to harm her, let alone kill her.'

'A nurse came into the room. 'Doctor's on his way, Mr Faudin.' And to the police officers. 'I'll have to ask you to leave, gentlemen.'

As Tansey stood up for the second time, Derek Faudin said, 'You understand that that was a voluntary statement, don't you, Chief Inspector? After all, I've not even been given an official warning.' He smiled wanly.

'Yes, I understand that, Mr Faudin,' said Tansey. But as he and Abbot left the room he added to himself, 'And I also understand a good deal more than you damn well give me credit for.'

CHAPTER 14

'We shall treat ourselves to a pub lunch en route to Long-acres, Sergeant,' Tansey said as they reached the hospital car park.

'To celebrate, sir?'

Dick Tansey laughed. Abbot noticed that for some reason the Chief Inspector had become considerably more relaxed since the interview with Derek Faudin.

'It's not exactly a champagne occasion,' Tansey said, 'but I'll stand you a pint if you find us a good place. You've got a reputation for knowing every pub within fifty miles of Kidlington.'

'That was before I was married, sir. I'm a reformed character now. But there's the Windrush Arms in Colombury that I could recommend. It serves good beer and good food.'

'OK. Make straight for it.'

Bill Abbot's recommendation was fully justified, and the two officers ate an excellent meal, during which inevitably they discussed what might be termed Derek Faudin's confession—a discussion which continued in their car afterwards. Tansey admitted that he was sceptical. He knew from the shape and positions of the bloodstains on the dining-room carpet that Faudin's account of what had happened was flawed, but he was prepared to concede that any inaccuracies might not have been intentional on Faudin's part. Nevertheless, there were other details that failed to fit and, in sum, he didn't trust Derek Faudin.

'Such a pity the nurse interrupted us when she did,' Tansey remarked, not for the first time since they had left the hospital, 'but you can't gainsay a doctor on his home ground. We'll have to go back to Faudin, but I'm afraid next time we'll be at a disadvantage. We've lost the initiative.'

'At least we've got a chance to check on the knife. It's

funny how everyone assumed it would be in the drawer next to the carving fork.'

'Yes. That was my fault. One should never make assumptions.' Tansey grinned wryly. 'Of course, Faudin could be lying, but somehow I doubt it. He must realize it would be simple for us to check. We'll talk to Mrs May as soon as we get to Longacres, Abbot, and then we'll have another go at Simon Faudin. Knowing as we now do that Pauline Brune was a blackmailer, I find it hard to believe that Derek Faudin's private talk with her was as innocent as he implied. How did it strike you?'

'A bit odd, sir. I'd have thought that if anyone had needed to tell Pauline it was time she went it should have been Cynthia Faudin's job. After all, she's an experienced woman, principal of an Oxford college. I suppose it might have been embarrassing for her, but she must be used to dealing with difficult situations.'

'True enough,' Tansey admitted. 'I agree. That's one of the reasons I don't entirely believe in Derek Faudin's story. He may well have wanted to get Pauline out of the house, but I'd bet there was more to it than that.'

'Then do you think she might have been trying to blackmail him, sir? Christopher Winter did say she'd been caught reading his private papers.'

The Chief Inspector didn't answer Abbot directly. Instead he said slowly, 'It could be something to do with Antonia Merridew. Remember that slip of paper we found in the Brune woman's room. When we tried the name "Merridew" on Faudin the question shook him, though he denied having ever heard of it. But surely he must have, even if Simon's godson was brought up as Mark Carter.'

'Simon himself wasn't too quick about recalling it, either. It was left to Valerie to have a sudden flash of inspiration,' Abbot reminded him. 'Of course, the Faudins aren't young, and the Merridews must have been dead for years.'

'Simon and Valerie aren't that old,' Tansey protested, 'and neither of them is stupid. Nor for that matter is Derek, though he's quite a lot older. For instance, he fully appreciated the advantage of making a voluntary statement. But I'll tell you something, Sergeant. If this is the "family secret" that Winter referred to, it's certainly not shared by Cynthia Faudin. I was watching her at the time we first mentioned the name, and I'm positive she didn't react.'

'Perhaps not, sir. It's the two brothers who are really close, I'd say. If whatever it was happened ages ago there was probably no reason to tell Cynthia. As for Valerie, I got the impression she was—was sort of acting, and none too well at that.'

'That's pretty perceptive of you, Abbot. So did I.' Tansey nodded his agreement. 'But maybe we can get things a bit clearer this afternoon if we ever get to Longacres. Be a good chap and put your foot down hard. I don't want another late night if it can be avoided.'

'Very good, sir. Here goes. But I hope you'll bail me out if I get done for speeding.'

In the sitting-room at Longacres the neat and efficient Mrs May was quite definite. There had to be rules in any household, she maintained, and most especially in an establishment such as Longacres. Rules helped towards the smooth running of affairs, and thus ensured a pleasant, well-organized life for the Faudins, and it was for this that she was paid. Mrs Faudin had no time to be bothered with minor domestic problems; she had vastly more important matters to pursue.

If there was a large house party, as there had been for Mr Derek's birthday, rules were adhered to more strictly rather than less. On Sunday morning, time had been especially pressing. After a late night, breakfast had been a protracted meal, but eventually it had been cleared. As usual, when they were returned to the dining-room, place mats, glasses and plates that would be used again for lunch would be left on the end of the table. All the cutlery, however, would be given a quick polish and returned to the drawers of the sideboard.

'Last Sunday I checked myself, Chief Inspector,' said

Mrs May. 'Beryl's a good girl, but she's only a teenager and occasionally she makes mistakes—and the house has been very busy, as you know. But nothing that should have been put away had been left out.'

Tansey was given the choice of believing Mrs May or Derek Faudin, and he was inclined to accept the house-keeper's version. There was no reason for her to lie about such a triviality. But, unless the knife had been taken from the sideboard deliberately by either Faudin or Brune in anticipation of the other's arrival, the drawer must have been opened and the knife extracted during their quarrel; he found it hard to visualize such a scenario.

Over the years Mrs May had learnt to be both discerning and tactful, and she sensed at once that Tansey was in some kind of dilemma. 'Would you like to speak to Beryl yourself, Chief Inspector?'

'It's scarcely necessary, but—' To his surprise, Tansey found himself a little embarrassed.

'Why not?' said Mrs May, giving him an understanding smile. 'It will relieve any doubts you might have. I can make mistakes too, Chief Inspector.'

'Not many, I suspect, Mrs May.' Tansey was grateful. 'However, it might be a good idea to get Beryl's confirmation. But stay here while we talk to her, please.'

And a nervous Beryl, fetched by Abbot, confirmed the rule that cutlery was never left out, but was always returned to the sideboard until the table was laid for the next meal. 'It's more hygienic and the silver doesn't get tarnished so quickly,' she explained to Tansey with an anxious glance at Mrs May.

'What happens when you're particularly busy—like last Sunday morning? Aren't you ever tempted to cut corners when Mrs May's not around?'

'She's always around, sir.'

Tansey laughed. 'She was certainly around on Sunday morning, and she assures me that there was no silver left out on the dining-room table.'

'Then I don't understand why you're—'

'Beryl, we're not trying to catch you out,' intervened Mrs May firmly. 'But you know that Miss Brune has been killed and Mr Faudin badly hurt, so this is important. Just think carefully. Could you have put anything in the wrong place—the carving knife, for example?'

'No. I remember—' Beryl stopped, and clapped a hand over her mouth. 'Oh, Jesus!' she said.

'Tell us,' said Tansey. 'Don't be afraid, Beryl. We know you had nothing to do with hurting Mr Faudin or Miss Brune.'

'Well—it was like this, sir. After breakfast I washed the silver and gave it a polish as usual and then, as I told you, I put it all back in the sideboard.' Beryl was nervously fidgeting with her apron. 'I was just replacing the carving knife when I remembered I'd not sharpened it, and Mr Faudin had complained the other day about it getting blunt. So I took the knife back to the kitchen to sharpen. When I got back to the dining-room Miss Brune was there. She didn't look too pleased to see me and—and so I just put the knife down on the table and left it there . . .'

Beryl's voice trailed away miserably. 'I—I'm sorry,' she said. 'I didn't mean any harm . . .'

'No need to be sorry,' Tansey said quickly, afraid that the girl might be about to burst into tears. 'You've been a great help to us, Beryl. Solved a minor mystery, in fact. There was Mr Faudin saying one thing and Mrs May another, and you've shown that they were both right. We're all grateful. Now perhaps you or Mrs May could ask Mr Simon Faudin to spare us a few minutes.'

'Don't worry, Beryl,' added Mrs May. 'As the Chief Inspector says, we're most grateful to you. Now go and get on with your work, while I fetch Mr Simon.'

Simon Faudin, the Chief Inspector decided, was as wary as Terry Danforth had been, but his aggression was less obvious and, Tansey reminded himself, before his retirement Simon had been the senior partner in a well-known law firm. It wouldn't be easy to force him to tell the truth, or even an approximation to it, if he wasn't prepared to do so. Guile would be useless. A straightforward attack, never exceeding police authority or trespassing on a potential defendant's rights, was in order here.

'A few more questions, if you don't mind, Mr Faudin,' said Tansey as an opening remark.

'And suppose I do mind? Does it make any difference, Chief Inspector?'

It was not a good beginning, and Tansey didn't respond to Simon Faudin's provocative questions. Instead, he deliberately paused before asking one of his own. 'Mr Faudin, have you spoken to your brother since he told us what he says actually happened in the dining-room here on Sunday morning?'

'Yes. I've spoken to him, but I've no intention of commenting on what he told me.'

Tansey tried a different tack. 'Does Mark Carter know that he was born Mark Merridew?'

'Yes, of course.' This time Simon had taken longer to answer. 'But what the hell has Mark got to do with you?'

'Mr Faudin, this is a murder inquiry—or at least one relating to manslaughter. If you won't cooperate, and it becomes necessary, I can always get the information I want from the New York police, but this might cause Mr Carter some embarrassment. You see, I've come to believe that Pauline Brune tried to blackmail you or your brother, or both of you, because of your connection with Mr Carter.'

'And what makes you think that?'

Tansey smiled thinly. 'You seem to prefer asking questions to answering them, Mr Faudin, but I'll tell you and, when I have, I think you'll accept that there's a fair amount of evidence in favour of my hypothesis.'

'All right. Go ahead, Chief Inspector.' Simon Faudin, his face merely expressing attention, leant back in his chair. 'I'm listening.'

The man's arrogance annoyed Tansey, but he controlled his temper. 'Your brother caught Pauline Brune going through some of his private papers. Next you were heard quarrelling with Miss Brune in the library; the excuse you made was that she wanted to take a book you were using— it was a pretty weak explanation, you must admit. Then when I asked Mr Derek Faudin if he knew of an Antonia Merridew he denied it, but he was clearly shocked and hastily rang for his nurse to avoid any further questioning. You too, Mr Faudin, were oddly slow to recognize the name and you had to be prompted by your wife, who is not a great actress. She sounded as if she were repeating lines she had learnt, and she wasn't exactly convincing.'

Deliberately Simon Faudin took out his handkerchief and blew his nose. 'Is that all, Chief Inspector?'

'Not quite, Mr Faudin.'

Tansey was as acerbic as Simon, and Abbot gave a warning cough; these coughs of his were becoming a habit, the Chief Inspector thought, but there there was no question of bullying an old or sick man. Simon Faudin was perfectly capable of looking after himself, more capable in fact than Terry Danforth.

'We also have irrefutable evidence that Pauline Brune was a blackmailer,' Tansey said quietly, 'and that she intended you to be a victim.'

'What evidence?'

'The statement of someone whom she succeeded in black-mailing,' Tansey replied, 'and there is circumstantial evidence that that was not her first effort.'

'Really? I accept what you say, Chief Inspector, but I still don't see how it concerns me.'

'Mr Faudin.' Tansey managed to contain his exasperation. 'When you searched Pauline Brune's room immediately—indeed, with extraordinary immediacy—after her death, ostensibly to trace a next of kin, there was something you missed—an envelope taped to the underside of a drawer. In it was a piece of paper giving the birth date of Mark Merridew and other information about him.'

Simon Faudin remained silent, but he had not been able to disguise the shock in his eyes and the tensing of the muscles around his mouth.

Tansey seized his advantage. 'The police are never on the side of blackmailers, Mr Faudin. You must know that from your experience as a lawyer. If the Merridew connection has nothing to do with Pauline Brune's death, then no reference will be made to it in public. Even if it does turn out to be relevant, no names will be mentioned.'

He waited and, when Simon Faudin still made no response, he added. 'It would be in the best interests of yourself and your family to cooperate, I assure you.'

At last Simon Faudin said, reluctantly but with a certain truculence, 'Yes. I expect you're right. Here's the whole story. Your silent sergeant sitting there by the window can take it all down.'

It was not an extraordinary story and Dick Tansey had already made a good guess at the substance of it. But Simon Faudin, in his dry, legalistic voice, brought it unexpectedly to life.

'Many years ago I had to go to New York on business,' he said. 'My client had interests on both sides of the Atlantic. Valerie didn't come with me—she had just had a second miscarriage, in spite of taking extreme care. The case in question dragged on, as they often do in the States, and my client, who was rich and influential, urged me to stay to see it through. Selfishly I agreed.

'I was well entertained and I met the Merridews at a party. They were a good-looking couple, and popular. Personally, I found David rather a wooden character and not very intelligent, but Antonia was beautiful.' Simon's voice shook. 'We were instantly attracted to each other, and I suppose that I was emotionally ready for an affair. Ours was brief. I had to go back to England, to Valerie, whom I dearly loved.'

He paused for a moment and then continued, 'Antonia and I had agreed not to write, and we kept to our agreement, but months later I received a letter from Dorothy Carter, David's mother, whom I'd also met. She said that Antonia had had a child, Mark, and that Antonia had told her I was the father. Antonia knew it couldn't be David's because

David was impotent. And, of course, David knew that too, and suspected that Mark was my son—or perhaps he forced Antonia to admit it. I don't know. Anyway, some newspaper cuttings were enclosed with the letter. David Merridew's reaction had been extreme—unbalanced, if you like. He had deliberately driven his car, with Antonia and Mark, who was only a month old, into a support of the Brooklyn Bridge. He and Antonia were killed instantly. Miraculously, Mark survived. Then, in brief, the Carters officially adopted the boy, and gave him their name.'

Simon Faudin heaved a sigh, and continued, 'I never told Valerie because I thought she would be devastated, not only because I'd been unfaithful to her, but because she yearned for a child but couldn't have one. Derek knew and made certain financial arrangements for me. And Pauline Brune saw some papers he'd left for a few minutes on his desk; I'm not sure exactly what she read, but it was clearly enough for her to put two and two together. That woman was a bitch! Yes, Chief Inspector, she did try to blackmail me, but she didn't succeed.'

'You expect me to believe that, Mr Faudin?' Tansey asked, as Simon stopped speaking.

'It's the truth.' The words carried conviction. 'Derek had warned me she might have gathered some information she ought not to have had, and at his birthday dinner I knew he was right. She made an unmistakable remark about "my son in New York". Actually I was so startled I upset a whole glass of wine. Then the next day she found me in the library. She asked for money, and I told her to go to hell. Chief Inspector, I've seen enough misery caused by blackmail in my profession. I wasn't going to become a victim.'

'So you appealed to your brother?'

'Yes. But if you're thinking he killed Pauline Brune to protect me, you can think again. In the first place I told Valerie at once, hoping that by this time it wouldn't hurt her so much, and she said she had guessed most of it anyway.' Simon shook his head, apparently in wonder at women's intuition. 'Then I told Derek that Valerie knew and he promised to confront the Brune woman and tell her to get out of Longacres or we'd accuse her of attempted blackmail. If I'd any idea that she might attack him physically I'd never have let him tackle her alone. What happened was really my fault.'

Simon became silent, and there was a thoughtful pause before Tansey said, 'Thank you for being so frank, Mr Faudin. You've explained a great deal. Incidentally, when you searched Miss Brune's room did you remove anything from it?'

'Yes.' The hesitation had been so brief that Tansey wasn't sure of it. 'A tin box. I thought it might contain material about the Merridews. In fact, it held a reel of old-fashioned ciné film and some photographs. These things meant nothing to me, so I destroyed them and threw the box away. I'm sorry, Chief Inspector. They were probably evidence of Brune's other activities.'

'They probably were, Mr Faudin,' Tansey agreed. 'A pity they've gone, a great pity. Well, I think that's all for now. Thank you again.'

'What about my brother, Chief Inspector?' Simon Faudin asked as the officers rose to their feet. 'Presumably he'll have to face charges. What will it be? Murder? Manslaughter? In any case, I'm sure he'll plead self-defence.'

'That won't depend on me, sir, as you know quite well,' said Tansey. 'When I've made my report to the Chief Constable, the matter will be out of my hands.'

'The Chief Constable? Ah yes. That's Philip Midvale, isn't it? I've met him. A good man.'

And a just and honest man, Tansey thought, so if you're hoping to influence him, forget it.

'So . . .' said Abbot when Simon Faudin had left the room.

'So . . .' answered Tansey pensively. However, he was not prepared to share his thoughts—or his doubts—with his Sergeant, at least not at that moment. He would save them for the Chief Constable.

CHAPTER 15

Detective Chief Inspector Tansey delayed his formal conference with the Chief Constable for a week, in the Micawber-like hope that something would turn up. He was disappointed; the week was entirely uneventful, though the routine continued, additional statements were taken and filed, the preliminary forensic reports were refined and amplified, the files were examined and re-examined. The net result was that no further evidence became available, and the Chief Inspector was reluctantly forced to the conclusion that, barring unforeseen and seemingly unlikely developments, the Faudin case was at an end.

Philip Midvale regarded Tansey speculatively across the desk in his office. It is not always the most brilliant officers who become Chief Constables, but Midvale was one of the most efficient in England and he prided himself on what he knew was now called 'man-management'; he preferred to think of it as 'knowing his men'. He made a practice of treating each of his more senior officers as an individual whom he was prepared to trust, and as a result of judicious selection his trust was rarely misplaced.

Dick Tansey was one of the officers for whom he had the highest regard and respect, but the Chief Constable knew that anyone was fallible. He had spent a large part of the morning reading and re-reading Tansey's report on the Faudin affair and, after his customary lunch at his desk—a sandwich, a piece of fruit and a cup of coffee—he had sent for the Chief Inspector. It was obvious from the report that Tansey had his doubts—doubts which Midvale himself had come to share—and the obvious next step was a discussion in an attempt to resolve them.

'A strange business, Chief Inspector,' he said. 'Don't you agree? We have a body. We have a confession. Yet somehow the conclusion is unsatisfactory—especially the recommendation concerning what Faudin should be charged with.'

This was precisely Tansey's feeling, but he merely said, 'I accepted that we can only go for manslaughter, sir, and that Faudin will plead self-defence.'

The Chief Constable agreed. 'You know the law as well as I do, probably better,' he said. 'One can use *reasonable* force to defend oneself. What's wide open is the interpretation of "reasonable" in any given circumstances. So much depends on the judge—especially his summing-up—and of course on the make-up of the jury.'

Tansey grinned wryly. 'And you can't control either or rely on either.'

'Unfortunately not—from our point of view,' Midvale agreed. 'I also find it infuriating when some character who's probably guilty up to his eyebrows gets off scot-free or with some risible sentence, which is later halved for good behaviour.'

Midvale shifted his heavy bulk in his chair as if prepared to confer for the next hour. 'Now, let's recap. You tell me what you've got to support our case.'

The Chief Inspector began marshalling his evidence for an oral statement. Knowing his superior's habits he saw no point in reminding Midvale that it was all lying on his desk in neat typescript.

'Primarily, there's the forensic evidence, sir,' he said. 'It contradicts the account Faudin gave us. The round blood spots on the carpet show incontrovertibly that when he received that knife wound he was standing still and, what's more, continued to stand still while he started to bleed. I suppose a good barrister could argue that that was immediate effect of shock—but, with a wound of that seriousness, is it conceivable? And of course, sir, it might be argued that he'd been taken by surprise, but he says that he then struggled with Pauline Brune for possession of the knife. If that's true his blood stains should be smeared, but they're not. You see the point, sir? The forensic people won't come out and say they can prove it, but it suggests the possibility that Faudin's wound was self-inflicted, incredible as that may sound.'

'I take your point. But wait a minute, Chief Inspector,' Midvale interrupted. He referred to the report in front of him. 'It says here there *were* some smeared bloodstains.'

'They were Brune's blood, sir, both from the relative positions of the bodies and the tests. Admittedly Faudin and Brune had the same blood group, but nowadays, as you know, the matching is much more subtle than that. Though I don't deny that in court you could probably get some experts arguing the point.'

'Yes,' said Midvale. 'Go on.'

'The blow that killed Brune was struck with considerable force. That implies real violence, sir—intent to harm rather than accidental wounding—at least in my book.'

Midvale was again studying the report. He said, 'But the fact that Faudin and Brune were of much the same height could be turned in Faudin's favour. A good barrister, as you call him—and Derek Faudin would certainly have the best there is—would claim that he needed to use force to overcome someone like Brune. It wasn't as if she were a slip of a girl.'

Tansey nodded. 'I appreciate that, sir.'

'And you can't show he had a good motive for killing her, Chief Inspector. Simon Faudin would swear he'd already told his brother that his wife, Valerie, knew about Mark Carter. So when Derek Faudin met Brune in the dining-room that Sunday morning he was aware that she was mistaken in believing she had any possibility of blackmailing brother Simon. Anyway, it seems weak to me to suggest that Derek would have killed Brune to stop his brother being blackmailed. Don't you agree?'

Tansey did agree. He had already realized the force of this argument—indeed, lack of motive was one of the main reasons he had abandoned any attempt to string together a case for a murder charge. 'Nevertheless,' he went on, 'I wish I could understand why Derek Faudin told us so many lies. First, he invented a non-existent thief, whom he claimed was interrupted by Pauline Brune and subsequently discovered by himself. Then he made a so-called "confession", withdrawing that story. He said that when he told Brune she'd outstayed her welcome at Longacres she had threatened to cause unpleasant publicity for himself and his wife—and had then attacked him. Regrettably he had caused her death, but it had been completely inadvertent and in self-defence.'

'Chief Inspector,' Midvale said quietly, 'we can't prove that this second story was a lie. We can't even be sure in our own minds that it was.'

'It was certainly a lie by omission, sir, if nothing else. He never mentioned the Merridew business or Brune's attempt at blackmail. Why on earth not, if he knew that Valerie Faudin had been told about Mark? It would have added substance to his story.'

The Chief Constable was again sifting through the report. 'I thought I read somewhere that you put that question to him,' he said doubtfully.

'Yes, I did, sir, but of course not at the time—not until after I'd heard Simon's account. Anyway, I don't consider Derek's answer satisfactory. He said that he was afraid the media would seize upon the tale and make a scandal out of it—to the detriment of his wife's career.'

'*His* wife? What's the Merridew affair got to do with Cynthia Faudin?'

Tansey shrugged. 'Absolutely nothing, as far as I can see, sir. But Derek Faudin appears inordinately anxious to avoid anything he thinks might lead to harmful publicity. It seems that it doesn't matter how much he misleads the police, as long as the Faudin family doesn't appear in a bad light.' He hesitated. 'It—it's almost as if he were slightly unbalanced about it, sir.'

'I take your point, Chief Inspector,' said Midvale. 'And I still can't see how Cynthia Faudin could be affected. There's very little doubt that public sympathy—even media sympathy—would be with the Faudins because Brune was a blackmailer. It could even be suggested that *she* was unbalanced.'

'Yes, sir,' said Tansey and, when the Chief Constable made no further comment, added. 'So the charge is to be manslaughter, then, sir?'

Philip Midvale nodded slowly. 'We'll go ahead with that. I'm sorry you're not satisfied, Chief Inspector. Nor am I, at the end of the day. Derek Faudin's behaviour has been inconsistent, to say the least. But on the evidence we have I don't see any hope of a more serious charge.'

'Very good, sir.' Tansey had no option but to accept the Chief Constable's verdict. 'Manslaughter it shall be.'

That same evening Detective Chief Inspector Tansey, quite uncharacteristically, abandoned an in-tray that, if not overflowing, was still uncomfortably full, and decided to go home. He was not in the best of tempers, and he knew it. As he admitted to his wife, he was thoroughly disgruntled.

'Why should I—and a lot of other people—work like hell to produce a—a—' he searched for a word and finally completed the sentence—'to produce a mouse?'

Hilary thought for a moment. 'In the interests of British justice?' she suggested finally.'

'Justice? A travesty of justice! Merely manslaughter, when I know in my bones it ought to be murder!' Dick Tansey exploded. The frustration that had been growing within him during the past week at last demanded an outlet. 'Motive's the main bloody problem. Lack of it means that all Derek Faudin will be faced with is a charge of manslaughter. He'll appear in a magistrates' court, plead self-defence and be remanded on bail, and I guess that in view of his position the bail will be derisory. In a few months' time he'll face a judge and jury. Considering that the police will admit that Pauline Brune was a proven blackmailer there'll be considerable sympathy for him—even Midvale admits that. I wouldn't be in the least surprised if he got off with something like two years—suspended!'

'Oh, Dick!' Hilary protested. 'You're not usually so bitter.'

Dick Tansey grunted. 'I'd have been vastly better employed these last weeks doing the work this house needs. Sure, the downstairs is fine, but the bedrooms badly need redecorating, and as for the garden, well—'

'It'll get done in time,' said Hilary soothingly. 'Anyway, you're much too busy. I think we should get someone in to do the decorating. We can afford it.'

It was three months since the Tanseys had moved from the house the Chief Inspector had owned before their marriage into their present house in North Oxford. They had been very fortunate. They had been shown over the place by an estate agent and had decided at once that it met all their needs and expectations. The rooms were bright and spacious, and there was a good-sized garden. It was, they thought, an ideal place to bring up the two children they planned to have when Hilary was fully recovered from her miscarriage during that disastrous last year when Dick was attached to the Met in London. But the price of the house was high, too high unless Hilary continued to work. Then, when they had given up hope and were looking for a smaller home, Hilary's aunt died suddenly and left her a moderately substantial legacy. At the same time their original choice came back on to the market and they were able to snap it up.

'I don't understand why Pauline Brune should suddenly have seized that carving knife and attacked Faudin but, on the other hand, if it didn't happen that way, I don't understand why he attacked her,' Tansey said ruminatively, ignoring his wife's last remark.

Hilary sighed. It was clear to her that Dick's mind was still completely absorbed by the Faudin case. She didn't blame him. Indeed, she knew enough about the pressures he faced to sympathize, but she was worried. He had been working too hard, not sleeping well, and was becoming over-tired. She wished she could persuade him to take the leave that was due to him, and which she was sure he needed, but she saw little prospect of achieving this. So, she thought resignedly, for the moment it was probably better for him to talk about the case, rather than brood on it in silence.

'Dick,' she said, 'there's a casserole in the oven, so we can eat when we like. I'll just have a look at it while you pour us a drink. Then I want to ask you about Pauline Brune.'

And, minutes later, the food checked and the sherries poured, Tansey sank back in an armchair and said, 'What do you want to know about the Brune woman, Hilary?'

'Well, haven't you learnt any more about her background? There must have been a lot of inquiries. Haven't any of them turned up anything?'

'Not really. As you know, her bank manager was very helpful, and has done all he promised. Brune seems to have operated in this general district, at least for the last ten years. She banked here in Oxford, mainly through other branches. She had a current account, which she used mainly to pay in her salary. And she also had a deposit account, into which she seems to have paid in her blackmail gains.' Tansey gave a shrug. 'There's no doubt. The woman was a small-time but efficient blackmailer. She probably did a lot of harm and deserves to be dead, but—'

'And where did she come from originally? Hasn't she got any relations? And what about the man she married? What was his name—Gaul or something?'

'She was born in Kent—near Tunbridge Wells. The CID there investigated for us, mainly in the hope of finding some next of kin, but they couldn't help much. We already knew from Cynthia Faudin that Pauline's father was a Church of England parson. Apparently in 1939 the Reverend Brune was transferred to a living in the Isle of Wight—to a parish in which the Courtlands—Cynthia Faudin's family—had their home. We've been on to the police there, too. Mrs Brune died towards the end of the war, and her husband a couple of years later in 1946, when Pauline was seventeen. And Pauline—their only child—was left more or less penniless and unqualified.'

'And after that she became a home-help to the Courtlands

and eventually to a succession of other people.' Hilary was pensive. 'What a sad life.'

'It doesn't excuse blackmail.'

'No, but—surely you must know more about her than that, Dick. The husband, for example?'

'You must remember it was all a long time ago, and not long after World War Two. People were still coming and going. No one seems to remember the Brunes at all clearly. As far as Pauline's husband's concerned, we know where and when she was married—the certificate, and that of her husband's death—were in her safe deposit box at her bank. Gaul married her in 1950 in London, so she couldn't have stayed all that long with the Courtlands. The Brune woman was unlucky, for her new husband died suddenly a year later. The Met looked into it for us, also in the hope of tracing a remote relative. They had no luck. Anyway, what does all this matter? As far as we know Pauline Brune hadn't got around to blackmailing anyone at that stage of her career.'

'Maybe not, but—' Hilary held out her glass for a second sherry—'let's get back to the Isle of Wight. It's the connection, isn't it? I mean, if Cynthia Courtland and Pauline Brune hadn't been children together Pauline would never have gone to Longacres. I wonder if they went to the same school.'

'I've no idea, Hilary! And they weren't exactly children together. Cynthia was five years younger than Brune, which is a lot at that age.'

'The local police don't seem to have been very thorough.'

'They were only asked in connection with tracing any next of kin.' Dick Tansey smothered a yawn. 'Darling, I'm hungry. How's that casserole doing?'

'I'll go and see,' Hilary replied at once.

But later that night, when they were in bed, and relaxed after making love, she returned to the subject.

'Dick, we're both due some leave and we've been promising ourselves a holiday soon. Why don't we go down to the Isle of Wight for a few days? I've never been there, but it's said to be a lovely place and we could combine pleasure with a little business—'

Tansey laughed aloud. 'A little business,' he said. 'I can't go haring off to someone else's patch without permission.' Then he reflected. 'But it's not a bad idea. I'll put it to the Chief Constable,' he said. 'I might even get some expenses.'

Part Three

CHAPTER 16

Dick and Hilary Tansey drove quickly down the A34 from Oxford to Southampton, and even more rapidly along the Motorway to Portsmouth, where they found the car ferry that would take them across the Solent to Fishbourne on the Isle of Wight. Tansey himself was looking forward to the short voyage. He had done some sailing when he was younger and had enjoyed—did still enjoy—wind and waves and the smell of the sea. And today, even from the security of the terminal, it looked as if there would be plenty of wind and waves.

Hilary took quite a different view; she knew that she was not a good sailor, and even her husband's reassurances as to the speed of the crossing failed to satisfy her. She had read somewhere that the Solent could at times be one of the most boisterous of the so-called sheltered waters around Britain, and this seemed likely to be one of those times. After a fine spell the weather had suddenly changed. There was even a hint of rain in the air and the sky was a sullen grey. It didn't presage well for what was intended to be, if not exactly a holiday, at least a pleasurable break with a certain amount of work to which the Chief Constable had readily given his blessing.

In fact, Midvale, who himself had been harbouring unexpressed doubts about the outcome of the Faudin case, had been glad when Tansey had suggested what amounted to a new line of inquiry. The Hampshire Constabulary had been approached, and permission easily obtained for the Chief Inspector and his wife to conduct further investigations on the Isle of Wight.

But Hilary was right about the weather and the sea-state. The middle of the sea trip found her sitting close by her husband on the open deck of the small ferry *Caedmon*, as the ship pitched and rolled and an occasional shower of spray broke over the side. Hilary shivered.

'Are you sure you wouldn't be better off under cover?' Tansey asked.

'Quite sure, thank you. In my present queasy state it's only the fresh air that saves me. I couldn't bear the smell of food or beer. I can't imagine why on earth they can't have an air or helicopter service across this wretched bit of water. Anyway, I'd rather be cold and damp than sea-sick.'

Tansey didn't point out that being cold and damp was not the best remedy for a poor sailor. Instead he said, 'It won't be long now. Look, you can see the entrance to the terminal at Fishbourne quite clearly. And listen—there's the announcement asking us to get down to our car.'

'Thank God,' said Hilary. And, indeed, the sea became much calmer as they neared the island, and they were able to descend to the car deck without incident. It was only fifteen minutes before they were driving up the ramp, on their way to Ryde. The Isle of Wight Division of the Hampshire Constabulary had been good enough to book them a room at a hotel, where they were to meet an Inspector Warwick from the local CID.

Hilary said, 'I may be on dry land, but it feels as if the deck was still going up and down under my feet.'

'That'll pass very quickly, darling,' said Tansey, thankful that the greenish tinge around Hilary's mouth was fast disappearing. 'We'll soon get to this hotel.'

They found the hotel easily—a modern building on the sea front—and drew up at the main entrance, to be greeted by a doorman who took their bags and volunteered to park their car. It had been a tiring journey, especially for Hilary, and they were glad to register quickly before going to their room to wash and relax for a few minutes. And it was only ten minutes before the phone rang and the receptionist told them that a Mr Warwick was asking for them in the hall.

As they stepped out of the lift they were accosted by a middle-aged man in a thick navy blue suit, who said quietly, 'Chief Inspector Tansey?'

Tansey nodded. 'That's right. I'm Tansey. You must be Inspector Warwick. Let me introduce my wife.'

The man held out a large hand and crushed Tansey's fingers. 'Welcome to the island, Chief Inspector—and Mrs Tansey. Or should I say Sergeant Tansey; you're in the force too, I understand.'

'That's right,' said Hilary, 'but I've really come along for the ride, as it were. We hope to see something of your island while we're here.'

'Good,' said the Inspector heartily. 'Is this your first visit to us?'

'Yes,' said Hilary, trying not to wince as he shook her hand.

'Not much of a day to start it, I'm afraid,' said Warwick. 'It must have been quite a rough crossing. Let's go into the residents' lounge. There won't be anyone there at this time, and we can get a drink—'

'That's a wonderful idea,' said Tansey.

As soon as they were settled around a small table in a corner of this comfortably-furnished and empty room, Tansey said, 'It's very good of you to come and meet us here. I know that your Headquarters is in Newport, and that's right in the middle of the island, isn't it? I've been studying the map.'

'Yes,' said Warwick, 'but it's only a few miles. The Isle of Wight's pretty small, you know. And anyway we're always happy to be of service to a colleague from the mainland. It's this Pauline Brune case, I gather. I handled the inquiries that have already been made here at your request. You've read my report, of course. Now there are some more details?'

'Yes,' Tansey admitted. This was a moment for tact. 'There are a few points that have come up. You did exactly what we asked—to try and search for any traces of next of

kin—but we're hoping a slightly different, wider approach
might produce some further useful evidence.'

'I see,' said the Inspector, who clearly didn't.

There was a slightly hesitant pause before he went on.
'Well, we recommended this hotel because it's a quiet and
efficient place with excellent service, and also because it's
within walking distance of the church where the Reverend
Brune was the rector. It's called St Michael and All Angels,
and at present it has a young parson called David Nightingale. He'll show you the records and direct you to
wherever you want to go. Do you want me or one of my
chaps to come with you, or would you prefer to operate
alone?'

'That's terrific, Inspector,' said Tansey. 'Many thanks. I
don't think we'll bother you, at least to start with, but we'll
keep you informed, of course.'

Inspector Warwick was not without his share of tact.
Sensing that Tansey was unwilling or unable to explain any
further, he turned to Hilary, smiling and saying, 'And you
hope to see some of the sights, you said.'

'Indeed we do,' said Hilary.

'There are plenty,' said Warwick and he went on to
mention a list of places of interest that the Tanseys must
be sure to visit—Carisbrooke Castle, Alum Bay with its
coloured sands, and the Needles, stretching out westwards
into the English Channel.

Eventually, the Inspector rose to his feet. 'I'll say goodbye,' he remarked. 'I'd beter get back to Newport. But
please don't hesitate to give me a call if you want any
assistance or there's anything we can do for you. And we
hope you'll find time to look in at our Headquarters and
perhaps have a word with our Chief Superintendent—he's
the senior officer on the island—before you go.'

'We certainly will,' Tansey promised. 'And, as I said,
we'll brief you on anything interesting we come across. And
thank you again for meeting us.'

'Thank you,' Hilary echoed. 'It was very kind of you.'

Once again Inspector Warwick offered his hand to each

of them in turn, though this time they knew what to expect. 'I wish you luck,' said Inspector Warwick.

The next morning turned out fine and bright, and the Tanseys found their way to St Michael's Church without difficulty, though it was not until they were leaving the rectory that Dick fully realized how ironic Inspector Warwick's parting wish had been. Warwick had already covered the ground—expertly and thoroughly in his opinion—and he had made it fairly evident that he didn't believe that a Chief Inspector, who was not even on his own patch, would get any further with the inquiry.

And, after talking to the present incumbent at St Michael's, Tansey was inclined to believe that Warwick's judgement was right. The Reverend David Nightingale had shown them the church records, repeated what he had told Inspector Warwick and had added that, since he had been interviewed by the Inspector, he had asked some of the more elderly members of his congregation if any of them remembered the Brunes. One or two did, but could recall nothing specific or useful about them.

'Well, that's a dead end,' Tansey said to Hilary. 'The Brunes don't seem to have made a great impression on the religious life of the island.'

'Maybe not, but if Cynthia Faudin remembered Pauline, others must also,' Hilary said with more optimism than she felt. 'I think we're asking about the wrong generation, Dick. It's a contemporary of Pauline's we should be trying to trace.'

'And how do you suggest we set about that?'

'Let's find some coffee, and consider the dates we've got.'

'Fine, let's, though I'm not sure how they'll help. It's the luck Warwick wished us that we need.'

'We could have a go at creating our own luck,' Hilary said with determination, leading the way into an attractive-looking café.

Dick Tansey was amused. He ordered coffee and cakes and said, 'OK. Now what about these dates, darling?'

'The Brunes came to the Isle of Wight in 1939 when the Reverend Brune was transferred to St Michael's, which was the church Mr and Mrs Courtland attended. Pauline must have been nine at the time, and she must have gone to school. Where? And what about her school friends? Not Cynthia, who was so much younger, but Pauline's contemporaries, as I say.'

Abruptly Hilary stopped speaking as if an idea had occurred to her. A waitress brought a pot of coffee and a plate of homemade cakes. Hilary poured the coffee and absent-mindedly began to eat a cake. Her husband waited, wryly expectant.

At last he said, 'Hilary, what is it?'

Hilary laughed. 'Sorry. I just thought of something. The Courtland family was on the Isle of Wight before the Brunes arrived here. Why don't we start with them? After all, we know that Cynthia Faudin's parents and Pauline Brune's parents, even if they weren't close friends, had some kind of social relationship. Otherwise the Courtlands would surely never have taken pity on Pauline and—'

'They might have wanted some cheap household help.'

'Dick!' Hilary was surprised. 'You're not usually so cynical. Anyway, it's a different approach, isn't it? We could try the schools first, and then—'

The owner of the café, brought by the waitress from the rear of the premises, was as happy to be of assistance as the rector of St Michael's Church had been. A plump and smiling woman, she became curious as soon as Tansey mentioned the name Pauline Brune, and told her some half-truths about seeking next of kin.

'You know,' she said, 'I guessed it must be the same Pauline—Brune's an unusual name, after all—and one can't help being interested. When I thought I'd been to the same school as she did, I read every word about her death in the newspapers.'

'You knew Pauline at school?' Hilary asked; it was too good to be true.

'Oh no, she'd left before I went there. She's a lot older than me. It was just that I remembered her as our vicar's daughter during the war.'

'Yes, of course,' Hilary said. 'How silly of me. But perhaps you know of someone around Pauline's age, who might have known her?'

Slowly the woman shook her head. 'No,' she said. 'I'm afraid not. For one thing, there was more class consciousness in those days, you know, and the girls who might have been friends with the vicar's daughter wouldn't have been likely to befriend me. My dad was a plumber.'

'At least as useful as a parson,' said Tansey. 'Some people would think more so.'

The woman laughed. 'More practical, at any rate. But I'll come to the door with you and point out the way to the school. They might be able to help.'

After the courtesy they had been shown by the owner of the café the Tanseys felt they had to visit the school though, with some justification, their expectations were not high. Although they hadn't made an appointment they were quickly and amiably received by the headmistress, who must herself have been considerably younger than Pauline Brune.

'I'm sorry, but I don't think we can be of much help,' she said, after Tansey had explained the reason for their questions. 'I read the story about this Pauline Brune in the papers, but it never occurred to me she might have been at school here. It must have been long before any member of our present staff. The oldest mistress is due to retire next year, but she'll only be sixty—about the same age as Miss Brune, I gather.'

The headmistress had rung for her secretary to show the Tanseys out and, standing in the open doorway of the study, the secretary had heard the end of the conversation. The headmistress added, 'If you like I'll get my secretary to check through the records and give you the exact dates Pauline Brune was here, but—'

'That really won't be necessary,' began Tansey, when the secretary intervened.

'Miss Parker,' she said, 'if we're looking for an elderly member of staff to remember someone, have you thought of Miss Fenwick?'

'Oh, Vera, how stupid of me not to think of her!'

'Miss Fenwick used to be a mistress here,' the secretary explained to the Tanseys. 'She's over ninety now, but her mind's still fine and she's extraordinarily active for her age. I'm sure she'd be delighted to have a visit from you. She lives in a sheltered home outside Newport. Shall I telephone and ask her?'

'Yes, do, Vera—if that's what the Tanseys would like.'

'Please!' said Hilary without hesitation, and to her husband she added as they left the school, 'See, we *are* making our own luck. What could be pleasanter this afternoon than driving through the island to have tea with a charming old lady who actually knew the Brunes. We could stop at this Carisbrooke Castle; the map suggests that it's not far out of our way.'

'Don't be too sure Miss Fenwick will be a charming old lady,' said Dick. 'She might be a fierce old biddy.'

In fact, it was difficult to class Isabel Fenwick as either. Certainly she was old, white-haired and slow-moving, but she carried herself like a Guards officer, her eyes were as bright as a squirrel's and, while she wore scarlet slacks, above them was a white, high-necked blouse with a cameo brooch at the throat. She greeted them warmly.

They might have been a nephew and niece whom she rarely saw, and it wasn't until cups of tea had been drunk and second slices of chocolate cake refused that Pauline Brune was mentioned. Then Miss Fenwick said, 'You know, in these violent days it's strange, but Pauline's the only one of my many ex-pupils who ever got herself murdered.'

'Murdered?' Dick Tansey exclaimed.

'Why, yes.' Miss Fenwick was quite calm. 'That's what I understood from what the media didn't say. Murder, though perhaps not premeditated. I expect she gave this Mr Faudin cause to attack her, but I very much doubt if she went for him first.'

'Why do you say that, Miss Fenwick? And how did you know it's the same Pauline Brune?'

'Because I guessed. I know—or rather knew—Pauline. If ever there was a "murderee", it was she. Oh, I can guess what you're thinking—that it was a long time ago—but in my experience an individual's basic character doesn't change. And Pauline wasn't in the least hot-tempered. Rather, she seemed merely cunning, accepting, but internally resentful of, any slight—real or imagined.'

Detective Chief Inspector Tansey and Detective-Sergeant Tansey were too well trained to exchange glances, but Miss Fenwick sensed their incredulity. 'Mind you,' she said, 'it wasn't surprising. I'll tell you.'

Pauline Brune had been the only child of elderly parents. Her mother had suffered from poor health, and the pregnancy so late in life had been unwelcome. Her father had devoted himself to his parish and his wife, and had little time for his daughter. Pauline had been fed, clothed and given suitable presents at Christmas and for her birthdays. She wasn't neglected in any sense, but she led a solitary existence, without companions of her own age.

'Didn't she make any friends at school?' Hilary Tansey asked.

'No. She didn't know how to deal with her contemporaries and she was discouraged from taking other children home to the vicarage. In addition, her father was a strict disciplinarian, almost Victorian in outlook. Thus, whereas most girls of her age were allowed out to have some fun, Pauline was expected to stay at home and help her mother. Her mother, incidentally, died when she was fifteen, and Pauline left school at once to be her father's housekeeper. Two years later her father died too, and there was Pauline—untrained, unattractive and more or less penniless.'

'You make her sound pitiful,' said Hilary.

'She would have resented pity, and she wasn't in the least

grateful to those who tried to help her.' Miss Fenwick's comment was abrupt.

'Like Mr and Mrs Courtland?' said Tansey casually.

'You would have known them too,' said Hilary.

'I knew of them,' Miss Fenwick corrected her. 'Cynthia was only at school for a short time. A clever child, as I remember. But she didn't like it at our school and they sent her to some boarding school on the mainland—I forget which, but Virginia Drinkwater might know, if it's important.'

'Who's Virginia Drinkwater?' Hilary asked.

'She's now Virginia Mercer. She was the daughter of Sir William and Lady Caroline Drinkwater.'

'And the Drinkwaters and the Courtlands were friends?'

'No, not really, though Mr Courtland and Sir William had been at Eton together. I believe the Courtlands were very well off at one time, but the money went somehow. Anyway, they lived here quite modestly.' Unexpectedly Miss Fenwick chuckled. 'I remember what a fuss Mr Courtland made when the school tried to charge him for an extra term because he hadn't given notice that Cynthia was leaving. He stormed around, saying he'd complain to his old friend Sir William—Sir William was a governor of the school at the time—but he paid in the end.'

'He sounds something of a snob,' Hilary said.

'Oh, I think he was,' Miss Fenwick agreed. 'But here I am gossiping about the Courtlands while it's Pauline Brune who interests you. But I don't believe I can remember any more about her.'

Suddenly, as old people are apt to do, Miss Fenwick had become tired. The Tanseys said goodbye, thanked her for the tea and her kindness and cooperation, and left.

In the car Hilary said, 'We can look the Mercers up in the phone book.'

'Tomorrow,' her husband said firmly. 'We've done enough for today. What I want now is a bath, a couple of drinks and a good dinner. Darling, we've collected enough material to form the background for a biography of Brune but you must admit we haven't furthered our own purpose much, have we?'

'No, I suppose not,' Hilary said reluctantly. 'OK, Dick. But perhaps we could call Mrs Mercer later this evening.'

It was fortunate that they did telephone Mrs Mercer that evening after dinner. She said she was catching the first ferry in the morning on her way to London, and subsequently to New York, and she didn't know how long she would be in the United States. Anyhow, what business was it of Chief Inspector Tansey—if he was Chief Inspector Tansey?

Referred to Inspector Warwick, Mrs Mercer became slightly more cooperative. Yes, she said she had read about Pauline Brune, and suspected it was the woman she vaguely remembered as a girl working for the Courtlands—though she hadn't thought of any of them for years. A pity that Mr Courtland was dead; he would have considered that Pauline had met her just desserts at last.

'Why do you say that?' Dick Tansey asked.

'Oh, he blamed her for Colin's death. It happened when they were on holiday in Jersey—it must have been in 1947, I should think. The Courtlands had relations there and they went to stay with them. Pauline was supposed to be looking after the twins—Cynthia and Colin, and Colin died of pneumonia. It doesn't sound very logical to have blamed Pauline, but there you are. I'd probably have done the same if it had been my son. Anyway, that's all I know, Chief Inspector.'

Tansey thanked her, and slowly put down the receiver. 'Hilary,' he said, thoughtfully, 'I think we might spend the second half of our holiday on an even smaller island.'

CHAPTER 17

Tansey's next step in the morning was to call Inspector Warwick and arrange to visit Newport. There he was welcomed by the Chief Superintendent who, when he learnt

the outcome of Tansey's inquiries on the island, had no
hesitation in offering the facilities of his Headquarters. In
fact, all Tansey needed was the use of a phone and some
travel information. He spoke to his own Chief Constable in
Kidlington, who readily approved a visit to Jersey and
promised to arrange matters with what appeared to be
called, oddly enough, the States of Jersey Police Force,
headed by a Chief Officer and not a Chief Constable.

Travel was the next question, and Tansey was surprised
to learn how simple that would be. Obviously going by boat
was not on the cards, both because of the time element and
because of Hilary's reluctance to undertake a lengthy seven-
or eight-hour sea trip. However, there were frequent flights
to Jersey from Eastleigh Airport near Southampton where,
as Inspector Warwick pointed out, parking facilities were
very adequate. The necessary reservations were easily made.

The return journey from Fishbourne to Portsmouth was
comparatively smooth, and the trip up the Motorway to
Eastleigh was uneventful. So was the short flight to Jersey,
where they were met at the airport by a plain-clothes officer,
who introduced himself as Detective-Sergeant Boulanger.
He was a fair-haired, blue-eyed man in his early thirties
but, he assured them at once, he was 'no relation of that
Sergeant Bergerac—if you watch that television series'.

'We do sometimes—and enjoy it,' Hilary said.

'But we rather doubt if a detective-sergeant's life here is
so dramatic—or so romantic,' Tansey added.

'It has its moments, sir,' said Boulanger, straight-faced.
Then he grinned. 'We've booked you in at the Hotel Pomme
d'Or in the middle of St Helier. You'll find it very comfortable and convenient. A hire car's being delivered there for
you after lunch. I'll leave you a Perry's Guide.'

'A what?'

'A Perry's Guide. Perry is a Guernseyman who's done
more to show Jersey people the way round their own Island
than anyone else. It's a little book of excellent and extremely
accurate road maps. All our patrol cars carry them. You'll
find it essential.'

'Really? On this little island—what is it, about nine by five miles?'

Boulanger was amused. 'Just about, sir. It seems small all right, but the longer you stay here the bigger it gets. And the lanes buried in the country parishes are like a maze. You'll soon find out.'

They had descended a hill and had turned on to a narrow undistinguished road, which suddenly, at another crossroads, became a dual highway, with the sea on the right—the only such highway in the island, according to the Sergeant. Here Boulanger increased speed, but still drove quite slowly. When Tansey commented, he said, 'There's an all-Island speed limit of forty miles an hour, sir, and in some places it's thirty or even twenty.'

Almost as soon as they had accelerated they were stopped by traffic lights at a complicated junction, and looking to the south they saw a massive building rising from the sea. 'That's St Aubin's Bay, and the building is Elizabeth Castle, where Sir Walter Raleigh lived when he was governor of the island,' Boulanger explained. 'It's a museum now, but you can get to it by amphibian at high tide or by walking across a causeway when the tide's out. You should visit it if you have time. It's a terrific place if you're interested in history.'

The lights changed and they moved forward again, reaching their hotel very soon afterwards. Sergeant Boulanger insisted on showing them in, and arranged to meet them at police Headquarters during the afternoon. He gave them detailed instructions on how to find the place, and wished them a cheerful *à bétôt*, leaving them with the famous Perry's Guide.

'A pleasant chap,' said Dick Tansey as they were shown up to their room, which overlooked a busy traffic round-about and a harbour. 'But what do you think his last words were?'

Hilary laughed. 'I wondered myself for a moment, but I imagine it's the Jersey-French for *à bientôt*,' she said.

'Of course,' said Tansey. 'Boulanger—it's French, prob-

ably a Jersey—name. He must speak Jersey-French. I suppose quite a lot of people here do. How intriguing!'

'Ye-es.' Hilary now sounded a little doubtful. 'You don't
think he was pulling our legs, do you? Can the police
Headquarters really be in a street called Rouge Bouillon—
Red Soup?'

Tansey had been studying his Guide, which included a
town plan of St Helier. 'It's here all right,' he replied. 'It
seems to be part of a kind of ring road around the town. It
should be simple enough to find.'

Hilary's doubts were finally resolved when after lunch
they drove up Rouge Bouillon and discovered their goal—
a complex of buildings almost opposite the central fire
and ambulance stations. They were greeted by Sergeant
Boulanger, taken to meet an officer of Tansey's rank who
was head of Jersey's CID, and then introduced to the Chief
Officer. Both offered any assistance in their power.

Finally, Sergeant Boulanger showed them around the
Headquarters, and explained the complicated policing arrangements in Jersey. Dick and Hilary were fascinated by
the combination of dual forces—the paid States of Jersey
Police, and the voluntary non-uniformed honorary police
elected by the residents of the twelve individual parishes.
Tansey had been unwilling to be totally frank about their
real mission on the island, and was relieved that their formal
visit had been little more than social.

The Chief Inspector, though he had enjoyed the afternoon, was very aware that from a professional point of view
he had achieved nothing; he was no nearer finding a more
credible explanation for Pauline Brune's death than when
he had left Oxford. He wondered how he would be able to
produce a remotely adequate report for his Chief Constable
back in Kidlington, and began to wish that he had never
listened to Hilary's idea of trailing around the offshore
islands of Britain. At present he was neither making progress
with the Faudin case, nor enjoying his much-needed holiday

But before they left the Headquarters, Sergeant Boulanger took them into a small office and invited them to sit down while tea was brought. He said, 'We haven't been exactly idle on your behalf, sir, in the short time we had. We were told you were interested in the story of an English boy called Colin Courtland who died when he was on holiday in Jersey in 1947, visiting relations, and that you were trying to trace any living relatives.'

'That's correct, Sergeant, but we don't want any publicity if we can avoid it.'

Boulanger nodded his understanding. 'I'm afraid there's no one in Jersey of that name. Of course, 1947 was a long time ago.'

'Yes,' said Tansey wearily. He was growing bored with this comment.

'And we were told the boy died of pneumonia, which was hardly a police matter, but would have meant an inquest. The hospital should have a record of his death, if they can trace it. However, I've been giving the matter some thought, and I guess the most useful step would be to consult the files of the JEP. I haven't had time to do this myself, so—'

'The what?' interrupted Tansey.

'Sorry, sir. The *Jersey Evening Post*. It's our local daily newspaper, and it comes out every afternoon except Sundays. The story would certainly have been reported there, and any connection with Jersey relatives would have been mentioned for sure.'

'They were publishing as far back as 1947?' Tansey asked, and regretted the question as soon as Hilary gave him a reproachful glance.

'Sir,' said Sergeant Boulanger rather proudly, 'the JEP started operations in 1890, and has continued ever since, even during the Occupation. I believe it has almost complete files, though some may have been microfilmed. 1947 should present no problem.'

'Right. That sounds a splendid idea, Sergeant. How do we get to see them?'

'The offices are at Five Oaks, and the records are there too. It's just north-east of the town, and I've made an appointment for you to go up there tomorrow morning at eleven to have a word with the editor. If that's not convenient I can easily change it. Incidentally, I warned him about the months you were interested in, but I didn't tell him why, though I know you can rely on his discretion.'

'Thanks a lot. Eleven will be fine. That's a great help,' said Tansey, relieved that the trail was not necessarily yet dead.

The next morning, having left plenty of time, the Tanseys arrived embarrassingly early at Five Oaks and the *Jersey Evening Post* offices—a low, modern building set back from the road by a circular drive enclosing a parking lot—and decided to go for a short drive. This was a mistake. Fifteen minutes later they were lost in a tangle of lanes. What was more, the Guide, so thoughtfully provided by Sergeant Boulanger, was still in their hotel room.

'Damn!' said Dick Tansey. 'Now we shall be late, which isn't a good beginning to the day.'

'There's a car coming. We can stop them and ask the way.'

'We'll certainly stop them, darling. Nothing's going to get by us in this lane but a bike with a thin rider.'

But the car coming towards them swung suddenly and effortlessly into the entrance to a field, allowing them to pass. Tansey edged slowly forward and lowered his window. 'Can you please help us?' he said. 'We're looking for the *Jersey Evening Post* offices at Five Oaks.'

'You're going in the wrong direction,' said the driver, a pretty blonde girl. 'Let me get out of here. Then you can turn and follow me. I work there.'

'Thanks,' said Tansey, and repeated his thanks after she had guided them to a parking place, and escorted them to the reception area. They were no more than five minutes late.

The editor greeted them warmly, offered them coffee and said he had arranged for the microfilm of the issues for the months they wanted to be ready for them, together with a microfilm reader. 'There's only one point,' he added. 'Normally, it's a rule that you should have a member of staff with you while you're searching the files. They're very precious to us, you know. But, seeing as you're police and vouched for by our own force, I'll stretch a point.'

'Thank you,' said Tansey. 'It really is important not to let our precise interests become public.'

'I understand,' said the editor. 'It's all organized.' He called to his secretary, who in a moment was taking the Tanseys to a small office, with the films and equipment.

Left to themselves, almost at once they struck gold. An issue of the *Evening Post* had a banner headline on its front page: BOY HAS TRAGIC ACCIDENT, it read.

'Accident?' said Hilary. 'I thought he died of pneumonia. No one's ever mentioned an accident.'

They read the screen together. It was a simple, sad story. Colin Courtland, on holiday with his parents, had been playing on the rocks at Le Dicq and it was assumed that a piece of the rock face had broken off and he had fallen. He had been found by his young cousin, Pierre de Chantal, who had summoned help. Colin had been taken to the General Hospital where, in spite of every effort to save him, he had died of pneumonia two days later.

'Pneumonia?'

'It happens, Hilary. The effects of shock and other trauma, I think, and, remember, in 1947, the doctors didn't have all the drugs and antibiotics that are available now. Let's look for the report of the inquest.'

At the inquest a verdict of 'accidental death' had been recorded. But the coroner had added a rider, a reprimand to Pauline Brune, whom he suggested had failed in her duty of ensuring the safety of her charges, Colin and Cynthia Courtland. Tansey noted, however, that the reporter had implied a certain sympathy for Pauline Brune, pointing out that she was scarcely more than a child herself.

'It doesn't say what Brune was doing at the time, Dick.'

'No. A pity. It doesn't tell us about Cynthia either.'

'But we've got the name of one of the Courtlands' Jersey relations. Pierre de Chantal. It sounds very French.'

'There'll be a lot of French names on this island, I expect, but we should be able to trace him without too much difficulty. Make a note of the dates and then go and ask the editor if we can have prints of these two issues. We won't say which page we're particularly interested in. I know that everyone's been very helpful, but it's a newspaperman's job to be curious.'

Hilary laughed. 'OK. Then we'll go back to the hotel and search the phone book.'

'Good idea, darling!'

And, as soon as they had reached their room at the Pomme d'Or Hilary looked up the name de Chantal. There were four listed and each one had a 'P' as a first or second initial.

'It could be much worse,' she said. 'Luckily it's not the most popular of names. Some of them go on for columns. Do you think they're all related, Dick?'

'One would assume so, on such a small island, but that doesn't necessarily make all four de Chantals related to Cynthia and Colin, and that's the question to ask.'

'True enough. Do you want to do the phoning, Dick, or shall I?'

'You,' said Tansey. 'I shall lie on the bed and watch.'

'Right,' Hilary said, and ten minutes later, when she put down the receiver, she glanced at her husband in triumph. 'Got him! Our man, Dick, is Pierre Louis de Chantal. He's a farmer and he lives at La Rondelle in an area called St Ouen.'

She was rewarded by a gentle snore. Dick Tansey, tired out, was fast asleep.

Refreshed, the Tanseys set off again after lunch. This time they remembered their Guide and, with much consultation of maps and the helpful advice of a road sweeper, they found La Rondelle Farm. Passing under a high granite arch, they drove into a cobbled courtyard surrounded by buildings.

These too were of granite with slate roofs, on the ridges of which were perched several large seagulls. The farm was clearly well-kept and prosperous. A shaggy-looking dog of indeterminate breed lifted its head as Dick and Hilary got out of their car, but almost at once lost interest and went back to sleep in the sun. However, a terrier appeared from nowhere and shattered the afternoon calm with its barking.

The front door of what was clearly the farmhouse opened quickly, and a girl came out. It was a moment before they recognized her. She was the girl who had led them to the *Evening Post* offices that morning.

'Hello,' she said. 'Have you been following me again?'

Hilary, laughing, shook her head. 'Do you live here?' she asked.

'No. Just visiting. Like you? Actually La Rondelle belongs to my husband's family.'

'We were hoping to have a word with Mr Pierre de Chantal,' Tansey said.

'And you are?'

'Our name is Tansey. We're trying to trace some Jersey relatives of an English family, and we believe Mr de Chantal might be one.'

'Really? What fun! You'd better come in and I'll fetch my father-in-law.'

The girl, whom they now knew was young Mrs de Chantal, showed them into a sitting-room. It was spacious, low-ceilinged and with a massive granite fireplace; the furniture was modern, the cushions and curtains in dramatic colours.

'How lovely!' Hilary exclaimed involuntarily.

'My mother-in-law is from Paris,' said the girl. 'She was an interior decorator before she became a farmer's wife.'

Farmer or not, the man with whom she returned a few minutes later fitted easily into the décor. He was in his late fifties, tall and broad shouldered, with dark hair and bright blue eyes. He wore black slacks and a yellow roll-necked sweater.

To Tansey's relief, de Chantal's daughter-in-law, having

introduced them, said she had work to do and withdrew.
De Chantal gestured them to chairs.

'Margot tells me you're trying to trace some relatives,' he
said. 'Everyone seems to be doing that in Jersey nowadays.
Relatives of your own family?'

'No, not exactly,' said Tansey. 'Mr de Chantal, we understand you're related to the Courtland family. Would you
mind explaining?'

'Not at all. There's no secret about it.' De Chantal smiled,
showing strong, white teeth. 'My mother, Margaret, had a
sister called Mary, who married one Theodore Courtland.'

'So you were the cousin of Colin Courtland, the English
boy who died in Jersey in 1947?'

De Chantal's smile had faded. He nodded slowly. 'We
were first cousins, yes. As I said, his mother and mine were
sisters. But—Mr Tansey, who are you exactly?'

The question had come sooner than Tansey expected.
Silently he passed de Chantal his Warrant Card. 'I'm
Detective-Chief Inspector Richard Tansey of the Thames
Valley Police Force,' he said, 'and my wife here is a
detective-sergeant in the same force. We are making inquiries, with the full cooperation of your own States Police, into
a woman called Pauline Brune who was recently killed in
somewhat strange circumstances. You've not read about
the case?'

'No. I usually skip that sort of story in the press, unless
it's local, and I don't think I've ever heard of—Pauline?'
He stopped suddenly. Then, 'Dear God! You're talking
about that wretched girl old Courtland blamed for Colin's
death. Well, I'm damned! I've not thought of her, or the
twins, in forty-odd years.'

'You've completely lost touch with them?'

'Yes. My mother died shortly after that visit, and the
Courtlands—or at any rate Uncle Theodore—considered
us to be Jersey peasants and not worth bothering about.'
De Chantal laughed. 'To give him his due, the island can't
have had happy memories for him. Colin was the apple of
his eye. He'd got the boy's future all planned. Eton, Oxford,

a commission in the Guards. Everything was for Colin. Poor Cynthia came a bad last. But I imagine it's Pauline you want to hear about.'

Tansey thought for a moment, and decided he had no alternative but to take de Chantal into his confidence. He said, 'First, I must impress on you that this is a delicate matter, Mr de Chantal. If we're asked about our interest in the deceased woman, we say we're searching for any next of kin, and I'd appreciate it if we could stick to this "tracing relatives" story. In fact, what we're interested in is the manner of Colin Courtland's death.'

De Chantal looked up sharply. 'I see,' he said at length. 'And you don't want headlines in the JEP. You can rely on my discretion, Chief Inspector.'

'Thank you, sir,' said Tansey. 'Now, will you be good enough to tell us what you recall of the day Colin Courtland was injured.'

'Of course, but I'm afraid it's not a great deal.'

In fact, Pierre de Chantal's memory was good. 'I was fifteen then, a schoolboy, about half way in age between the twins and Pauline—' he began.

It appeared that the Courtlands were staying at a hotel in Havre des Pas, and on the day of Colin's accident Mrs de Chantal and Pierre had been asked to lunch there. While the adults had their before-the-meal drinks, Pierre had been sent off to join Pauline and the children, who were playing at Le Dicq nearby—an area of beach where there was a steep rocky outgrowth and also a fine stretch of sand. He—Pierre—had not been too pleased to be excluded from the adults' company, and he had taken his time about getting to Le Dicq. The tide was out and he had wandered slowly along the beach.

'It was Pauline I saw first,' de Chantal continued reminiscently. 'She was using a camera, as she often was; it was her hobby and she was good at it. But even if she'd been standing close to Colin I doubt if she could have saved him. Of course, I suppose she ought never to have let Colin and Cynthia climb around those rocks, though all the local

children did. But the twins weren't used to it, and they'd
been told not to go there. Actually, come to think of it, it
was odd that Colin was brave enough to do so. He was a
timid boy, though Cynthia was bold and she often dared
her twin to do things he didn't want to.'

'You found him?' Hilary asked.

'Yes. He was lying on the beach among the rocks and
had obviously fallen and hit his head on a great jagged bit
of granite. There was blood and—and—and at the time it
seemed to me appalling! I had nightmares about it for weeks
afterwards.'

'What did you do?' said Tansey.

'Shouted to Pauline that there'd been an accident. Told
her to collect Cynthia and go for help. It wasn't long before
Uncle Theodore arrived with a lot of other people, and
eventually an ambulance took Colin off to hospital. The
Courtlands went with him, and Mother and I came home.
Colin died a couple of days later.'

'Dreadful for the Courtlands,' said Hilary. 'Was Cynthia
very upset? Twins are usually close.'

'Colin and Cynthia weren't at all close,' de Chantal
commented at once. 'They quarrelled quite a lot. I think
she was jealous because, as I indicated, being the son of his
father, he got everything, and she had to make do with the
pickings.'

'What sort of boy was Colin?' Hilary asked. 'You said
he—'

'Was timid, yes. He was also quiet, fond of his own
company. They came here to the farm a couple of times,
but he didn't want to join us in anything. I think he most
enjoyed reading. Poor kid!' De Chantal shook his head
sadly.

'And Pauline?' said Tansey. 'What happened to her?'

'My father collected her from the hotel the day after the
inquest and drove her down to the boat. He said she had
the remains of a black eye and her face was bruised. We
thought Uncle Theodore had hit her. She had her ticket,
but very little money—evidently the Courtlands hadn't paid

her—so Dad gave her a couple of quid and she sailed away. And that, Chief Inspector, is all I can tell you.'

Fifteen minutes later, having expressed their thanks to Pierre de Chantal, the Tanseys were on their way back to St Helier.

'Dick, are you thinking what I'm thinking?' Hilary said suddenly.

'There's no evidence for it, and it's the merest supposition, just a feeling in the bones, but if you mean that Cynthia might—just might—have murdered her twin brother on those rocks—then yes,' said Tansey. 'But I wonder how on earth I'm going to put the suggestion to the Chief Constable.'

Part Four

CHAPTER 18

The Chief Constable shifted his heavy body in his large swivel chair. 'So what you've done, Chief Inspector, is to produce another mystery—and this time one that's forty years old.'

'What I've done, with respect, sir,' said Dick Tansey, his voice tight, 'is to shed some light on this old mystery and at the same time provide a credible motive for Pauline Brune's murder.'

Philip Midvale grinned. 'OK, Chief Inspector. Just give me a précis of events, as you see them. I accept that some of what you're about to say must be logically reasoned guesswork rather than fact that can be established—but go ahead.'

'Very well, sir. I'll try.' Tansey concentrated. 'On the day in question,' he began, 'Colin and Cynthia Courtland were sent to play on the beach. They were in the care of Pauline Brune, but Pauline was more interested in her photography than in the children. Colin was a timid boy—I stress that, and there's evidence for it—but Cynthia persuaded him to climb up over the rocks. There's evidence, too, that she was accustomed to dare her twin to attempt things that normally he wouldn't contemplate.

'Well, suddenly she realized that he was in such a position that here was her chance. A blow from behind between his shoulder-blades, and she could rid herself of a brother she didn't particularly like, and at the same time ensure that the money which was to be spent on him could be spent on her—as indeed it was. She must have thought herself perfectly safe, but in fact Pauline saw her and took at least one photograph to prove it.'

Tansey paused, and then added, 'There's even a suggestion from Simon Faudin's statement that she might have captured the scene on ciné film. And I also gathered from something Simon Faudin said that this may be a particularly tricky time for Cynthia's reputation, so the hint of a scandal might have put her effectively at Pauline's mercy.'

'Yes, but . . .' the Chief Constable objected. 'It's pretty thin, isn't it? If Pauline knew that the boy's fall wasn't an accident, and had photographic evidence to prove it, why on earth didn't she say so at the time? In any case the whole operation seems a bit much for a twelve-year-old girl, which is all Cynthia Faudin was.'

'As to your first point, sir, perhaps Pauline did say something. Perhaps she told Mr Courtland what she'd witnessed, which was why he hit her. After all, she was only seventeen, and it wouldn't have been difficult to call her a liar and intimidate her, especially if Cynthia denied any responsibility. What's more, she wouldn't have been sure she had evidence, until the film was developed, and by then she was far away and must have been worrying about her future. I doubt she would have thought of blackmail immediately at her age.'

'And what about Cynthia's age?'

'Ah, your second question, sir. All I can say is that it's clear from her subsequent career that she developed into a woman of considerable intelligence and determination— and rather a self-centred one; there's no reason why she shouldn't have demonstrated qualities like this in her early years. Besides, if she did push her brother to his death it was probably on a sudden impulse.'

'Well, but . . . Anyway, go on, Chief Inspector.'

Tansey drew a deep breath. 'When we meet Pauline next she's sixty and an accomplished though small-time blackmailer. I think she may have read about Cynthia Faudin in the press and decided that here was her opportunity to make a killing—Sorry, sir, no pun intended. I mean that Pauline, now no longer young, saw a great chance to increase her nest-egg for her old age.'

Tansey paused, and the Chief Constable said thoughtfully, 'Have we any evidence whatsoever that Pauline was trying to blackmail the Faudins on account of Colin Courtland's death? And have we any evidence to suggest that Pauline's meeting with Cynthia Faudin in Oxford was by anything other than pure chance?'

'No, on both counts, sir,' Tansey admitted. 'All we do know is that Pauline was generally unpopular at Longacres, and yet the Faudins didn't ask her to leave. To let her stay on week after week, when she had originally come for a few days, would seem an excess of altruism. They didn't owe her anything. She wasn't related to them. She hadn't seen Cynthia in years—as far as we know, not since the Jersey holiday.'

'I take your point, Chief Inspector. But what about those vital photographs that Pauline may or may not have taken? You must admit they were never found in her room or anywhere else.'

'Unfortunately I've got to agree, sir.' Tansey thought of Simon Faudin, and wondered. Had he lied? Had he looked at the reel of film—it was 16 millimetre, after all, and would only need to be held up to the light. Had he recognized Cynthia as a child, and understood the significance of the camera's record? And, had he then asked himself why Pauline had kept them? It wouldn't have taken much thought for a man as astute as Simon Faudin to put two and two together.

'Well, go on, Chief Inspector,' said Midvale, as Tansey remained silent. 'Finish the story. I take it that Derek Faudin arranges to meet Pauline in the dining-room that Sunday morning after his birthday. He intends to tell her she must go, and say that if she makes any trouble they'll accuse her of trying to blackmail Simon. But she replies that the wife he loves so much is a murderer. So he sees red, and promptly kills her. Is that really what you think happened?'

Tansey sighed. 'It fits the facts better than any other scenario we've got, sir. After all, Derek Faudin has admitted killing the Brune woman.'

'But what about his own wound? I know the forensic people suggest it could have been self-inflicted. If they're right—and they admit they can't be sure—why would he have done that? Frankly, it's one of the points that puzzles me.'

'Yes, I agree, and I've given it some consideration, sir. It's possible he heard sounds in the hall and was afraid someone was coming into the room, so he hurriedly tried to stage what looked like a fight.'

'M—mm.' Midvale shook his head. 'There's an awful lot of "perhaps" about all this. I've been making some inquiries too, Chief Inspector. Derek Faudin has the reputation of being a level-headed and competent businessman. True, he's said to be devoted to his wife, and one could imagine him slapping Brune's face if she accused Cynthia of fratricide. But sticking a knife in her in a fit of temper is something else again. Surely not. It would be completely out of his character, as I understand it. In my view, Faudin could only have done it in self-defence.'

'So the charge will still be manslaughter, sir?'

'Yes, Chief Inspector. I'm sorry. I appreciate that you've put in a great deal of work on this case, but there's no concrete evidence that Colin Courtland was ever pushed off those Jersey rocks and, without that, there goes this new motive.'

'But if the manner of Colin's death could be substantiated, if those photographs of the film could be found,' said Tansey, thinking of Simon Faudin, 'it would certainly weaken the defence, wouldn't it?'

'Ye-es, I suppose so,' Midvale agreed. 'However, as I said before, Chief Inspector, you'll need strong evidence to convince a judge and jury—let alone the DPP—that a man of Derek Faudin's character and reputation would suddenly act so violently without physical provocation.'

*

Detective Chief Inspector Tansey returned to his office, to sit at his desk and stare blindly at the wall in front of him. He knew—or he believed he knew—what had happened in the dining-room of Longacres on that fatal Sunday, but to prove it was another matter. He wasn't even sure that any further attempt would be worth the effort. The Chief Constable had made up his mind; Derek Faudin was to be charged with the manslaughter of Pauline Brune.

'So much for bloody justice!' said Tansey in disgust, and thought what a waste of time and effort the inquiry would have been if, as seemed highly probable, Derek Faudin was found guilty but got a mere suspended sentence.

Then his phone rang, and resignedly Tansey picked up the receiver. It was Sergeant Abbot, who had met the Smithsons in the Headquarters reception area. They would like to see the Chief Inspector for a moment or two if he could spare the time. They were on their way south, and didn't expect to be near Oxford again before they flew back to the States.

It was the mention of the United States that reminded Tansey that the Smithsons, Andrew and Janet, were Derek Faudin's American cousins. 'OK, Sergeant,' he said. 'Bring them along, and arrange some coffee for us, will you?'

Five minutes later he was welcoming the Smithsons, asking about their visit to Stratford and their future plans. Derek Faudin wasn't mentioned until a tray of coffee and biscuits had been brought in, when Andrew Smithson said that they would be having a brief visit with their relatives at Longacres, but not staying overnight.

'It's splendid that Cousin Derek's home again,' said Janet Smithson, 'and such a relief he wasn't fatally hurt. That poor woman Pauline—'

'Brune,' her husband prompted.

'Yes. Of course we've called regularly to ask after Cousin Derek while we've been up north, and we've read your newspapers, but we're not really informed as to the progress you've made, Chief Inspector.'

'Not much, I'm afraid, Mrs Smithson.' Tansey saw no

reason to tell them that Derek Faudin was about to be charged.

'We read that you've traced the young man we saw on our way to church, and he turned out to be Clare's fiancé.'

'Yes, and he's been cleared—completely.'

'I'm glad of that, at least. Chief Inspector, we hope you find the villain, whoever he was. Cynthia said he didn't succeed in stealing anything.'

Tansey noted that the Smithsons seemed still to believe in Derek's original story, but otherwise he scarcely listened to what they were saying. Then he caught the word 'photograph'. 'Photograph?' he heard himself repeat stupidly.

'Yes. Such a thoughtful gift,' Janet Smithson said. 'I'm sure Cousin Derek will treasure it, not only for sentimental reasons but because it was so charming. You know, Chief Inspector, Cynthia can't have been more than twelve at the time, but everyone agreed that it was quite clearly Cynthia.'

'Pauline Brune gave Mr Faudin a photograph of his wife as a child?' Tansey's mouth felt dry, and he hoped his voice didn't sound as forced to the Smithsons as it did to him.

'Yes. In a little leather frame. It was her birthday present to Derek,' Andrew Smithson explained. 'Pauline might have been quite a photographer if she'd taken it up professionally.'

Tansey was tempted to say that Brune had taken up photography professionally, but hardly in the sense that Andrew Smithson meant. He smiled at them, hoping for more, but the Smithsons were standing up, apologizing for keeping him from his work and preparing to leave. He said he would see them out.

They were in the reception area when he remembered Hilary's suggestion that he should try to make his own luck. 'Strange that Pauline should have kept that particular old photograph,' he remarked casually.

'Oh, it wasn't just that one print, Chief Inspector,' Janet Smithson corrected him quickly. 'Pauline said she had some other photographs of Cynthia and her brother Colin when they were children. She promised to show them to us, but then she never had the chance.'

'What a pity,' said Tansey.

He said goodbye to the Smithsons, wished them a pleasant journey and returned to his office. Cynically he thought of Cynthia and Simon Faudin and their unnatural eagerness to search Pauline Brune's room immediately after her death, supposedly to discover her next of kin. Simon's actions were explicable in terms of Pauline's attempt to blackmail him over the Merridews, but Cynthia's could be explained only if she had been looking for the photographs—or an incriminating film—which Pauline had mentioned at the birthday party. And, he thought, remembering Mrs May's tale of the spider under the bed, that might not have been Cynthia's first attempt to find them, either.

The day was Friday. The Chief Constable had decided that Derek Faudin would not be charged until after the weekend, when his doctor would have less excuse for claiming that his patient was too weak to respond to the situation. Tansey had made no attempt to object.

So now he had a choice. He could have a quick lunch in the canteen, tidy up his desk and for once go home early to spend a quiet, enjoyable weekend with his wife. Or he could . . . Without consciously making a decision, the Chief Inspector reached for his phone and tapped out the Longacres number. He asked to speak to Mr Simon Faudin.

Tansey had given Simon Faudin little option. He had said that a point had arisen that he would prefer not to discuss on the phone, and he would like to talk to Mr Faudin in person as soon as possible. Could Mr Faudin come to police Headquarters that afternoon? He had counted on Simon's curiosity, and had been rewarded. After the briefest of hesitations Faudin had agreed to meet him at three o'clock.

At five past three Sergeant Abbot ushered Faudin into the Chief Inspector's office. He took the chair which Tansey indicated on the other side of the desk, and crossed his legs, seemingly completely at ease. But Tansey didn't miss the searching glance he gave to the Sergeant who, on Tansey's instructions, had seated himself at a small table in a corner of the room and produced a notepad to make a record of any conversation that was to follow.

'Well, Chief Inspector, I hope it really was necessary to bring me into Kidlington this afternoon. My wife and I are going home on Monday, and we were hoping to enjoy our last weekend at Longacres in peace.' Clearly, Simon Faudin did not propose to be on the defensive.

'I take it your brother's health is considerably improved, then?' Tansey remarked coldly.

'You mean, as we're leaving? Yes, it is. He even gets up for part of the day, but he's somewhat depressed, which isn't surprising in the circumstances. It must be a dreadful thing to cause someone's death, however unintentionally.'

Tansey made no comment on Simon Faudin's last remark. Instead, he said conversationally, 'His wife will be glad to have him home again and recuperating. I gather she's very fond of him, though of course her own career must take up much of her time.'

'Yes, it does,' said Faudin flatly, when Tansey didn't continue.

'When a man marries a much younger woman it's usually the man who's the more devoted of the couple. Would you say that applied in your brother's case?'

'Yes, I would. But what the hell are you getting—' Faudin swallowed what he had been about to say, and went on more calmly. 'Chief Inspector, I really don't understand how the details of my brother's marriage can be of any interest to you.'

'Oh, everything interests me, Mr Faudin.' Tansey had been riffling through some papers on his desk. 'Here it is!' he said triumphantly, extracting what was obviously a report. He smiled at Faudin. 'Now, let's get down to business. In a previous interview you admitted that you took a black metal box from Pauline Brune's room after her death because you believed it might contain material about the Merridews.'

'Yes. I told you. I didn't see why that—that business should be involved in what was obviously going to be a police inquiry.'

'Quite. What did you do with the box?'

'I threw it away.' Faudin's hesitation suggested he had been expecting a different question.

'Where? Where did you throw it, Mr Faudin?'

'I burnt it.'

'Burnt it? How?'

'Chief Inspector, a house like Longacres generates a great deal of rubbish of one kind or another. We have quite a large incinerator in the grounds, beyond the kitchen garden. That's where I tossed it. But if you're hoping to find the box, I'm afraid the thing's lit up once a week.'

'Why did you take the trouble to dispose of it there, Mr Faudin, once you'd removed the contents?'

Faudin looked irritated at Tansey's persistence. 'I suppose I felt slightly ashamed at having it, once I'd discovered that the contents had nothing to do with me or my family.'

'Your family? Meaning your wife and your son, Mark—Carter?'

'Yes.'

'The box contained photographs and negatives, of course, which you removed and you say you destroyed. In the same way?'

'Of course. I took them all out to the incinerator.'

'This was after you'd assured yourself you didn't recognize anyone in them.'

'That's right.'

'Pauline Brune gave your brother a birthday present. I understand it was a photograph of his wife as a child in a leather frame. You didn't find the negative of that print?'

'No. I repeat, the photographs meant nothing to me.'

It wasn't exactly how Faudin had phrased his statement previously, but Tansey let the matter pass. 'Well, thank you very much, Mr Faudin. It was good of you to come in.'

'You mean that's all you wanted?'

'Yes. That's all. My sergeant will see you out, sir, if you'll excuse me. I've a lot of work to do. It's been accumulating while I've been in Jersey.'

Slowly Simon Faudin got to his feet. His whole body was taut, like a coiled spring that might suddenly unwind, but somehow he managed to control himself. His tongue came out and licked his lips.

'Jersey?' he said.

'Yes, that's right. Goodbye, sir.'

Almost reluctantly Simon Faudin nodded. But Sergeant Abbot was holding the door open for him, and he went through it.

Alone in his office Tansey drew a deep breath and let it out slowly. Now we wait and hope, he thought grimly; God, how we hope!

CHAPTER 19

Detective Chief Inspector Tansey would have found it impossible to define in detail exactly what he anticipated. In broad terms, he hoped that Pauline Brune's killer would be brought to justice—which, as a police officer, he had to believe meant being charged, receiving a fair trial and, if found guilty, an appropriate sentence. But he knew that his personal responsibility was limited. He could present a case to his Chief Constable and, through him, to the DPP, but there his brief ended; others would decide on the further course of events. Nevertheless, to Tansey it was a matter of personal integrity that any case he did present was as accurate and free from blemish as he could make it.

Regrettably he was unable to tell himself that these criteria were satisfied by the current state of the Faudin affair. He was bitterly aware that he had been unable to provide Philip Midvale with an adequately reasoned account, backed by evidence, of what he now believed to be the truth.

The trouble, he knew, was that he had been slow in

interpreting events, and had reached his conclusions belatedly, perhaps too belatedly. And it was only after the visit to Jersey and the emergence of the possibility that documentary evidence of Cynthia's fratricide might have existed—or even might still exist—that it had occurred to him that, though Derek coulid now be shown to have a real reason to protect his wife's reputation, Cynthia herself had an even better reason to protect her own. Even an attempt to face down such a rumour would lead to scandal. And to someone as ambitious as Cynthia Faudin appeared to be . . .

In practical terms, he had realized there was little he could do, except retreat to an age-old ploy. He was hoping that, by shaking Simon Faudin from his shell of complacency, he would cause a reaction at Longacres that might help to disentangle the web of lies and deceits that the Faudins and their house guests had woven.

So, when the telephone rang as the Tanseys were breakfasting on Sunday morning, the Chief Inspector leapt to answer it. 'Yes,' he said. Then, 'Yes' and 'yes' on an ever-decreasing scale of enthusiasm.

There was a pause while he listened. 'Right. You've got everyone in action?' Another pause and finally, 'Good. I'll be waiting.'

He returned to the breakfast table and sat, silently contemplating the eggs and bacon that were fast congealing on his plate.

'What's wrong, Dick?' Hilary asked at once.

'I tried to be clever, and was too damned clever. Derek Faudin's committed suicide.'

'Oh no! But that's not your fault,' his wife said quickly. 'Darling, you can't blame yourself. Why should you?'

At that moment Tansey found it impossible to explain; it was too complex and would take too long. Instead he said, 'Bill Abbot's picking me up in fifteen minutes.'

'Then you've got time to finish your breakfast.'

'Hilary—'

Automatically Dick Tansey began to eat again. He tasted

nothing, and couldn't have said afterwards whether he had
had marmalade or honey with his slice of toast. His thoughts
were on the Faudins, especially Derek Faudin. When the
front doorbell pealed he started, and nearly spilt what
remained of his coffee.

'That'll be Abbot,' he said. 'Tell him I won't be a minute.'

He went into the bathroom, relieved himself, washed
his hands and regarded himself in the mirror over the
washbasin. What he saw didn't please him, and he turned
away in self-disgust. He remembered Abbot's disapproving
coughs when in the Sergeant's opinion he had overstepped
some unstated mark and pressed old Winter and Derek
Faudin too hard. He wondered if Abbot would be coughing
all the way to Longacres.

The fancy amused him, and in spite of his inner feelings
he was grinning as he went into the kitchen where Hilary
was washing up the breakfast dishes. He kissed her fondly.
'No need to say I'll be back as soon as I can.'

'No need,' she agreed, smiling and relieved at his apparent
change of mood. 'Good luck!'

The front door of Longacres was opened to them moments
after Tansey had pressed the bell. Clearly, Vernon had been
waiting in the hall. He greeted them solemnly. He said that
Mr Simon and Mr Peter were in the sitting-room with Dr
Gouray. The doctor had given Mrs Faudin a sedative and
she was resting. Mrs Simon Faudin had gone over to Mr
Danforth's caravan to break the sad news to Miss Clare and
had not yet returned.

Tansey thanked him for this résumé of the situation,
warned him that more police officers and the pathologist
were on their way, and said they would like Dr Gouray to
accompany them to Mr Faudin's room. The two officers
waited at the foot of the stairs and Dr Gouray appeared
almost at once. Vernon again took up his position by the
front door.

The doctor bade them a gruff good morning and said, 'A
great tragedy this, a great tragedy—for the family, and for

me personally. I've known Derek for years and I'm going to miss him.'

'I've been told it was an overdose,' said Tansey.

'Yes. Drugs I prescribed to make him relax and sleep,' said the doctor. 'I'll give the details to the pathologist; I'm sure he's on the way.'

'He is,' said Tansey. 'When did you see Mr Faudin last?' he asked.

'I dropped in yesterday morning after surgery—an unofficial visit. I had a drink with him, and a bit of a chat. He seemed depressed, but I never dreamt . . .' The doctor shook his head sadly. 'He talked a lot about the wickedness of believing that killing someone—anyone—was an act of little consequence. Perhaps Pauline Brune's death was preying on his mind, or perhaps he couldn't face the prospect of a trial, with all the inevitable publicity and—and a dubious verdict. I don't know, Chief Inspector. I'm an old-fashioned general practitioner, not a psychiatrist.'

'You don't remember his exact words—about it being a serious matter to take someone's life—do you?' asked Tansey.

They had climbed the stairs, with Abbot a few steps behind them, and now stood outside the bedroom where Derek Faudin had died. It was not the room he normally shared with Cynthia, nor the adjoining dressing-room where he sometimes slept. At his request Mrs May had arranged for him to have one of the guest suites while he was recuperating.

'No, I don't.' Dr Gouray frowned as he tried to recall the conversation.

'Right,' said Tansey after a pause. 'Let's go in then, shall we?' he continued, motioning to the doctor to precede them.

The room was comfortable and elegantly appointed, but impersonal, as if not often used. Derek Faudin's body lay, a neat mound, in the centre of the twin bed nearer to the bathroom. The sheet had been drawn up over his face. Tansey pulled it back gently. In death Derek Faudin looked sad and vulnerable and, as Tansey drew the bedclothes further back, he saw that someone had crossed Faudin's hands over his breast. On the table by the bed were a glass, a quarter-full bottle of Chablis, and the scattered remains of half a dozen blister packs that had once contained capsules.

'Was he like this when you arrived?' Tansey asked.

'He was lying on his back, yes, but he'd thrown off the bedclothes. I examined him briefly, but there was nothing to be done. I would say he'd been dead since four or five this morning. It was about half past eight when I saw him,' he added, forestalling Tansey's question.

'And the things on the bedside table?'

'As far as I know they've not been touched, but you'll have to ask Simon. It was he who found Derek. He woke Peter, who had come down to Longacres for the weekend to see his father, and then phoned me and your Headquarters.' The doctor paused.

'And—' prompted Tansey.

Dr Gouray went on, 'Peter brought Cynthia—Mrs Faudin—in while I was still here. She closed Derek's eyes, arranged his arms in the traditional position and covered him. Naturally she was very upset. She kept on repeating, "Why? Why? I don't understand." She sounded almost angry. I told Peter to take her to her room, and later I gave her a sedative. Mrs May's keeping an eye on her—and that's all I can tell you, Chief Inspector, except—'

'Except what?' asked Tansey.

'I gather he left a note—'

'I was going to ask about that,' said the Chief Inspector. 'Do you know where it is now?'

'Simon has it, I believe. I've not seen it.'

'I see,' said Tansey, a frown belying his words. 'Didn't Mrs Faudin ask about any note?'

'Yes, and Peter said his father hadn't left anything for her.' The doctor looked embarrassed. 'Simon had already told me that Peter had found one, but I don't know who it was addressed to, though one would have expected . . . Anyway, I didn't think it was my place to intervene, or inquire further.'

'Thank you, doctor. I'll have to ask them about it,' said Tansey, as if the matter were of no special significance. 'In any case, Sergeant Abbot and I must go along to the sitting-room and have a word with them now.'

'If you'll excuse me, I'll look in on Mrs Faudin.'

By this time they were outside the guest room door. Tansey said, 'But you'll wait for the pathologist? He should be here any minute, with the rest of my crowd.'

'Yes, of course,' answered Dr Gouray.

'Thanks very much, doctor,' said Tansey.

The doctor went along the corridor, and Tansey and Abbot started down the stairs. 'Poor Derek!' said the Chief Inspector. 'The bitch wasn't worth it.'

Abbot stared at his superior officer in some surprise; it was unusual for Tansey to express himself with such vehemence and, though there was no excuse for blackmail, Pauline Brune had paid a heavier price than the law would have extracted. Besides, Abbot's father, who had also been a police officer, had taught him that the dead, whatever they had done, should be respected by the living, for they would all get their due desserts in the fullness of time.

'You mean, sir, that Derek Faudin's life was worth more than Pauline Brune's?' the Sergeant asked tentatively.

Tansey shook his head. 'No, Abbot, that wasn't what I meant. I wasn't thinking of Pauline.'

To Abbot's annoyance Tansey led the way into the sitting-room so rapidly that he had no chance to ask for any explanation. Simon Faudin, hands behind his back, was standing at the window, staring into the distance. Peter Faudin was sprawled in an armchair, staring down at the Chinese carpet. Both seemed to flinch as the officers opened the door and came in.

'Good morning,' Tansey said. 'My condolences. I'm truly sorry that this should have happened.'

Simon had turned away from the window and Peter straightened his back. They both nodded in acknowledge-

ment of the Chief Inspector's words. Simon waved Tansey
and Abbot to chairs and himself took a seat on a small sofa.

'We've ordered some fresh coffee,' he said. 'I expect you
could do with it.'

'Thanks.' Tansey was appreciative. 'Now perhaps you'd
tell me what you know about this morning's unfortunate
events.'

Peter gestured to his uncle and Simon Faudin said, 'I
wasn't sleeping too well, and I got up around seven. I went
along to the library, but I was restless and thought I'd go
and see if Derek was awake. So I found him—' Simon's
voice broke. 'It was obvious he was dead, and how it had
happened—the wine and the remains of the pill packaging
on the bedside table—but I felt for a pulse and got a shaving
mirror from the bathroom. There was no sign of breathing.
Then I went to tell Peter and immediately phoned Dr
Gouray and you people.'

'Why did you tell Peter first?'

'I—I don't know. I think I just thought that someone should be with the—the body. Isn't that a normal reaction?'

'Yes, I suppose in a way it is. Did you touch anything in
your brother's room?'

'Only Derek himself. Nothing on the table, if that's what
you mean. Derek must have knocked his letter on to the
floor. If I'd been less upset I might have looked for a—a
note, but I suppose I was too shocked.'

'Of course,' Tansey said, thinking that in the circumstances Simon seemed to have behaved with extraordinary
composure. 'And the letter?'

'I found it,' Peter said. 'It was half-hidden under the bed.
It's pretty devastating,' he added.

'Here you are, Chief Inspector.' Simon took an envelope
from his inside pocket and passed it to Tansey. 'As you see
it was addressed to me, and I've shown it to Peter. But no
one else. It is, as Peter says, pretty devastating, but perhaps
more so to him than to me.'

Tansey looked at the envelope. It had 'Simon' scrawled

on it in handwriting, but the letter inside was typewritten, except for the signature. Carefully holding the sheet of Long-acres engraved notepaper by its edges, Tansey read:

Dear Simon,

Forgive me, but I can't go on. I have loved Cynthia utterly. I would have gone on trial gladly for her sake. My one thought when I came on her in the dining-room that Sunday morning just after she'd killed Pauline Brune was to save her, to take the blame for her. Even then she had the presence of mind to murmur 'sneak thief' as she left me, but I only had time to slash myself before, as I now know, old Christopher came in.

Cynthia told me later that Pauline had been trying to blackmail her over a somewhat unsavoury affair she'd had with a married don while she was an undergraduate. On reflection I decided that this story of Cynthia's was probably a lie. Anyway, she said she lost her temper, that she'd only meant to threaten Pauline, and at the time I believed that, perhaps because I wanted to.

All this was before you told me about her brother and showed me that film. Now I accept that Cynthia is prepared to kill anyone who stands in the way of her inordinate ambition—and, what's worse, she feels no remorse.

So I cannot bear to go on—either standing trial in her place—which she would gladly accept—or, if you're right and Tansey already suspects, watching her go to prison.

My love to you and Val, and to Peter and Clare. Thank God they don't take after their mother.

Your brother,

Derek.

Slowly and thoughtfully Tansey returned the letter to its envelope, without showing it to Abbot. He made no direct comment on its contents, but merely said, 'You know I shall have to keep this, Mr Faudin?'

'Of course,' said Simon, and added, 'I told Derek you'd.

been in Jersey, and I could guess why. I had to tell him. I had to warn him. I never dreamt he would—'

'And the film?' demanded Tansey.

'I lied to you, Chief Inspector. I kept the contents of that black box. I didn't destroy them. I thought of doing so, but . . . And once you'd hinted that you'd been making inquiries in Jersey, I knew that Derek should see them. Neither Valerie nor I are particularly fond of Cynthia, I must admit. It seemed to us that she showed a calculating and selfish purposefulness in getting Derek to marry her rather than a widowed friend of ours to whom we expected him to become engaged, and we've never had reason to change our minds about her.' Then he added, almost reluctantly, 'But she's been a good wife to Derek, and we've got along with her, for his sake.'

Simon Faudin reached into the briefcase beside him. 'Anyway, here's the reel of film,' he said. 'You don't need a projector, though of course that would help. It shows the whole sequence of events quite clearly, even to Cynthia gazing down after her brother's fall. And the date the film was processed is printed by the sprocket holes. To my mind there's no doubt that Cynthia pushed her brother to his death on those Jersey rocks, and that this was the real hold that Brune had over her.'

Tansey took the film, and examined it curiously, unreeling it and holding it up to the light. It was 16 millimetre film so the frames were not that small and, as Simon had said, the evidence was quite clear. It would be still better when they got it on to a screen. He turned to Peter Faudin. 'You knew nothing of this.'

'Not until Simon told me, and showed me that film. It—it was an awful shock, but—but it's Dad's death I can't get over. I'll never forgive Mother for that—never. She killed him as surely as if she'd stuck that bloody knife into him instead of the wretched Brune woman and, as far as I'm concerned, if someone's got to be blamed for Pauline Brune's death, I'd rather it was my mother than my father.'

A tap on the door interrupted them. Vernon announced

that 'the other gentlemen from the police' had arrived. In fact, for some minutes they had been aware of the crunch of tyres on the drive and moments later voices in the hall.

'Thank you,' said Tansey. 'I'll be right with them.' And to the Faudins, 'We'll have to talk again, of course, and you'll both be asked to make further statements. I must warn you that there will be a number of formalities before any action is taken, and I must request that in the meantime you do not mention the contents of the late Mr Derek Faudin's letter, or what we have just been discussing, to anyone else—anyone at all. You understand?'

Both the Faudins were on their feet. 'Yes, Chief Inspector,' said Simon at once, and Peter nodded his acquiescence.

Tansey stared at them for a moment, then turned on his heel and left the room, followed by a somewhat bemused Sergeant Abbot.

CHAPTER 20

During the first week of Oxford University's Trinity Term Cynthia Faudin, née Courtland, was arrested and charged with the manslaughter of Pauline Gaul, née Brune. At the hearing in the Magistrates' Court she was refused bail, on the grounds that she might contemplate taking her own life.

'Do you really think a woman like that would commit suicide, Dick?' Hilary asked over supper that night.

'Personally, I don't, though we thought we'd better take no chances, and the magistrate agreed. In my own opinion, she's fighting mad,' Tansey said. 'But on the other hand she's a strange mixture. She appears extraordinarily cold-blooded and calculating, but I believe she does act impulsively on occasion. For instance, it seems to me unlikely that a twelve-year-old lured her brother up on to those steep rocks intending to push him over the edge, and she can't have planned to kill Brune as she did. Neither act can have been premeditated, though . . .'

He hesitated for a moment, then went on, 'If you'd seen the famous film projected on to a screen, you might think twice about premeditation. Every detail's clear, even her expression as she delivered the fatal blow, and as she looked down over the rock face with a satisfied smile to make sure she'd done the trick. There's even a moment, just after that, when she glances into the distance, apparently in some alarm. We've wondered if she could possibly have caught a glimpse of Brune and her camera. In any case, she must have hated Brune, loathed her. She had a very great deal to lose.' Tansey finished his soup, and waited until Hilary returned with the next course. 'You don't know this, but Simon says that Derek told him in confidence that Cynthia was to be made a Dame in the next Honours List, and that she hoped to become the first woman Vice-Chancellor of the University. Whatever happens, she won't get either of those plums now.'

'What do you mean, whatever happens? You don't think she'll get off, do you?'

Tansey cut into his pork chop. 'No, I don't, though it's anyone's guess what sort of sentence she'll get. An awful lot depends on whether the judge will admit the evidence about the brother and his death. If he does, it'll damn her, even though she was only twelve at the time—and the letter Derek left plus the film and Simon's evidence will clinch the matter.'

Hilary regarded her husband curiously. 'Dick, tell me, between you and me, are you satisfied? You do believe Cynthia's guilty, don't you?'

'Oh yes. I believe she killed her brother because he was the apple of her father's eye and she envied the education he was to have at her expense, and she killed Brune because Brune was blackmailing her on account of that old crime.'

'That's definite enough,' said Hilary. 'You've no reservations, then?'

'About Cynthia Faudin's guilt, no.'

'What then?'

'My God, Hilary, you must be psychic or something!' Dick Tansey exclaimed. 'All right I'll tell you.' He held out his plate for more vegetables.

'So?' said Hilary.

'As you said, between you and me, darling, I—I do have my doubts, but about Derek's last letter. I find it almost incredible that a man who's just out of hospital and who intends to kill himself should go calmly into his study and accurately type out such a long, detailed, lucid and coherent explanation of events.'

'But—but who, then?'

'Simon, of course! He admits that Derek had confided in him, so he knew all the facts. I'd bet—though there's absolutely no proof—that Simon found Derek's body a good deal earlier than he has admitted. He also found the brief and conventional note that Derek had left on the bedside table in an unsealed envelope. He thought for a while and then went to Derek's study, took the top sheet of paper from the pad there in the hope there'd be some of Derek's fingerprints on it—and there were. He already had an envelope in Derek's writing, and all he had to do was type a new note and forge Derek's signature, which he had in front of him. Then he went back to the bedroom and dropped the note on the floor for Peter to find.'

'But why, Dick, why?' demanded Hilary at once, pouncing on the weak link. 'Why on earth should Simon want to stir up more trouble for the Faudins? He may dislike Cynthia, but he's fond of Peter and Clare.'

'Trust you to ask the right question, Hilary. It must be my training,' said Tansey. 'I think there were two reasons. First, he was very attached to his brother, and didn't want him—even in death—to carry the opprobrium for something he hadn't done. And secondly because he considered it—and this is pure surmise—unjust that Cynthia should benefit from three deaths. He blamed her for Derek's death too, as did Peter.'

'I see,' said Hilary doubtfully. She began to clear away the remains of supper. 'Have you told the Chief Constable any of this? Have you made any attempt to check if the signature was a forgery?' she asked.

'Good heavens, no! There's no point in raising hares at this stage. I intend to let justice take its course,' Dick Tansey said firmly.

Death's Long Shadow

CHAPTER 1

At one moment Jean White was in a deep sleep. The next she was fully awake. She lay still, breathing carefully. She could feel her heart thumping. In the twin bed beside her, Greg, her husband, emitted gentle snores. Slowly Jean opened her eyes.

The curtains were partly drawn back to allow a gentle breeze to blow through the open window into the room, and by the light of the night sky Jean could see the familiar objects around her. She relaxed. She had thought that some noise, some unwelcome sound, had woken her, but now she told herself that she must have been feeling the effects of a menacing dream.

Then the noise was repeated. But this time Jean was awake and the sound didn't frighten her. She knew that there was someone downstairs and she assumed that it was her daughter, Rosemary. She glanced at the clock on the bedside table. Its illuminated hands pointed to three o'clock.

Three o'clock! Jean threw back the duvet and got out of bed. She was angry. Against her better judgement she had agreed that Rosemary might go to a birthday party with Tony Pulent, the son of their next door neighbour. Rosemary had sworn she would be home by twelve-thirty. In Jean's opinion this was far too late for a girl of sixteen who had to be at school the following day, but Rosemary had pleaded that this was a special occasion, and it had been difficult to refuse her.

And Greg had been no help. Jean frowned at her husband's sleeping form as she slid her feet into slippers, pulled on a robe, and brushed back her short, dark hair. He had said that she shouldn't fuss, that Rosemary was a sensible girl and Tony a responsible boy. Of course he was right, but what he didn't seem to realize was that his daughter looked at least two years older than her age and had become an extremely attractive young woman. As for Tony, it wasn't a great demonstration of his much-vaunted responsibility to keep Rosemary out until the small hours like this.

Seething with anger, Jean opened the bedroom door and started along the corridor. The moon shone through an uncurtained window and she had no need to switch on a light. The north Oxford house was comparatively modern—Greg's parents had helped them to buy it twenty years ago when they had got married on the strength of Greg's election to a Fellowship at St Xavier's College—and Jean knew that no squeaky boards would betray her. She planned to surprise Tony and Rosemary and tell them precisely what she thought of their behaviour.

There were more sounds from below. Jean stopped. By chance she was standing by Rosemary's bedroom door and, as the sounds downstairs ceased, she heard other gentler sounds that were not quite snores coming from her daughter's room. Her heart began to thump again. Carefully she turned the handle and opened the door a few inches so that she could see inside.

Rosemary was in bed. She was lying on her back, her mouth slightly open, her dark hair framing a pretty face that in sleep looked surprisingly childish and vulnerable. She stirred and Jean quickly shut the door and leant against it.

Jean White was not normally a nervous woman, but there had been several burglaries in the neighbourhood recently, in one of which the householder, an elderly woman, had been beaten up so badly as to require eight weeks of hospital treatment. Jean had no desire to face violent men by herself. She crept back to the bedroom she shared with Greg.

Greg was still asleep. He was tired. He had had a wearing week and the previous day, although a Sunday, had not

been a day of rest as far as he was concerned. It was just
after the beginning of the Michaelmas Term and therefore
of the University year—always a difficult time with the
influx of new undergraduates who had to be welcomed to
the college and settled into a way of work that was strange
to many of them, used as they often were to much stricter
supervision at their schools.

Further, there were innumerable administrative details
to be attended to, and personal problems to be faced and
solved. In a small college such as St Xavier's a Fellow and
tutor was expected to deal with everything from homesick-
ness or the need for a particular diet to a request to read a
different subject from the one for which the student had
been awarded an exhibition.

On the whole, Greg enjoyed his work. He was a good
teacher, and he was interested in those he taught. His lectures were always well attended, and if some of his less
popular colleagues claimed that this was because he was
a good-looking man, over six foot and with an attractive
manner—he didn't give a damn. He made no effort to set
out to please. And for the most part his students achieved
their potentials, which was often more than was expected
of them.

Jean complained that he spent too much time on student
affairs and college matters, to the detriment of his academic
career, and it was true that he had published very little;
what was intended to become a *magnum opus* on Milton—his
subject was English literature—remained unfinished after
five years. But Greg was not ambitious, which was why he
did his best to shun involvement in the intricate backbiting
that inevitably characterized the internal politics of all colleges. In this way he saved himself a lot of hassle, though
sometimes, when he was not present, he found that
decisions of which he did not approve had been made for
him.

Something like this had happened just before the beginning of term. Dr Cathcart, who was responsible for teaching English language at St Xavier's, had collapsed with peritonitis and was expected to be away for some weeks. Who was to take on his work? Greg ignored the ensuing wrangle, only to discover that Cathcart's first-year students had been assigned to him—thus adding to his workload.

'Too much,' he muttered in his sleep. 'Can't remember —damned stuff. Years since I did any Anglo-Saxon. Too much. Got my own.'

Irritably he twitched away as Jean shook him by the shoulder. He mumbled something else that she didn't catch and she shook him harder. 'What—is—it?' he demanded sleepily. He wished she would go away. He had no desire to wake up. In his dream he had been telling Sir Philip Pinel, Master of St Xavier's College, Oxford, that he refused to be imposed upon, that he'd got more than enough to do without taking over—

'Greg! For God's sake wake up, Greg!'

'All right, darling.'

Greg White forced himself awake. He sat up in bed and yawned. Then he smiled at his wife. He took in the fact that she was wearing her robe, and suddenly her anxiety communicated itself to him.

'What is it, Jean? Isn't Rosemary home yet?'

'Not so loud, Greg. No, it's not Rosemary. She's in bed asleep, as she ought to be at three in the morning. But there's someone downstairs. I heard them moving around. I thought it might be Rosemary and Tony but it's not. We've got burglars.'

'Damn!' Greg threw back his duvet and slid his legs over the side of the bed. Then he said, in a loud whisper, 'Are you sure, Jean? I can't hear anyone.'

'Quite sure!' Jean bit off the words. 'We ought to get the police.'

'How can we? The phone's downstairs. I always said we should have one by the bed too.'

'So what can we do?'

'We certainly can't phone anyone.' Without thinking, Greg had put on his dressing-gown and slippers. It was stupid but it made him feel slightly less defenceless. He looked about the room. 'There's not a thing up here that would do as a weapon, not even a golf club.'

'You're not going down?'

'There's not much choice, is there? I'll put on all the lights as I go and make a lot of noise. With luck they'll run.'

'For heaven's sake, Greg! They didn't run from old Mrs Porteous. They beat her up. She was in hospital for eight weeks.'

'I'm not a feeble old lady. Besides, we don't know that these are the same chaps.'

'They could be. The police never caught the others. Greg, it's not worth it. We've scarcely anything that can't be replaced and we're insured.'

'Underinsured. But that's not the point.'

Greg would have found it difficult to explain exactly what the point was. He didn't think of himself as a brave man, but nor did he consider himself a coward. He didn't want to go downstairs and possibly confront a couple of violent louts equipped with knives and knuckle-dusters. On the other hand some atavistic instinct was prompting him to do just that.

'Greg, please don't—'

'Jean, I must—'

The frantically whispered argument reached no conclusion. It was interrupted by a shrill scream of terror, abruptly cut off. Greg and Jean froze. Then they ran, fear for Rosemary overwhelming any fear for themselves.

Greg was quicker than Jean. He dashed into the corridor ahead of her—and stopped. Jean, who couldn't see round him, ran into his back. He half-turned, reached behind him and took her hand, pulling her close to him.

'Stay exactly where you are,' a voice said.

The voice was without noticeable accent, though not especially well-spoken. Its source was clearly to be seen in the light through the window—a stocky, broad-shouldered man, about five feet nine in height, with a round head and rather short legs. He was dressed completely in black—black shoes, black trousers and jacket, black gloves and a black stocking pulled over his face to disguise his features and render him unrecognizable. He exuded a sense of purpose, emphasized by the serviceable-looking revolver he held in a firm grip.

'Oh God!' Greg heard Jean mutter. She was clutching his hand tightly. 'Greg, where's Rosemary?'

Her question was answered without Greg's intervention. A second man had appeared in the doorway of Rosemary's bedroom. He was dressed like his companion, but was taller and thinner and gave the impression of being the younger of the two. He was pushing Rosemary in front of him. He had bent her arms behind her back and he had the muzzle of a small automatic pistol pressed against her neck.

'Dad! Mum!' Rosemary whimpered. In her short woollen dressing-gown and bare feet she looked like the child she was. 'He's hurting me!'

Greg started forward. 'Leave her alone, damn you!' he cried.

'Stay where you are!' the older man snapped. 'And listen carefully. If you do what you're told you won't be harmed, any of you, but we're not fooling—and you'd better believe it.'

'Very well.' Greg controlled himself with difficulty. 'But let my daughter go.'

The older man nodded to his companion, who released Rosemary. The girl ran to Greg and pressed herself against him. She was sobbing, but stopped almost at once as he fondled her hair.

'It's all right, darling. Be brave.'

'I'll try.' Rosemary found a handkerchief and blew her nose hard.

With his family close to him Greg was less inclined to be amenable. He confronted the two men. 'Who the hell are you? And what do you want?' he demanded.

His belligerence had no effect. The older, shorter man, who was clearly in charge, merely gestured with his gun. 'You're to follow me downstairs. Slowly. Don't try any tricks. My—my mate will be behind you and he won't hesitate to shoot. Nor will I.'

Somehow, in spite of his vicious tone, Greg wasn't convinced that the men would shoot. But it was not a judgement he could risk. He tried a last protest.

'Now, look here. Just let us go back to the bedroom. There's nothing worth taking there. Steal what you like in the rest of the house. We shan't try to stop you.'

This approach elicited no response, except a repetition of the order to go downstairs. Greg could feel the pressure of Jean's hand on his back, urging him forward. There seemed no alternative, and the strange little party with its stranger escort went meekly down the stairs to the front hall.

'Into the dining-room,' the man leading them ordered, and there was satisfaction in his voice.

The dining-room in the Whites' house was at the rear, overlooking the garden. It was not a big room. The oval table would seat some six in comfort, and eight with care; they rarely had eight people in for a formal meal. Jean preferred to give casual buffet parties which, as there was always plenty of wine and the food was excellent, were very popular.

When Greg and Jean had gone to bed the door to the dining-room had been shut for the night. Now it was open, the curtains drawn close and the light on. The chairs around the table had been rearranged, so that three of them were on one side, facing the curtained window, and the other five pushed back against the wall.

'Sit down! The girl in the middle, between you.'

They obeyed. Later Greg was asked why they had submitted so tamely. The question annoyed him. What else could they have done? The surprise, the guns, the disbelief in what was happening had numbed them all. And yes, they were afraid. The men might not want to kill, but they had shown that they wouldn't hesitate to hurt, possibly maim, if they didn't get what they wanted. And what the hell did they want? They were no ordinary thieves—that was for certain.

'Hold out your hands, palms facing.'

Again they obeyed and, while the shorter man kept them covered, the other produced from a bag—previously unnoticed in a corner of the room—a collection of handcuffs. It took him a minute to fix them on. Then he got down under the table.

'Ankles together!'

Greg felt the cold metal against his flesh and heard the snap of the cuffs. Then the man went to Jean; Greg saw her shift in her chair. Neither of them had protested. But Rosemary cried out and tried to push herself away from the table.

'No! No! Don't! Leave me alone!'

'What is it, darling?'

'He was—was trying to—to touch me up, Mum.'

'You filthy beast!' Greg staggered to his feet. 'Don't you dare lay another finger on her or I—'

'Or you'll what?' The man had emerged from beneath the table, and it was obvious, in spite of his stocking mask, that he was grinning broadly. 'Or you'll what?' he repeated.

And Greg, feeling sick, knew he had no answer. If he had been going to act, he should have acted before, though God knew what he might have achieved. Now, at least for the moment, he was helpless.

CHAPTER 2

The two men stood in the doorway of the dining-room, muttering to each other. Greg studied his manacled hands. He felt deflated and useless, unable even to offer encouragement to Jean or Rosemary. Rosemary was making an unsuccessful effort to curl herself up into a ball and Jean, who was the most lightly clad of the three of them, had begun to shiver. The muttering ceased.

The younger man left the room, but returned at once. 'Do any of you take sugar?'

Sugar! In the circumstances it seemed the most irrelevant of questions and no one answered.

'In your tea,' the man said patiently. 'I'm going to make us tea.' He spoke as if he were explaining something simple to a group of mentally deficients.

Jean found her voice. 'No. None of us take sugar but—but we'd love some tea. It's cold in here and we're only wearing our nightclothes.' She hesitated. 'There's a thermostat in the hall. Would you please turn it up?'

'Oke!'

Jean, with her placatory manner, was achieving more than he was, Greg thought, as the man departed and a click indicated that he had turned up the central heating as she had asked. But the situation was incredible—two characters, two presumed villains, who were prepared to make tea for their—their victims? What in God's name did they want? Then he remembered old Mrs Porteous and he was fearful, for Rosemary and Jean—and for himself—but especially for Rosemary. He stared intently at the masked gunman who was sitting across the room from him.

'Tell me what you want!'

'Later.'

But Greg felt a need to make him talk. 'You're not common burglars?'

'No!'

'Bank robbers. Abingdon.'

Rosemary had spoken in a whisper and the man gave no sign that he had heard. Greg gave his daughter a startled glance. Could she be right? He knew what she meant. A few months ago the family of a bank manager in Abingdon had been held hostage at gunpoint while he was forced to drive to the bank and open the safe for the thieves. Something had gone wrong, a teller had alerted the police and the would-be robbers had been caught. But crimes were often copied. This might be an example, except—

'Did you hear what my daughter said? Are you hoping to rob a bank? Because if you are you're out of luck. You've come to the wrong house. I'm a don, a university teacher. Mr Pulent, who *is* a bank manager, lives next door.'

There was a hoot of laughter from the taller man, who had returned carrying a tray with three mugs of tea on it. He placed one in front of each of the Whites, who had to manage as best they could with their handcuffed wrists.

'Yours is in the kitchen, boss. I've had some.'

'Ta! We'll have a talk when I get back.' The older man addressed Greg. 'Meantime, the answer's no. We aren't planning to rob a bank, and we didn't come to the wrong house. It's you we need to help us—Mr White.'

'How on earth can I help you? Since you know who I am you must know I told you the truth. I'm just a teacher at St Xavier's.'

'Later! Drink your tea before it gets cold.'

Rosemary giggled hysterically. 'That's just what Mum used to say when I was small.'

'It's good advice, darling.' Jean was already struggling to lift her mug.

Greg marvelled at his wife's resilience. Now that she had got over the first shock Jean seemed to be accepting the

situation. He wished he could be so sanguine. Perhaps it
had been too much to hope that this couple of unspeakable
but curious customers had mistaken him for his neighbour,
but at least it would have made some sense. His imagination boggled when he tried to think of what he could possibly do for them that would warrant this treatment of
himself and his family. But it was useless to speculate. Presumably he would soon be told. With difficulty he lifted his
mug between his manacled hands and drank. The tea was
surprisingly comforting.

The man whom the other addressed as boss returned to the
dining-room. He drew up a chair and sat at the table. His
companion lounged in the doorway, but his gun was ready
and he was watchful. They were taking no chances.

'I'm going to ask you some questions, and I want straight
answers.' The man opposite them looked from Greg to
Rosemary to Jean and back to Greg. 'Cooperate and you'll
come to no harm, as I said. You've my word for it. But try
to trick us and you'll be sorry. You've my word for that
too. Do you understand?'

They nodded in unison, without speaking. They understood that the threat was real—but that was all.

'First you, Rosemary. Today's Monday. You expect to
go to school, don't you?' He didn't wait for an answer.
'Well, you won't be going today. You'll be staying at home
with your mother. What happens when you miss a day?'

'I—I don't know what you mean.' She resented the
patronizing way in which he was questioning her.

'You must miss a day sometimes,' he said patiently,
'when you have a cold or just feel sick.'

'Mother telephones my housemistress. If I'm away more
than a few days—'

'You won't be. You'll be at school tomorrow—if your
father's sensible.' He turned to Jean. 'What time would you
phone, Mrs White?'

'About eight forty-five.'

'You'll do that, then.' It was an order. 'Now, what had *you* planned for today?'

Jean hesitated. 'Nothing much. Monday's washing day as a rule.' She stopped, fighting for control. Her simple, mundane statement had brought their predicament home to her. What *was* she doing? How could she be thinking of clothes washing when she and Greg and Rosemary were sitting in their own dining-room, bound hand and foot and menaced by a couple of armed thugs? It was absurd but— she mustn't appear hostile. 'A dull day,' she concluded.

'You haven't arranged to go out anywhere?' And when Jean shook her head. 'Are you expecting anyone to come to the house?'

'No. No one.'

'What about the milkman, the postman—other deliveries?'

'The bottles are by the side door. The milkman only rings on Fridays, when he's paid. The postman puts the letters through the box. If it's a parcel he'll ring but if there's no answer he'll leave it in the back porch. I'm not expecting anyone else, except the newspaper boy, but he'll put the papers through the letter box too.'

Why am I telling him all this? Jean wondered. It's stupid. Now he knows that he can do what he likes with us because no one will come to help. But he had said they wouldn't be hurt, that Rosemary would be at school tomorrow, and somehow she believed him. Of course he had also said that it depended on Greg. She glanced sideways at her husband, who gave her a wry smile. Whatever they wanted of him he wouldn't refuse, she thought. He would do it—whatever it was—for Rosemary's sake, and hers.

'That's oke then, Mrs White. Mr White?'

'Me? You want to know about my day? Well, first of all I'm due at the regular Monday morning meeting in the Master's Lodgings at St Xavier's at nine-thirty. The meeting will probably last a couple of hours or more, depending on the length of the agenda. Then the Master will offer us a sherry—'

'Enough, Mr White. It's not going to be like that. Not this Monday morning. We have other plans for you.'

'I gathered you might have.' Greg was grim. 'I only wish you'd tell me what they are. I assume you'll want my wife to phone the College to say I'm ill. I won't mind that. I find these meetings extraordinarily tedious and I'll be glad of a chance to miss one.'

There was no immediate response as Greg stopped speaking, and the silence lengthened. It had the effect of making Greg feel foolish. He glared at the man opposite him.

Suddenly the man said, 'You must dress now.'

'Dress? What about washing and shaving?'

'We'll look after all that, Mr White. My—my mate here will remove your cuffs and take you upstairs. But don't try any funny business. Remember, I'll be down here keeping an eye on your wife and your daughter. A smashed shoulder wouldn't be much fun for a young girl.'

Greg nodded; he couldn't bring himself to speak. He had no means of knowing if there was any substance in the threat. But the threat was enough by itself. He couldn't risk Rosemary being shot, and probably pointlessly.

He was escorted up to the bedroom and bathroom, where the younger man watched as he took off his dressing-gown and his pyjama jacket. He washed briefly and shaved with his electric razor. He glanced at his companion and took the opportunity to use the lavatory. Then he returned to the bedroom to put on underpants, clean shirt, trousers, tie, sweater, jacket, socks, shoes. He combed his hair. He slipped on his watch and filled his pockets with the usual assortment of articles that he kept overnight on a small tray on his chest of drawers. All he needed was his briefcase, he thought, and he could have set off for the College; no one would have noticed anything amiss or unusual. But for what was he ready?

It was a surprise when, as soon as they returned to the dining-room, the older man ordered him to sit down again at the table, and his ankles, though not his hands, were manacled. Because he was dressed and Jean and Rosemary were still in their nightclothes he felt alienated from them, as if he had taken an unfair advantage. He glanced at his watch. It was past seven. He had heard the grandfather clock in the hall strike while he was dressing, but had mis-counted and thought it had struck six. It was hard to believe that the time, which had borne so little relation to reality since Jean had woken him, had passed so quickly.

'Now breakfast,' said the older man.

There was a gasp from Rosemary. In spite of the extra-ordinary circumstances, the threats and the fear, she was hungry. She hoped that the suggestion of breakfast wasn't a malicious joke, but a genuine offer.

'Are you proposing to cook it for us?' Jean asked coldly. Seeing Greg dressed as if ready to depart somewhere, she felt her fears for Rosemary and herself magnify.

'Tea and toast only, and make the most of it. It may be some time before you get anything else.'

'What do you mean by that, damn it? Stop talking in riddles! Tell us—tell *me* what you want!' Greg banged a fist on the table. 'One moment you utter appalling threats, the next you make us tea, offer us breakfast. It makes no sense. What the hell do you want?'

'Later, Mr White, as I said before.'

'No! Now! Tell me now, or you can stuff your breakfast.'

'You've decided not to cooperate? You intend to be difficult?'

'I want to know—'

'Oke. That'll be breakfast for two then as Mr White and his family don't want any. Sure you won't change your mind, Mr White?'

'Dad, please! He said it might be ages before we got anything else—all day, perhaps.'

'Greg, for heaven's sake! What have we got to lose?'

Greg drew a deep breath. What *had* they got to lose? Pride maybe, but that was already lost. Nevertheless, he felt that every time they obeyed a simple order or accepted a favour they were weakening their will to resist and putting themselves even more at the mercy of the two thugs who menaced them. Yet what was the alternative? To deprive Jean and Rosemary of a cup of tea and a slice of toast that they might well be grateful for later seemed a pretty worthless act.

'All right. Forget what I said. We'd like breakfast.'

'Good. That's sensible of you, Mr White.'

'Don't you think you might free my wife and daughter's hands so that they can eat decently, and enjoy the meal you're so kindly providing?' Greg tried to combine irony with a little authority.

'No call to be sarcastic, Mr White. They can manage. It doesn't matter if they spill a bit on themselves. It's different for you. We wouldn't want you going to your College with marmalade down your tie, would we?'

Greg said nothing. The altercation over the breakfast hadn't achieved much, but at least he had gathered one piece of information. They intended him to go to St Xavier's. He knew better than to ask why.

Time passed. Breakfast arrived, was eaten and the dirty plates and mugs removed. No one attempted to make conversation. They were all growing tired; strain and lack of sleep were beginning to tell on them. But the two men, who had taken turns to eat in the kitchen, didn't relax their vigilance.

There were several minor alarms. The milkman's cheery whistle and the clank of his bottles made them stiffen, as did the thud of the newspapers and a little later the letters, circulars and magazines that cascaded into the hall. The younger man brought in the milk and collected the news-papers and the mail. He flung the *Telegraph* and the *Independent* on to a chair and leafed through the post.

'Not very interesting,' he commented. 'A couple of bills, a postcard from Majorca and a billy-doo for the lovely Rosemary.'

'Shut up!'

'Oke, boss. Sorry. Anyway, there's nothing important, Mr White. It can all wait till you get back.'

Back from where? Presumably from St Xavier's. Greg had no time to ponder the matter. The telephone in the hall had started to ring. But it was scarcely eight o'clock, too early for most people to phone. Greg thought at once of his father, who had recently suffered a stroke.

'Are you expecting a call? You didn't mention it.' The older man was suspicious.

'No, but it could be my mother. My father's been ill. You must let me answer it. Bring the phone in here. It's on a long lead. Please!' Greg gritted his teeth.

They did as he asked and, to his relief, the call was for Jean; the woman who organized the rota of voluntary helpers at the local Oxfam shop wanted Jean to replace someone who had a cold. Jean said it was impossible, as Rosemary was sick and couldn't be left.

And the waiting continued. The telephone, the Whites' link with the outside world, remained on the dining-room table, but it only served to mock them. It offered no means of getting help.

CHAPTER 3

Greg became conscious that for the last five minutes Rose-mary had been fidgeting in her chair, She leant forward over the table, then bent back. She moved her shoulders.

She looked about her. Catching what appeared to him a desperate glance from her, Greg, whose wrists were not cuffed, patted her hands and for a moment she clung to one of his fingers.

'Don't touch each other!'

Greg took his hand away. He wondered if Rosemary were trying to tell him something, but he couldn't imagine what. The time was now twenty past eight, still too early for Jean to telephone Rosemary's housemistress to say she was unwell. Perhaps she really was unwell. She was fidgeting more than ever.

'I'm sorry!' she suddenly burst out. 'I'm sorry, but I've got to go to the loo—the lavatory.'

Greg thought that he could do with another pee himself, but it was not imperative, and Jean never seemed to have an overpowering need. 'For heaven's sake, let her go,' he said quietly. 'She's not going to run away. You can wait outside the door.'

'I'll take her.'

Inevitably it was the younger man who had volunteered. Greg saw Rosemary's mouth set and her chin come up, but she didn't protest. She started to make an effort to stand, which proved abortive.

'Oke,' the leader said; it was a word of which he and his companion were fond, in spite of their reasonably grammatical speech, and Greg was to remember it. 'But no fooling!'

The other man drew Rosemary's chair back from the table. He unlocked the manacles on her ankles and then her wrists, and she spent a minute massaging them before she again tried to stand. She walked uncertainly to the door without a glance at either of her parents, and they heard her begin to mount the stairs.

Rosemary went up a step at a time, pulling herself along by the banisters and half dragging one leg. She hoped she was giving an impression of a cowed girl who was in some pain. This way she planned to take by surprise the revolting smarmy guy following close behind her. She was thankful that he had raised no objection to going upstairs as she had feared he might.

In fact, there was a cloakroom on the ground floor of the house. It was in the hall to one side of the front door, and from the outside looked like a coat cupboard. Rosemary could have gone there more easily but, while it was true that she did want to use the lavatory, she had another purpose which could only be served by the bathroom at the top of the stairs.

For Rosemary had suddenly remembered that the night before, when Tony had brought her home from the birthday party, he had promised to pick her up at eight-thirty the next morning and drive her to school. This meant that in a very few minutes he would be ringing the front doorbell and when no one answered the door he would think it very odd.

She could make a guess at what he might do. He might try shouting through the letter-box or he might go around to the back of the house and look through the kitchen window. He would wonder why the dining-room curtains were drawn and the light was on; he would surely catch a glimpse of it through the edges of the curtains. So he might bang on the windows—and when there was still no response? He would go home and tell his father. Help would arrive!

That was one conceivable outcome, but Rosemary was a sensible girl and was aware there might be others. Tony might try phoning when he got home, and accept the excuse that she was ill. Or, something she feared much more, if Tony made a nuisance of himself outside the house, the front door might be opened to him and, before he realized what was happening, he could be pulled inside to join them at gunpoint in the dining-room. Somehow she had to warn him and, if it proved at all possible, make him get the police.

By now Rosemary was almost at the top of the stairs. The bathroom, its door ajar, was immediately opposite. She wished the guy behind her was not so close, but she had to take her chance. Without warning she kicked backwards as hard and as viciously as she could. She heard the man grunt with pain, but with a bare foot the blow was less devastating than she had hoped. He dropped his automatic, but managed to save himself from falling by seizing the banister.

Nevertheless, her action gave Rosemary a few precious seconds. She was in the bathroom, the door slammed, the bolt shot, before the man had regained his balance. But she hadn't even unlatched the window, which gave out on to the flat roof of the garage a few feet below, before he was pounding on the door panel and shouting at her.

'Open up, you bitch! Open up!'

Rosemary had no intention of obeying, and he knew it. He stopped his futile shouting and ran at the door, hurling himself shoulder first against it. The door was solid but the bolt was weak. At his third attempt it gave, and he was in the bathroom.

It was not until the banging and shouting started that Greg and Jean, and the man guarding them, realized that some kind of altercation was taking place on the floor above. Instantly they were alert, apprehensive. But they scarcely had time to react before there was the jarring crash of the bathroom door being slammed back against the wall. Moments later Rosemary screamed.

Several things happened simultaneously. The older man, shouting to Greg and Jean to stay where they were, raced from the dining-room. He was back almost immediately to scoop the telephone from the table, just as Jean was stretching out her hands to pull the instrument towards her. Greg, meanwhile, forgetting his cuffed ankles, had leapt to his feet in his desire to go to Rosemary's aid, and after one attempted stride had fallen heavily. As he lay on the floor, entangled in his chair, he could hear the older man calling up the stairs.

'Bring the girl down. Now! At once. Do you hear, Tom? Bring the bloody girl down!'

For a minute there was no response. Rosemary had been half way out of the bathroom window when the man, whose name she had just learnt was Tom, burst into the room. He had seized her around the waist and pulled her back. As she struggled to resist him they had fallen together to the floor and before she could stop him he had rolled on top of her. He was much bigger and heavier than she was, and she felt that his weight was pressing the breath out of her, but still she struggled.

It was her struggles that aroused him. It was when she felt his hand pulling down her pyjama trousers and forcing her legs apart while the other hand unzipped his fly that she screamed. And then she did the one thing that could have saved her. Instinct made her claw at his face. Chance caused her to grasp his stocking mask. She tugged at it and it came over his head, revealing short sandy hair, blue eyes and the top of what once might have been a broken nose.

The impression she received was fleeting but strong. He had thrust himself away from her, and was staggering to his feet, while at the same time trying to replace his mask. He kicked Rosemary hard, twice, and she cried out.

There was a renewed shout from the stairs. 'Come down! Bring the girl! Do you bloody hear me, Tom?'

'Coming!'

This was followed by a stream of abuse that only Rosemary heard; many of the words she didn't even recognize. But she knew that she was safe, at least for the present, and she didn't care when, zipping up his trousers, Tom kicked her again.

'You bitch! You stupid little bitch! Just you wait. I'll get you.'

Rosemary ignored the threat. Pulling her pyjamas together and her dressing-gown around her and tying the belt tightly, she stood up. She half expected him to hit her again, but he merely gave her a shove as she edged past him. She walked carefully down the stairs. She had noticed that he was no longer carrying his gun, but knew she had no chance of making a dash for the front door and escaping. The other, older man was standing on the bottom stair, revolver in hand, the telephone tucked under his other arm.

'Come on, girl. Hurry! I don't know what you've been up to, but you've done no good to yourself or your family.' He gestured with his gun to the dining-room door. 'Get back in there.'

Rosemary ran past him. She hugged her mother first because she was nearer, then went to her father, who had managed to free himself from the chair he had knocked over as he fell, and was standing up. He folded her in his arms and held her to him.

'You're all right?'

'Yes. I tried to get out of the bathroom window but he caught me. He—' She stopped. She had an idea that if she explained more explicitly what had happened it would only cause extra animosity towards her on the part of the man called Tom. She also had an idea that Tom resented his companion's authority since it had in effect interrupted his attempt to—She refused to think about it further.

'Thank God you're all right. I was afraid—'

Greg didn't say what he was afraid of; in his turn, and for different reasons, he didn't dare to put it into words. Over Rosemary's head he exchanged glances with Jean. He knew that she had shared his fear. The last few minutes—only minutes though they had seemed endless—had been hell, not least because he had been incapable of any action, useless, when Rosemary had needed him.

The two men had entered the room close behind Rose-

DEATH'S LONG SHADOW

mary. The older one banged the telephone down on the table; he was obviously angry.

'Sit down, all of you!' he ordered.

They sat. Without being told, Tom replaced the manacles on Rosemary's wrists and ankles; he was rough, but made no attempt to touch her more than necessary. He had found the gun he had dropped on the stairs, but it was clear that either the incident in the bathroom or fear of his companion had subdued him. He was quiet and sullen.

'What happens now?' Greg demanded. 'You are—you're beyond my comprehension. You make no sense. Why won't you say what you want? And then perhaps—How can I know unless you tell me?'

'Mr White, be patient. I'm about to tell you what we want—what I'm sure you're going to do for us.' He shook his head. 'If you love your wife and daughter, as clearly you do, you really don't have much choice.'

'Suppose you stop these pointless threats and get on with it, then.'

'Oke, though there's no hurry. You won't be leaving for about half an hour. Just before nine o'clock, Mr White, you will go out of the house—' He stopped; the front doorbell had rung. 'Who'll that be? You said you weren't expecting anyone.'

'We're not,' Jean said quickly.

'Yes, Mum. Tony. He promised to drive me to school.'

'Who's Tony?'

'Tony Pulent. My boyfriend. He lives next door. I forgot he was coming.'

'You forgot?' The doorbell pealed again. 'Will he go away if no one answers?'

Rosemary shrugged. 'I don't know.'

'Of course he won't. He's expecting you to be here.' The older man pointed towards Greg's ankles. 'Undo him,' he ordered Tom. 'Hurry! Mr White, you're going to answer

the door, tell the boy Rosemary's ill and get rid of him. I'll
be right beside you, where he can't see me. But I'll be able
to see you, and if you make the smallest gesture or speak
one wrong word, I'll have this Tony inside the house with
the rest of you before you can—'

'I understand.' Greg was rubbing his ankles, and he
thought how absurd it was that at such a moment he should
notice that the chain had made a hole in his sock.

'Come on then! Quick! And, remember, your wife and
daughter will be in here.'

'How can I forget that?'

Greg tried to smile at them as he obeyed the gesture of
the older man's gun to go ahead of him into the hall, but
neither Jean nor Rosemary met his gaze. Jean was wondering what she might do if she were in his place, and hoping
he wouldn't be rash; Rosemary was torn between worrying
about Tony's safety, and wishing Tony would do something
heroic that would save them from this present nightmare.

Greg opened the door. 'Hello, Tony.'

'Hello, Mr White.'

Tony straightened himself. He had been bending down
to peer through the letter-box and had seen, or thought he
had seen, two pairs of trousered legs coming towards him,
but now there was only Greg White. Automatically Tony,
who had known the Whites all his life and considered their
house a second home, made to step into the hall. Greg
blocked his way.

Tony was surprised. 'I promised I'd pick Rosemary up
and drive her to school this morning.'

'Yes, so she said, Tony. Unfortunately she's not well.'

'Not well?' Tony frowned. 'But—'

Tony was nineteen, in his third year at St Xavier's,
reading Law. He was, he knew, not the most brilliant of
students, but he was working hard and hoped to get a
reasonable degree; later, if all went well, he planned to go
into politics. As he had a pleasing extrovert personality,

plenty of common sense and appeared to like people, there seemed no reason why he shouldn't succeed.

He ran his hand through his thick fair hair. 'Mr White, I don't understand. Rosemary was perfectly well when I dropped her off not many hours ago. What's the matter with her?'

'She running a temperature. I—I don't think it's anything serious. I hope she'll be all right tomorrow.'

'Have you sent for the doctor?'

'No, no. I'm sure she doesn't need a doctor.'

'Then she can't be too bad. I can come in and have a chat with her, cheer her up. I don't have a lecture till eleven.'

'Tony, I'm sorry.' Greg was getting more and more conscious of the man with the gun hidden from Tony. He had to get rid of Tony before the man beside him decided to act; it wasn't fair to involve the boy. 'Look, she'll call you tomorrow. I promise.'

'But, Mr White—I—I don't understand. Is something wrong?'

'No. Everything's fine.' Greg forced himself to grin. 'Goodbye, Tony. See you.'

Greg shut the front door firmly and leant against it. He prayed that Tony would go away and not ring the bell again. 'I did my best,' he said.

'Sure. You did all right, Mr White, but only just. Another minute and I'd have had that young man in here. Now, back to the dining-room and I'll give you your instructions.'

CHAPTER 4

'I've got rid of Tony. I promised you'd phone him tomorrow, Rosemary.' Greg's voice was tight, though he was doing his best to sound normally cheerful.

'Good. I—I'll do that, Dad.'

Rosemary wasn't sure whether or not it *was* good. She hadn't wanted Tony dragged into the house, but on the other hand she had been hoping against hope that he could be given a hint that all was not well. He had been their last chance of getting help, and now that seemed to have evaporated. She wondered if she would ever see him again, or if, in spite of their claims, these horrible, revolting men intended to kill them.

'Time for you to phone the school, Mrs White. Early perhaps, but near enough. You know the number?'

Jean nodded. The instrument was pushed across the table to her and she tapped at the keypad. She had considered calling the Pulents instead of the school, or when she got Rosemary's housemistress, who was a sensible woman, saying—what? 'Help us! Get the police!' It was unlikely she would have the chance to say more. And how would the men react?

As if reading her thoughts the older man said, 'Don't try to be a clever-clever, Mrs White. You'd be sorry. Understood?'

Jean understood. She asked for Miss Westlake and briefly explained to her that Rosemary wouldn't be coming to school because she had a temperature; she hoped it was nothing serious and Rosemary would be there tomorrow. The housemistress was sympathetic, but had no reason to be concerned, and Jean put down the receiver with a small sigh. Like Rosemary, she had been wondering about the extent to which they could depend on their captors' assurance that if they cooperated they would not be harmed. But it was the only hope they had.

The older of the two immediately reinforced that hope. 'I'll tell you what we want Mr White to do, what we intend him to do, and I repeat that we won't harm any of you if he agrees to help us. We've got nothing against you. That's on the credit side as far as you're concerned. On the debit side—but Mr White isn't going to let it come to that, are you, Mr White?'

'I don't know.'

'You soon will if you refuse, because we're bloody determined to carry out our plan. You'd better believe that. Whatever the cost to us, or to you or your family, Mr White, we're not calling a halt now.' The man's voice had become almost hoarse with suppressed passion, which was frightening.

Greg suppressed a shiver. The man might be mad, must be mad, but he had to be believed. There was a steely determination about him, and the phrase 'whatever the cost' was chilling.

'All right. Tell me what you want of me,' Greg said quietly. 'I may be lacking in imagination but I can't conceive what it may be. What happens if it's impossible—if I can't do it? Have you considered that?'

'You'll be able to do it. It's not in the least difficult, as long as you follow our instructions exactly.'

'Go on,' Greg said warily.

'You'll leave this house shortly before nine. You'll take your usual route to the College, down the Banbury Road, and you'll park your car in Broad Street.'

'Supposing there isn't a parking space? I often take the bus because parking's so difficult.'

'Then you'll just have to park at one or other end of the rows of cars and hope you won't get a ticket. You'll walk fast down Turl Street to the High Street and your College. We've timed it half a dozen times, doing what you'd call research, Mr White, and you should get there shortly before nine-thirty. Anyone you meet that you know you just say ''Morning' but you don't stop for a chat. You go straight to your Master's Lodgings, as you call them, and to this meeting of yours. No funny stuff, you understand. No delays. Timing's of the essence, as they say.'

'And I'll be watching you, Mr White,' Tom broke in.

'Any try at being clever and I'll be popping along to the nearest phone and calling the boss. He'll be right here in your house, waiting, and if I tell him you've double-crossed us, you won't recognize your wife or daughter when you next see them.'

Greg clenched his hands so that the nails bit into his palms. He yearned to counter threat with threat, to swear that one day he'd make sure their positions were reversed, and when he had them at his mercy he'd see them in hell. But he knew they'd only laugh at any such outburst. And why not? At this moment any threats he could make were worthless.

'So, to continue, Mr White. You've arrived at your meeting in the Master's study. I take it these meetings start punctually?'

'Yes.'

'Good. So it won't have started yet. You sit down, put your briefcase beside you and then excuse yourself. Say you have to go to the toilet, if you like. Instead you leave the Lodgings, return to your car and come home. We'll be watching you, like before, though you may not spot us. If you do just what I've said you'll find your family safe. Not difficult, is it?'

'No, but—' Greg's face twisted into a grimace. 'There's a catch. It's the briefcase. I don't take that with me when I leave the Master's Lodgings, do I?'

'No, Mr White. It stays in the Master's study, beside the chair you sat in, until at exactly twenty-five minutes to ten, when the meeting's well under way, it explodes!'

'Dear God!' whispered Jean.

Greg was shaking his head in disbelief. 'You *are* mad! You can't really believe that I'd blow up the Master and—and several of my senior colleagues and wreck part of the College just to please you. Why in hell's name should I?'

'It will please me, yes, but that's not why you'll do it, Mr White. Perhaps you'd be happy to die instead of these colleagues of yours. But what about your wife and daughter? Have you forgotten them? You'll do it for their sake, I'm sure.'

'I'm damned if I will. They wouldn't want me to.' But Greg spoke without conviction. 'Anyway, I don't believe you. You're bluffing.' He felt on stronger ground here. 'What would you have to gain?'

'It's what *you've* got to lose you should be thinking about. I said we were determined to carry this out, no matter what the cost to ourselves, or to you, Mr White, and I wasn't joking.'

'But why? Why?'

'That's our business. It doesn't concern you. All that concerns you is doing what you've been told.'

'And if I refuse?'

'Mr White, do I have to repeat everything? You're supposed to be a clever man. Sure, you can refuse, but then you'll take the consequences, you and your family. The one thing I'm not doing is bluffing.'

'He means it, Dad.' Rosemary was frightened.

'Greg, she's right. He *does* mean it,' Jean repeated. 'For God's sake consider what he's saying.'

'But there would be no point. If I refuse his plan's failed. Don't you realize that? It would be stupid to hurt any of us. The police won't bother overmuch about—about what's happened so far, but if—'

'Mr White, if you refuse—and I don't think you will once you've considered the matter—we'll have to find another don who can be persuaded to help us—and try again.' He held up his hand to stop Greg's reply. 'I know what you're going to say, but you're wrong. You won't have warned the police about our plan, because when we go away from here, we'll have left you cuffed and helpless with the briefcase just out of your reach. You won't be telling anyone anything.'

There was a gasp of horror from Jean. 'Greg—'

'You murderous swine!' he cried, and choked.

This was a nightmare. He stared at the two men. The fact that they were dressed from head to foot in black made them ludicrously unreal. They were like characters from a bad melodrama. They didn't behave consistently; sometimes they didn't even seem sure of their lines. Cups of tea, and toast, closely followed by unspeakable threats of violence. And why me, he thought, why did they pick on me? He was unaware that he had spoken aloud.

'Do you wish we'd picked on someone else, Mr White? Would you rather be in your Master's study at nine thirty-five this morning when the briefcase explodes, or on your way home to your wife and daughter?'

Greg didn't answer. He had been tempted to say, yes, he would rather be in the Master's study, ignorant of what was to happen—and innocent of anyone's death. But that choice wasn't his. It had been made for him, and he'd been lumbered with a far more difficult, indeed an impossible choice between Rosemary and Jean on the one hand, and several people, most of whom he liked and respected, on the other. But ... He put his elbows on the table and buried his face in his hands.

'I'll give you five minutes to decide, Mr White. That's all we can spare. But don't hope we'll change our minds. If you refuse to help us you'll die at nine thirty-five, all three of you.'

'And I might have a bit of fun first.' The younger man, leaning in the doorway, laughed suddenly. 'I quite fancy your daughter, Mr White.'

'No!' Rosemary cried immediately. 'No, not that! Dad, please don't let him.'

'You can't, Greg. For God's sake! I'd take their damned bomb myself if I could, rather than—Rosemary's a child, your child, with her whole life in front of her. You can't believe the Master and a lot of old men are more important than she is. Don't you love her?' Jean was incensed.

'They're not all old men,' Greg said absently. 'They're

mostly around my age and married, with their own wives and children.' He sighed. 'And of course I love our daughter. Rosemary, you know that, don't you, darling?'

'Yes, Dad, I know that, but—' She shivered. 'I can't bear the idea of that—that guy—'

'No. I can understand that.' Greg was bitter. He squared his shoulders. 'All right. They win. I'll take this blasted bomb. I'll blow up the Master's Lodgings. I'll kill a few of my colleagues. And God forgive me!'

'Would you prefer God to forgive you for letting your daughter be raped and all of us murdered?' Jean's voice was harsh, showing the strain she was under.

'No,' Greg said. He felt numb. He had made his decision and he would stick with it. He had no choice. In fact, he thought, the decision hadn't been his. Jean and Rosemary had made it for him. Jean had hardly understood that there was a decision to be made. To her his hesitation had been a kind of betrayal. 'When do I go?' he asked dully.

'Right now!' There was relief as well as satisfaction in the older man's voice. 'Two minutes for my mate to get going, then I'll be watching you leave, Mr White. Remember he'll be following you all the way.'

'I'll remember.' Greg pushed back in his chair; his ankles were still manacled. 'I'll need to walk,' he said.

'Natch.' The younger man, Tom, thrust himself off the doorframe against which he was leaning. He dived under the table and freed Greg's legs. Then he tossed the key to his companion. 'I'll be off.' He gave the Whites an exaggerated salute.

'Put the phone back in the hall as you go.'

'Oke. Be seeing you, Rosemary dear.' He blew her a kiss as he went.

Greg stood up. He leant both hands on the table and addressed the remaining man. 'I'm doing what you want,' he said, 'but I swear to you that if that yobbo ever comes near my daughter once this is all over, I'll kill him.'

'He won't, Mr White. He won't. You'll never see or hear from either of us again. Just deliver the briefcase and return to your family. Then you can forget about this little lot.'

Greg didn't bother to contradict him. He knew he would never forget the two men, or the horror they had brought with them. And it wasn't over yet. 'Where is the bloody briefcase?'

'In the hall, by the front door. Treat it with care. Put it on the seat beside you while you're driving.' He got to his feet. The revolver was steady in his hand. 'Come on now. I'll see you out.'

Greg gave Rosemary a quick hug and leant across her to kiss Jean, who offered him her cheek. None of them spoke. There was nothing to be said. Rosemary was near tears.

Jean twisted in her seat so that, moving her cuffed wrists, she could entwine her fingers with Rosemary's. She felt the girl start as the front door slammed.

'Dad's gone,' Rosemary whispered.

'Yes. Don't worry, darling. Everything will be all right. He won't let us down.'

'No, but—Such a lot can go wrong. He could easily be delayed. Another car could run into him or he could knock down a pedestrian or—or—'

Or he could try to do something clever, and fail, Jean thought, but she didn't voice the notion. She didn't trust Greg over this. In his place she wouldn't have hesitated; surely the family had to take precedence over half a dozen academics, some of whom he didn't particularly like. True, they had wives and children too, but in the circumstances his own family should come first.

'And these men, Mum? They said the explosion's going to happen at nine thirty-five, but are they sure? I suppose they made this bomb themselves. How expert are they?

Bombs don't always go off when they're meant to and—
and I'm afraid for Dad.'

'So am I, Rosemary.'

It wasn't a lie. She *was* afraid for Greg, but she was more
afraid for Rosemary and herself. Rosemary was right. Even
if Greg didn't attempt some silly heroic act, the bomb might
go off at the wrong time and in the wrong place—and what
would the gunman do then? When he learnt that they had
failed to achieve their purpose would he shoot the pair of
them out of pure vindictiveness?

He had returned to the dining-room, and it was clear to
them that he was feeling the strain as much as they were,
for he paced up and down in front of them and glanced at
his watch every few seconds. Once Jean asked him the time,
but he didn't answer.

Nevertheless the minutes had to be passing, however
slowly—and still the phone didn't ring. They had to assume
that Greg was carrying out his task as ordered and that
nothing had interfered with him. Jean began to hope that
after all the worst wasn't going to happen; she refused to
think about the Master and the others who might be killed
or maimed with him.

Then suddenly their captor stopped his pacing. He
swung round and levelled his gun at the pair of them. Rosemary gasped.

'Has—has the bomb exploded?' Jean asked quickly. 'We
wouldn't have heard it from here, would we? But no one's
phoned.'

'It's only twenty minutes past nine. Your husband ought
to have parked his car by now and started to walk down
Turl Street, so I'll say goodbye. I'm off.'

'You're leaving? Now! You mean you'll kill us although
Greg's doing what you want? But you said—you promised—we'd come to no harm if—'

'Mrs White, I know what I said. There's no need to
remind me. I'm not going to hurt you, so you don't have

to worry. Just you wait there as you are till your husband or someone else arrives. I'll put the keys to your cuffs in the lounge.'

Jean bit her tongue. She had nearly said thank-you, but to thank a criminal who had physically and mentally abused them because he was kind enough to spare their lives would have been absurd—or was she falling for the so-called Stockholm syndrome? Nevertheless, in her relief, she had difficulty in stemming the tide of gratitude she felt.

'All right.'

'Only one thing. When the police question you, as they will, you can't describe me or my mate. You don't remember a thing about us. And that goes for Mr White too. Understood?'

'We couldn't describe you if we wanted to.' Jean spoke with conviction; she didn't notice that beside her Rosemary had suddenly tensed.

'Oke. Then I'll be off.'

They didn't answer, but they listened. They heard him go into the sitting-room. From there he went to the kitchen, and they waited. It seemed a long wait, and certainly he didn't leave the house immediately. But after two or three minutes the side door slammed.

Jean released her breath, 'Rosemary, I think—I think we're safe.'

'I hope so. But—but what about Dad? What's happened to him?'

CHAPTER 5

As soon as he emerged from the dining-room Greg had seen the briefcase standing, handle upright, on the floor of the hall. It was very like his own. He gritted his teeth. The next hour was going to be a period of terrible stress and anxiety, and he told himself that he must forget Jean and Rosemary, and forget the consequences of his imposed mission. It was essential to concentrate on carrying out the task accurately and without arousing the least suspicion on the part of Tom and any other watcher whom the pair of gunmen might have stationed outside.

His car, a red Ford Fiesta, five years old, was parked in the short driveway in front of the garage which housed their new Rover. He placed the briefcase carefully on the gravel, unlocked the front left-hand door of the Ford, placed the briefcase carefully on the seat and relocked the door before going around the car and getting behind the wheel. He wondered if he should try to wedge the case upright, but he had nothing with which to do this.

His hand was unsteady, but his second attempt to insert the ignition key in its place was successful. He started the engine and backed the car into the road, wincing as it bumped over the gutter. Some fifty yards behind him a plain white van drew away from the kerb, and further back he saw a motorcyclist wearing a yellow crash helmet, but otherwise dressed in black. Either or both of these could have been the escort he had been promised.

He drove the length of the street. A neighbour, busy working in her front garden, waved to him and he waved back. A party of schoolboys, laughing and jostling each other, strayed off the pavement and he gave them a warning hoot. There was a normality about the scene that was reassuring. Even the slight smell of the fruit drops which Rosemary liked to suck and which had permeated the Ford over the years was comforting. But there was no way he could forget the briefcase on the seat beside him, and the enormity of what he had to do appalled him.

He stopped at the corner on to the Banbury Road, and waited for a gap in the southbound traffic. To his dismay he noticed on of his students standing at the bus stop nearby. And Jack Graham had seen him! Greg swore. He could not possibly have Jack in the car. He knew nothing about the bomb except that it was due to go off at nine thirty-five and he had been told to treat the briefcase with care. He had no idea how volatile the damned thing might be. For all he knew it might explode at any moment, and he couldn't risk an unnecessary life. In any case, any attempt to stop for a hitch-hiker might well trigger a tragedy at his home.

So, staring straight ahead of him, Greg turned the corner and drove past the bus stop. As he went by he caught a glimpse of Jack Graham's face, and in other circumstances the change of expression from grateful anticipation to stunned disbelief would have made him laugh. But he was in no laughing mood. The incident had brought home to him the fact that he was a menace to anyone near him— the occupants of a passing car, a pedestrian waiting to cross the street, a cyclist delayed beside him at a red light.

The man in black gear with a yellow helmet whom he had seen when leaving his house had overtaken him, and was disappearing into the distance on his motorbike, but the white van was still behind him. He wondered if he had any option but to drive to the centre of the city and go to his College. If he had thought earlier he might have driven to Parks and abandoned the car with its deadly burden in an open space where an explosion would destroy grass, trees and flowerbeds but, with luck, not a single human being. But then again, what would have happened to Rosemary and Jean?

Anyway, it was too late now. He was heading for the most populated area of Oxford. Even as he accepted this frightening fact and what it might mean, he saw a traffic warden step into the road and hold up a warning hand. He braked sharply, too sharply. The briefcase started to fall forward but, thrusting an arm sideways. he just managed to save it.

His car stopped on the edge of a pedestrian crossing and

the traffic warden glared angrily at him. A woman wheeling a double pushchair of the kind made for twins began to walk across the road. To Greg she moved with agonizing slowness. A taxi with an elderly couple in the back drew up beside him. A motorbike suddenly appeared in the narrow space between his car and the taxi. Behind Greg was a bus, and on the opposite side of the road were several stationary vehicles heading north. Two women were standing on the pavement close beside him, chatting.

Greg shut his eyes. No, he prayed, not now! If the bomb exploded—He refused to contemplate the horror that would ensue. But, after all, if it did happen he would know nothing about it; that was the only consolation.

There was a loud hooting behind him. The traffic warden stepped forward and banged on his windscreen. Greg opened his eyes and swallowed hard. The woman with the twins had reached the opposite pavement. The traffic, except for the lane he was blocking, was once more flowing freely.

Hurriedly Greg got into gear and drove off. He reached the lights in St Giles'. They showed red and he prepared to stop again. He was beginning to worry about the time. If he were late reaching the College . . . He looked in his rear-view mirror. The white van had overtaken the bus and was still behind him. But the lights had changed and thankfully he accelerated away.

He turned into the Broad. As he had expected, there was a solid double line of cars parked in the centre of the wide road, and no space was available. Then a Mini started to pull out. Greg drew up and waited. The woman at the wheel of the Mini was not the most efficient of drivers and seemed to have difficulty in reversing. Greg hooted impatiently and she waved an apologetic hand as she drove off. Greg ignored the friendly gesture.

He parked quickly. Broad Street is entitled to its name, and it occurred to him that if he merely abandoned the briefcase in his car here the bomb might explode without harming anyone and with the minimum of devastation. But of course he couldn't think of such a solution. He was still being watched. The white van was parked outside Balliol. Even if he went and accosted the driver, whom he assumed to be Tom, he couldn't depend on holding him until the police came and, if Tom got away, what might happen to Jean and Rosemary? Once more he was faced with the same dreadful dilemma.

He wiped his face and hands on his handkerchief. He was sweating badly and he knew he had to hurry. Time was passing. If he sat there much longer he would be blown to pieces and the likelihood was that he wouldn't have saved Jean and Rosemary. He got out and went round the Ford, opened the passenger door and gingerly picked up the briefcase. He crossed the road and started to walk down the Turl.

He moved at a brisk pace, wishing there were not so many people about. As he passed Exeter College a student dashed out of the lodge. He knocked heavily against Greg and in a vain effort to save the pile of books he was carrying nearly wrenched the briefcase from Greg's grasp.

'Sorry, sir!'

'You—'

Greg bit back the expletives. He leant against the wall of the College and hugged the briefcase to his chest. For a split second he thought he was about to collapse.

The student, already on his knees collecting his books, looked up at him curiously. 'Are you all right, sir? I'm awfully sorry.'

Greg nodded. He pushed himself away from the wall and continued down the Turl, carefully shielding the briefcase from passers-by. In his anxiety he had lost all sense of time, and even forgotten that he was wearing his watch. Now he remembered, and glanced at it. It had seemed to him an age since he left home, and he was both surprised and relieved to see that he had over five minutes in hand *if*—*if* the bloody thing had been timed accurately.

But now he was committed. Whatever wild ideas he might have had before, there was no longer any alternative. He was taking the briefcase and its unholy contents to St Xavier's. This way he could at least expect with some confidence to save Rosemary and Jean, and everyone other than those for whom the bomb had been intended. He lengthened his stride, not bothering to look back to see if he could spot a follower; there were too many people about to make this feasible.

'Greg, my dear chap, just the man I want a word with.'

Even in ordinary circumstances Greg wouldn't have welcomed the intervention. The man standing squarely in front of him and blocking his way was the acknowledged bore of St Xavier's Senior Common Room. He was a massive character whose habit was to get someone in a corner to have 'a word' and then keep his unfortunate victim there for half an hour. He was the last person Greg wanted to meet.

'Sorry, Christopher, I haven't time at the moment.'

'It will only take two ticks. It's about one of your students, young Morrison. He has rooms above me on 'C' Staircase and—'

'Complain to the Bursar!'

Greg dodged into the road, circumventing the large bulk that was obstructing him, ignoring the man's surprise at his brusque rudeness and causing a passing cyclist to fall off his machine. He hurried on, oblivious of the angry cries behind him, reached the High Street and dived into the porter's lodge of St Xavier's College.

St Xavier's was a relatively new College. It was not large, and by modern Oxford standards rather exclusive. Built on the corner of the Turl and the High, it occupied the sites of what had once been the Mitre Hotel and some of the eclectic shops behind it. It consisted of three quadrangles.

The Master's Lodgings were in the first quad to the right of the porter's lodge and, though an integral part of the College, constituted in effect a small, self-contained house.

Greg returned the porters' greetings and walked rapidly across the quad to the Lodgings. In these days of security consciousness a stranger might have been asked to state his business and open his briefcase, but no one would have thought to question a Fellow as well known as Greg White.

He went up the two steps to the heavy oak door, which was already unlocked in preparation for the meeting that was about to take place. He entered the short, square-shaped hall in time to see the Bursar go into the Master's study. He could hear a murmur of voices and guessed he was among the last arrivals. Then Ailsa Mackay came out of her office.

Ailsa was the Master's secretary. She was a plain, shy woman, one of Greg's first pupils, and she had been expected to get an excellent degree. But her father had died, there had been family difficulties, and she had gone down at the end of her second year. Subsequently she had returned to Oxford to take a secretarial course, and Greg had been influential in her getting her present post. If she carried a torch for him, she never let it show. They were friends, no more.

But Greg liked her, admired her, and was sorry for her, though he wouldn't have admitted the last. He had also completely forgotten about her. Her sudden appearance, a sheaf of papers in her hand, made him realize that she, who had never had the best of luck, would be sitting in the Master's study taking shorthand notes when the bomb he was carrying exploded. Faced with such a potential—and totally innocent—victim of the act he was about to commit he knew at last that he couldn't go through with it.

'Greg, are you all right? You've gone awfully pale.'

'Yes. Yes. I'm all right.'

He had to think and he had to think quickly. There was

very little time left. What could he do with the bloody
briefcase? He could not take it into the study, but he could
not leave the Lodgings and the College with it still in his
hand. He must put it somewhere—the lavatory?—and then
walk out of the College, showing himself to the watching
Tom as empty-handed, and set off up the Turl to his car—
and home, to Jean and Rosemary.

'Greg, what is it? Something's wrong. Tell me! I'll help
if I possibly can.'

'It's nothing!' She was holding his arm and he pulled it
away, being careful not to jog the briefcase. 'Tummy upset,
that's all. Must go to the loo.'

Conscious of Ailsa gazing after him, Greg strode towards
the cloakroom which was off the hall. He was wondering
about the best place to put the briefcase. He thought of the
cistern but that wasn't big enough. In the end he managed
to find room for it behind the lavatory pan. He activated
the flush and left. He could only hope that no one would
go in there for the next few minutes, and that two thick
walls would provide some protection for those in the study
across the hall.

Thankful that Ailsa hadn't waited for him to emerge he
let himself out of the Lodgings. There were several people
in the quad, among them Tony Pulent, who was leaning
against the wall of the Lodgings chatting to Hugh Fremont
and a younger man whom Greg didn't recognize. It was
impossible to ignore them.

'Hello, Greg. I was hoping to see you. I'm just here for
the day. Let me introduce my kid brother, Richard.'

'Hugh—' Greg began.

Hugh Fremont was one of the most brilliant students
that St Xavier's had produced. He had gone down a year
ago and was at present a Third Secretary at the Foreign
Office; great things were expected of him.

'How do you do, sir.'

Richard Fremont held out his hand and Greg, shaking it

briefly, was made aware of the dampness of his own palm. He couldn't stop. There was no time. But he couldn't leave the trio where they were; they were much too close to the wall of the cloakroom for safety, and any second now—

Tony, who knew him best, was regarding him anxiously. 'Mr White, are you unwell?'

'Listen!' Greg snapped. 'Do as I say and don't ask questions. Go to my rooms—all three of you! Now! At once!'

Without waiting to witness their amazed reactions, Greg sprinted across the quad to the lodge. As he reached it he caught a glimpse over his shoulder of the three young men moving slowly, very slowly, away from the vicinity of the Lodgings in the direction of his staircase. He wanted to scream at them to hurry, but he had to save his breath. To impress Dobson, the head porter, with the need for action was the more immediate necessity.

He burst into the lodge, and forced himself to speak emphatically and authoritatively, but without panic. 'Dobson, this is an emergency! There's a bomb in a briefcase in the cloakroom of the Master's Lodgings. It's due to go off any moment. Clear the Lodgings! Phone the police! You know what to do.'

Dobson had been a sergeant-major before he was invalided out of the army. He was used to emergencies and to taking and giving orders. Greg had scarcely finished speaking before he was shouting at the junior porter, a youth called Fairchild, who was open-mouthed at what he had just heard, to 'get over there and get everyone out'. At the same time, Dobson himself was dialling 999.

Greg didn't wait. He had done all he could. Now he must make sure of Jean's and Rosemary's safety. He paused for a moment outside the College. The High Street was busy with cars and bicycles, its pavements thronged with pedestrians. But there was no sign of a white van and, if the watchful Tom was on foot, Greg had no means of identifying him. Quickly Greg set off for his car, and home.

CHAPTER 6

The bomb exploded exactly on time just after Greg had turned the corner into Turl Street. The dull boom was loud and clear, and Greg even thought that he could feel the pavement shake for a moment beneath his feet. He realized at once that his warning had been too late. There was no hope that everyone had been able to comprehend a warning, appreciate the need for immediate action and leave the Master's Lodgings. Indeed, there was every possibility that the meeting had just started and they would all be in the study. All? Suddenly he remembered Lady Pinel and the cook-housekeeper; until that moment he had completely forgotten about them.

Feeling physically sick, he ignored the surge of excitement that surrounded him. Pedestrians stopped dead, and so did the traffic, brought to a halt at the corner of the High. Drivers left their vehicles. Everywhere startled faces expressed anxiety, curiosity, apprehension.

But almost immediately some individuals, mostly men, realizing the significance of the sound, began to run towards its source. Others shrugged and continued on their way. Greg himself hesitated, then decided to join the latter group. Questions would undoubtedly follow him, sooner rather than later he imagined, but his first priority was the welfare of his family. For the moment he must forget the consequences of his enforced action.

When the bomb went off, Fairchild, unaware that the main door of the Master's Lodgings was unlocked, had rung the bell and was pounding on the brass knocker. His senior, Dobson, had left the lodge and was running towards him, repeating his instructions to go in and get everyone out.

Tony Pulent and the two Fremont brothers had reached the middle of the quad, and there were perhaps half a dozen other dons or graduate students or undergraduates in the vicinity. All were startled, but none appreciated the immediate significance of what had happened.

One undergraduate who was leaning out of his window on the far side of the quad talking to a friend below, had an excellent view of events. Later, he described them graphically. 'There was a sound like an enormous muted bang,' he said. 'The shock came up through the floor. Part of the front wall of the Lodgings bulged outwards and then seemed to disintegrate. Stone and rubble showered down, overwhelming poor Fairchild. The blast knocked Dobson to the ground, but even as the dust settled he was staggering to his feet. The door to the Lodgings had been blown out and the chaos inside the hall was visible. It was horrific.'

Inside the Lodgings the meeting in the Master's study had just started. It was late, three minutes late, the amount of grace the Master had allowed Greg when Ailsa Mackay had said that Mr White had gone to the cloakroom and must be coming any moment. Sir Philip Pinel, as everyone in the College knew, was a stickler for punctuality and was not prepared to wait until—to use his own words—'Mr White condescended to grace us with his presence'.

It was ironic that the Master should have made such an acid remark about a man who, by his quick thinking and his actions, had almost certainly saved his life and the lives of the Bursar, three senior dons and Ailsa Mackay. For there was no doubt, according to the subsequent report of the police bomb squad, that had the explosion taken place in the study it was highly unlikely that anyone in the room would have survived.

As it was, though the study wall giving on to the hall stood up to the blast, the door was flung open and a small tornado engulfed the room. The window shattered, throwing glass splinters everywhere. Pictures fell to the floor, small objects, some of them surprisingly heavy, flew through the air like missiles, inflicting damage to people and property. Dust made breathing difficult and, as it settled, there became visible a nightmarish scene.

The Master lay slumped in his chair, blood streaming into his eyes from a cut in his brow inflicted by a heavy glass ashtray. The Bursar, who had chronic asthma, was gasping for breath. Ailsa had been hit in the face by a silver cigarette box and was badly bruised, her nose bleeding. Dr Harold Dawson, Senior Tutor of the College, seemed to be unconscious, though the reason was not immediately apparent. All those in the study were covered with small splinters of glass from the shattered window and all were suffering from shock. The room itself was a shambles.

Then, as the noise and dust subsided, from the hall came a high-pitched wailing scream that went on endlessly.

It was audible in the quad outside. It galvanized Hugh Fremont who, followed by his brother and Tony, raced towards the Lodgings. Dobson was already pulling at the rubble with his bare hands in an attempt to free young Fairchild. Hugh Fremont ignored him; others, recovering from their initial surprise and horror, were coming to help. Hugh led the way into the Lodgings.

The source of the screaming soon became clear. It was Lady Pinel, the Master's wife. She had been in her bedroom, dressing to go out, at the time the bomb exploded, and she had started to run downstairs, only to find that the last half-dozen steps were missing and that the hall was in a state of devastation. Stunned, she had retreated up the stairs and sat down, screaming hysterically.

'Give me a leg up,' Hugh ordered his brother.

'It may collapse,' Richard pointed out quickly.

But he did as he was told and Hugh, having tested the banister at the height of his reach, managed with a heave from Richard to pull himself on to the stairs. He crawled gingerly towards Lady Pinel, whose screams continued until he slapped her across the face, once, twice. He admitted afterwards to Greg that it had given him a good deal of satisfaction. Beatrice Pinel was not one of his favourite women.

Luckily, however, she was tall and thin and he was able to lower her down to Richard, who took her out into the quad and sat her on the grass, where she received help from a woman student who seemed to know what to do. Meanwhile, the Bursar had of his own accord staggered outside and was gasping and choking as he struggled for breath. The two dons who had suffered least, Dr Desmond Ansley and Mr Brian Mead, were doing their best to carry the Master from the Lodgings. Tony led Ailsa to safety and others carried out the unconscious Harold Dawson. Hugh, who had been forced to jump down from the staircase and had twisted his ankle, limped after them. In a matter of minutes the Lodgings had been cleared.

No one had been killed. Indeed, it seemed at the time that no one was to suffer permanent injury as a result of the outrage, though Dawson, an elderly man, had a minor heart attack and Fairchild was to spend some weeks in hospital with concussion and a broken leg. The remaining injuries were comparatively slight. Nevertheless, it had been an appalling incident, and a large part of the ground floor of the Master's Lodgings had been wrecked.

When the authorities arrived—first, two police officers from a patrol car, closely followed after a radio call by police reinforcements, ambulances, the fire service, and a little later senior police officers and the Thames Valley police bomb squad—the front quad of St Xavier's resembled the aftermath of an air raid combined with a battlefield casualty clearing station.

The fire service was not needed, but the ambulances were, and the more seriously injured were soon on their way to hospital. As soon as it was realized that the cause of the incident was almost certainly a bomb of some kind, the police started to clear the whole area—the College itself, the neighbouring buildings and the High Street, where a crowd of sightseers had gathered; some had even come into the College quad itself to gawp at the results of the explosion. They went without argument, aware now of the danger to themselves if there should be a second explosion—women with shopping-bags, a party of foreign visitors, some undergraduates. The only person who gave trouble was the Pinels' cook-housekeeper, who had been on a shopping excursion to the covered market nearby. She protested strongly at not being allowed to enter the College and only permitted to leave her heavy basket in the porter's lodge after it had been searched.

Among those who had managed to view the scene inside the quad was a young man, fairly tall, thin, with sandy hair, blue eyes and a crooked nose. He was wearing black trousers and a green leather jacket over a black shirt. There was nothing unusual about him—except perhaps for an ill-concealed grin—and he made no impression on the police officers. This was a pity, for Tom had left his white van in Broad Street, followed Greg to St Xavier's, seen him emerge without the briefcase, and noted with satisfaction the time of the explosion.

CHAPTER 7

It was at least fifteen minutes before the Thames Valley Police control room at their Kidlington Headquarters fully appreciated the situation. A bomb at St Xavier's College? Part of the Master's Lodgings destroyed? A number of casualties? Sure, there had been bombs in other parts of the area covered by the Thames Valley Police—one such

incident near Reading was even now under investigation—
but never before in the very centre of Oxford city. The idea
was, at first, unthinkable.

But training and reason reasserted themselves and the
Inspector on duty alerted Sir Philip Midvale, the Chief
Constable, who was immediately faced with a dilemma.
Normally, outrages of this kind would not be treated as
ordinary crimes, and the inquiries—demanding, as they
usually did, coordination and cooperation with technical
personnel, specialized forensic experts and even the Special
Branch from the Met.—would be handled by a specialist
officer and his team. But the officer in question was already
in Reading, and there was nothing for it but to hand the
matter over to the Serious Crime Squad. Fortunately, he
reflected quickly, Tansey was available.

Detective Chief Inspector Richard Tansey was far from
being a stupid man and, now in his late-thirties, he had few
illusions about human nature and would have claimed that
nothing could surprise him. But he was surprised now,
when he answered the Chief Constable's urgent call.

His first reaction mirrored that of the Inspector in the
control room. The area covered by the Thames Valley
Police was not without its quota of crime. There were the
usual numbers of burglaries, murders, rapes, acts of violence and less serious offences every year, not least in Oxford
City itself. This, however, was the first occasion that had
seen wanton destruction—and destruction apparently
caused by a bomb, of all things—inflicted on the persons
and property of a College and, what was more, apparently
within the College.

'Get along there at once, Chief Inspector, and take over-
all charge. You'll find a uniformed Inspector called Carey
holding the fort and doing what he can till you arrive. The
bomb squad technical boys are also on the job.' There had
been an edge to the Chief Constable's voice as he was
briefing Tansey—a minimal briefing, for few details were

available at that point. 'Until we know more, you'll report direct to me.'

'Yes, sir.' Tansey thought with regret of the pile of files remaining in his in-tray. 'You say there was a warning?'

'Apparently. Given by one of the dons, according to the head porter who called us originally. But it was much too late. Now, as I say, the bomb squad's already there, and they'll tell you what they require, if anything. I imagine the first thing will be a preliminary search for another device, if that's not been started already, and then a fingertip search of the immediate area—but the bomb boys will probably do that themselves; they know what to look for better than we do. Anyway, you know you can count on my full support.'

'Thank you, sir.'

Tansey had no need to ask why the Chief Constable was taking such a personal interest in this case. First, there was its seemingly unique character and, secondly, Tansey knew that Philip Midvale had himself been up at Oxford, and was attached to his old university.

'We must find the villains, Chief Inspector, and quickly.'

'I'll do my best, sir,' replied Tansey a little doubtfully. He knew that such inquiries sometimes stretched over long periods, even years, before anyone was brought to justice.

'I'm sure you will.' Midvale heaved his large bulk out of his outsize chair, signifying not only that the interview was at an end, but that he was unusually tense. His comment matched Tansey's private thoughts. 'Though I've got an idea this may not be all that elementary a case.' He gave Tansey a wry smile.

The remark and the smile brought an answering grin from the Chief Inspector. Tansey liked his Chief Constable and over the years had developed a close relationship with him. He also had an immense respect for his superior's judgement and instinct. But he hoped that on this occasion, their instincts had let down both Midvale and himself, and it would prove a simple case,—preferably, for example, an attempt at vandalism that had somehow got out of hand.

Tansey returned to his own office and acted rapidly. He sent for Detective-Sergeant Abbot, whom he planned to take with him. Bill Abbot was a cheerful, extrovert type, born and bred in Oxfordshire, and his knowledge of local people had often proved useful in the past. Tansey was aware that the explosion at St Xavier's probably had no local connections, but Abbot was always an excellent support

And since the Chief Constable had given him a free hand, Tansey decided to include a woman in his team. He chose a uniformed officer, WPC Robertson who, though young, was a plump and motherly type, but extremely shrewd. He knew that St Xavier's had begun to admit women undergraduates some years ago, and thought that Robertson might prove useful.

Tansey briefed Abbot and Robertson as well as he could, and they set off. It was a straight run from the Headquarters of the Thames Valley Force in Kidlington to the centre of Oxford, and Abbot drove fast. Yet by the time they arrived they found that some order had been restored in place of the initial chaos.

They were met by Inspector Carey who, with the help of the Bursar, had been busy setting up an incident room and an interview room. At least the College had plenty of space for such activities, and the Bursar—his name was Peter Lacque—was an efficient character who would probably have risen to the very top of the business world had he not been plagued with asthma all his life. In the present crisis, once he had regained his ability to breathe normally, he had assumed control of St Xavier's and was proving his worth.

Tansey introduced himself and the two officers with him, and Carey started his briefing without being asked. First and most importantly, the College had been subjected to a

preliminary search for further devices, and at least the front
quad declared safe. The end of Turl Street and part of
the High Street had been cordoned off for the present. In
response to Tansey's inquiry about casualties, Carey said
that ambulances had taken the Master and Lady Pinel, and
a Dr Harold Dawson and the young porter, Fairchild, to
hospital. A woman secretary, Ailsa Mackay, though
bruised and bloodstained, the side of her face swollen and
discoloured, had accepted first aid, but refused to go to
hospital. Dobson had returned to his lodge, and had also
obstinately refused to budge from his place of duty.

As a first step Tansey instructed WPC Robertson to
obtain from the Bursar and Dobson a complete list of members of St Xavier's, from the Master to the most lowly
undergraduate, with the position that each individual held.
He also wanted a list of all the employees and staff who
helped to keep the College running. And, in particular, he
needed to know who had been seen near the scene of the
crime before, during and after the explosion. They had all
been evacuated, of course, and Robertson was to try to
discover their present whereabouts.

Next the Chief Inspector went with Abbot to the Master's
Lodgings, where it was obvious that a detailed so-called
'fingertip' search of every square inch of the ground floor
and the area outside the building was already in progress.
The head of the bomb squad, a quiet, bespectacled young
man, came out to meet them.

'Quite a mess, sir,' he said, by way of a greeting. 'But it
could have been much worse. Whoever planted the device
put it in a damned stupid place—from his point of view, I
mean. It was in the downstairs cloakroom, jammed behind
the toilet pan, and the pan partially shielded the rest of the
house. Even so, it was a powerful little trinket. It was lucky
no one was killed.'

'I'd like to see inside.'

'Of course, sir. There's no danger. I expect Inspector

Carey's told you that this quad has been declared safe, and I'm practically certain there isn't another bomb elsewhere in the College. Incidentally, from the debris we've found already, I'd guess that this one was in a leather bag of some kind.'

Tansey and Abbot followed him into the building. Two men were still examining the cloakroom. One of them said, 'I've found a bit of a timing device. It looks pretty primitive to me.'

'What about the bomb itself?' asked Tansey. 'It's done an impressive amount of damage, I would say, but could it have been someone's idea of a black joke that misfired?'

The three experts shook their heads in unison. 'Definitely not,' said the senior man. 'We shan't be certain what explosive was used until we get everything we find back to the lab, but I can tell you now that this was no prank. It was for real, all right. Whoever planted the thing must have had a fair idea of the impact it would have. On the other hand . . .'

'Yes?' Tansey prompted.

'It's early days yet. I don't want to stick my neck out. But somehow this hasn't got the hallmarks of a professional job. For one thing, if it was an act of pure terrorism, why choose a small and not particularly well-known College? Why not Balliol or Christ Church?' He grinned suddenly. 'I'm afraid I'm usurping your territory, Chief Inspector.'

Tansey laughed. 'I'm always open to suggestions. If you have any more, add them at the end of your report.'

'Will do, sir.'

Tansey and Abbot picked their way through the rubble of the hall, had a look at the truncated staircase and then inspected the Master's study. The rest of the ground floor, except for the odd picture that had fallen off a wall, appeared largely undamaged.

'What next, sir?' asked Abbot as they emerged into the quad. 'The Bursar?'

'Not yet. We'll give him a little more time to help Inspector Carey and settle us in. We may be here for some while.' Tansey was already striding towards the porter's lodge. 'Let's have a chat with this chap Dobson. It was he who gave the warning, late though it was.'

In the lodge Ailsa Mackay had been disinfecting the cuts on Dobson's hands and, in spite of his protests, putting dressings on the worst of them. She had borrowed a white coat from a science student to cover the bloodstains on her blouse and skirt, but she couldn't disguise her swollen face. Nor was her appearance improved by her worried frown at the trend of her talk with Dobson.

'I don't understand, Miss Mackay,' Dobson reiterated. 'If Mr White knew there was a bomb in the Lodgings—'

'I don't understand either, Dobson, but I'm sure Mr White will have a perfectly good explanation.'

'What about the police? What shall I tell them?'

Ailsa sighed. 'The truth. Answer their questions. But—but there's no need to volunteer information, Dobson.'

The porter laughed. 'I learnt that long ago in the army, Miss Mackay.'

The arrival of Tansey and Abbot prevented further private conversation. Ailsa gave her name, hurriedly excused herself and then made her escape, although she knew that she was probably only securing a temporary respite. Tansey made no attempt to detain her, but he thought her eagerness to depart interesting.

'William Dobson, sir. At your service.'

'Thank you, Mr Dobson. I was sure the police could depend on your help, which is why we came here to start our inquiries, once we'd surveyed the scene.' Tansey wondered why he was being so unctuous, and realized that he had been copying the porter; neither of them was entirely sincere. 'It was you who gave the alarm, wasn't it?'

'You could say that, sir.'

'And just what could *you* say, Dobson?' Tansey's manner had changed. 'Was it or was it not you who called 999 and said there was a bomb in the cloakroom of the Master's Lodgings here? Yes or no?'

'Yes—sir.'

'How did you know?'

'Mr White—he's a Fellow of the College here—he came into the lodge and told me.'

'So what did you do?'

'Mr White said to ring the police, which I did, and I sent Fairchild—that's my junior who's in hospital now, poor chap—to get everyone out of the Lodgings. But the bomb went off while he was at the front door.'

'You were still here?'

'No. I was on my way across the quad to help Fairchild.'

'And this Mr White? What did he do?'

'I've no idea, sir.' It was a lie; Dobson had seen Greg White leave the College, but he had no intention of saying so. As he had told Ailsa Mackay, he didn't understand Mr White's behaviour, but he agreed with her implied suggestion that it wasn't up to him to tell tales to the police.

'I see,' said Tansey thoughtfully. 'And there's nothing more you can tell us that might help with our inquiries?'

'I don't think so, sir.'

'I see,' said Tansey again. 'Well, many thanks—for the moment, Dobson.' He turned to Abbot. 'Sergeant, I think it's time we went and had a talk with the Bursar. And in the meantime we'll ask Inspector Carey to see if he can track down this Mr White.'

Directed by Carey, they found the Bursar in his office on the ground floor of one of the front quad staircases. After Tansey had expressed his consternation at the attack on St Xavier's, he asked Mr Lacque about that morning's meeting.

'These meetings are held every other Monday in term-time,' the Bursar explained. 'They start punctually at nine-thirty and usually last an hour and a half to two hours, depending on the agenda. They're chaired by the Master, of course, and attended by his Secretary, Miss Mackay, the department heads, myself and often, if there's a particular problem to be discussed, one of the other Fellows.'

'The routine was well known?'

'Throughout the College. Oh yes.'

'And this morning's meeting was seemingly no different from any other?'

'In composition, no, though we were rather light on the ground—fortunately, as it happened. Let me see. Who was there? The Master, Miss Mackay, Dr Ansley, Dr Dawson, Mr Mead and myself. Mr Chapman, who's an athletic type, was painting his house over the weekend and fell off a ladder, so he had made excuses. Mr Beale's wife phoned to say he was laid low with a temperature. You've got all that?' He addressed the query to Abbot.

'Yes, sir. Thank you, sir,' Sergeant Abbot acknowledged by holding up his notebook. 'I can check the spelling of the names with the list of members of St Xavier's.'

'Good. And Miss Mackay will provide any further details you need, and tell you about Mr White. I'd prefer she did that herself. He was due to attend the meeting but he never arrived.'

The Bursar looked at his watch. 'Chief Inspector, with the Master and Dr Dawson, the Senior Tutor, both in hospital I've a hundred and one things to see to, as you can imagine. Could we possibly continue this later? I'm sure there are other people you wish to interview.'

'Of course, Mr Lacque. Thank you for giving me such a clear general picture of the situation, but just one more question. Can you think of anyone who might have committed this crime?'

'No, I can't, Chief Inspector. We're a very peaceful

College. We've never had any sort of political or racial trouble here.'

The Bursar was clearly eager to leave, and Tansey didn't press the point, though he had not himself been thinking in such broad terms. He rose to his feet with Abbot and left the office.

Outside in the quad they found Inspector Carey waiting to escort them to the rooms that the College had set aside for the use of the police. They were normally used by a Dr Cathcart, who was in hospital recovering from peritonitis, and they overlooked the front quad from the ground floor of a staircase near the Bursar's office. The set consisted of two rooms, opening off a small hall, as did a small bathroom. The rooms were usually furnished as a study and a bedroom. Now a couple of uniformed constables were moving in desks and equipment from a van parked outside in the quad. The original study—the larger of the two—would become the incident room, and the bedroom Tansey's office and the interview room. Tansey nodded his approval.

'Mr White doesn't appear to be in the College, sir,' said Carey. 'At any rate, he can't be found. He was last seen heading towards the porter's lodge a few minutes before the incident. But Dobson wouldn't commit himself. I went over the same ground that you did, but all he'd say was that Mr White *might* have left the College. Dobson wasn't exactly cooperative.'

Tansey grinned. 'I noticed that too.'

'I tried to phone the Whites' house—they live in North Oxford—but the line's dead. The phone company's looking into it. Shall I put out a call for this Mr White?'

'No-o. It's a bit soon. But you might send an officer out to the Whites to make sure everything's all right there. If White himself is at home bring him back here.'

'Will do, sir. Here's WPC Robertson for you, sir.' Carey held the door open for her.

'People are trickling back into College, sir, now that it's

been searched,' she said. 'I've got the list of members—that was simple. I've also got a preliminary list of possible witnesses. It's long, sir, and still may not be complete, but I've done my best to sort out the ones you might like to see first. There's one young student, Peregrine Courcey, who claims to have witnessed 'the whole show' as he called it from the window of his rooms.'

'Really? Sounds too good to be true.'

'It probably is, sir,' Abbot remarked cynically.

'Nevertheless, we'll have him in.'

Peregrine Courcey proved to be an elegant character, who was not in the least abashed at being interviewed by two detective officers. He said good morning cheerfully, sat and crossed his long legs, carefully adjusting the creases in the trousers of the checked suit he was wearing. He also had an embroidered waistcoat and his hair was unfashionably shoulder-length. All in all, he looked more like a dilettante (in the true sense of the word, thought Tansey, who was keen on the correct usage of English) than an undergraduate.

'I saw it all,' said Courcey, 'or almost all. I had a wonderful view, a front seat in the dress circle, you might say.' He gave his graphic description, and concluded, 'I must admit those three chaps impressed me—dashing into the place to rescue people like that. There could easily have been another bomb.'

Tansey glanced questioningly at his Sergeant, who referred to his notes. 'Mr Hugh and Mr Richard Fremont, and Mr Anthony Pulent.'

'That's right,' Courcey continued. 'Actually, they were jolly lucky. They were standing right by the wall that collapsed, when Greg White came out of the Lodgings. He spoke to them for a few moments. From his gestures it almost looked at if he was ordering them away—but they'll tell you about that, of course. If they'd not moved, they'd have been buried like the porter chap.'

'Where did they go?'

'They just started to stroll across the quad, and then the bomb went off.'

'And Mr White went with them, did he?'

'Oh no. He went over to the lodge.'

'Was he carrying anything?'

The question puzzled Courcey. 'What sort of anything?'

'Forget it. Would you say this was a quiet, peaceful college, Mr Courcey?'

The question was greeted with a hoot of laughter. 'After this morning? You must be joking, Chief Inspector.'

Tansey had not been joking. 'Let me put it another way,' he said. 'You're in your fourth year here?'

'Yes. I'm reading Greats.'

'Then you should know the place well. Would you say there was any element in St Xavier's College which felt strongly about politics or race or religion, for example?'

Courcey stared at Tansey. 'You're thinking this was a terrorist bomb?' he asked. Then he added, 'I doubt it, myself.'

Sergeant Abbot was entertained to see that the Chief Inspector had been taken aback. Mr Peregrine Courcey might appear to be an elegant fop, but he wasn't lacking in imagination. Head on one side, he appeared to be considering the matter further. Tansey remained silent.

'Terrorism?' repeated Courcey at last. 'No, Chief Inspector. We do have a certain number of chaps who aren't white Anglo-Saxon Protestants, and I myself wouldn't vote Conservative. But, praise be, there's never been any violence here till today, and if this was meant to be some kind of demonstration I can't imagine why an outsider should pick on us. To be honest, though we've been criticized for being fairly snobbish in our choice of undergraduates, in reality we're a pretty dim place—especially since people like Amanda Hulton and Hugh Fremont and that set went down.'

'So who were Amanda Hulton and that set?'

Courcey considered the Chief Inspector for a moment. Then he said, 'Well, I suppose *you* might have called us bright young things, Chief Inspector. I was one of them myself, though I wasn't their year. But I was at school with Hugh.'

'I see,' said Tansey. 'So all you've said would suggest the bomb was a personal attack on the Master and those who attend these regular meetings.'

'The hierarchy of St Xavier's? I suppose it would, Chief Inspector, but I couldn't begin to guess who'd do such a thing, or why.'

'Well, thank you very much, Mr Courcey.'

'My pleasure, Chief Inspector.'

Tansey was thoughtful as Peregrine Courcey left. He had been impressed by the young man, whose instinct had helped to support his own growing belief that St Xavier's College had not been the victim of an act of terrorism, but of something more personal. For this reason his interest in Gregory White was increasing. There was still no news of White.

Courcey was followed by Hugh and Richard Fremont and Tony Pulent. As soon as they were seated, Tansey congratulated them on their efforts at rescuing the occupants of the Master's Lodgings. Then he asked, 'Did Mr White say anything to you about a bomb when he came out of the Lodgings just before the explosion?'

There was a brief silence, then: 'A bomb? Certainly not!' This from Hugh Fremont. 'How could he know?'

'As I understand it, Mr White went straight from talking to you to the porter's lodge, where he told Dobson to call the police and warn everyone in the Lodgings.' Tansey let them absorb this information which he suspected they were already aware of. 'Are you sure he didn't warn you? Did he seem upset at all?'

'No.' Hugh was casual. 'I introduced my brother, whom

he'd not met before, and we had a brief conversation. Incidentally, who says he told Dobson there was a bomb in the Lodgings?'

Tansey didn't answer. Instead he asked a question of his own. 'Did you notice if he was carrying anything—a briefcase, say?'

'No,' said Hugh Fremont.

'Yes,' said his brother.

Tansey addressed Richard, whom he had recognized as the most vulnerable of the trio. 'Do you mean Mr White *was* carrying a briefcase?'

'I mean, I did notice, and he wasn't. I shook hands with him and I'd have seen it,' Richard mumbled.

'What about you, Mr Pulent?'

Tony shrugged. 'I didn't notice, but I can tell you one thing, Chief Inspector. If you're accusing Greg White of being responsible for that explosion, you're making a big mistake. I live next door to him and his family. I've known him all my life. And there's not a better man anywhere.'

'I'd second that,' said Hugh.

'I'm not accusing Mr White—or anyone else,' Tansey said mildly. 'It's much too early for anything like that. I'm just trying to build up a general picture of the quad and the incident.'

This was not untrue, but clearly they didn't believe him. They answered the rest of his questions guardedly, almost sullenly, and he learnt nothing more of value from them. After they had left he turned to Abbot. 'What do you think, Sergeant?'

'This Mr White seems an odd bloke.'

'Quite,' said Tansey shortly. 'Let's try the secretary. What's her name?' He looked at the list in front of him. 'Ah, Ailsa Mackay, of course.'

Ailsa Mackay proved a great help. Her files were in her office in the Master's Lodgings, but she had a good memory and without difficulty produced confirmatory information about those who had been present at the Monday meeting, and those who should have been there but for one reason or another had not attended. It was only when Tansey asked her to describe the events of the morning and mentioned Mr White that he sensed she had become wary.

'You say Mr White was the last to arrive. You met him in the hall. Was he carrying a bag?'

'His briefcase.'

'Did you actually see him go into the cloakroom?'

'Yes. I watched him because ... He'd said his inside was upset and he looked ill.'

'You didn't see him leave the cloakroom?'

'No. I went into the Master's study. I expected Mr White to arrive, but he didn't. I imagine he didn't feel well enough. The meeting started and then there was this explosion.'

Tansey, who felt rather sorry for the woman—her poor swollen face would have roused anyone's pity—thanked her. As she turned to go she glanced out of the window which gave a good view of the quad and the porter's lodge.

'Here's Mr White now—just coming into College,' she said suddenly, unable to hide her relief.

CHAPTER 8

Greg White reached Broad Street with relief. He got in his car and automatically started for home, driving in a trance. It was not until he was turning off the Banbury Road that his mind cleared and it occurred to him that he was perhaps behaving foolishly. As far as he could recall there had been no sign that the white van had followed him home—in his dazed state he had forgotten to check whether or not it had gone from the place where he had last seen it outside Balliol—but the gunman whom he had left at his house might well still be there, ready to add his corpse to those of Jean and Rosemary. He had trusted the man because there had been no choice, but he need not walk into a trap now. He could go to a neighbour's—the Pulents, obviously—and call the police. But explanations would be complex and lengthy. Could his family wait? No. He must act himself, in case . . .

Nevertheless, he parked his car a little way along the road, and walked to the house. It looked quiet and peaceful, normal in every respect. If anyone had noticed that the curtains upstairs and downstairs were not yet drawn the fact probably wouldn't have been given a second thought. He went up the drive and cautiously circled the house. At the end of the sitting-room window most distant from the front door, a slight gap had been left in the curtains and he peered in.

'Oh no!' he said under his breath. 'Please God, no!'

Rosemary was lying on the carpet. She was motionless and it was impossible for Greg to tell if she was breathing, but he could see that the manacles were still on her ankles.

Without further hesitation he ran to the front door and thrust his key into the lock, flung open the door—and stopped dead. Jean was lying on the floor of the hall in much the same position as her daughter.

But, hearing him, she had raised her head. 'Greg!' she cried. 'Thank God you're back! We thought you'd been— We thought you'd never come.'

He knelt beside her. 'Darling, are you all right?' It was a stupid question, but—

'Yes. Yes.' Jean was impatient. 'The man's gone. He went ages ago and he kept his promise; he didn't hurt either of us.' Her voice rose to a shout. 'Darling, it's Daddy. He'll get the keys.'

'What keys?'

'The keys to these damned handcuffs, of course. The man said he'd leave them in the sitting-room. We waited and waited, but when no one came we decided to try to reach them ourselves.' Jean was impatient. 'But it's almost impossible to walk with one's ankles and hands chained like this. Rosemary was better at it than I was, which is why she's in there now.'

'Hold on a moment.'

Greg hurried into the sitting-room. 'Oh, darling!' He gave Rosemary a brief hug. 'The keys?'

'They're on the mantelpiece. I can see them, but I can't get to them.'

Greg found the keys and, after some fumbling, unlocked Rosemary's manacles. She rubbed her wrists and legs, and he lifted her up and sat her in an armchair.

'Be with you in a moment,' he called to the hall.

'Dad!' Rosemary stopped him from leaving her. 'The bomb? Did it explode? Was anyone hurt?'

'Later.' Greg didn't wait. He had no wish to discuss the situation, not yet. 'I must get your mother. We'll talk in a few minutes. Then I'll have to go.'

'Go? Where?'

Greg didn't answer. He returned to the hall and freed Jean. He didn't know if it was because of his relief at finding them both safe and unharmed, but he suddenly felt exhausted. As he supported Jean into the sitting-room he noticed that the telephone socket had been ripped from the wall. It meant that he couldn't phone Lorna Pulent or anyone else for support, couldn't ask anyone to come and stay with Jean and Rosemary. On the other hand, he couldn't leave them alone. Nevertheless, it was vital that he returned to the College as quickly as possible. His first reaction to what had or had not been the results of the explosion had now been overcome by an urgent need to know the worst.

'I'm going to pop next door and fetch Lorna,' he said. 'She'll come and stay with you, keep you company. Would you like her to phone the doctor?'

'Greg, we don't want a doctor. And we don't want Lorna.

First, make us some coffee and tell us what happened at St
Xavier's. Then we'll get washed and dressed. We're quite
all right now it's over, shaken naturally, but—'

'I can't leave you alone.'

'We won't be alone. You'll be here—or are you going
somewhere?'

'I must get back to the College.'

'For God's sake, Greg, *why*? If people have been killed
there's nothing you can do about it.'

'Maybe I can help in some way, and in any case I have
to talk to the police, tell them what I did. They'll want to
talk to both of you too, I'm sure.'

'But not immediately.'

'The sooner the better. Those men were dangerous.
They've got to be caught.'

'Of course, but—Greg, this has been a pretty harrowing
experience for all of us. Surely we're entitled to a brief
respite, just to be together for a few minutes as a family.
and feel safe again. It's not much to ask.'

'Jean, there's something you should know, you and Rosemary. I didn't do exactly what they wanted. In the end, I
couldn't.' Greg thought for a moment of Ailsa Mackay. 'If
I'd left the briefcase in the study, I think everyone there
would have been killed.'

'So what *did* you do?' Jean's voice had become cold and
distant.

'I put the briefcase in the downstairs loo at the Lodgings.
I hoped it might save . . . And then as I left the College I
warned Dobson, told him to call the police and get everyone
out of the Lodgings before the bomb went off.'

'Oh, Dad, that was clever of you—and brave.' Rosemary,
who had been listening intently, was admiring.

'It was neither clever not brave! Don't be stupid, Rosemary! What your father did has put us all at risk again.
Once those men discover he's deceived them, God knows
what they'll do.'

'I'm sorry, but I don't think it's as bad as that. They may not even find out. I was careful to make sure that there were no signs of an emergency before I'd left. That's one of the reasons I must get back to College, discover who—who was hurt, and what damage was done. A lot may depend on that. Then, as I say, I have to talk to the police—the senior officer—whoever's in charge there. Darling, try to understand.'

'I understand all right.' Jean rose to her feet. 'But don't expect me to agree with you, Greg. Clearly we've got different priorities. So don't worry about us. I'll get the coffee and I'll cope here. You go back to your beloved College.'

She stalked out of the sitting-room without a glance at him, and Greg sighed heavily. Jean didn't understand, he thought, but he couldn't blame her. He was not altogether sure that he understood himself. Perhaps he'd been wrong. 'Perhaps I was a fool,' he said aloud.

'No, Dad! No! You were right.' Rosemary had no doubts. She came to him and hugged him, and Greg thought that if anything happened to her—or to Jean—because of what he'd done, or not done, he would never forgive himself.

In fact, Greg did not leave home immediately, but forced himself to stay to drink coffee with Jean and Rosemary. He told himself that Jean was considerably more upset than she appeared to be on the surface, and that he owed it to her to give her love and support. But if his intentions were good, the results were the reverse. Jean remained bitter, and frightened at what might happen to them because of what she considered to have been Greg's uncompromising attitude. She refused to forgive him for not putting her and Rosemary first, before the welfare of his colleagues.

They bickered with ever-increasing intensity until Rosemary simply left them and went upstairs to dress. She still hadn't told them that she had seen Tom's face. Somehow there had never been a suitable moment before, and she realized that now it would be yet another bone of contention between her parents. Her father would feel she should tell the police; her mother, after the warning they had been given about not describing the gunmen, would want her to forget what she had seen. She heard the front door slam as she got under the shower, and she knew that her father had gone again.

He had not parted from Jean happily. Her last remark— indeed, it was a statement—still rang in his ears as he went towards his car. 'Don't expect anyone except Rosemary to think you a hero, Greg. You've achieved exactly *nothing*! You've put your family in great danger again, and the chances are you'll be charged with blowing up the College and causing bodily harm—or worse—to your beloved colleagues, whom you care about more than your family. So let them visit you in prison, because I shan't.'

Then Jean had picked up the coffee mugs and gone into the kitchen. He could hear her angrily stacking china and cutlery in the dishwasher, uncaring whether any piece became chipped or broken. He no longer cared, either. Without calling goodbye he went, slamming the front door behind him. As he got behind the wheel of his car he was shaking.

Until Jean's last virulent attack on him, it had not occurred to him to consider what the consequences of his actions might be for himself. His primary concern had been for Jean and Rosemary and the need to protect them; then he had done his best to save Ailsa and whomsoever might be in the study when the explosion took place. The fact that, according to Jean, he had failed in the first of these efforts made it even more important that he should find out what success he had achieved in the second.

So once again he set off for St Xavier's. Once again he

was lucky and parked in Broad Street without any trouble, but he found his way barred half way down the Turl. The street was still cordoned off and traffic redirected along Ship Street, though members and staff had been allowed back into the adjoining colleges. Obviously representatives of the media were there in force, though they too were compelled to remain outside the barricade.

It took Greg several minutes to persuade a police constable to allow him to go as far as St Xavier's lodge, and as he was allowed through, his passage was followed by the clicking of cameras.

In the lodge he was greeted by Dobson. 'Mr White, am I glad to see you! Everyone's been looking for you, sir, asking where you'd got to.' Dobson carefully didn't say, 'gone to'. He went on. 'There's a Chief Inspector, name of Tansey, wants to speak to you. The Bursar set him and his sergeant up in Dr Cathcart's rooms.'

'If you'd come along with me, please, sir.' The police officer who was sharing the lodge with Dobson spoke politely but with authority. He had been warned that White might appear; the officer who had left for the Whites' house had phoned Inspector Carey to report that, according to Mrs White, her husband was on his way to the College.

'One moment!' Greg was adamant. 'Dobson—Dobson— was anyone badly hurt—or killed?'

'Not too badly, sir. Four of them have been hospitalized, but I gather they'll all survive.'

'Thank God for that.'

Greg felt weak. This was better news than he had dared to hope for; any damage to the Lodgings—and, looking across the quad, he could see from here that it was extensive—was insignificant beside the loss of life there might have been. The police officer was showing impatience, but Greg ignored him.

'Who?'

'The Master and Lady Pinel, sir, and the Senior Tutor
and Fairchild. It's the young lad's situation that's the most
worrying. He lives with his mother who's a bit of an invalid
and—'

'Mr White, sir!' the police officer was becoming annoyed.

'I'm right with you. Don't worry, Dobson, I'll cope with
the Fairchilds.'

Greg followed the police officer across the quad. His
thoughts were chaotic. He knew he should be concentrating on his coming meeting with this Chief Inspector
Tansey; he hoped the man would prove intelligent and
understanding, and not be some blockhead eager for
promotion. But his spirits had soared. No one had been
killed. No one had been permanently maimed or Dobson
would have said so. Almost euphoric in his relief, he
bumped into Ailsa Mackay as she came out of the
staircase he was entering.

'Greg! Are you all right?'

'Yes. I'm fine, but you—you—your poor face. My dear,
I am sorry.'

'It's not your fault. I'm sure of that, Greg.'

Ailsa squeezed his arm, and gave him what she hoped
was an encouraging smile though, distorted by her bruises,
it was more like a grimace. But Greg knew what she was
trying to convey, and he was grateful.

'Ailsa, I may be some time with the police. Could you
arrange to let Fairchild's mother know what's happened,
and give her whatever help's needed?'

'The police have already informed her and Hugh Fremont is driving Margaret Sandown out to Iffley, where the
Fairchilds live.' Miss Sandown was a junior don. 'She's a
sensible girl. She'll cope.'

'Good. I hope to see them as soon as I can. Meantime,
if there's any question of money—'

'Greg, don't worry about the Fairchilds.' Ailsa wanted
to add, 'And don't blame yourself, whatever's happened,'

but with the police officer standing near it didn't seem a
politic comment.

'Chief Inspector, I'm the man responsible for planting that
bomb in the lavatory of the Master's Lodgings.'

Tansey hesitated for a moment, wondering about the
applicability of the Judge's Rules in this unique and bizarre
situation—a situation he had never before faced. Then he
said, 'May I take that as a voluntary confession, Mr White?'

'Certainly. But the act itself was the reverse of voluntary.'

'Ah,' said Tansey. 'So—'

While Greg told his story Tansey and Abbot listened and
observed. They noted what appeared to be anomalies in his
account. They noted how his voice broke when he described
his fear for his daughter when she had been prevented from
escaping. They noted the warmth with which he spoke of
Ailsa Mackay and Tony Pulent, and his seeming restraint
when he mentioned his wife. They noted his self-disgust at
what he described as his own inadequacies, and his relief
that no one had been killed or permanently maimed.

'. . . and that's about all I can tell you,' Greg concluded.

Tansey sat quite still for a moment, considering. Then
he glanced at Abbot, said 'Excuse me', and went through
the hall into the incident room, where he found Inspector
Carey. Briefly he passed on the story—was it a 'story', he
wondered fleetingly, or was it the exact truth?—that Greg
had told, and immediately gave his instructions.

'Get some uniformed men out to that house at once.
Whatever the rights or wrongs of the matter, the occupants
may be in danger. A marked car outside, and some
uniformed men. And make sure one or two are armed. Then
get a scene of crime team into the house. One of them can
pick up White's dabs here. I know he says these gunmen
wore gloves all the time, but they must have gone for a pee
at least once, and you don't often keep gloves on for that.
Get the loos checked for unusual prints. Get the place

searched. Get those damned handcuffs White talks about—there should be four or six sets. See if there's anything to support White's story. But make sure no one questions his wife or daughter. I'll do that myself later.'

'Will do, sir,' said Carey laconically as Tansey went back to his office.

Here Greg and Abbot were sitting in an almost companionable silence. Tansey knew that Abbot had done the best possible thing, and made sure that White was relaxed and at his ease; that was just how he liked his witnesses—or suspects.

'Now, sir,' he said, sitting behind his desk, 'you remarked that you'd told us all you could, but I doubt it. Witnesses always know more than they think they do. Perhaps we could go through what you've said again. Then we'll have your statement typed and get you to sign it.'

'Will it take long? I'm worried about my wife and daughter.'

'Quite a time, I'm afraid. But don't worry about your family; they'll be taken care of.' Greg looked up in surprise, but Tansey didn't answer the implied question. Instead, he said, 'Let's start at the beginning again.'

In fact, the process took longer than either of them expected, because Tansey found it necessary to interrupt frequently, so that the interview became an interrogation. When Greg hoped he had satisfied one query, there were always one or two more, such as precisely what he had said to Tony Pulent and the Fremont brothers.

'Why did you tell them to go to your rooms, Mr White?'

'It was the first thing that came into my head. I had to get them away from that wall.'

'You didn't mind about Miss Mackay or your colleagues in the Master's study?'

'Of course I minded! Haven't I made that clear? But if I'd tried to warn them they'd have come streaming out of the Lodgings and this Tom might have seen what was happening from outside the porter's lodge. I had to make sure he saw me come out of the College without the briefcase *before* the bomb went off. At that point there was every chance he'd make a getaway himself. Don't you see, I couldn't risk Rosemary and Jean. I've risked them too much anyway, or so Jean thinks, by not obeying orders, as it were.'

It was an admission that explained some of the anomalies in White's story, and Tansey was becoming increasingly sympathetic with the man and his dilemma. Nevertheless, he had a job to do. Whatever White's motivation, he had committed a crime which might have produced an horrendous result.

'Mr White, I must ask you what I'm asking everyone. Do you know anyone who might have had a grudge against the Master, Sir Philip Pinel, or against St Xavier's?'

Greg wiped his brow with the back of his hand. He was tired. He had been woken shockingly in the early hours and had been under great strain ever since. Somehow during the Chief Inspector's questioning his euphoric relief that no one had been seriously injured had waned. By now he was having difficulty in thinking clearly.

'Not off-hand, Chief Inspector,' he replied at last. 'The Michaelmas Term has just started and the last university year was quiet and uneventful as far as I recall.' Greg hesitated. 'We did have a case of petty pilfering shortly before Christmas last year. It turned out to be one of the scouts and he was sacked, but—'

'His name?'

Greg shook his head. 'I can't remember. He hadn't been with the College very long. Ailsa—Miss Mackay—would know. But isn't it a bit far-fetched to imagine—'

'We have to consider every possibility, Mr White. Is there anyone else you can think of?'

'No!' Greg regretted having mentioned the scout; clearly Ailsa had forgotten the incident, or not thought it worth mentioning.

'All right, Mr White. I'll pass you to Inspector Carey now. He'll arrange for your statement to be typed and get your fingerprints taken—for purposes of elimination when we go through your house. By that time Sergeant Abbot and I should be ready to call on your wife and daughter. You can come with us, and an officer will bring your car. Don't be surprised to find uniformed men on duty outside the house—you can guess why; in fact, you've already shown that you're aware of the possibilities. And there will be some officers examining the house, too, but they won't worry you. I'll be there myself to talk to your wife and daughter.'

'Of course, Chief Inspector.' Greg's smile was wry, as he wondered how Jean would accept the idea of house arrest.

CHAPTER 9

Tansey had declared a half-hour break from the inter-viewing, and on the Bursar's orders one of the scouts had brought soup, sandwiches and tankards of beer from the buttery to the set of rooms formerly occupied by Dr Cath-cart. The Chief Inspector and his sergeant ate in silence. Abbot was thinking about his wife and his first child, soon to be born; Tansey was considering what Greg White had said, and its implications. It was this difference between them, as Bill Abbot had once humorously remarked, that had made Dick Tansey a Chief Inspector, while he himself remained a sergeant.

After the meal, at Inspector Carey's request, Tansey went out to make a brief statement to the media. A tele-vision crew had been allowed into the quad, and was busy filming the ruined frontage of the Master's Lodgings. Press and radio reporters—both locals and stringers from the national press—were questioning anyone who would talk to them, under the watchful eyes of a couple of uniformed officers. But as soon as Tansey appeared, they surged towards him, shouting their queries.

'How big was the bomb?'—'Who was it intended for?'— 'Why St Xavier's?'—'Was it the IRA?'—'The Red Brigade?'—'What about casualties?'—'Anyone killed?'—'Who was hurt?'—'Any ideas yet?'

Tansey held up a hand. 'I always have ideas, but at this stage I prefer to keep them to myself. It's only a few hours after the incident, so I'd have to be a genius to answer all your questions. I hope that tomorrow I'll be able to give a full press conference. Meanwhile, I'll tell you two things. First, four people have been hospitalized—including the Master of St Xavier's College and his wife—but I understand that none of them is in any serious danger. Secondly, I'll hazard a guess: this was not the work of any terrorist or political organization, but of two or three individuals who had some personal reason for their action.'

In the surprise which greeted his last comment Tansey was able to make his escape and return to his room. He knew that he would be quoted, and probably misquoted, and that if his guess—which after all was no more than a reasonable surmise—proved to be wrong, he would have to bear the brunt of the criticism that would inevitably follow.

Tansey found Dr Ansley and Mr Mead waiting for him. In appearance they made a somewhat comical duo. Desmond Ansley was a tall, almost gaunt-looking man in his fifties; Brian Mead, not yet forty, was short and podgy, with a round baby face. Although physically unharmed except for a few superficial cuts from the shattered study window, they had both suffered from shock and had done their best to recover from it by a large intake of wine during lunch. As a result, though they were not drunk, they were by no means totally sober.

Tansey listened patiently while, in a kind of double act, the two dons described their experiences before and immediately after the explosion. He complimented them on their behaviour in rescuing Dr Dawson and asked them some general questions. He had little hope of learning anything fresh from them, but in this he was proved wrong. They had had time to consider the situation and, being far from stupid, had come up with some interesting ideas.

'Terrorism in some form would appear to be the obvious answer,' said Ansley, 'but we decided to reject it. We couldn't imagine any terrorist group worth its salt planting a bomb in the Master's downstairs loo.'

He paused while Tansey waited, and eventually continued, 'Look, we know it's no joking matter, but—the downstairs loo, where it would do the least harm. The idea's almost laughable. And even if one or two of us had been killed, what on earth would have been achieved? As far as we know, none of those in the study has even been involved with politics or the armed forces or even the police.'

'The alternative would seem to be someone with a grudge against the College in general, or the Master as a symbol of the College,' Mead intervened. 'If it were against any particular senior member other than Sir Philip, it would have been much simpler to attack him—or her—at home, rather than in the Master's Lodgings. On the other hand, as the day and time were clearly chosen so that the explosion would coincide with the start of one of our regular meetings, it's arguable that the Master was not the sole target.'

'Quite,' said Tansey. 'There's a good deal in what you say. In fact, my own thoughts have been running along similar lines.' Ansley and Mead exchanged satisfied glances. Then Tansey, expecting a largely negative reply, added, 'And have you any suggestion as to who might be the—the culprit or culprits?'

'Several,' they replied in chorus.

Tansey hid his surprise. 'Then perhaps you'd be good enough to elucidate.'

'Certainly,' said Ansley. 'Between us we've gone back over our memories of the last university year and, as I said, we've come across several possibles. Mind you, Chief Inspector, some are more 'possible' than others.'

'That's understood,' said Tansey a little impatiently.

'Well, we begin with Harry, who was a scout at the College. We can't remember his surname, but Miss Mackay will know. Just before last Christmas there was a spate of pilfering from undergraduates' rooms. It was finally traced to Harry, and he was kicked out.'

'Prosecuted?'

'No. The Master decided that a prosecution would create bad publicity for the College. Harry was a poor wretch, and there were extenuating circumstances.'

'There always are,' said Mead. 'Extenuating circumstances, I mean. Personally, I think we made a mistake. We heard afterwards that Harry was swearing in his local that he was innocent, and he'd make the Master regret sacking him.'

'He might have been drunk,' Tansey commented, 'but we'll look into him. Who else?'

Ansley and Mead again exchanged glances—this time almost mischievous glances—and Tansey began to think that, however clever the two dons might be, they were taking an almost childish delight in analysing the situation and were welcoming this opportunity to outline the latest College scandals. Mead belched gently and gave a self-satisfied smirk, somehow implying that he was responsible for the next suggestion though he would allow Ansley, as his senior, to offer it.

'Then, in the Hilary Term we had a spot of bother with drugs. Nothing unusual in that these days, of course, but not to be countenanced, nevertheless.' Ansley spoke ruminatively. 'Oddly enough, or so it seemed to me at the time, those involved were a dull bunch. I don't mean academically. I mean they were hard-working, serious types—the kind who finish up with good Second Class degrees if they're lucky. None of your gilded youth.'

'We did have a small coterie of those,' Mead remarked. 'You know, the sort who never appear to do any work, but manage to finish up with good Firsts all the same. Bright in every way. But they nearly all went down the summer of last year. Most of them—like Hugh Fremont and the Hulton girl—got plum jobs, largely provided by rich and influential parents or relations.' Mead sounded vaguely envious.

'Anyhow, they're irrelevant,' Ansley interrupted. 'And frankly I can't see any of our druggies planting a bomb in the Lodgings. Certainly not Davies.'

'Who's Davies? And why not him?' Tansey asked quickly.

'Ah! Apparently Davies was the supplier. He and his girlfriend were both sent down. We don't know what happened to her, but Davies continued in his bad ways and your people caught up with him. He's now doing seven years. The others who were involved were rusticated for the rest of the term, but were allowed to return to take their Schools—their final examinations—so they really have no cause for complaint. In my opinion the College was pretty lenient—too lenient—with them.'

'You didn't inform the police?' asked Tansey curtly.

'No, we didn't,' Ansley admitted.

'Perhaps if you'd been less lenient and done so, Davies's career might have been cut off sooner,' said Tansey. 'Or was this another example of St Xavier's avoiding adverse publicity?'

Sergeant Abbot coughed loudly. He knew that the Chief Inspector held strong views about drug pushers, and he himself shared his superior's views, but it was not advisable

to antagonize witnesses of this kind. Both Dr Ansley and
Mr Mead had already become more reserved.

'No one likes bad publicity, Chief Inspector—not even
the police force.'

'Granted, Dr Ansley. However—have you thought of
anyone else who might have a chip on his or her shoulder?
People might have been employed to manufacture and
place the bomb, we must remember.'

Mr Mead opened his mouth and shut it quickly as Dr
Ansley shook his head. Tansey cursed himself. He hadn't
needed Abbot's warning cough to know that he had made
a mistake.

'Would you say that Sir Philip Pinel was a popular Master?' Tansey tried a different tack. 'I gather it's only five
years since his election. Was it welcomed in the Senior
Common Room?'

'The Senior Common Room elected him,' said Ansley.
'But opinions varied, all the same. The Master is an administrator—as indeed he needs to be—but there were some
who considered that his academic qualifications were rather
inadequate. Nevertheless, the College has flourished under
his guidance.'

'Do you know of anyone who was passed over in Sir
Philip's favour, as it were—anyone who might be bitter
about that kind of thing?'

Ansley shrugged. 'People always have aspirations, but—
no.' Suddenly he smiled, showing large uneven teeth. 'If
you're thinking of Mr White, the answer's still in the negative. I'd say that Greg White's wife is considerably more
ambitious than he is.'

'Why should I be thinking of Mr White in particular?'

'It was he who went to the cloakroom in the Lodgings
and then warned Dobson about the bomb, though much
too late to be any use, wasn't it? Why didn't he warn us
himself? It would have been vastly quicker.'

So the grapevine was already at work, Tansey thought, and gossip was spreading. He felt sorry for Greg White; the man was going to have to take a lot of shit in the next few days and weeks. 'So have you any reason to believe that Mr White had a grudge against the Master?'

'None!' Ansley admitted at once.

'None!' Mead echoed firmly.

Tansey got to his feet. 'Well, thank you very much for your help, gentlemen. I may have to talk to you again, but for the moment, that'll do. Of course, if you think of anything else, however trivial, you can always get in touch with me through Inspector Carey, or the incident room we've set up next door.'

The two dons rose. Standing side by side they made a ludicrous pair, but Tansey knew they were not to be underrated. They were intelligent men, and men with principles. As they reached the door he saw rather than heard Brian Mead murmur something to his colleague, and Ansley stopped, turned and came back into the room to confront Tansey.

'Mr Mead has just reminded me, Chief Inspector,' he said smoothly. 'Last term there was some trouble over one of our women dons. I don't know the ins and outs of the matter, so I won't attempt to tell you about it. It may not be relevant—most probably it isn't—but if you're interested Miss Mackay would know the details.'

'The answer to all our questions would seem to be Miss Mackay,' Tansey said as soon as Ansley and Mead had left. 'Unfortunately I'm not sure that at present she's being totally candid with us. A little ingenuous, would you say, Abbot?'

Detective-Sergeant Abbot, who was used to these sudden ruminative questions on the part of the Chief Inspector, merely nodded, and Tansey went on, ' Still, I'd be interested to see her reactions to the names of the potential villains that have been suggested. We'd better have her in again.'

'Now, sir? Time's getting on.'

'I'm afraid so. It's going to be a long day. But we can't keep White and his family waiting indefinitely. We'll be as quick as we can.'

'I'll get someone to fetch Miss Mackay, sir.'

Stifling his reluctance, Abbot went across the small hall to the incident room, in what had been Dr Cathcart's sitting-room. How well these dons did themselves, he thought—good pay, long vacations, no shift work, freedom to set their own hours within reason and bags of prestige— very different from being a cop, even a Chief Inspector. And their wives were luckier, too.

Greg White looked up hopefully as the sergeant came into the incident room, where he was waiting, but when he heard Abbot ask for Miss Mackay, he returned to the magazine he was pretending to read. He had protested several times that he must return to his wife and daughter; each time he had been met with polite sympathy, but the comment that the Chief Inspector was anxious that they should go back to North Oxford together. By now his state- ment had been typed, read and signed, but that had made no difference. Inspector Carey had assured him that his house and his family were under police protection and he need not worry about them. But how could he not worry? The minutes dragged.

'Miss Mackay has gone home to change her soiled clothes and have a bit of a rest,' Inspector Carey was telling Abbot. 'She'll be back later.'

'Can I help?' The Bursar, who had entered the room and heard the exchange, addressed the Sergeant. 'I can spare some time now.'

'Chief Inspector Tansey has some queries that he hoped Miss Mackay could assist us with, sir, but perhaps you—'

'I'll do my best.'

Peter Lacque followed the Sergeant out of the interview room, and Abbot explained the situation to Tansey. The Chief Inspector was more than happy. He had found Ailsa Mackay with her swollen face and wary, slightly unco-operative attitude less easy to deal with than the Bursar.

'Mr Lacque,' he began, 'what's your opinion of Mr White?'

The Bursar was taken aback. 'Were you intending to ask Ailsa Mackay that?'

'I'm asking you—and it's a serious question.'

'Worthy of a considered reply?' The Bursar took the minor snub in good part. 'Right. Let me marshal my thoughts.' The Bursar was a small man, with heavy tortoiseshell-rimmed spectacles too large for his face. He paused for only a moment. 'Greg White has been a Fellow of this College for about twenty years. I've known him for ten. He's a conscientious tutor and a good teacher. He's popular with his pupils, but some of the Senior Common Room despise him because he publishes very little—if any—original work of his own. I'd say that during his time here he's served St Xavier's extremely well.'

'I see. And as a person? Would you call him a friend, for instance?'

'I'd be proud to do so, Chief Inspector. I know there's a wild rumour going around the College that he dashed out of the Lodgings without warning those of us in the Master's study. The gossip has various versions. Frankly, I don't believe any of them. Greg wouldn't save himself at someone else's expense. He's not that kind of man. He'd be much more likely to throw himself on a live hand grenade so as to save others. I can only believe that, if there's any truth in the gossip at all, Greg White was acting under some greater compulsion.'

For a minute Tansey was silent. He was impressed by what the Bursar had said—and by his concluding sentence. It confirmed his own opinion, but, coming from an individual who had known White for many years, was a most useful endorsement. He decided to retail to Lacque the version of events that White had provided.

'Good God! It's unbelievable! So I was getting close to the truth,' Lacque said as Tansey finished. 'And, if that's what Greg White maintains, I believe him. But who the hell are these men? And why should they—?'

These were obviously rhetorical questions, but Tansey chose to answer them. 'Villains with a grudge against St Xavier's would satisfy both your points, wouldn't they, Mr Lacque? I've been offered various suggestions and I'd like to know what you think of them.'

The Bursar listened carefully as Tansey outlined what he had been told. 'All right,' he said, 'I'll give you my comments. The scout—his name was Harry Batsford—was a youth with an unfortunate background and I'm glad he wasn't prosecuted. I believe he's been going straight since he left here. He's working in a garage in Cowley, I gather. There's no way I can imagine him undertaking a crime like this.

'The drug business was a different matter. I think we— those of us in the College with responsibility, and among those I include myself—behaved atrociously. We should have disregarded the possibility of publicity and called in the police, but the Master wouldn't have it. Davies was a bad lot. So was his girlfriend, one Betty Fergus. But Davies is in prison now. I don't know what's happened to Fergus.'

'We'll have to look into them—and Batsford.'

'Of course.'

Tansey waited, but the Bursar volunteered no more, and the Chief Inspector had to prompt him. 'Any other hidden scandals, Mr Lacque?'

The Bursar shook his head, and then stared at Tansey in some surprise. 'You're not thinking of poor Emma Watson, are you?' he asked. 'If you are, you have been raking through our dirty linen, Chief Inspector.'

'Just tell me about Emma Watson.'

'She was a history don, early thirties, very attractive—too attractive for her own good, perhaps. In many ways we're a small-minded, closed community.' Lacque paused, and then went on. 'Anyway, Emma became pregnant. There were several rumours as to the father.' He hesitated again. 'In the end, she—she lost the baby, and was quite ill. She didn't come back to the College. She's teaching in a school in Abingdon.'

'I see,' said Tansey, who didn't really see the relevance of the Watson story. In any case time was pressing and he must get away to the Whites' home. Deliberately he looked at his watch. 'Time we were off, Mr Lacque. We'll be back tomorrow, no doubt. Meanwhile, thanks for your help. I shall probably need it again. Contact Inspector Carey if you're worried about anything in the meantime.'

The Bursar nodded. 'Anything I can do, Chief Inspector—I want this business cleared up as much as you do.'

But it was not going to be simple, Tansey thought. The Chief Constable had been right. The case, even on the first day, showed every sign of becoming curious and complex.

CHAPTER 10

'In the back, if you will, Mr White.'

Greg climbed into the rear of the unmarked police car, thankful that the waiting was over and at last he was on his way home. Tansey, glad of a respite, however brief, from the chore of interviewing, got in beside him. Abbot drove, with beside him a police constable who was to drive Greg's car to his house. Greg had already handed over his keys.

'That's it. That old red Ford Fiesta,' Greg said as they reached Broad Street.

Abbot, regardless of the traffic rules, drew up directly in front of the Ford. The police constable got out, walked around the car, glanced underneath and was about to open the door when Greg made an inarticulate sound, and pointed.

'You bloody people have made me get a parking ticket!' he cried.

Tansey drew a deep breath. 'Mr White, we're not as used to dealing with explosives as you appear to be. For a split second I thought you'd spotted some sort of device—a booby trap, perhaps. It was a nasty moment.'

'I'm sorry. But it's damned annoying.'

'Not to worry. I'll fix your parking ticket if I have to pay it myself.'

'Good! I'll keep you to that, Chief Inspector.'

Tansey grinned. He was beginning to like Greg White and, as he learnt more about him, he was also beginning to trust him—and his account of recent events. The man was clearly under a great strain, and it was difficult to believe that, in the circumstances, if he were acting he could be so convincing. Nevertheless, Tansey reminded himself that he must keep an open mind; if they found—as he personally hoped they would—corroborative evidence of White's story at his house, it would be a different matter. He signalled to Abbot, who drove off, leaving the Fiesta to follow, and it was not until they neared their destination that Tansey spoke again.

He said, 'Mr White, as I mentioned earlier, I'm afraid you'll find that your home's rather full of police, and there'll be a couple of our cars outside. They're there partly to protect your family, just in case—

'In case of what?'

'Oh, come on, Mr White, you know what I mean. In fact, you've hinted at the possibility yourself. In case these men take further action once they've realized that their bomb hasn't been entirely successful. Though as they must also realize that by this time you've told your tale to the police, I should think they'd have to be very stupid or very determined to do anything but lie low.'

'Of course you're right, Chief Inspector. You were saying—'

'And partly to search for clues to help us with our investigation.'

'I understand.'

'Of course you'll want to greet your wife and daughter. After that I shall have to ask you to wait with Sergeant Abbot, while I hear what my men have to say. Then I'll talk to your family.'

Greg nodded. Her knew he had no choice, so there was no point in objecting to this procedure. But after the harrowing experiences of the morning he seemed to have done nothing but wait and, though he hated to admit it, he didn't altogether trust Jean to be fully cooperative with Tansey.

His misgivings increased when they arrived at the house. Jean gave him a cool cheek to kiss, and barely acknowledged the Chief Inspector and Abbot. He was glad to turn to Rosemary, who hugged him, then offered her hand to both police officers. Reluctantly he left them and showed Abbot to his study.

'Obviously I want to talk to you, Mrs White,' Tansey said, 'and to Miss White, but first I must speak to my colleagues.'

'Is my husband under arrest?'

'Good heavens, no! Most certainly not.'

'Just helping you with your inquiries?' Jean was sarcastic.

Tansey's smile was thin, but all he said was, 'I shan't be long, Mrs White.'

He found the inspector in charge of the scene of crime team in the kitchen, with the uniformed senior constable in charge of the protective squad. The scene of crime officer was a small, morose character, who was rarely happy whatever incriminating evidence his men managed to uncover.

'Any joy?' Tansey asked him.

'Not really, sir.' He lowered his voice and pointed vaguely in the direction of the sitting-room. 'That stupid—lady! The villains drank tea and ate toast. Maybe they kept their gloves on, but there could have been saliva, for example—and what does the lady do? As soon as she can she puts all the damned crockery into the dishwasher! There it is—it's just finished swishing away the evidence. We got here much too late to stop her.'

'Too bad!' Tansey refused to commiserate further. 'What about prints elsewhere?'

'There are plenty all over the place. Presumably the family. At first the—lady objected to having her dabs taken, but I persuaded her; the girl was amused and interested. But there'll be a lot of elimination to do—the cleaning woman, friends, relations, odd callers. There are some prints that seem to recur a good deal, so that's likely to be a frequent visitor. The girl's boyfriend, perhaps. Even if we can't place them all, there's no guarantee that the ones that we're left with belong to the villains,' he added gloomily. 'Incidentally, there are a lot of smudges that we guess have been left by gloved fingers. I think our chummies were very, very careful.'

'So?' said Tansey.

'Well, it's obvious, sir. *If* you catch anyone, and *if* they've been careless—in a bathroom, for instance—the dabs here might help. Otherwise . . .'

Tansey noted the officer's pessimism, but he didn't comment. Clearly the bathrooms had been checked, and he knew better than to ask about the toilet and its flushing handle. However discouraging the man might be, no one had ever found cause to doubt his efficiency.

'Right,' Tansey said. 'Anything else? What about those cuffs that White talks of?'

'Oh, we've got those all right. They're cheap objects—almost the kind you might buy in a joke shop. Fair enough for the job they had to do, though given a little time any professional would manage to free himself. Hard to trace, too, sir; I should be very surprised if they provided any useful information.'

'I'm sure you're right.' Tansey suppressed a sigh.

'Before we go we'll show you how we think the men got in, and probably out, sir? OK?'

'Fine. I'd like to have a look around by myself first.'

Tansey gave instructions to the constable about protective arrangements for the Whites, and then left the kitchen, seeking to acquaint himself with the layout of the house in order that he might better understand the sequence of events that morning. He walked around the dining-room and went upstairs. He found the Whites' bedroom, came out into the passage, and glanced into a room that was obviously Rosemary's. He spent a few minutes in the bathroom from which she had tried to escape, inspecting the broken door bolt and studying the view from the window. The girl, he thought, had guts and so, in his way, had her father—if his story was true; and indeed everything he had seen in the house up to now appeared to confirm it.

Slowly Tansey went down the stairs. As he reached the last step a young uniformed WPC came into the hall. She looked pleased.

'Sir, I'm one of the team looking after the Whites—they thought a woman officer should be here. But I think I've discovered how those men got in. Would you like to see? Or have you been told already, sir?'

'Lead on, Constable.' Tansey, amused by her enthusiasm, was not prepared to frustrate her.

She led the way through the kitchen to a utility room which contained a washing machine and a tumble-drier, just leaving enough space for an ironing board to be erected. The room, though small, had a surprisingly large, low window.

'It's made like that so on a fine day you can lean out of the window and hang up your washing, which dries much fresher in the open air than in a machine,' the girl explained earnestly.

Tansey, who was a married man and a recent father, refrained from saying that he had much the same arrangement in his own house. He stared at the latch which, like most of the others in the Whites' home, was far from secure. Then he caught his breath. The wretched girl had undone the window, flung it open and was leaning out.

'It's OK, sir.' She gave him a wide smile to which he didn't respond. 'The whole surroundings have been checked over, no prints, but a couple of black threads caught on a nail. Incidentally, the villains came in this way, but almost certainly went out by the side door. It locks itself, but there's a bolt inside and that was open. Mrs White assured us the door was properly locked up when they went to bed last night, but—'

'Right.' Tansey just saved himself from appearing brusque. Somehow the girl, with her obvious determination to impress him with qualities which might lead her into the CID, made him feel old. He began to turn away, but he was not an ungenerous man, and he remarked, 'Good work!' before he moved off.

'Thank you, sir.'

Tansey went through the kitchen into the hall. The scene of crime team had now finished and were packing up their gear. He spoke to the officer in charge, saying that he'd been shown the utility room. The officer, as expected, was not hopeful that any really useful evidence had been unearthed, though he was prepared to admit that what had been found tended to support rather than dispute White's story.

And now for Mrs White, Tansey thought. Squaring his shoulders as if to gear himself to face a difficult encounter, he entered the sitting-room where Jean and Rosemary sat in an uncompanionable silence, pretending to read.

*

'I'm sorry to have kept you so long, Mrs White.'

'That's all right, Chief Inspector. We're not going any-where—unless you intend to take us to some police station.'

'Why should I do that?'

'To charge us with being accessories to a crime, of course,' Jean snapped.

'Accessories? Not victims, Mrs White?'

Jean didn't answer. She carefully put a marker in the book and shut it. Tansey noticed that she was pale, and her hands were shaking slightly. Rosemary, on the other hand, seemed to be reasonably relaxed.

'Mrs White, I'd like you to tell me what happened from the time you heard a noise downstairs in the middle of last night.'

'Surely my husband's told you all that already.'

'Yes, naturally. But you may be able to fill in more detail—and I hope that Miss White will help too.'

'I'll try,' said Rosemary.

'Rosemary! Don't—don't start inventing things.' Jean gave Tansey a weak smile and waved him to a chair. 'The young are so fond of dramatizing,' she said.

Tansey nodded an agreement that he didn't feel. Jean White, he decided, was frightened, probably more for her family and her home than for herself. He took it for granted that the villains had threatened dire consequences if the Whites provided any evidence against them.

'Well, I woke my husband—' Jean began.

Tansey listened attentively. Her account, which grew less hesitant and more fluent as it continued, differed from her husband's only in emphasis.

In conclusion, she let her feelings show, She reiterated, 'As I said, Greg had no choice though he seemed to think he had; but really it was either doing what these men ordered, or let-ting Rosemary and me be killed—and probably raped first. Of course he didn't want to blow up the Master and the other people at that meeting, but—' she shrugged angrily. 'Well, in the end he didn't, did he? His courage failed him. God knows what will happen to us all now!'

'Mrs White, until these men are caught, or we believe they've ceased to be a danger, you and your family will have police protection, I assure you.'

Jean laughed. 'Chief Inspector, I must speak candidly. In my opinion your assurance is worth precisely nothing. Police protection's a joke—and as for these men being caught, I suspect the likelihood of that is minute.'

'I hope you've misjudged the situation, Mrs White,' Tansey said soberly, and thought he understood why she was afraid; she had reached the conclusion that the villains might try to take vengeance for the minimal success of their plan, and indeed he had to admit it was a possibility. But it seemed grossly unfair of her to blame her husband. 'However, to continue—'

'I don't agree with my mother!' Rosemary could contain herself no longer. 'Dad was great, Chief Inspector! He did everything he could, everything right when those ghastly men were here. Actually, the oldie wasn't too bad, but that disgusting Tom!'

'Rosemary!'

Rosemary paid no attention to Jean. 'As for Dad putting the bomb in the loo, that was a brilliant idea. A part of the Lodgings may have got destroyed, but it's only a modern building anyway and no one was seriously hurt. What else could he have done, Chief Inspector? What would you have done in Dad's place?'

'I don't know, Miss White.' Tansey hesitated, then replied honestly. 'Tell me about this Tom. You struggled with him on the bathroom floor. Did his breath smell—of tobacco or liquor or chewing gum, say?'

Rosemary shook her head. 'Not that I noticed.'

'Did you notice anything particular about either of them—any mannerisms, for example? What about you, Mrs White?'

'No, nothing!' Jean spoke too quickly.

'You must have got some impression of them.'

'They were dressed from head to toe in black. The older one—at least the one who seemed to be in charge—was short and square. Tom—if that was his real name—was taller and thinner. At the time they were horrible, terrifying! They threatened us. But they did make us tea and toast, and in the end they *kept their word*. They said they had nothing against us, and wouldn't hurt us if we followed their instructions—and they didn't. Of course when the older one left here he didn't know what Greg had done.'

'They sound an unusual couple,' said Tansey mildly. He was tempted to add that Mrs White sounded as if she were siding with the villains rather than the forces of law and order. Certainly she was not being helpful. And he had noted the emphasis she had put on the phrase 'they kept their word', clearly implying that her husband had not.

'It's interesting that they denied having anything against Mr White,' he commented. 'I don't think he mentioned that point. Mrs White, would you say these men were acting on their own behalf, or were being paid to do a job?'

'It was their own show!' Rosemary answered before Jean had time to give a shrug to express ignorance. 'It was some personal matter to them, I'm sure.'

'Why? What makes you so sure?'

'I—I don't know.'

'Rosemary dear, really! You must not pretend you know things when you don't. I'm sorry, Chief Inspector.'

Tansey waved aside Jean's apology on behalf of her daughter. He grinned at Rosemary. 'A funny internal feeling, eh? I get them myself sometimes.'

Rosemary returned his grin. 'A strong feeling,' she said, and gave her mother a challenging glance.

'OK.' Tansey didn't want to exacerbate the festering disagreement between mother and daughter. 'Now—' He stopped. Rosemary had made an inarticulate sound. 'What is it?'

'Chief Inspector, when you said 'OK' just now, it reminded me. And I'm not making it up. You can ask Dad. Both Tom and the other man kept saying 'oke' instead of 'OK'. They repeated it several times. Of course, I've heard people say 'oke', but not all the time, and not recently.'

'Do you recall that, Mrs White?'

'Yes,' Jean said reluctantly. 'But I doubt if it's important. Lots of people use out of date slang.'

'It helps to build up a picture,' Tansey said, and thought that it was turning out to be a damned funny picture. 'Now, what about their voices?'

'Not particularly well educated, but of course they were distorted by their masks.' Jean was giving away as little as possible.

'And is there anything else either of you can tell me?'

Tansey looked hopefully from Jean to Rosemary; as he had expected, the interview had been hard going. They both shook their heads, but Rosemary gave him a curious stare that he couldn't interpret. He wondered if she did have further information that she wasn't prepared to mention in front of her mother.

'Then we'll call it a day, Mrs White—Miss White. If anything else does occur to you, you know how to get in touch with me. Meanwhile, thank you both very much for your help. Incidentally, there'll be two officers—a constable and a WPC—inside your house overnight, and another in a police car in the street, so I trust you'll be quite safe. Not that I think you need expect any trouble, but it's a form of insurance.'

Tansey stood up. Mindful of the lectures that he occasionally had to give to new recruits on the importance of maintaining good relations with the public, he suppressed his personal feelings and ignored Mrs White's studied silence. 'I'll say goodbye then, for the present.'

Neither of them answered, though Jean gave him what could only be called a nod of dismissal, and Rosemary produced a rather worried smile. He left the room thoughtfully, to encounter Greg White coming out of the downstairs cloakroom. 'Ah,' he said, 'I wanted a word with you before I go. I think we'd better have a tap on your phone, which'll be repaired any minute now. It'll mean having another officer in the kitchen with an instrument and a recorder. You and your family can answer the phone as usual. My man will only intervene or record if the call's other than personal.'

'Fair enough,' replied Greg. 'Have you told my wife?'

'No,' said Tansey. 'I thought I'd leave that to you.' He gave Greg a sympathetic glance before he continued, 'And what about tomorrow? I take it you'll want to go in to St Xavier's.'

'Yes, naturally,' said Greg, surprised.

Tansey sighed. 'OK. I'll have a man with you all the time.'

As he went out he was reflecting that he was now convinced that Greg White's account of events had been truthful, and for that at least he was grateful. One obstacle on the way ahead had been cleared.

CHAPTER 11

At two o'clock the following morning, Dr Harold Dawson, the Senior Tutor of St Xavier's College, died as a result of a second—and this time massive—coronary. The staff at the hospital did everything they could to save his life, but to no avail. His wife and son had been hurriedly summoned, but arrived too late to see him alive. Mrs Dawson was unexpectedly bitter. Unrestrained in her grief, she loudly blamed the College for their slack security precautions which had enabled someone to plant a bomb in the Master's Lodgings, thereby causing her husband's first heart attack and subsequently his death. She threatened to sue, though on precisely what grounds was not clear. She became hysterical, declaring that 'dear Harold' had been murdered.

Eventually, escorted by her son and a nurse, the unhappy widow went sobbing along a corridor to the lifts. In spite of their efforts to calm her, she made a considerable amount of noise—enough to wake one of the patients in a small ward nearby.

That patient was Bert Fairchild, the junior porter at St Xavier's. He had remembered nothing of what had happened from the time he had dashed across the quad on Dobson's orders to warn everyone in the Lodgings that there was a bomb in the toilet, until he had found himself in hospital with a broken leg, multiple bruising, several cracked ribs and concussion, and had been told about the explosion. He was in a great deal of pain, but an injection had helped, together with some sedatives, and he had managed to get a little rest. But once he had been woken by the weeping Mrs Dawson, he had been far too uncomfortable to manage any more sleep.

Hoping to find comfort in a chat with a nurse, and perhaps a hot drink even if he were not allowed another injection or more pills, Fairchild rang the bell. It was several minutes before a nurse appeared; the hospital was having a busy night. But Fairchild didn't mind waiting. He considered that he had been treated extremely well since his arrival at the hospital—almost like a hero—and once he had learnt that his own injuries were considerably more serious than those suffered by anyone else involved in the bomb incident, he had allowed himself to relax. After all, he reflected, if he had done wrong no great harm had come of it, and he was suffering more than others. It didn't occur to him that this was a very specious argument.

A nurse appeared eventually, promised him a glass of hot milk and went away again. Fairchild dozed, in spite of his discomfort. Hot milk reminded him of his old mum. He had been glad to see her yesterday afternoon. It had been good of Mr Fremont and Miss Sandown to bring her, very kind. Then there had been messages from Miss Mackay that he was not to worry—about his mother, his job or anything; the College was grateful for what he had tried to do, and she could assure him that it would show its gratitude.

Fairchild winced suddenly. He had shifted his position in the bed, and a pain shot though his chest. He swore vividly under his breath: these damned ribs; they were quite the most uncomfortable of his injuries. He was sorry that Ailsa Mackay had been hurt; she was a nice lady. As for Miss Sandown, he rather fancied her, but he knew he wouldn't stand a chance against someone like Hugh Fremont. Apart from anything else, Fremont already owned a sports car, and she wouldn't want to ride on the motorbike that he, Bert Fairchild, was trying to save for with so much effort. He was dreaming of the Yamaha TZR that was almost within his reach when the nurse returned.

'Here we are,' she said cheerfully, but in a whisper so as not to wake the other patients on the ward. 'But I don't know what you think you're doing, pretending you can't sleep after all the drugs you've been given.'

'I *was* asleep until there was a lot of noise in the passage outside; it sounded like a woman crying her eyes out.'

'Oh yes, poor Mrs Dawson.'

'Dawson?' Fairchild nearly choked on his milk. 'You don't mean Dr Harold Dawson's wife? Why should she be crying? Has anything happened to him?'

The nurse was nearing the end of her shift, and because the floor was short of staff she was tired, and she momentarily forgot that her patient and Dr Dawson were victims of the same outrage. 'I'm afraid Dr Dawson died a short while ago,' she said quietly.

'Died? How did he die? He was—'

'He had what you would call a major heart attack.'

'But it was the result of that explosion, wasn't it? Wasn't it?' Fairchild insisted. 'If it hadn't been for the bomb he wouldn't have died.' His voice had risen.

'Mr Fairchild, please!' The nurse gave no direct reply, but took the half-empty glass away from him. 'Speak quietly and don't get so excited, or I'll have to send for a doctor.'

Fairchild didn't answer. He had pulled the sheet up over his face. He didn't want the nurse to see how scared he was, but she heard him murmur, ' Now they can say it's murder.'

Over breakfast the Whites had almost had a family quarrel, though it was difficult to row in what Jean had aptly termed a 'house under siege'. The quarrel was partly a continuation of the argument that Jean and Greg had had the night before about the presence of yet another policeman in the house, this one manning an extra phone. Jean had refused absolutely to have the man in the kitchen, so that he had been relegated to the utility room.

Now, Jean, Greg and Rosemary sat at the small round table at one end of the kitchen, and tried to keep their voices low. It was shortly before eight. None of them had slept well.

A further point of dissension was what they should do during the day, and how they should cope and behave. Normally, such questions posed few problems, but their present situation was new to them, to say the least.

It was Greg who had precipitated this particular aspect of the argument. He had just told Jean that he had arranged with Tansey to go into College that morning. He explained that he had to lecture on Milton at ten o'clock, and on

Protestant Literature at eleven, and from five to seven that evening he was due to give two tutorials. He saw no reason why the disruption caused by the explosion and the inevitable police inquiries should affect his students, whatever his personal feelings might be.

Jean made no effort to hide her disagreement and disgust. 'Get along to your College then, Greg, since you believe your students are more important than we are. Anyway,' she added unpleasantly, 'you'd better make the most of it. As soon as Sir Philip recovers he'll kick you out of the place!'

'I'm not so sure he can,' said Greg, and wondered if planting a bomb under duress in the Master's loo counted as 'reprehensible conduct likely to sully the name of St Xavier's College', as the Statutes put it.

'Just wait!' Jean said softly.

'All right, Jean. And this afternoon I was thinking of going to the hospital, if Tansey will let me. I want to see poor young Fairchild, and I could pay a duty visit to the Master. Perhaps he'll be more understanding than you assume. Meanwhile, when I've had some more coffee, I'll be off to the College.'

'And I'll be off to school,' said Rosemary.

'Oh no you won't!' Jean was determined on this at least. 'Your father may be prepared to face the cameras and reporters lying in wait outside the house—but not you. Have you looked out of the window and seen them?'

'No, but—'

There was a tap at the kitchen door, and one of the police officers who had spent the night in the house poked his head in. 'Chief Inspector Tansey wants you on the phone, Mr White, sir.'

'Coming.'

Greg returned in a very few minutes. His expression was bleak and he made no attempt to soften the blow. 'The Senior Tutor died early this morning,' he said bluntly. 'It was another heart attack, and there's little doubt it was a direct result of that damned explosion.'

'Dear God! So now it's become murder,' Jean said, unwittingly echoing Bert Fairchild.

Greg made no attempt to contradict her. Probably for the first time in their married life he was thankful to leave the house and his wife. Ignoring the cameras and the clamouring reporters and the stares of a small group of curious bystanders, he got into the police car on which Tansey had insisted, closed his eyes and tried to make his mind a blank. The drive was over too soon. But the College was not unwelcoming. It was no longer cordoned off, though there was a police officer on duty in the lodge, and everyone going in was questioned and searched.

Dobson greeted Greg with evident pleasure, and in the quad he met Ailsa Mackay carrying a heap of files. The bomb squad had moved out of the Lodgings temporarily, and the debris in the Lodgings had been partially sifted and cleared, so that with the help of a scout Ailsa could move her vital documents and equipment to a room that the Bursar had found for her.

Greg relieved her of the files. He was concerned for her. She looked ill, her eyes black-circled, her face still distorted by the bruising.

'Ailsa, are you all right? Should you have come in today?'

'I'm fine, Greg, and there's so much to do. Peter Lacque can't manage everything.' She hesitated for a moment. 'You've heard about Dr Dawson?'

'Yes. The Chief Inspector phoned me.'

'He phoned the Bursar too, and now the entire College seems to know—at any rate all the Senior Common Room. Oh, Greg, it makes the whole thing so much worse, doesn't it?'

They had reached the room that was to be Ailsa's temporary office, and she pointed out where to put the files. She waited until the scout had gone, then she turned to

Greg. 'It's you I'm worried about,' she said. 'Oh, I know it's not my business. You've got your family and—and so many friends. But in a way it is—my business, I mean—because of the College and because—' She bit her bottom lip to stop herself, terrified at what she had been about to say, and winced as pain shot up her cheekbone. 'I'm sorry. I'm being incoherent.'

'Yes, I'm afraid you are.' Greg took her by the shoulders and gripped tightly. 'I'd shake you—' He had nearly said 'kiss you'. 'But it might hurt. Ailsa, what's the matter?'

'All these rumours—that you could have warned us but you saved yourself instead, that you actually wanted the Master to be blown up and didn't care about the rest of us, that—that it was you who planted the bomb.'

'That's true,' Greg said quietly.

'What!'

'I did plant the bomb, Ailsa—but not willingly.'

Ailsa listened without interruption as Greg told his story, and it was not until he reached the end that he realized that he had been trying to explain to her the nature of his emotions and just how he had felt, torn between one ghastly alternative and the other. It was not something he had made a great effort to explain even to Jean, he knew, but then he had not expected her to be sensitive or compassionate.

Ailsa offered him no sympathy, but her eyes were full of tears. 'Thank you for telling me, Greg. At least now I can set the record straight—and bugger anyone who says anything against you!'

Greg laughed. Ailsa rarely, if ever, used such words. 'Let's hope the Master won't be one of them. Jean seems to think he might be.'

'She could be right. He and the Senior Tutor were great friends. How—how is Jean, Greg—and Rosemary?'

'Rosemary's been terrific. Jean—Jean's taking it rather hard.'

As soon as he had spoken Greg felt that he had been disloyal to his wife. He had no wish to discuss his family with Ailsa, and he was glad that the scout chose that moment to return with another pile of files.

Jean was indeed taking it hard, and perhaps she had good reason. Greg had disappeared to St Xavier's, leaving her to cope—as she thought of it—with whatever might arise. Rosemary had retired to her room, saying that, if she weren't allowed to go to school, at least she could do some reading. Jean felt abandoned. On a normal Tuesday she might have done some gardening, gone shopping, written letters—but this was certainly not a normal Tuesday. With three police officers now in the house, including the one manning the phone in the utility room, and others outside, plus the media and the curious onlookers, she felt restless and could settle to nothing.

Lorna Pulent had phoned shortly after Greg had gone to ask if there was anything she could do. She had suggested coffee, lunch, whatever Jean would like or would be useful. Jean had thanked her, but refused her offers. She was fond of Lorna but wasn't prepared to face the inevitable questions. Another friend phoned to commiserate about St Xavier's and, as yet unknowing of the Whites' connection with the disaster, had hoped it wouldn't prevent them coming to dinner the following evening.

The next caller was Tony Pulent, who asked to speak to Rosemary. Rosemary came downstairs willingly enough, and occupied the phone for at least five minutes. She had scarcely put the receiver down when the phone rang again and, thinking that Tony had forgotten something, she picked it up and said, 'Hi! What is it, Tony?'

The call was brief. For a minute after it had ended Rosemary leant against the hall table. Her mouth was dry and suddenly, as her mother came out of the sitting-room, she shivered. She was unaware that she had become very pale.

Jean was startled. 'Darling, are you all right?'

'Yes. I—I—'

'Rosemary, what's the matter? What did Tony say?'

'It wasn't Tony. I mean, it was Tony the first time. He's coming in later. The other call was—was Tom.'

Jean took her by the arm and led her into the sitting-room. 'Tell me!' she said fiercely; she hadn't realized that there had been two calls.

Rosemary pulled her arm away. 'There isn't much to tell. He said that we needn't worry, Dad had done well enough and they were satisfied.'

'Is that all?'

'No. He said that we were to remember to keep our mouths buttoned up, or else—He sounded his nasty, threatening self, as usual.'

'I'm sure he did. He's a horror! But let's be thankful they're satisfied in spite of your father doing his best to trick them. It's a great relief.'

'If it's true.'

'Why shouldn't it be? They've kept their word so far.'

Rosemary shrugged. 'Yes, I suppose they have. Anyway, I'm going back to my room. I've plenty of work to do. And the chap in the utility room will have heard everything. Tom put his receiver down before I remembered to try to keep him talking.'

'That's all right, darling. Forget the police, and let's take care of ourselves.'

Rosemary shook her head doubtfully. And when she reached her room she sat for some while at her desk, staring unseeingly at her open book. After Tom had warned that they were to keep their mouths shut he had added, 'That goes for you especially, Rosemary, sweetie.' And she knew why.

She wondered what the police would make of it.

Tony stared at Rosemary in disbelief. He failed to under-stand. He thought of her not only as attractive, but as intelligent and practical as well; he was proud to have her as his girlfriend, and knew that he was often envied. Most of the time he forgot that she was just sixteen, but that fact had been brought home to him sharply now. He was astonished that she was behaving so stupidly.

'Why on earth didn't you tell your parents—and the Chief Inspector? Don't you realize how important it is that you can identify this guy Tom?'

'But I—I'm not sure I can! I saw his face for a mere second! I'd never be able to pick him out on a—an identity parade.'

'You could describe him. You've just described him to me.'

'Yes,' Rosemary said sulkily.

She kicked at the leg of the chair on which she was sitting. After Tom's threatening phone call that morning she had needed to tell someone, and Tony had seemed the obvious person. Her father wasn't there and anyhow he had enough problems of his own without extra worry about her. Her mother, she was certain, would either have scorned what she had to say, or have sworn her to silence, probably both. And, like Tony, they would have demanded to know why she hadn't mentioned it before.

'Don't you want these chaps to get caught?' Tony was exasperated.

'Yes, of course, but—'

'But what? You don't sound too sure, Rosemary. Don't you realize that until they're caught your father's going to be under a certain amount of suspicion, After all, it was he who—'

'Shut up! How dare you suggest—' Rosemary sprang to her feet.

'I'm not suggesting anything against Greg. You know I admire him more than anyone I know.' Tony was placatory. 'But other people may.'

Rosemary subsided. 'All right! But I've tried to explain.

There was never a good moment to admit I'd seen Tom's face—and now Mum will be furious. I think she wants the whole affair to be forgotten as if it never happened. And it's not as if I believed I could identify him.'

'Nevertheless, the Chief Inspector *must* be told what you know. It could help enormously.' Tony paused. 'Rosemary, would you like me to—to tackle Tansey for you?'

'Would you?'

'Of course! Go over it again so I'm sure I've got the facts straight.'

Rosemary did her best. There wasn't much—short, sandy hair, blue-grey eyes, reddish face, crooked nose. It could have been the description of countless men.

'And that's all I can tell you, Tony—or the police. I had no more than a brief glimpse—and I was busy at the time—you know what I mean?'

'I know,' Tony said gently.

Rosemary suddenly went on. 'The only funny thing is I feel certain I've seen Tom—or someone very like him—somewhere before. I'm sure I'm not imagining that.'

CHAPTER 12

It was not until the evening of that day, Tuesday, that Detective Chief Inspector Tansey went to make his report to the Chief Constable. In the interval his time had been busy but fruitful, though mostly in a negative sense, or so he then believed. Certainly, he admitted to himself that he had made little positive progress, though he had 'cleared some of the undergrowth', as he put it. He comforted himself with the thought that, at this stage of the case, that was more or less to be expected.

His first task had been to give a formal press conference, at which he provided a sympathetic account of Greg

White's action, and repeated his firm belief that the bombing was an attempt at a revenge killing, Then, in company with Detective-Sergeant Abbot, he had set off for the hospital in the hope of interviewing Sir Philip Pinel, the Master of St Xavier's College, whom he had never met. Having dispatched Abbot to interview Fairchild, Tansey found Pinel sitting up in bed in a private room, and thought him an impressive figure, even though his great domed head was swathed in a bandage. It was not until he was to see the Master standing up that Tansey was to revise this opinion; unfortunately, the Master's splendid torso ended in very short legs.

Apart from his appearance when seated, Pinel was in fact not a specially impressive character. He was impatient and irascible; his main concern seemed to be what harm the bombing might cause to the College Fund, as if a fall in such contributions was more important than the death of his friend Dr Dawson, or Fairchild's broken leg or the shock that had been suffered by everyone exposed to the explosion in the Lodgings.

'We're a small College,' said the Master. 'With costs rocketing as they are, we need all the support we can get, and no one—old St Xavier's man or not—is going to lend his name or give money to a cause that's not reputable. I simply do not understand Mr White. How could he bring himself to plant that infernal weapon? Has the man no sense of duty? When it becomes known that it was one of St Xavier's own senior members who—It's totally disgraceful!'

'Mr White was acting under duress, Sir Philip.'

'So he maintains. But why, I ask, should these supposed men have chosen Gregory White as their—their messenger of doom—rather than anyone else?'

Tansey ignored what he assumed to be a rhetorical question. 'Can you think of anyone who bears you a grudge, Sir Philip—or St Xavier's?'

'People always bear grudges,' said Pinel shortly.

But few, Tansey thought, worked them off in such a violent fashion and, when the Master continued to be unhelpful, he was forced to prompt him by mentioning the thieving scout, the student expelled for drug pushing and the don who—The Chief Inspector got not further with his recital. Sir Philip had gone red in the face and was ringing for his nurse.

'No loyalty!' he stuttered. 'Have they no loyalty—telling you these dreadful tales about the College, making the place sound like a den of thieves and whores and drug addicts?'

Thankfully Tansey withdrew from the presence. At the nurse's station he inquired about Lady Pinel, but was told that there had been no need to detain her overnight. Apparently she had gone to stay with her sister and brother-in-law, who lived in Norham Gardens in North Oxford. Tansey decided to forget her, at least for the present. He joined Abbot, who reported that Fairchild had been uncommunicative and, as expected, had produced only confirmatory evidence.

From the hospital the two police officers had driven out to Cowley. Ailsa Mackay had found the name and address of the garage—a small but seemingly perfectly reputable firm—where Harry Batsford was now working. Batsford was not pleased to see Tansey and Abbot when he learnt who they were.

'What do you want?' he demanded aggressively. 'I done nothing wrong.'

'We'd just like to ask you a few questions,' said Tansey, using the time-honoured sentence.

Batsford glared at them. He was a thin, white-faced boy in overalls that were too big for him and, in spite of his attitude, Tansey understood how he could arouse sympathy. He looked a pathetic creature.

'You'd better come into the office then.' Batsford led the way into a minute box-like room, decorated like the offices of all small garages with calendars featuring semi-naked girls in glamorous poses. He pointed to two hard chairs and seated himself on the edge of a desk. 'Lucky the boss isn't here at the moment or you'd be getting me the sack. He doesn't like coppers.'

Although he had been less than welcoming, Batsford was far from reticent. He seemed to have no hesitation in pouring out information. Perhaps he had hopes of getting rid of Tansey and Abbot before his boss returned.

He freely admitted that he had lost his job as a scout at St Xavier's for petty pilfering. It had been just before Christmas and he'd been skint, as he said. 'But I didn't take 'alf the things they said I did. That Betty Fergus, Davies's bint, she claimed I pinched a diamond ring he'd give her, but I never set eyes on it. Nor had she—set eyes on one—I bet. Now, if it had been Amanda Hulton—' He paused ruminatively. 'She was a peach, that Amanda, and rich, but I wouldn't have stole from her or Mr Fremont or any of that set. They always treated me right. But they got their degrees and off they went, except for Peregrine Courcey and poor old Steve.'

Tansey knew about Courcey. So, 'Who was this Steve?' he inquired.

'Steve Sarson? Oh, he wasn't really one of them—a kind of hanger-on, you might say. Me, next term I was moved to another staircase with a ripe lot of sods, treated me like dirt, some of them did.'

'So you thought them fair game,' said Tansey.

Batsford heaved a theatrical sigh. 'OK. I agree. I'm not quarrelling with you. I was wrong, but I paid for it. I lost a good job and I learnt my lesson. I've gone straight since.'

'You know you were heard threatening to get your own back on St Xavier's?'

'Oh, that was months before Mr White got me taken on here, and if you think I've anything to do with blowing up the blasted place, forget it. I'm happier doing garage work than being a servant to sods no better than what I am, for all their gowns and airs.'

'Where were you yesterday?'

It was Abbot who asked the question, surprising Batsford, though he answered immediately. 'Right where I am now,' he said. 'You can ask my boss, and we had one or two regulars come in. They'll speak for me.'

'Fair enough.' Tansey stood up. 'Mind if we look around before we go.'

'Same if I do, ain't it?'

But Batsford showed them around the premises without outward resentment, and indeed with a certain amount of pride. There was no sign of a white van. Abbot suggested that they might fill up with petrol and have the oil checked, a request to which Batsford responded quickly and efficiently. They parted from him on reasonably good terms.

Tansey had been thoughtful as they drove away from Cowley. He didn't doubt that Harry Batsford's alibi was genuine—it would be too simple to check—and probably the young man *was* going straight now. But it was interesting that he would possess all the information required to know when and where the bomb should be placed, and also that he had a good reason for not wanting Gregory White, who had obviously befriended him in his troubles, to be blown up. What's more, Batsford could still be bearing a chip on his shoulder, in spite of what he said and however irrational it might be. In Tansey's experience people were very often irrational.

They might have gone directly to Abingdon to talk to Emma Watson, the woman don who seemed to have scandalized the hierarchy of St Xavier's, but a call from Headquarters came through on the radio. Mr Tony Pulent had been trying to get in touch with Chief Inspector Tansey; he claimed to have urgent information, but refused to divulge it to anyone else.

Slightly irritated to have his plans changed for what he thought would probably be a waste of time, Tansey had nevertheless directed Abbot to St Xavier's, where Tony had said he would be for the rest of the morning. It was always possible that Pulent had happened on some detail that might prove useful, and a visit to the College would show the authorities that the Chief Inspector was taking the case seriously. Tansey, while not overly ambitious, knew that a good word from the University would do him no harm.

And, in the event, the diversion had proved well worth while. The police now had a description of one of the villains, however vague, and Rosemary might still remember why he had looked familiar to her, though such a resemblance could easily turn out to be coincidental. Tansey was not displeased. He had also had an opportunity to speak to Inspector Carey, and to agree that there was no objection to Greg White visiting the Master and Fairchild in hospital later in the day.

After a quick lunch Tansey and Abbot had once more set out for Abingdon. He had hesitated about phoning Emma Watson to warn her in advance of his coming, and had decided against such a move. It was term time, and she would almost certainly be at the school, so there was no reason to forgo the element of surprise. On the other hand, he had no wish to cause her undue embarrassment, and therefore gave his name to the maid who answered the front door as Mr Tansey, adding that he and Mr Abbot would wait if that would be more convenient for Miss Watson.

The surprise was theirs, however. When Emma Watson appeared she greeted Tansey as Chief Inspector. 'I read the newspapers,' she said by way of explanation, 'and I listen to the local radio. I take it you've come to see me about this bomb at St Xavier's. I can't imagine any other reason.'

Miss Watson was a petite woman, blonde and blue-eyed, with a good complexion and a slightly upturned nose. She was not pretty in the accepted sense of the word, but there was no doubt that she was attractive. Her black skirt, a modest calf length, and a demure white blouse accentuated rather than minimized her sexiness, and she was perfectly self-possessed, giving both Tansey and Abbot a small polite smile. She waited for one of them to speak.

Tansey recovered quickly. 'We're interviewing everyone who might have felt ill will or malice towards the Master of St Xavier's or the College,' he began.

'And I come into that category, of course. I hate that old Puritan bastard, Chief Inspector. I won't pretend I don't. The same goes for many of his colleagues, too.'

'Not all of them? What about Mr White?'

Emma Watson gave a wide impish grin. 'Greg White's a nice man, too nice for his own good perhaps, but I never had an affaire with him, if that's what you mean. Nor with the Bursar, though I think Peter Lacque wouldn't have minded. However, I was involved with another man at the time; he and his wife have since gone out to Australia. If you want details about undergraduates, I had a brief fling with Hugh Fremont, and an even briefer fling—in fact, you could call it a one-night stand—with poor Steve Sarson after Amanda Hulton had let him down. And that's all. I smoked pot a few times, but I never slept with any of the druggies, as was rumoured. I'm afraid my reputation far surpassed my achievements, Chief Inspector.'

'I see,' said Tansey. 'Nevertheless, you were asked to leave the College, Miss Watson, and I gather I'm right in assuming you were unable to find an equivalent position.'

'Damned right, Chief Inspector, if you mean I couldn't get a reasonable job. Otherwise I wouldn't be teaching— or trying to—in this crummy second-rate school—and lucky to be here, I suppose, after the rotten reference old Pinel gave me. Incidentally, I had classes all yesterday, so I've a splendid alibi. I can't have been blackmailing Greg White into planting that bomb.'

'Someone else might have been acting on your behalf, Miss Watson.'

Emma Watson laughed. 'Come off it, Chief Inspector. Who? And what for? Money? I haven't got any. Love? I don't rate that sort of devotion.' For the first time she sounded bitter. 'If you're thinking of the father of my dead child, think again. He departed at a rate of knots and he's since married his childhood sweetheart, or so they tell me. By the way, he had no connection with the College and I've no intention of giving you his name.'

'So you can't help us?'

'No!'

Tansey had believed her, but he had suspected that even if she could have helped them she wouldn't. What he had not realized was that inadvertently she, like Harry Batsford, the former scout turned garage hand, had given him a valuable lead. He could hardly be blamed for not recognizing this among the welter of information and misinformation he was receiving, but the delay in following up the point was to lead inevitably to further violence.

It had been a long hard day, and Dick Tansey had to smother a yawn as he seated himself across the desk from the Chief Constable. He handed over his typed report, and waited until Midvale had skimmed through it. It was a quirk of the Chief Constable's that, on any important matter, he preferred to read reports in the presence of the author and then ask for them to be supplemented with a less formal oraldissertation, before conducting what was in effect a *viva voce*. Not all his senior officers enjoyed a procedure of this kind, but Tansey had always found it rewarding. However, on this occasion he was glad to see that Midvale had already changed into a black tie, which presumably meant that he had a dinner engagement, and that the session couldn't last too long.

'You've certainly covered a lot of ground in a short space of time, Chief Inspector.' Midvale shifted his heavy bulk in his chair. 'And I agree with your main thesis. This crime has all the hallmarks of a revenge killing which failed to achieve its ultimate object—thanks to Mr White. No terrorist organization has claimed responsibility for it and, unless evidence to the contrary emerges, I accept that we must seek someone with a grudge.'

'We've found several of those already, sir, and there may well be more. For instance, we've barely touched on the drugs scandal that the College suppressed last spring.'

Midvale grunted. 'There's always a lot of feuding going on in these in-grown societies,' he said. 'And mixing the sexes hasn't helped; I'm not sure it's not made things worse, in spite of what some claim. But it's not usual for the combatants to resort to such extremely violent measures. Usually they prefer a more subtle approach.'

'I wouldn't say this was an unsubtle crime, sir.' Tansey felt bound to protest. 'It seems to me to have been well planned, and carried out with great efficiency. Whoever organized it knew a great deal about the College and its organization, and must have been in a position to judge the White family's likely reactions.'

The Chief Constable nodded. 'You think it was an inside job then, and that Tom and the other chap were hired?'

'The Whites don't believe that, sir, for some reason. They were positive the two men were personally involved.' Tansey shrugged. 'Of course, they could be quite wrong.'

'I suppose their neighbours haven't produced any useful evidence?'

'No, sir. We've made the usual house to house inquiries, but no joy. A woman noticed a white van parked in the road early yesterday morning, but she couldn't give any details, and white vans are two a penny around Oxford. Unluckily for us the Whites live in the sort of neighbourhood where people don't pay much attention to each other's affairs.'

Midvale glanced at his watch and raised Tansey's hopes that he was about to end the interview, but the Chief Constable continued. 'There were three people who should have been at that meeting, but failed to attend it—Chapman, Beale and White. Have Chapman and Beale been checked yet?'

'Yes, it's in the report, sir. Mr Beale has a high temperature. There's no doubt he's genuinely ill. The police officer who went to their house met the doctor. As for Mr Chapman, his injuries are genuine too. I suppose that if he'd known about the explosion he could have fallen off that ladder on purpose in order to avoid the meeting, but the idea seems a bit far-fetched.'

'Which leaves us with Mr White.' The Chief Constable referred to his watch again, and this time got to his feet. 'I'm afraid I must be off. I've a dinner date. We'll talk later in the week, Chief Inspector—or earlier if you think it would help. Meanwhile, I've one suggestion. Try to find out why White was picked. Was it just because he was suitable, a good subject with his wife and daughter to be threatened, or was it because the villains had some reason to like him?'

'Yes, sir,' said Tansey dutifully, though at the time he failed to appreciate the importance of the Chief Constable's suggestion.

CHAPTER 13

For Greg White the next couple of days were among the worst he had ever experienced in his married life. Jean dusted and vacuumed in a state of barely suppressed fury;

her cleaning woman had telephoned to say that she was unwell and could not come that week, an excuse Jean scorned. She cooked meals and made polite conversation with her husband and daughter, but she remained aloof, and disdained to show either of them any affection, complaining at intervals about the continuing presence of the police in and around the house. Greg had given up trying to win her over.

Rosemary was only a trifle more responsive. Jean had forbidden her to leave the house, and she sulked, spending most of her time in her room on the grounds that she needed to keep up with her school work as much as she could. Only Tony's visits seemed to rouse her from this lethargic pose.

In the circumstances Greg couldn't be blamed for taking refuge in the College, where he was also safe from the attentions of the media. Although Tansey had done his best to state Greg's case in the most favourable light, the popular tabloids had not been kind to him. That their attitude was largely based on a statement issued by the Master from his hospital bed only made the situation worse. Sir Philip Pinel, without quite putting the point in so many words, had effectively accused Greg of cowardice, and a failure to do his duty to his colleagues and the College.

Greg had been appalled by this attack. Certainly, the Master had been cold and unfriendly when he had visited him in hospital the day after the explosion, but he had not seemed so alarmingly hostile, and the press reports had come as a surprise. What was more, these same reports had tended to complicate still further Greg's relationship with his wife.

Even safe within the College Greg felt something of a pariah. It was not that anyone was positively antagonistic, though he wondered if this atmosphere might change when the Master returned to his duties. But sometimes a silence would fall when he entered the Senior Common Room;

groups in the quads or the passages would mysteriously
dissolve when he approached; and he was not asked to join
the small committee formed to arrange a memorial service
for the Senior Tutor.

By Friday Greg found himself keeping to his rooms, and
emerging only when it was strictly essential. But he didn't
lack visitors. Ailsa Mackay was the most frequent; she came
without excuse and Greg was always glad to see her. Peter
Lacque, the Bursar, busy as he was, also made a point of
looking in. And there were others, though not many, both
dons and undergraduates, who were prepared to show their
continued affection for and trust in him.

As noon—the time for his last scheduled lecture of the
week—drew near, Greg was toying with the idea of finding
some pretext or other to cancel it. Neither the subject nor
the hour made it popular, and he expected a poor attend-
ance. Suddenly it all seemed a waste of time. The Bursar
had just informed him that the Master would be returning
to St Xavier's on Monday; he would be unable to use the
Lodgings and would be staying with his wife's sister and
brother-in-law in Norham Gardens, but he would require
a suite of rooms in College. For Greg this was dispiriting
news.

'I've heard,' he said, as Ailsa came in a little later.

'Heard what? Oh, you mean about the Master? He's
going to have the Senior Tutor's rooms.' She laughed.
'What with the Lodgings out of commission and the police
usurping so much space we're getting positively crowded.'

'I'm surprised no one's suggested I should move out.'
Greg was bitter. 'Or is Pinel to have that privilege himself?'

'Don't be an idiot, Greg!' Ailsa spoke sharply. 'I know
things are bad for you at the moment, but they'll get better.'

'They could scarcely get worse,' Greg replied resentfully.

Ailsa ignored the remark. 'Anyhow, that's not what I
had to tell you. I went to the hospital yesterday evening to
visit Bert Fairchild. Physically he's doing fine, but mentally

he seems in a bad way. He'd hardly speak to me. I gather from the nurse he was no problem to begin with, but now he's suddenly become sunk in gloom. He doesn't want to eat or talk or do anything.'

'How odd! I looked in on him when I was at the hospital on Tuesday, but he seemed to be asleep and I didn't disturb him.'

'You wouldn't try again, would you?'

'Wouldn't Margaret Sandown be better, or Hugh Fremont if he's at home and not gone back to London? They're the ones who took his old mother to see him, and—'

'Greg, Margaret's a very junior don. At the time she was available, and as she's a sensible girl and Hugh volunteered to drive them, it was the best solution. Peter Lacque has been to see him since, but Fairchild wouldn't talk to him either.'

'What makes you think he'd be any more likely to talk to me?'

'Perhaps he won't, but—'

'But you consider it's my duty as I'm responsible for him being in hospital?' The clock on the mantel struck twelve. 'Good Heavens! Ailsa, I must fly. I'm due to lecture. Too late to cancel it now.' He struggled into his gown and collected his books and notes. 'All right. I'll pay young Fairchild a visit this afternoon. I might as well make use of my chauffeur-driven police car.'

'Thanks, Greg. Bless you!'

Feeling inexplicably more cheerful after this conversation with Ailsa, Greg ran down the staircase and hurried through the archway into the second quad. He was slightly out of breath as he reached the lecture hall, and he paused to calm himself. There wasn't a sound from within, and he decided that if there were fewer than a dozen students he would send them away.

He opened the door, took two or three steps into the hall, and stopped. The place was packed. As he walked slowly towards the platform, climbed the three or four stairs to it and placed his books and papers on the table in front of him the audience rose to its feet and started to clap. Even when he held up a hand in an attempt to end the demonstration the clapping continued, steadily and rhythmically. For a brief moment Greg was convinced that this was a hostile slow hand-clap, but the expressions on the smiling faces of those before him quickly disabused him of this idea. Clearly, they were on his side.

He waited—there was nothing else he could do—and while he waited he scanned the audience. Many were his own students. Some, such as Tony Pulent, he knew socially. Some he had noticed about the College, though he couldn't put a name to them. Yet others were a surprise. What were Hugh Fremont and Amanda Hulton doing there, seated on either side of Peregrine Courcey? They had both graduated the summer before last, and had no reason to attend his lecture.

Suddenly, as if at a given signal, the clapping stopped and there was a scurry of noise as they all resumed their seats. Greg realized that he must make some suitable reply, though he found it difficult to choose the right words.

'For the life of me I—I can't think why I should have deserved that,' he began.

'It was a vote of confidence,' shouted a voice from the back of the hall.

'Well, thank you—thank you very much. Believe me, I appreciate it. My morale's not exactly high at the moment, and that reception's given it a great boost.' He paused. 'And now I'm about to deliver a normal lecture so, if any of you would like to depart, I'd quite understand.'

No one moved. He gave them a minute, then started to talk about the effect of Milton's religious beliefs on the poet's work. They listened, though it was not the most inspired of lectures. There was very little fidgeting. Some individuals even took notes. He had never had such a large and attentive audience before, but his voice was hoarse and he was glad to bring his discourse to an end after some three-quarters of an hour.

Hurriedly scooping up his books and papers, he said, 'Thank you again, everyone.' He gave a wave of his hand and escaped from the hall. He was touched. After that reception, he thought, if the authorities tried to get rid of him he would fight. He would do his utmost to remain at St Xavier's.

If the last two days had been depressing for Greg White and his family, they had been frustrating for Detective Chief Inspector Tansey. A lot of officers had done a lot of work on his behalf, but the results had been meagre in the extreme. To put it bluntly, the investigation had made no progress.

Tansey, concentrating on the 'grudge' theory, as he had come to call it, had interviewed the young man who had been sent down from St Xavier's and was at present in jail, but he found no reason to connect him in any way with the explosion at the College. The same was true of his former girlfriend, and of the other 'druggies' whom the Master had treated more leniently.

Tansey had also given serious consideration to the proposition suggested by the Chief Constable, that the choice of Greg White to plant the bomb might have some special significance, but the Chief Inspector had found no evidence to support—or, for that matter, deny—his superior's suggestion. White was not the only St Xavier's don with access to the meeting who held hostages to fortune. Chapman, Beale and Mead were all married. Chapman—the man who had fallen off his ladder—had three small children; Beale had a teenage son; Mead had a son and a daughter. And, as far as Tansey could judge, they were all reasonably popular characters. Yet Greg White had been preferred by the villains, who had nevertheless seemed to

stress the fact that they wished him and his family no direct
harm.

'Of course, there could easily be someone we've not heard
of, someone who's been cherishing resentment against the
Master and the College in secret.' Tansey was in a ruminative mood.

'You mean from way back, sir?' said Abbot.

It was the tail end of Friday, and the two detectives were
in the Chief Inspector's office in Kidlington. Tansey, with
promptings from Abbot, had been trying to sum up progress with the case so far. It was this attempt which had
caused his frustration.

'Possibly,' he replied. 'To date we've only considered the
last academic year. Whatever occasioned this malice could
have been rumbling on over a long period, but it's got to
be something important—unless we're dealing with a crazy
villain. No one's going to blow up the Master and his senior
colleagues because they weren't invited to a party, say!'

'There's another point too, sir. This bomb. I know you
can learn how to make one from books, though it must be
jolly risky, but the forensic boys say it was comparatively
sophisticated, and it must have taken time to assemble the
ingredients and construct it. Maybe that could account for
any delay.'

'Yes. That idea—anyone trying to purchase suitable
materials and so on—is being looked into, as you know.
But no joy up till now.'

The telephone rang, and Abbot answered. 'Mr White
wants to see you urgently, sir. He's at the College, but if
it's convenient for you he'd prefer to come by here before
he goes home.'

Tansey hesitated. It was already after seven. Hilary
would have put the baby to bed, and would be wondering
whether to have supper by herself or wait for him. 'All
right. Tell Mr White that'll be fine'. But he had seen the
shadow pass across Abbot's face as he put down the

receiver, and he added, 'No need for you to stay, Bill.'

'Thanks, sir!'

Tansey grinned at him. He didn't mind some time to himself. He called his wife to say he would be late, thankful that as a former detective-sergeant she was understanding, and he concentrated on the paperwork in his in-tray until Greg White was announced.

'I'm sorry to keep you, Chief Inspector, but I was some time at the hospital and then I had tutorials.'

Tansey waved him to a chair, 'You've been to the hospital again?'

'Yes. Ailsa—Miss Mackay—suggested that I should visit young Fairchild. She said he was down in the dumps and perhaps I could cheer him up—you could argue it's my fault he's there at all, at least that's how I reasoned, but I wasn't altogether right.'

'Mr White, I'm sorry, but you're not being very clear.'

'No, I'm not, am I?' Greg gave a rueful grin. What with lack of sleep and general strain he was not feeling at his brightest. 'Let me try again. This afternoon, after talking to Miss Mackay, I went to the hospital to see Bert Fairchild. I felt some responsibility for him. I didn't really think I could help him, but I was wrong. He was worried and scared and by the time I got there I found he'd been wanting to talk to someone. He believed I'd understand and would help him, because I was involved in this bomb business too. So he chose me as his father confessor.'

'People seem to make a habit of picking you to help them, Mr White.'

'I wish to God they didn't.'

Tansey laughed. Then, suddenly serious, he said, 'So what did Fairchild have to confess?'

'As he told it, it was a lengthy story. I'll try to keep it brief. Fairchild rides a bicycle, but he yearns for a motorbike, and he's saving up for one—a powerful and pretty expensive Yamaha, I gather—so he needs money. This

summer he was knocked off his bicycle by a white van.
The driver blamed himself for carelessness and was full of
apologies. He insisted on taking Fairchild to a nearby pub,
where he learnt all about the motorbike. He said he might
be able to put some cash in Fairchild's way, and they
arranged to meet again.

'When they did, this chap asked Fairchild a lot of curious
questions, about his job, where in the College he could go,
how the Master lived, if he still had meetings of the tutors
in the Lodgings, and who went to them.' Greg stopped as
he sensed Tansey's quickened interest.

'Are you sure about those last questions? They suggest
the chap had some knowledge of the College.'

'Fairchild seemed sure. Of course, you'll have to talk to
him yourself, but I questioned him carefully. He admits he
got a bit drunk and can't remember all he was asked, but
he's positive about those points. And he's not stupid, Chief
Inspector.'

'Go on.'

'There's not much more. The chap said he was sorry,
but the job he'd had in mind for Fairchild had fallen
through. He gave Fairchild twenty pounds—compensation
for the bicycle accident he called it—and Fairchild's never
seen him since. I'd guess he felt uneasy about the incident
for a while, and then forgot it until the explosion—and
especially the death of Dr Dawson, which seems to have
bothered him. As I said, he's not stupid, and he's an honest
enough boy, so that once he put two and two together his
conscience has been bothering him.'

'Did he give any description of his benefactor?'

'Fairly tall and thin. He wore jeans and a leather jacket,
and the sort of peaked cap that painters wear. It covered
his hair, but his eyebrows were very black. He had tinted
glasses, a reddish face and a crooked nose. It's not a bad
description, is it?'

'No, indeed not,' said Tansey thoughtfully. 'Mr White,

between ourselves for the moment, has your daughter ever told you that she saw Tom's face?'

'No, by God, she hasn't! How could she?'

'It was when she was struggling with him on the bathroom floor. She pulled his hood off.' Tansey paused, then went on, 'Mr White, you mustn't think I'm intruding, but naturally I know something about the situation in your household. I imagine Rosemary was half afraid to admit she could identify one of the villains in case her mother became even more upset. Anyway, she told Tony Pulent, who told me. I've not spoken to her myself yet, but now I'll have to. Her description ties up reasonably well with Fairchild's description of the man in the pub. Many thanks for your intervention. I'm most grateful to you.'

'I see,' said Greg. 'You may well be right—about Rosemary's attitude, I mean. But I'm glad she had enough sense to come clean, if only indirectly.'

'So am I,' said Tansey. 'Now, is there anything else? Any ideas of your own on the matter?'

Greg shook his head. 'Not really. I'm still convinced that Tom and the man he call 'Boss' were personally involved, and not bribed or hired by anyone else, and I've wondered—'

'Yes—' Tansey prompted.

'It may sound snobbish, but they didn't sound to me as having ever been university material, as it were, and if one of them had been a scout or a member of the quite large staff that keeps the College running and in good repair they wouldn't have needed to ask all those questions about the Master and the Lodgings. I know this seems to contradict the idea that they were personally involved, unless—and this is just a vague thought—unless they were trying to—to avenge someone close to them, a brother perhaps, who had been at the College in some capacity.'

Tansey appreciated the argument, but he also saw its

weakness. The villains wouldn't have needed to cross-question Fairchild if the individual they were avenging was available. The Chief Inspector nearly raised this point, but he was sorry for Greg White who, tired and unhappy as he obviously was, nevertheless had done his best to be helpful. Tansey let the moment pass. It was a mistake he was to regret.

CHAPTER 14

The week that followed was uneventful. Life at St Xavier's quickly reverted to near-normality. True, there was still a police presence in the College, but it was no longer obtrusive. Inspector Carey continued to occupy the set of rooms he shared with Chief Inspector Tansey, but his staff had been cut and there was now only one officer on duty in the lodge. The Master had returned. Each day he sorrowfully inspected the Lodgings, where progress was slow; the hammering and banging as renovation began was a constant which most people came to ignore, though the dust that was raised didn't help the Bursar's asthma. The media, temporarily at least, seemed to have lost interest.

The White household had also returned to comparative normalcy. Greg now drove himself into central Oxford or caught a bus. At the College he lectured and gave tutorials and went about his usual business; he avoided the Master as much as possible. Rosemary was once more back at school, and was not displeased to find herself the centre of attraction. For her part, Jean was thankful to be rid of police in the house. There had been no more telephone calls from Tom, and the obscene calls from strangers that unpleasant publicity always seems to bring in its wake had ceased. To an extent she too had resumed her customary routine, though her relations with Greg were still strained and she remained angry with Rosemary for not having admitted earlier that she had glimpsed Tom's face.

As for Tansey, he was far from happy with the situation, but there was nothing he could do about it. He had insisted on a round the clock watch over the Whites' house, but there was no surveillance on them as individuals. He regretted this. He was especially fearful for Rosemary in case Tom believed she could identify him, but he accepted that it was impossible to offer her personal protection. For one thing, there had been a large number of influenza cases throughout the Thames Valley, and the police, hit badly, had even less staff available than usual.

Nor was Tansey pleased with the way the case was progressing, or rather failing to progress. Forced to carry the workload of a sick colleague, he had been unable to give it as much time and attention as he would have wished. But by dint of working long hours he had managed to interview more members of the College, both academic and other staff, and to study the many reports that had continued to pour in. Unfortunately, none of this effort was helpful, and he had to tell the Chief Constable that he was getting nowhere.

'I suppose you've considered getting the girl to help make a photofit of this man Tom, and distributing it to the local forces, Chief Inspector?' Midvale asked tentatively.

'Of course, sir. But I've been hesitating because I was afraid that too wide a distribution would put Rosemary White at greater risk. I suspect Tom would guess she was the main source; he can't believe that Fairchild's description would be of much use to us by itself. There's another point too, sir. I've never had much luck with photofits, and I've been wondering whether something a bit less mechanical and formalized might appeal to the girl and get more out her. In other words—Stanhope.'

Stanhope was a local artist sometimes employed by the

Thames Valley police. 'I take your point,' said the Chief Constable. 'Very well. Let's try him first.'

'As a matter of fact, I've already organized a session, sir. For tomorrow morning. As it's a Saturday Rosemary won't be at school so it can be done without a fuss.'

'Good idea,' said Midvale.

Rosemary arrived at the Headquarters of the Thames Valley Force at ten o'clock the next morning. She was accompanied not by her mother, as Tansey had feared, but by Tony Pulent. Sergeant Abbot met them in the reception hall and took them along to Tansey's office, where they were introduced to Robert Stanhope.

Stanhope had set up an easel with a thick pad of paper. He explained to them how he started—with a round, an oval or a square—to represent the approximate shape of the face. Then, as Rosemary filled in the details the portrait could take shape. It was essential that Rosemary should advise him and correct him so that eventually a likeness of the man she knew as Tom might emerge.

'It's a rather demanding exercise, I'm afraid,' he said, smiling at Rosemary, 'but it's interesting, and everything depends on you. Don't hesitate to tell me if I go wrong. I'll just flick over to the next sheet and we'll try again.'

Rosemary returned his smile. She hadn't expected the artist to be so young and attractive. Stanhope was in his late twenties, dark-haired, blue-eyed and fully aware of his charm.

'I'll do my best,' she said, and added, 'I saw him—Tom, I mean—last night.'

Tansey and Abbot were astounded, but Stanhope spoke first, 'What? But that's great!'

'She thinks she saw him,' Tony said, addressing Tansey. He had taken an instinctive dislike to Stanhope. 'It was probably imagination.'

'I tell you, I saw him! And he saw me!' Rosemary didn't enjoy being contradicted.

'Where and when?' Tansey intervened.

'Outside the Apollo Theatre, yesterday evening. We were queuing for tickets and he passed on the pavement. I could almost have touched him. He stared directly at me as he went under a street lamp, and I saw his expression change. I did *not* imagine it. I recognized him, and he recognized me.'

'Well,' said Tansey, 'that suggests he may be a local man, which could help to narrow the search. Incidentally, Miss White, you said before that Tom reminded you of someone. You've not yet remembered who, have you?'

'No. It niggles at me, but I don't get anywhere.'

'Probably some pop singer,' Tony grunted.

Rosemary threw him a glance of disgust, and turned to Stanhope. 'Tom has a round face,' she began, 'and a crooked nose . . .'

Stanhope drew charcoal sketch after charcoal sketch, making minute revisions as Rosemary instructed him. Tony, in spite of his irritation with her, was fascinated by the growth of the portrait. At last Rosemany slowly shook her head.

'It's not quite right,' she said, 'but I don't know why. Colour might help.'

'Of course,' Stanhope agreed at once. 'Give me about twenty minutes.'

'What about coffee in the meantime,' Tansey suggested.

He took them along to the officers' mess and brought coffee and pastries from the bar. On a Saturday morning the place was three-quarters empty. Tony chatted about St Xavier's and told Tansey of the surprise ovation that Greg White had received.

'He never said anything at home,' Rosemary remarked. 'I didn't know about it till Tony told me.'

'He deserved it,' said Tony. 'He's a great man, Chief

Inspector. For his sake you've got to clear up this business. It'll be a crying shame if he's forced to leave the College because of it.'

'Is that likely?'

'The Master's got it in for him all right, and Pinel's a pretty powerful figure.'

They were interrupted by Stanhope, who declared he was finished and led the way back to Tansey's office. He had arranged the easel so that the portrait faced them as they came through the door. Rosemary gasped when she saw it.

'That's wonderful,' she exclaimed at once. 'It *is* Tom. You've made his hair a bit too red, but otherwise it's as I remember him. Mind you, I only saw him for a second or two, but—but it wasn't a moment I'll forget easily. And I wasn't wrong, Tony. It *was* Tom I saw yesterday evening.'

Tony didn't answer immediately. He was frowning at the picture. At last he said, 'Extraordinary! Absolutely extraordinary!'

'What is it?' Rosemary demanded.

'I know whom he reminds you of. It's poor old Steve. Steve Sarson.'

'Steve? Yes. So it does. That's right. How silly!' Rosemary sat back in what was not a comfortable chair. 'I'm sorry, Chief Inspector.'

Tansey knew that he had come across the name before, but rather than search the files he asked, 'Who's Steve Sarson?'

Tony answered. 'Steve was up at St Xavier's. He was two years ahead of me, the same year as Hugh Fremont. He was a scholar and pretty bright. Everyone expected him to get a First.'

'And he didn't?'

'I honestly don't know, but somehow I rather doubt it. He didn't seem to do much work in his last year.'

'Dad would know,' Rosemary said. 'Steve was a pupil of

his. That's how I came to meet him. At one time he used to come to the house for tutorials or extra coaching, and he was occasionally invited to the supper parties that Mum gives. But does it matter, Chief Inspector? Surely it must be just chance that there was a resemblance between Steve and that horrid Tom.'

'Was?' asked Tansey. 'What's happened to Steve?'

'He's dead. He was drowned in the Cherwell the summer before last.'

'An accident?'

'No. He committed suicide,' Tony said. 'Everyone was horrified, especially Amanda—Amanda Hulton. She blamed herself, but in a way it was as much Hugh Fremont's fault or Peregrine Courcey's. They didn't bother to keep in touch with him. Steve was a nice guy, quiet and clever and he should have got his First and gone on to be an academic somewhere. That's what he wanted.' Tony was having difficulty in explaining.

'But—' Tansey encouraged.

'For some reason in his last year he was moved to a different staircase. Among others Hugh and Peregrine had rooms there, and through them Steve met Amanda. The three of them 'took him up', as people used to say. But he was never really one of them. He had no money; he'd come from a comprehensive school and was dependent on his scholarships and grants. His background was quite different from theirs. He'd never been abroad or done any of the things they'd done. They were a pretty high-powered lot, you know, and you could say he didn't speak the same language. Then of course, to make matters worse, he fell head over heels in love with Amanda.'

By now Tansey had remembered where he had heard the name of Steve Sarson. The one-time scout, Harry Batsford, had mentioned him in connection with Amanda Hulton, and the sexy Emma Watson had said she'd had a 'one-night stand' with him.

'I assume Amanda jilted him,' Tansey said.

'Jilted? That's an old-fashioned word, Chief Inspector. But no, she didn't jilt him. She simply never considered him in that light, and I'm sure she made it perfectly clear.' Tony shrugged. 'You can't blame her—or him, but it's a pity it should have happened that way.'

'Poor old Steve,' Rosemary said. 'It was no reason for him to drown himself.' She studied the portrait on the easel. 'It's strange—creepy—that he should be so like Tom. Of course Steve's nose was straight and he was younger and more—more innocent-looking.'

'Perhaps they were related.' Tansey voiced his thoughts and was at once aware that the remark sounded feeble. He smiled apologetically. 'But even if they'd been brothers, Tom would scarcely have tried to avenge Steve's death by bombing St Xavier's and the Master, would he? The target would surely have been this Amanda Hulton.'

'So the picture's been no use?' Rosemary was disappointed.

'It most certainly has,' Tansey assured her. 'We'll circulate it—though not publicly—and with luck an officer will recognize Tom, or spot him in the street as you say you did. Then we'll make some inquiries and when we're sure it *is* Tom, we'll try and trace his companion, put a case together and charge them.'

'How simple you made it sound, sir,' said Sergeant Abbot when Stanhope had packed up his possessions and departed with Rosemary and Tony.

'I wish it were. It seems to me to get more and more complex. Why did this chap Sarson, who seems to bear a strong resemblance to one of the villains, have to have some connection with St Xavier's College? Why couldn't he have been at some other college—or preferably at Cambridge? It's too much of a coincidence, Bill, and I don't like coincidences.'

*

Officially neither the Chief Inspector nor Sergeant Abbot were on duty that afternoon, but because it was a lovely day, because his wife's sister had come to spend the week-end and he knew they would enjoy a good gossip together, because he was restless—and because he disliked coincidences, Tansey decided to pay a sudden call on Amanda Hulton.

He knew that the Hultons lived in the Cotswolds, and he got the address from St Xavier's. That Amanda Hulton would not be there was a chance he was prepared to take; Ailsa Mackay had told him that Amanda was at present working at home on a biography of one of her ancestors, but it was unlikely that she would be occupied with it on a beautiful Saturday afternoon.

Tansey didn't bother to recall Abbot and drove himself at a leisurely pace. The sky was a pale grey-blue, the leaves already in their autumnal colours, the rolling Oxfordshire hills looking their best, and once he was off the main road there was very little traffic. He stopped in the market town of Colombury to ask the way. Even so he passed the entrance to the Hultons' place and had to turn back.

The house was called Broadlands and, from all he had heard of Amanda Hulton, he had expected it to be of a fair size. But he had not expected the Palladian-style mansion that confronted him at the end of a long drive bordered by lime trees. A white-coated houseman opened the door to him and, once he had identified himself and explained his errand, showed him into a rather large and formidable book-lined room.

It was some minutes before an extremely pretty girl appeared. She was tall and slim, with long fair hair pulled severely back from her face and held at the nape of her neck by a black bow. She wore black slacks and a long-sleeved sweater which Tansey assumed was made of cashmere. She was completely self-possessed, although her colour was high.

'Good afternoon, Chief Inspector. I'm Amanda Hulton. I can't imagine why you should want to talk to me, but come along to my sitting-room. It's more comfortable than the library.'

She led the way across the hall and along a corridor, then stood aside to allow Tansey to go into the room ahead of her. It was, as she had said, more comfortable than the library. The furnishings were modern, and there were bright modern paintings on the walls. But he scarcely had time to appreciate it.

Hugh Fremont rose to greet him, hand outstretched. 'Hello, Chief Inspector, I didn't expect to meet you here.'

'That goes for me too, Mr Fremont,' Tansey refused to be disconcerted.

Amanda waved him to a chair and sat herself on a sofa next to Hugh. They held hands. They smiled at Tansey, who was in no hurry to start the conversation. He waited.

Hugh gave a deprecatory gesture. 'You must be the first to congratulate us, Chief Inspector. We've just got engaged.'

'Really? Then I do congratulate you, and I apologize for having intruded at such an inappropriate time.'

'That's not important, Chief Inspector,' said Amanda. 'But why have you come? It's over a year since I graduated from St Xavier's, so it can't be about the explosion there.'

'I've come primarily to ask what you can tell me about Steve Sarson,' Tansey said.

'Oh no.' A shadow passed over Amanda Hulton's face. 'Steve? Not that again! I hoped that business was all over.'

'Steve's dead, Chief Inspector,' put in Hugh Fremont. 'He drowned himself in the Cherwell. There's no doubt it was suicide. He left a note saying he was so unhappy he no longer wanted to live. You can find it all in your files, I'm sure.' Hugh sighed. 'Of course, we were horrified. We felt that if we'd realized we might have saved him, and we blamed ourselves.'

'Rightly, too,' Amanda said. 'He was almost penniless by our standards—his father was a carpenter or a plumber or something like that—and we treated him as—as a kind of pet. We took him to restaurants and the theatre and dances, and to London, to nightclubs. We took him racing. We gave him expensive presents on his birthday. Then it was time for Finals, and we couldn't have made it more clear that this was goodbye. He wasn't going to be part of our future.'

'And you believe that was why he took his own life?' Tansey asked, thinking that she had provided a useful gloss on what Tony Pulent had already told him.

'Why are you raking up this old dirt now, Chief Inspector?' Hugh sounded suddenly indignant.

'Because I need to know, Mr Fremont,' Tansey replied curtly.

'Hugh, it doesn't matter. If we don't tell him someone else will.' Amanda released her hand from Hugh's and sighed. 'Steve asked me to marry him. It was a—a preposterous idea, and I refused. Probably I was less kind than I might have been, but he took me by surprise. I'd never encouraged him, though it was suggested at the inquest that I had.'

'Did you ever receive any threats after Steve was drowned, Miss Hulton?'

Amanda looked surprised. 'Threats, Chief Inspector? No! Why do you ask that?'

'You did imply that someone thought you might have been to blame for his death.'

'Oh, you mean—But that was my tutor, Dr Dawson.'

'The one who's just died?'

'Yes. The Master was unwell and poor old Harold stood in for him at the inquest.'

'It would have made more sense if it had been Greg White who had blamed Amanda and the rest of us,' Hugh intervened. 'Steve was his pupil, not Dawson's, and it's true we stopped Steve working as hard as he should have done if he was to get a First.'

'What sort of degree did he get?'

It was an idle question. Tansey had decided that he had learnt all he was likely to get from the present interview. Hugh and Amanda exchanged glances and together shook their heads.

'I don't know,' Hugh said. 'Probably a Third. Certainly not a First. In any case, he was dead by the time the Honours Lists were published.'

It was a pathetic obituary, Tansey thought as he drove back to Oxford. They hadn't really cared a damn about Steve Sarson. Amanda had admitted it. They hadn't even bothered to look for his name in the examination results. Not out of malice but from pure thoughtlessness they had tempted Steve with a way of life he could only envy, and he had not been strong enough, mentally or physically, to resist the temptation. But this tragedy—and it *was* a minor tragedy—had happened over a year ago. There had been no threats then and, if someone had taken his time to avenge Steve, why had he attacked the Master and the senior members of St Xavier's, who could scarcely be held personally responsible? The idea made no sense at all.

CHAPTER 15

While Chief Inspector Tansey was driving through the Cotswold lanes on his way home, Rosemary White was playing tennis. She had cycled a couple of miles to a friend's house, and had already played two strenuous sets of singles, winning one and losing one. It was now three-all in the third set, and she was determined to win. She was enjoying her afternoon.

Eventually, after a great struggle she did win the final

set. She accepted a glass of lemonade, but refused to stay
for tea. Her friend's mother had returned, and Rosemary
had no wish to face a barrage of questions about the
explosion at St Xavier's College and the White family's
involvement with it.

'Thank you,' she said politely, 'but I ought to get back.
Mum's visiting a neighbour who's sick, and Dad's alone.'

They didn't try to keep her. Rosemary mounted her
bicycle and set off for home. What with the morning spent
at police headquarters and winning the match that afternoon she decided it had been a satisfactory day. It was not
until she was turning into her own road that she became
aware of a white van behind her.

For a moment she panicked, but she could see her house
and the policeman lounging against the low wall in front of
it. He straightened as he saw her coming towards him. She
kept close to the side of the road and pedalled fast. The van
overtook her, then without warning swerved right in front of
her, braked hard to a full stop and immediately accelerated
away.

Rosemary had no chance. She rode straight into the rear
of the van as it stopped, hitting it with considerable force.
Her front wheel buckled and the bike slithered sideways.
The effect on Rosemary was the same as if she had been
riding a horse that had refused at the last moment to take
a fence. She was flung out of her saddle, described a para-
bola in the air and landed on the pavement. She was lucky
not to have hit her head on the van.

She lay, stunned. Momentarily she blacked out, but she
had regained consciousness by the time the police officer
had reached her. He was kneeling beside her, choking back
his curses, as she opened her eyes.

A passing car stopped and the driver got out. A pedestrian hurried across the road. The owner of the house
opposite, who had been looking out of the window and
seen what had happened, came to offer help. They were all

witnesses, but no one—not even the officer—had had the
sense to note the number of the van, and they couldn't
agree as to whether it had been an accident or a deliberate
attempt to maim, if not kill. Rosemary herself had no doubt,
but her one desire was to make light of the incident.

'Get me home!' she ordered the policeman.

He helped her to her feet. There was a gash down her
leg, which was bleeding, and she felt bruised and shaken,
but no bones seemed to be broken. She was able to walk,
though her ankle hurt her and she leant heavily on the
officer as they went slowly towards her house. The neighbour and the passer-by came behind them, carrying her
damaged bicycle and her tennis racket and shoes.

Greg opened the door. 'Dear God!' he said when he saw
the little procession. 'Darling, what's happened?'

At the sight of her father, Rosemary's courage finally
deserted her. 'Dad! Oh Dad!' she sobbed, and flung herself
into his outstretched arms.

Tansey heard the news on his radio phone as he approached
north Oxford and drove straight to the Whites' home. He
spoke briefly to the police officer and was about to ring the
bell when the door opened. It was Greg showing out the
doctor.

The Chief Inspector waited until the doctor had reached
his car. Then, 'How is she, Mr White?' he demanded without preamble.

'You know what happened?' asked Greg.

'Oh yes,' said Tansey. 'I've heard all the details—or as
many as my wretched man was able to give me. I'll put an
extra officer on duty for a few days.'

'Fine,' said Greg. 'As far as Rosemary's concerned, she's
not too bad, thank heavens! She's got a nasty cut on her
leg, a sprained ankle and a few bruises. I think the worst
thing is probably the shock. Do you have to see her? She's
resting. The doctor gave her a mild sedative.'

'No, I don't need to see her now. I just wanted to make sure she was—all right.'

'Kind of you. Come in.' Greg led the way to his study. 'My wife's out, which is lucky. She's pretty tense at present, understandably—and this isn't going to help.'

'I'm sorry.'

Greg nodded. 'It's a bloody business,' he said with a sudden spurt of anger. 'If only they hadn't chosen me.'

'Then you might be in hospital—or dead.'

'I realize that. Nevertheless, I find it hard to count my blessings, especially after this—this attack on Rosemary. Chief Inspector, tell me honestly, are you managing to get anywhere with the case?'

Tansey hesitated; he didn't want to raise too many false hopes, but finally he said, 'I think so, yes. Did Rosemary tell you that she thinks she saw the man we know as Tom last night, and that he saw her? That could be important. For one thing, it would explain the attack on her today. She'd only seen him fleetingly before, and he may have thought he was safe. But if she showed some signs of recognition—well, he knows she can identify him. And indeed it would seem she might, because, as you know, this morning she helped a police artist to produce what she claimed was an excellent likeness. Incidentally, Mr White, she said it reminded her of your old student Steve Sarson. What was more, Tony Pulent—who was with her—agreed.'

'Steve! Steve Sarson! But he's dead.'

'Quite. I know. I was talking to Amanda Hulton and Hugh Fremont earlier this afternoon. Steve Sarson, I gather, committed suicide because Miss Hulton had scorned his proposal of marriage, and she and her friends made it clear that once they'd gone down from the university they didn't expect to continue with what Sarson had assumed would be a close and enduring friendship. Would you agree with all that, Mr White?'

'From what I know of the situation, I couldn't disagree, though I wouldn't have put it quite so brutally.'

'But did his suicide surprise you? What sort of man was Steve Sarson?'

Greg White gave the Chief Inspector a long stare. 'Yes, it did surprise me. Certainly, he'd been bowled over by Amanda Hulton. He'd been entranced by a way of life to which he was not accustomed. But he wasn't an innocent. He was used to fighting for what he wanted, or with his background he'd have had more difficulty in winning a place at Oxford. After a short "down", I'd have expected him to get a grip on himself and say, "OK, I'll show you. I'll get to the top, and then—" It might have been a pipe-dream and come to nothing, but in my opinion he was the kind of chap who'd have tried.'

'That's most interesting. But what about this short "down", as you call it? This period of depression? Mightn't he have drowned himself then?'

'I don't know. I can only guess, though if my interpretation of his character's accurate he'd have been more likely to get stinking drunk, go to a brothel or find some tart.'

Which is more or less what he did do, Tansey thought, remembering what Emma Watson had said about consoling Steve after Amanda Hulton had turned him down. 'Nevertheless, he did take his own life, Mr White. There seems no doubt about that.'

'None. He left a note, and there were no suspicious circumstances—at least none that surfaced at the inquest.' Greg shook his head sadly. 'I was away at the time, conducting a summer course in the States. It happened several weeks after the end of the Trinity term, you know. I was horrified, shocked, when I returned and learnt about it. I couldn't help reproaching myself. Who knows, if I'd been here . . . ? I always got on well with Steve.'

'Is there any possibility that he took his life because he'd discovered that he'd got a worse degree than he'd hoped for? As far as he was concerned, this might have been the last straw, so to speak.'

'But—Chief Inspector, you're misinformed on two counts. Steve was already dead when the results were announced. And he didn't get a poor degree. He didn't get a degree of any kind. He failed.'

'Failed? Completely? That's unusual, surely?'

'Yes. I couldn't believe it. When we discussed his papers immediately after the exams he was pretty happy about how he'd done; he was possibly over-optimistic, I thought, but I never imagined he'd made such a mess of things. I even went to the Master to see if I could get his papers reviewed for the sake of Steve's family, but Sir Philip took a poor view. He said Steve had brought enough disgrace on St Xavier's by committing suicide because of a love-affair that he should have known was impossible, and it was best to forget the whole matter.'

'Did you ever meet Steve's family?'

'Yes. I went to see them. I felt I should. They were a surprisingly elderly couple to have such a young son. He must have been an afterthought, and as so often happens in such cases he was their favourite.'

'There were other sons?'

'Two, I believe, but—'

'Did you tell the Sarsons you'd tried to get Steve's papers re-assessed?'

'No. Definitely not. I told no one, and there was no one else present when I went to see the Master except the Senior Tutor, Dr Dawson.'

'The Dr Dawson who died?'

'Yes. He agreed with Pinel about Steve, and that was the end of it. But, Chief Inspector—'

'You can guess what I'm thinking, Mr White. This is the best lead I've had so far. I admit the motive's weak, but supposing Steve had somehow learnt about his failure and told his family, and then decided he couldn't face the future without the Hulton girl and without a degree.'

'I don't see how he could conceivably have known the results in advance.'

'Maybe not, but it's a possibility to think about. Anyway, I'll have to look into the Sarsons. Meanwhile, Mr White, I hope you'll consider the conversation we've had this afternoon as strictly confidential.'

'Of course, Chief Inspector, of course.' Greg sighed. 'And I hope to God you're right. When I think of Rosemary being hurt I desperately want an end to this business before—before anything else happens.'

Sunday was another beautiful day. Greg, who was by nature a sedentary man, felt the urge to go for a long walk in the country, but he knew that this was impossible. Jean had been naturally upset when she had returned home the afternoon before to be confronted with what had happened to Rosemary. She had blamed Tansey and the police, Greg and even Rosemary herself. The argument—still unresolved—about what Rosemary should do during the week to come had been bitter. No, thought Greg, a walk was out of the question; Jean would consider it to be a form of desertion. He retreated to his study, and sank into a chair.

He had been awake during much of the previous night, brooding over his talk with Tansey. He had assured the Chief Inspector that Steve Sarson couldn't have known about his exam results before he had decided to kill himself, but doubt about the validity of this assurance had begun to worry him. Could he have been wrong? Had Steve somehow learnt of his failure before the lists had been published?

Greg's original self-reproaches had returned to bother him again. He felt that as Steve's tutor he should have been insistent about inquiring fully into Steve's pathetic results. But he had been exhausted after a hectic time in the States, the boy was dead—making his lack of a degree irrelevant—

and the Master, backed by the Senior Tutor, had been very firm on the subject. In retrospect he wondered why they had been so adamant; a few words in private with the Chairman of the Examining Board would surely not have revived the scandal of Steve's suicide. Of course the Master had claimed that he had already made inquiries and had been informed that Steve's papers had been abysmal.

But why had they been so abysmal? Steve certainly was not stupid. Admittedly he had been slack during his last year, but he had done enough work in the preceding two to enable him to get at worst a Third, and he said he had liked the papers. He had even remarked that he had been lucky in the topics he had chosen for his last minute revisions.

Sighing, Greg got to his feet. The door of the study was open, and he could hear sounds suggesting that Jean was getting tea. At least he could carry a tray up to Rosemary, who was spending the day in bed, and save Jean a journey. He was in the hall when the crash came. Jean ran out of the kitchen.

'What was that?'

'I don't know. It sounded like breaking glass. I think it came from the sitting-room.'

Greg was right. There was a shattered pane in the middle of the window that faced the road, and shards of glass were scattered far into the room. The cause lay on the carpet, a reddish-brown object, rectangular in shape, about nine inches by four inches, with a large luggage label tied to it with a piece of string.

'Are you all right, sir?' The anxious face of the policeman on duty appeared outside the window. What with Rosemary being knocked down, his failure to get the number of the van, and now this, he was having a bad weekend. 'I'm sorry. I tried to catch him but he was too quick for me.'

'We're all right.' Greg was studying the object on the floor. For a moment he had feared it might be a bomb, but

now he saw that it was obviously a simple brick. He bent
to pick it up.

'Don't touch it!' said the officer.

'But it's only a brick.'

'Still, you never know, sir. May I come in?'

'Of course.'

The officer spoke into his mobile phone as Greg, ignoring
Jean's protest, went into the hall to open the front door for
him.

'Was it the white van again, Constable?'

'No, sir. A chap on a motorbike, which took me by surprise. It was a mighty throw,' he added, his voice tinged
with admiration, as he inspected the object.

'And what do you mean by that?' Jean demanded. 'He
could have blown up the house while you were admiring
his throwing arm. You call this protection?'

'Jean!' Greg protested.

'What does that label say?'

The officer had put on a glove and, without moving the
brick, held up the label by its edges. They could all see
that letters and whole words from a newspaper had been
carefully pasted together so as to form a text. It read: 'That
was a warning. R, keep your mouth shut or next time it
will be for real.'

'It's meant for Rosemary, Jean. A threat.'

'Obviously.'

'Don't touch it or move it, please,' repeated the officer.
'They're sending a couple of men up to take it away.'

'God! Not more police,' said Jean.

The constable tactfully remarked that he would go and
wait for his colleagues outside, and Jean turned on Greg.

'Now perhaps you'll listen to me,' she said. 'Those men
told us they were satisfied with the results of their bomb,
and that there'd be no more violence and no harm would
come to us, *providing* we kept our mouths shut and played
dumb. But did we? Were we sensible? No! You and Rose-

mary have both gone out of your way to help the police—
especially Rosemary. I suppose she likes to feel important,
but she was following your example. It's madness, I tell
you! All that's happened is that the three of us are at risk.
Greg, don't you realize that we're the only witnesses? Without us—'

Greg cut her short. 'Which is all the more reason why
we should do our best to put these men behind bars. We
won't be really safe till they are. We had to go along with
them in the beginning, allow ourselves to be blackmailed
because the odds were so much against us. But the situation's changed, Jean. We're in a much stronger position.
We've got to fight back.'

'What for? Abstract justice? I've never heard such bloody
nonsense. It's not as if you cared about old Pinel.'

'Maybe not, but—' Greg thought of Ailsa Mackay and
the Bursar and Tony Pulent and the Fremont brothers; he
cared about all of them. 'We'll talk about Rosemary later,'
he said forcefully. 'I think maybe it would be best if she
goes to stay with my parents for a while, even if it means
missing some school. She can always have some extra
coaching later.'

'In that case,' said Jean coldly, 'I shall go and stay with
my sister. I'm sure you'll be happy in your damned College,
Greg.'

But by Monday morning Rosemary was running a high
temperature. The doctor diagnosed the virus that was
prevalent throughout the Thames Valley. He said it wasn't
serious and she would be fine in a few days, but there was
no question of her going to stay with her grandparents at
present.

CHAPTER 16

When the Chief Inspector arrived at St Xavier's on Monday morning he found Greg White in the room which had become Ailsa Mackay's temporary office. He inquired after Rosemary, and was glad to hear that, as she seemed to have caught a virus, there had been no difficulty in persuading her to stay at home.

Pleasantries over, he said, 'Miss Mackay, I wonder if you could give me any information about the Sarson family?'

'The Sarsons? Steve Sarson's family?' Ailsa couldn't resist glancing at Greg before she answered.

Tansey was amused. 'Have you been doing my job for me, Mr White?'

'Not really. I'm trying to salve my conscience. Steve was my pupil and I'm certain he ought not to have failed his Finals. So at last I intend to look into the matter. Rather late in the day, I admit.'

'Have you got anywhere?'

'I've confirmed that Steve drowned himself *before* the results of his Finals were made public. I've also looked up the name of the professor who chaired the examining board that failed Steve. I know him, though not well, and I thought I might go and have a word with him. Is that all right with you, Chief Inspector?'

'I don't see why not.' Tansey was hesitant. 'But don't mention any police interest in the Sarsons. Make some other excuse for your inquiry.'

'Of course.'

'Why *are* the police interested?' Ailsa inquired.

Again Tansey hesitated. Then, 'In confidence, Miss Mackay, it's possible that the Sarsons might have considered they had a grudge against St Xavier's because of Steve's death.'

'And so they decided to blow up the Master's Lodgings?' Ailsa was incredulous. She shook her head. 'No, Chief Inspector. After Steve was drowned I went to see his parents in Colombury—that's in the Cotswolds not very far from here—'

'I know it,' said Tansey.

'Well,' went on Ailsa, 'the family had been living there for some years. I know, because we've still got Steve's file and it shows that it was from a Colombury address that he applied for a place at St Xavier's. The family ran some sort of business there, I believe. Anyway, his mother and father were a pleasant old couple, dreadfully upset when I saw them, naturally. Steve had obviously been the apple of their eye and they were tremendously proud of him, but as far as I could make out there was no question of them blaming St Xavier's. On the contrary, they kept repeating how kind Greg had been to Steve, giving him free extra coaching and inviting him to his home and so forth.'

Tansey refrained from remarking that Greg White as an individual was not quite identical with the College as an institution, and certainly not synonymous with its Master.

'Miss Mackay, you said they *were* a pleasant couple?' he remarked.

'I see what you mean. Yes, 'were' is right. Unfortunately Mrs Sarson died a few months after Steve. I'm not quite sure, but I think Mr Sarson stayed on in Colombury and a daughter or daughter-in-law keeps house for the family.'

'I see,' said Tansey. 'About the family—Steve had brothers, didn't he?'

'Two.' It was Greg who answered. 'Older than he was, and apparently not academic material. I think they probably left school at sixteen. Steve was the clever one.'

'His cleverness doesn't seem to have brought him good

fortune,' said Tansey, who himself had always regretted that his own education had been curtailed by his father's early death.

Half an hour later Chief Inspector Tansey was once more on his way to the Cotswolds, but this morning Sergeant Abbot was driving him. Bill Abbot had been born and brought up in Colombury and, though he no longer lived there, he knew the small market town well, had retained many contacts in the place and had often proved a useful source of information on the area.

'Sergeant, do you know a Colombury family by the name of Sarson?'

'Sarson? That's the name of the boy that drowned himself, sir.' Abbot took his eyes off the road and looked at his superior inquiringly.

'Yes,' replied the Chief Inspector, without further comment.

Abbot knew better than to ask further questions. Instead, he said, 'There's a furniture business called that in Colombury, sir, but it's not been there long, about five years, I think. I don't know the people who run it.'

'What sort of furniture business?'

'Nothing superior, sir. Not a real antique business or anything like that. I believe they buy second-hand stuff, do it up and sell it. There's a fair demand, and I'd imagine they make a reasonable living. But Sergeant Court will be our man. He's the authority on newish people in Colombury.'

'Yes, I suppose so. Anyway, we'll have to make our mark at the police station before we do anything else.'

Tansey hoped he didn't sound too reluctant. Sergeant Court was indeed an authority on Colombury and its inhabitants, and protocol demanded that they should call on him if they were to operate on his patch. But Court, now on the point of retiring, had always been a slow-speaking, slow-moving, slow-thinking officer who loved a good gossip, and Tansey visualized hours wasting away over cups of sugary tea.

He was not far wrong. By the time they left the Colombury police station he and Abbot were ready for a pint of beer and a good meal—both of which were readily obtained at the Windrush Arms. Nevertheless, the conversation with Sergeant Court had not been a waste of time. They had learnt quite a lot about the Sarsons.

Abbot had been correct when he said that the Sarsons had come to Colombury five years ago, and Court had been able to add that they had moved from Reading. They had bought a derelict house on the outskirts of the town with a variety of outbuildings, and had set up their business there. At that time the family had consisted of the elderly couple, Mr and Mrs Roger Sarson, and their son Bert and his wife Meg, who had two children. Bert's two brothers, Tom and young Steve lived at home and completed the group. They appeared to be an exceptionally close family, but they were not disliked in the town. They worked hard and had made a comparative success of their enterprise. They had never given the police any trouble—there had never been any suspicion of dealing in stolen goods, for example—though among the girls in the district Tom had a good or bad reputation, depending on the individual concerned.

The family had been devastated by Steve's death. Mrs Sarson had died shortly afterwards, and her death was said to be a direct result of the loss of her favourite son. As far as Sergeant Court knew, there had not been the slightest suggestion that the Sarsons blamed the University or St Xavier's College for Steve's suicide. The reasons generally accepted for the tragedy had been overwork and an unhappy love-affair.

'Not very encouraging,' Tansey said as he and Abbot finished their meal. 'These Sarsons sound an exemplary bunch—except perhaps for Tom. But his name, common as it may be, is another coincidence. I think we'd better go and have a look at them, Sergeant.'

Following Sergeant Court's instructions, Abbot had no difficulty in locating the Sarsons' establishment. It was not impressive, merely a collection of untidy buildings on an uncared-for area of land. One building bore a dilapidated sign: 'Sarson & Sons, Reconditioned Furniture'. As Abbot drew up, two toddlers, playing with a ball on a scrubby piece of grass in front of the ugly red-brick house, stopped their game to stare, and a mongrel dog, chained to its make-shift kennel, began to bark furiously.

The police officers had scarcely got out of their car when a woman appeared at the front door of the house. She was about thirty, and thin to the point of scrawniness. As if for protection, the toddlers at once ran to her and clung to her apron.

'Yes?' she said, pleasantly enough. 'What can I do for you? I'm afraid my husband's out, but if there's anything you were particularly looking for, I'm sure I could—'

'We're police officers,' interrupted Tansey. 'Detective Chief Inspector Tansey and Detective-Sergeant Abbot from the Thames Valley Police,' he announced, holding out his warrant card.

The woman's manner changed perceptibly. 'And just what do you want?' she demanded aggressively. 'We've never had no trouble here.'

'What we want is to speak to Mr Sarson?'

'Which one? I told you my husband was out.'

'Mr Roger Sarson—Mr Sarson senior.'

'Why?'

'We'll tell him that when we see him.'

'He's an old man and none too well. He had a stroke a few months ago. I'm his daughter-in-law, Meg Sarson.'

'Mrs Sarson, we still need to speak to your father-in-law.

I'm sorry about his health, but we'll be as considerate as we can.'

Meg Sarson gave a shrug of disgusted resignation. 'Oke!' she said.

She turned away before she saw the expression on Tansey's face as she used the slightly unusual—almost old-fashioned—slang. Shooshing the children back outside, she led the two men into the house and showed them into a front room. It was neat and clean, but gave the impression of being little used.

'Sit down,' she said, somewhat more amiably. 'I'll fetch him.'

Tansey sat, but Abbot strolled across to the fireplace and studied the photographs on the mantel. He had been attracted to them because they seemed to be mostly of the Sarson children at various ages, and he liked children. But, close to them, his attention was immediately seized by a coloured print of a bride and her groom. The bride was a younger, plumper version of the woman who had let them into the house; the groom, several inches shorter—a square-set, sandy-haired man—was presumably Bert Sarson, and he was in an army sergeant's uniform. Abbot stared at the photograph, then suddenly stiffened.

'Sir, you'd better have a look at this,' he said hurriedly as there were sounds in the passage outside the door.

Tansey had just time to take a quick glance at the wedding photograph and resume his seat before Meg Sarson brought in her father-in-law. Like his eldest son, he was a short, thick-set man. His greying hair showed signs of having once been sandy, and his eyes were a watery blue. He moved slowly, dragging his carpet-slippered feet across the floor, until he sank into an upright chair. Probably he was only in his mid-sixties, but it was difficult to visualize him as the father of Steve who, had he lived, would have been twenty-two or twenty-three by now.

'We're sorry to bother you, Mr Sarson, but we wonder

if you'd mind answering a few questions,' Tansey said.

'Same if I do,' said Sarson, clearly a man of few words.

'You've heard about the explosion at St Xavier's College in Oxford,' Tansey began.

'Saw about it on the telly.'

'Your son, Steve, was a student there. You must have been proud of him.' Tansey paused as Sarson grunted his assent. 'And his death must have been a great shock.' Sarson grunted again. 'Did he enjoy being at the College?' This time Sarson nodded without speaking. 'What did he think of Mr White, his tutor?'

At last there was a positive response. 'Steve liked Mr White and his family very much. Mr White's a good man, and he was kind to Steve. We're glad he wasn't hurt by that bomb.'

'But his daughter's been hurt, deliberately knocked off her bike.'

Involuntarily Sarson looked at his daughter-in-law, as if for confirmation. 'I—I didn't know,' he said. 'Why? I don't understand.' He sounded miserable and upset.

'How could you know, Pa?' Meg Sarson was quick to intervene. 'There's been nothing on the telly or in the papers, has there?' She addressed Tansey. 'How was the girl knocked down?'

'By a white van.'

'Really. There's lots of those about. We've got one ourselves, to move light furniture around.'

Tansey didn't bother to ask where the van had been on Saturday afternoon. He spoke directly to the old man. 'To return to Steve, Mr Sarson, were you annoyed when, after all the sacrifices you and your family had made, he didn't manage to get a degree?'

When Sarson didn't answer at once Tansey thought he hadn't heard the question. Then Sarson burst out. 'It was a lie! A lie! Steve was a clever boy. He didn't—'

'Pa!' In three strides Meg Sarson had crossed the room

and was standing over her father-in-law, shielding him from
Tansey's sight. She muttered something inaudible, and the
old man started to whimper. She turned on the Chief
Inspector. 'See what you've done. You've upset him. I told
you he wasn't well. Half the time he doesn't know what
he's doing or saying. You'd better clear out, the two of you!'

'Yes, of course, Mrs Sarson.' Tansey made no attempt
to argue with her. Signalling to Abbot, he rose to his feet.
'Goodbye, and thank you for your help.'

'What help?' she demanded, but received no answer.

As Tansey and Abbot came out of the house the dog
started barking again, but the children had disappeared.
Their voices could be heard calling to each other from one
of the outhouses. Then a white van, a table tied to its
roof, trundled up the lane and parked beside the unmarked
police car. Two men emerged; they were both sandy-haired,
blue-eyed and red-faced. The taller and younger man had
a crooked nose, which looked as if it might have been broken
in a fight.

'Good morning, sirs,' the older of the pair greeted them
politely. 'How can we be of help? We've some nice stuff at
the moment. Sorry we weren't here when you arrived, but
we've been to a sale in Chipping Norton. Incidentally, I'm
Bert Sarson. My brother, Tom.' He gestured.

'Police officers, not customers,' Tansey said, announcing
their names and ranks. 'My warrant card.' He held it out,
but Bert waved it away.

'What's the trouble? Stolen goods? We never deal in
them, Chief Inspector.'

'Nothing like that, Mr Sarson. We came to see your
father.'

'Pa?' Did the laugh that followed ring hollow? 'What on
earth would you want with Pa? He hardly leaves the house,
and I doubt if he's got the brains to mastermind a crime
any more—if he ever did.'

'Nevertheless, he was most helpful.'

'You've seen him?' Bert sounded wary.

'What was he helpful about?' It was Tom who couldn't resist the question.

'About your brother Steve.'

'He's dead!'

'Yes, indeed. I commiserate.' Tansey opened the car door and started to get in, then seemed to have second thoughts. 'By the way, Mr Sarson, when did you leave the army?'

'Five years ago, Chief Inspector. I'd done my time and I decided not to sign on again.' Bert Sarson spoke casually, but to Tansey he appeared to have tensed. 'I was married and my wife was expecting our second baby. It seemed sensible to settle down in business with my father.'

'Very sensible,' said Tansey, turning to the car. Then once more he changed his mind. 'May we have a look at your stock now we're here? You never know—'

There was only a slight hesitation before Bert answered, 'Of course.' He led the way to the largest of the outbuildings, while Tansey and Abbot glanced around curiously. 'This is the showroom,' Bert added a trifle pompously. The workshops are over there.' He pointed to a couple of rusty Nissen huts.

Tansey seemed satisfied with only a cursory inspection of the varied collection of bits of furniture and other bric-à-brac that Sarson & Sons were offering for sale. Then he said, 'Well, many thanks. We must be off. Goodbye to you.'

As they drove away Abbot said, 'You saw what I saw in that photograph, sir? It was a clear print, and the regimental badges were unmistakable. Bert Sarson was a sapper—a Royal Engineer.'

'I saw,' replied Tansey. 'And did you notice the motorbike between a couple of those derelict buildings?'

'Indeed, sir,' said Abbot.

Tansey relapsed into silence. He was glad he couldn't read the Sarson family's thoughts. He guessed that one or two of them at least were wishing him every ill. Nevertheless, he was elated. He was sure in his own mind that he had traced the villains. The next step was to prove it—and he guessed that would be far from simple.

CHAPTER 17

'You've put up a reasonable case, Chief Inspector.'

He didn't add, 'But not good enough.' It wasn't necessary. Tansey knew the Chief Constable's habits. He would now delve and probe and, unless Tansey could produce convincing arguments to support his hypotheses, his so-called case would be shredded.

'You're happy about it, in your own mind?' Midvale inquired, shifting his bulk in the large chair that had been specially made for him. 'No doubts? No doubts at all? But of course you've got doubts.'

'Of course, sir.' Tansey found he had no alternative but to acquiesce.

The Chief Inspector glanced around the Chief Constable's office, hoping to gain inspiration from somewhere or something—the Bratby hanging on the wall behind Midvale's desk, for example, or even the plain Wilton carpet on the floor. The more he had considered Bert and Tom Sarson, the more convinced he had become that they were guilty of the bomb outrage at St Xavier's; but he was fully aware that the evidence he had so far obtained against them was circumstantial, and their apparent motive terribly weak. In other circumstances he would have been content to wait, to dig deeper, to repeat interviews, to follow up seemingly useless leads. But now he was fearful, pressured by a need for urgency.

He was fearful for the Whites, and for Rosemary in particular. She was the only witness who might be able to identify Tom—and Tom probably knew it. What was more,

Tom, unlike his brother Bert, appeared to be an impulsive character, lacking in common sense. It had been foolish in the extreme to attempt to rape Rosemary after her abortive effort to escape through the bathroom window, when his brother was waiting downstairs and highly unlikely to coun- tenance such a crime. And, in fact, if he had not made this stupid attempt, Rosemary would never have seen his face.

It had been equally foolish to knock her off her bicycle— especially with a van that could have been identified—and equally foolish to threaten her. This last effort had merely tended to confirm that she could have and indeed had rec- ognized him. And it followed that, once Tom felt that the police were moving in on him, he would try some other violent means to silence Rosemary.

'Let's consider just what you've got on this family,' said the Chief Constable. As he spoke he ticked off the points one by one on his broad fingers. 'Fact one: the brothers are the right height and build to fit the villains as described by all the Whites, and one is called Tom. Two: the Sarson family have a connection with St Xavier's through Steve. Three: because of Steve they knew of Mr White and liked him, and the senior villain emphasized throughout the epi- sode that they intended no harm should come to the Whites. Four: Bert was a sapper, and it's possible he could have had a knowledge of explosives—incidentally, have we been on to the Met to ask the Ministry of Defence about the details of his record?'

'Yes, sir, but it's taking time.'

'Well, let's go on. Fact five: The Sarsons run a white van and a motorcycle. Six: they seem to favour the word 'oke' rather than the more usual 'OK'. And seven: Rosemary White believes she can identify Tom.'

Midvale sighed. 'As I said, Chief Inspector, taken together the points I've enumerated add up to quite a good case, but all the same I can't see the DPP buying it. Quite apart from a competent barrister, any third-year law

student would take it fact by fact, and treat them individu-
ally with derision. The DPP would argue that any cumulat-
ive effect would be lost in the confusion of a trial. In fact,
what you've done is prove that the Sarsons—together with
a few other people—*might well* have committed the crime.
Even Rosemary White's identification isn't worth much.
The girl admits she only caught a glimpse of the villain's
face, and any defence counsel would make a lot of the point
that she was under considerable stress at the time. Then he
would argue that Rosemary White saw Tom Sarson in the
street and, because of a chance resemblance, she imagined
that he and her assailant were one and the same. An identity parade would be useless. You follow my train of
thought, Chief Inspector? You agree?'

'Yes, sir,' said Tansey. There was nothing else he could
say.

'And as yet we haven't come to the major weakness in
the case against the Sarsons—the fact that they have no
clear motive. Steve had already taken his exams and gone
down from the University when he drowned himself. The
family had no reason to connect his death with St Xavier's,
especially as, according to the evidence at the inquest, he
had taken his life because at the time he was depressed over
a love-affair that had turned out badly.'

'Are you suggesting I should forget the Sarsons, sir?'
Tansey was becoming slightly annoyed at this shredding of
his case.

'No! Don't be silly, Dick. I'm merely suggesting that
you should keep an open mind.' Unexpectedly the Chief
Constable gave Tansey a broad smile. 'And I also suggest
that you review the case from the beginning. You may well
be right about the Sarsons, but you need to plug the holes.'

Dick Tansey sat in his office, thinking of holes and man-
holes and manhole covers. The Chief Constable had done
his best to fragment his case, but he still believed in it.

Admittedly, some of the evidence he had collected could be applied against persons (so far unknown) other than the Sarsons—but only when taken item by item. Nevertheless, there were two holes that were really worrying: the lack of motive, a most annoying point that he had appreciated all along; and Rosemary's identification, about which he had previously felt reasonably secure.

He decided to tackle the second, and simpler, part of the evidence first. Obeying the Chief Constable's injunctions, he re-read the files that related to Rosemary's description of the man who had attempted to rape her—or whom she thought was about to attempt to rape her. He had always been impressed by the common sense that the girl had shown, and the lack of diffidence with which she had treated the matter. He was pleased to note now that from the beginning, before she had helped the artist create an impression of Tom, and before she had seen Tom in the street, she had mentioned his crooked nose. This was not a characteristic that she was likely to have invented and, he was sure, it went a long way towards validating Rosemary's identification. That hole could fairly be said to have been plugged.

The lack of motive presented far more of a problem. If the Sarsons were the villains, the motive had to be connected with Steve, and the Master had to have been the prime, though perhaps not the sole, target of the bomb attack, for no one could have known in advance precisely which of the senior dons—apart from Pinel himself—might or might not be present at a particular meeting in the Lodgings. It followed then that the Sarsons—if they were guilty— believed, rightly or wrongly, that Sir Philip Pinel had done Steve some immeasurable harm—a harm that had to be avenged.

But what harm or injury would warrant such a violent attack on the Master, his senior staff and the College, Tansey failed to imagine. Nor were the files any help. In spite of his sense of urgency, he realized that he would have to start again, interviewing the same individuals, but possibly asking different questions. He needed to know a great deal more about Steve Sarson than had so far been unearthed.

Since he felt that it was vital not to arouse any suspicions in the minds of the Sarsons that the police had more than a passing interest in them, Tansey decided to ignore them for the moment and to commence his new round of inquiries with Greg White. From what he already knew of Steve, the young man's behaviour seemed to have been reasonably understandable, except in one respect—his failure to get any sort of degree. Clearly this fact had puzzled White, who had been his tutor, and old Mr Sarson's reaction to a query about his son's misfortune had been, to say the least, peculiar.

Was there any way in which the results of Steve's examinations could have been wrong or misinterpreted? Tansey put the question to Greg, whom he found the next morning in his rooms in the College, in conversation with Ailsa Mackay. Neither could produce an adequate answer.

At last Ailsa said, 'Isn't it possible that old Mr Sarson refuses to believe that his clever son could have failed?'

'Sure,' Tansey agreed, but he remembered how quick Meg Sarson had been to interrupt her father-in-law, and to emphasize that he was not altogether a 'responsible' witness.

He said, 'Mr White, you told me you were going to contact the head of the examining board about Steve Sarson.'

'Yes. I've done that, Chief Inspector, and I've also talked again to Dr Cathcart. At present Cathcart's at home recovering from peritonitis, but normally he's in charge of the language side of St Xavier's English teaching. He repeated what he'd told me before. He had been surprised that Steve hadn't got a degree, and when he asked about Steve's language papers he had been informed that they had been perfectly adequate. He had left it at that. It seems that it was the papers on English literature—my responsi-

bility, Chief Inspector, and Steve's strong side—that had
let him down. Professor Massey-King, the examiner, confirmed that.'

'Something odd must have happened. You mustn't
blame yourself, Greg,' Ailsa said as he shook his head in
disgust. 'Perhaps Steve didn't feel well when he sat the
papers, or he misread the questions or—'

'Nonsense!' Greg said savagely.

Ailsa shrugged; she knew his anger was not directed at
her, and she insisted, 'There must be some explanation,
Greg.'

'What I don't understand is why Steve should tell me
that he'd liked the papers, that he'd been lucky in what
he'd chosen for last-minute revision work and was sure he'd
done well. It makes no sense. Why should he lie to me?'
Greg demanded. 'He must have known he'd made a mess
of his chances.'

'What exactly did Professor Massey-King say?' Tansey
asked, trying to deflect Greg White from his futile recrimi-
nations.

'He wasn't very forthcoming.' Greg gave a somewhat
bitter laugh. 'In fact, he was damned unhelpful. All he'd
say was that what Steve had offered in the way of literature
papers had made it impossible to award him a degree of
any kind.'

'Is Massey-King always so uncooperative?' Tansey
inquired.

'I don't know him well, but I wouldn't have thought so.'
Greg was doubtful. 'Perhaps he'd had a bad egg for breakfast when I saw him. Anyway, he flatly refused to discuss
the subject further. He said it was past history, and it would
be a mistake to rake over the dirt now. Steve was dead. It
was a great pity, but nothing could be done about it.'

'How unkind!' said Ailsa. 'He sounds appalling.'

Tansey hesitated. 'Mr White, Professor Massey-King
used the word dirt?'

'Yes. I must admit I thought it a bit odd.'

'Well, this may sound an odd question, but did it strike you that Massey-King was at all nervous or personally upset that you'd re-opened this matter?'

'I'm not sure what you're getting at, Chief Inspector.' Greg looked questioningly at Tansey. 'Professor Massey-King is not a nervous type, but in retrospect I suppose I did have an impression that he was irritated—or perhaps embarrassed—but I could easily be wrong.'

'I see. Many thanks, Mr White,' said Tansey, and thought that it might be a good idea if he himself were to pay a call on this Professor Massey-King.

Professor Massey-King was a tall and handsome man, with grey hair and a florid complexion. He had an autocratic air and, as soon as his secretary had shown Tansey into his study, distanced himself from the Chief Inspector by waving him to a chair without speaking. He did not rise from behind his desk, nor did he offer his hand. Instead, he continued to glance through some documents for a moment or two, remaining perfectly polite but implying that he was in a commanding position and that his time was valuable.

'What is this about, Chief Inspector? My secretary says you refused to tell her. It sounds unduly enigmatic.'

'Not really, sir, but it *is* confidential, which is one of the reasons I have come without my sergeant. I'm making inquiries about a member of the University who drowned himself last year. His name was Steve Sarson.'

'Steve Sarson? Why come to me? He wasn't at this College and I never taught him.'

Professor Massey-King spoke in a mildly bored tone and his expression remained calm, but Tansey was watching his hands which, fingertips together, had been forming a casual pyramid on his desktop. Tansey was sure he saw the fingers tense, then relax, and he knew that this Professor was not at ease.

'But I'm told you were responsible for his failure to get a degree, sir.'

'Not I, Chief Inspector. Sarson was responsible for that himself.'

'I'm sorry. I see your point. I worded my sentence badly. But perhaps you'd be good enough to explain exactly what *you* mean, sir. I gather he was a clever young man.'

'That's as may be. All I know is that the English literature papers he offered were not adequate for him to be awarded a degree.' Massey-King paused; if he had briefly felt insecure, the moment had passed. 'Chief Inspector, I don't imagine you understand how the system functions, but there could have been nothing personal about the examiners' decision to fail Sarson. Papers are anonymous when they are marked and classified.'

Tansey, feeling frustrated, tried another tack. 'Could Sarson have known about his failure before the results were published? Could this have been a contributory cause for his suicide?'

'It's—possible, Chief Inspector.'

Tansey noticed the hesitation. He saw Massey-King stare at him, and sensed that the Professor would very much prefer to bring the interview to a close. Though Massey-King had appeared to be completely frank, he had shown a certain tension that one wouldn't have expected if he had been indifferent to, or objective about, the subject under discussion.

'I must ask you a direct question, sir,' Tansey said quickly. 'To the best of your knowledge, did Steve Sarson know about his failure to get a degree before he committed suicide?'

Massey-King took his time before answering. At last he said, 'Chief Inspector, I don't think I'm prepared to answer your question unless you can give me a good reason for it.'

'That's simple, sir.' Tansey was blunt. 'The Master's

Lodgings at St Xavier's College have been partially destroyed by a bomb. People have been injured. The Senior Tutor has since died—'

'I know! I know all that.' Massey-King interrupted. His air of superiority had deserted him, and he was clearly shaken. 'But what's that to do with Steve Sarson? It's over a year since the suicide and the boy's dead. It never occurred to me that there could be any connection with the St Xavier's bombing.'

'To be honest, sir, I'm not certain there is a connection, but there's circumstantial evidence pointing in that direction, and I need to know if the Sarsons had any reason to harbour a grudge against the Master and St Xavier's.'

'I see. The simple answer to that is no!'

'I have to judge that for myself, sir.'

Massey-King gave Tansey a calculating stare. 'Very well, Chief Inspector,' he said reluctantly, 'I'll tell you what happened, as simply as I can.'

Steve Sarson had sat his Finals and his papers had been duly marked. Except for three of the English literature papers, he would have got a Second Class degree. These three papers were brilliant, and would have assured him a First. But—and this was a big but—they were too brilliant. A careful study of them revealed that Sarson had possibly seen the questions in advance and been able to prepare for them.

'You mean he'd cheated?'

Tansey was amazed. He remembered old Mr Sarson's words. 'They lied,' he'd said, 'Steve was a clever boy. He didn't—' Then his daughter-in-law had shut him up. Didn't what? Didn't cheat—or perhaps didn't need to cheat?

'If you want to put it like that, yes, he cheated!' said Massey-King.

'How is it that this didn't become public knowledge?' Tansey asked suspiciously. 'I'm surprised it wasn't a scandal at the time. Surely the media would have made a splash with it—especially after Sarson's suicide. Yet not even Mr White, Steve's tutor, knew about it.'

Massey-King nodded slowly. 'The whole affair was hushed up. With hindsight this may have been a mistake, but at the time . . . Chief Inspector, Sir Philip Pinel, the Master of St Xavier's, is a friend of mine. We were at school together and our families are close. When I suspected that Steve Sarson had cheated I went to see Philip Pinel. Naturally he was extremely upset. He had always had a very high regard for the reputation of his College, maintaining that one couldn't expect support for an institution with poor standards of conduct. Pinel was afraid that the College would hardly survive such a scandal.

'Anyway Pinel sent for Steve and confronted him with the the evidence for our suspicions. The Senior Tutor was also present, I believe. At first Sarson denied the accusation vehemently, but then he admitted it and agreed to have the papers in question withdrawn. Twenty-four hours later his body was pulled out of the Cherwell.'

'Poor young man.'

'Yes. It was sad, Chief Inspector, I agree. It also left us with a problem. In the circumstances he couldn't be awarded a degree, even posthumously, as it were. That would have been highly immoral. On the other hand he was dead, and there was no point in a scandal that would harm his memory and his family—'

'And St Xavier's College?'

'That too!' Massey-King gave a thin smile. 'So the papers in question were destroyed and his name was omitted from the published class lists. I had some words with the examiners who had seen them, and scarcely anyone else inquired about the case. If they did, it wasn't difficult to dissemble.'

'His family?'

'Not as far as I know. I imagine they were too concerned over his death to worry about exam results, and the Master would have dealt with any questions they might have had

easily enough. It was made plain at the inquest that Steve
took his life because of an affair with a girl that turned out
badly. This could also have affected how he coped with his
examination and explained why he failed to get a degree.'

'Yes indeed,' Tansey said absently. He was thinking that
yet again a scandal threatening St Xavier's and its Master
had been conveniently avoided.

CHAPTER 18

'I do not believe it, Chief Inspector.' Greg White emphasized each word separately. 'I know you've told us that
Massey-King says that Steve admitted it to the Master, but
in spite of that I'd as soon believe that Tony Pulent—whom
I've known all his life—was a cheat. I grant that Steve
Sarson was an odd mixture. He was to some extent street-
wise, as they say, but he was also disingenuous. Above all,
he was proud, proud of what he'd already accomplished,
and of what he hoped to achieve in the future. He would
not have stooped to cheating.'

'Not even if he'd been afraid of getting a poor degree?'
Tansey asked tentatively. 'You said yourself that he hadn't
done much work in his last year.'

'He already had a good job lined up, hadn't he?' Peter
Lacque remarked before White could answer.

The three men were in the Bursar's office where Tansey
had tracked down Greg White. The Chief Inspector had
told them in confidence what he had learnt from Professor
Massey-King. He was intrigued by their reactions.

'Yes. He'd been offered a lectureship at London University.' White replied to the Bursar's question, and added for
Tansey's benefit, 'Not terribly well-paid but a fine beginning for an academic career. London would naturally have
been disappointed if Steve hadn't got his First—and so

would he, though he'd not really done enough work recently to deserve it, as you suggested, Chief Inspector. Nevertheless, I doubt if they'd have reneged on their offer, not unless his results had been very poor.'

'All right,' said Tansey. 'I accept your opinion, as far as it goes. Steve Sarson was an unlikely character to cheat, and there was no great pressing reason for him to do so. But still, what about opportunity?'

'That's something I fail to understand,' said Lacque. 'How could he have seen the papers in advance? They're always most jealously guarded.'

'Have there been similar cases before—proved cases, I mean? Have papers ever been sold, for instance?'

'Not to my knowledge, though I suppose it could have happened in the past, when security might have been more lax.'

'Anyway, I'm sure Steve wouldn't have had the money to buy them—or know how to set about it,' White objected.

'Then what would you say to accident?' asked Tansey. 'Accidents do happen. The most responsible people seem to leave briefcases full of vital documents in taxis or trains. Couldn't a forgetful professor have left the exam questions out on his desk, and mightn't Steve have been tempted?'

'What forgetful professor, and where?'

'You tell me, Mr White!' Tansey had momentarily lost patience with the conversation, which was getting him nowhere. 'Let's face the fact of Steve's admission. I reiterate that Massey-King claims that Steve Sarson admitted to your Master, Sir Philip Pinel, that he'd cheated. Now you're trying to persuade me that Steve couldn't possibly have done so. Can you explain that anomaly?'

'No, I can't, Chief Inspector. You'll have to ask the Master. Let's hope he can explain, though I have my doubts. All I know is that no one at St Xavier's can have had any advance knowledge of or connection with the examination papers for the English School. So how and where could Steve have seen them?' White turned to the Bursar. 'You agree, Philip?'

'Yes, Greg, I—I agree.'

But Tansey noticed the slight hesitation in the Bursar's reply. He watched as Peter Lacque picked up a pen from his desk and played with it, before seeming to come to a decision.

'I do have a thought about a possible connection,' he said. 'I'm afraid it's pretty far-fetched, but—'

'That doesn't matter,' Tansey said quickly. 'The oddest scrap of information sometimes helps.'

Lacque still seemed reluctant to speak, but eventually he said, 'It's about Emma Watson, who was on the staff here until recently.' He spent a couple of minutes repeating what both his listeners knew before he came to his point. 'I remember that in the Trinity Term before last she did some work for Professor Massey-King. His secretary was ill, and this was a particularly busy time for him. I'd heard he was in need of assistance, and I was aware that Emma could well do with some extra money, so I—I suggested she should help him out.'

'You mean there's a possibility she might have seen the English Literature question papers?' Tansey said bluntly.

'Yes, a vague possibility,' Lacque admitted, 'but even if she had why should she have told Sarson about them?'

'He wasn't one of her pupils,' said White. 'She taught history, and I doubt that if she'd met Steve in the quad she could have put a name to him.'

'Well, thanks all the same. I value your opinions.' Tansey thoughtfully looked at his watch. He had decided to keep his own counsel about Emma Watson's relationship with Steve Sarson. 'Quite clearly, I must make an effort to see Sir Philip.'

*

The Chief Inspector's interview with the Master of St Xavier's was brief and largely pointless. Pinel made no pretence that the revival of the story of Steve Sarson's death and its probable causes had taken him by surprise. He was the first to introduce the subject.

'I've been talking to Professor Massey-King,' he said, 'and he tells me you're interested in Sarson's failure to get a degree, Chief Inspector. I follow your train of thought. You believe the Sarson family may have blamed me and the College for this misfortune, and decided to take matters into their own hands and exact some kind of revenge.'

'Yes, sir,' said Tansey. He couldn't refrain from adding, 'You've put the case very clearly.'

'Then I'll put this clearly too, Chief Inspector. That theory is all hogwash. Steve Sarson cheated over his examinations. He admitted it to me, and to save a lot of adverse publicity it was agreed that he would withdraw the papers in question—which meant that he hadn't offered sufficient to warrant a degree. He had reason to be grateful to me, not the reverse. It could have been very unpleasant for him if I hadn't offered him this way out, but had taken further action.'

And it would have been unpleasant for the College too, Tansey thought. Aloud he said, 'Did the family ever ask you about Steve's failure, sir?'

'No. I believe Miss Mackay, my secretary, went to see Sarson's parents, and I know that Mr White visited them later, after he came back from the United States. Of course, neither of them knew anything about the cheating.'

'Did Steve Sarson explain to you how he managed to cheat?'

'I don't quite understand.'

'Did he say where and when and how he learnt the details of the examination questions?'

'No.'

'And you didn't inquire?'

'No,' Sir Philip said shortly. 'Chief Inspector, surely this is all irrelevant. If the Sarsons harboured any malice against me and St Xavier's over Steve's death, why didn't they take action months ago instead of waiting for more than a year?'

As he took his leave of the Master, Tansey had to admit that this was a valid point. Information he had received from the Ministry of Defence via the Met made it clear that Bert Sarson, as a result of his training and experience in the army, had the ability to make a simple explosive mixture and construct an explosive device whenever he wished. So why this long delay? Tansey could think of no answer to this poser.

The Chief Inspector's next move was to phone Emma Watson and ask her to meet him. She had been fetched out of a class and was not in the best of tempers. She said she was busy during the rest of the day, but when Tansey insisted agreed to meet him at the Saracen's Head in Abingdon at six o'clock that evening.

She arrived at six-thirty. Tansey was conscious of the admiring glances she received from the men leaning against the bar as she came across to the corner table he had secured. She didn't apologize for her unpunctuality. She sat down, unbuttoned her jacket to reveal a low-cut blouse and gave him a provocative smile.

'What, no sergeant, Mr Tansey? You're brave to come alone. What about your reputation?'

Tansey ignored the taunts. He summoned a waiter and ordered drinks. He had already decided how to deal with Miss Watson. In silence he waited for the return of the waiter.

Then he said suddenly,' Why did you lie to me the last time we met?'

'Lie to you?' Emma opened her eyes wide.

'You told me you'd had what you described as a 'one-night stand'with Steve Sarson. You knew him much better than that, didn't you?'

'What if I did, Chief Inspector? My sex life and his are no concern of yours. Especially now the poor boy's dead—'

'Because of you!'

'Me? Don't be a fool, Tansey. Steve would never have drowned himself for love of *me*. It was that Amanda Hulton he wanted, but I thought he'd more or less got over her. He told me he'd accepted that she wasn't for him. That's why his death was such a shock. I was really upset when I heard. I liked the boy. He didn't treat me like a tart as— as classy guys like Hugh Fremont did. He was a—a genuine person.'

Tansey stared at her. He had to believe what she said. It would have taken a fine actress to put on such a performance without warning. Emma Watson had cared for Steve Sarson. She had done her best to comfort him. She'd assumed he'd taken his own life because of his unrequited live for Amanda Hulton. She obviously knew nothing about the accusation of cheating.

'I'm sorry,' he said, though he wasn't sure why he was apologizing. He hurried on. 'Miss Watson, I have other questions to ask you. During the Trinity Term of last year you did some work for Professor Massey-King. Is that correct?'

'Yes. That's right, but—'

'You knew he was the Chairman of the Examining Board for students taking their English Finals?'

Emma Watson nodded. 'Of course. I did a lot of work for him while his regular secretary was away.'

'And some of that was confidential work, Miss Watson. It would have been a great breach of confidentiality if you had betrayed any details of the examination papers to anyone—and particularly to anyone who was going to sit the examinations, wouldn't it? In fact, it would allow such an individual to cheat.'

'Yes, I suppose—' Emma stopped abruptly. 'Ye gods!' she exclaimed. 'You're talking about Steve. But it wasn't like that. At least it wasn't meant to be. Steve would never have cheated, not knowingly.'

She gulped down the remains of her gin and tonic and held out her empty glass; she had become quite pale. Tansey waved to the waiter and ordered another drink for her. He had scarcely touched his own whisky. He looked at Emma anxiously. She was clearly upset, but by the time the fresh drink had arrived she had largely regained her composure.

'Tell me what happened,' Tansey said gently. 'How could someone cheat unknowingly?'

'Well, one night Steve was explaining that it was impossible to revise everything, and how there was a lot of luck in what one chose to do with limited time—which is true enough. And—and I don't know what got into me, except that I felt sorry for him. Anyway, I said, "I'll make five choices for you," and I did. Later he told me that three of them had proved to be right. I'd known they would be, because I'd seen the papers. Massey-King sometimes left various drafts on his desk.'

'Didn't Steve suspect?'

'No. Why should he? He didn't know Massey-King was to be the chief examiner. He thought my choices were pure chance. Anyway, he could easily have decided to revise those particular subjects himself. And I didn't enlighten him. Term ended and I had other things on my mind.'

'I'm afraid what you did was *not* trivial, Miss Watson. It was very important. Steve was accused of cheating, and as a result failed to get any kind of degree.'

Emma was aghast. 'And that's—that's why he committed suicide? You mean it was my fault? Oh shit! Why didn't he explain? I'd have supported him. Not that it would have helped him—not if that bastard Philip Pinel had anything to do with it.' She paused, then ended miserably, 'Oh poor,

poor Steve! He was a clever boy. He didn't need to cheat.'

'It's a sad story,' Tansey agreed, 'and it's not finished yet.'

'What do you mean?' Emma was still thinking of Steve.

'Miss Watson, I'm telling you this in confidence. If any persons considered they had cause to bear a grudge against St Xavier's and its Master, surely they would be the Sarson family. And there are other reasons for suspecting that Steve's brothers, Bert and Tom, may have been responsible for the recent bomb outrage.'

'Is that why you've been asking me all these questions?' Emma stared at him in horror. 'Of course,' she answered for herself. 'How stupid of me. I should have realized but—but it was so long ago. Why should they have waited till now?'

It was the same weakness in the case against the Sarsons that Sir Philip Pinel had spotted immediately. But, having found an excellent motive, Tansey was sure there would be a reasonable explanation—if only he could light upon it. He decided to pull in Bert and Tom for questioning the next day.

But a great deal was to happen before then.

Even in retrospect no one could blame the Chief Inspector's decision to wait until the next day before taking further action, or for the consequences of his decision. Where Tansey could be faulted was in his judgement of Emma Watson. He was right in his assessment that she had been appalled when she learnt that what had been intended as a friendly gesture towards a young man she liked had had such disastrous results. What he failed to appreciate was the extent of Emma's hatred for the Master of St Xavier's.

At eight o'clock that evening, as Dick Tansey and his wife Hilary were sitting down to supper, the telephone rang in the Sarsons' house on the outskirts of Colombury. Bert and Meg were upstairs putting their children to bed. The old man was asleep in front of the kitchen fire. Tom answered the phone.

When Tansey learnt of this much later he was convinced that Emma Watson had been the caller, but there was no proof of this and he never bothered to pursue the matter. There was only Tom's evidence that an anonymous voice had said, 'The police believe you're responsible for the St Xavier's bombing. Take care.'

For Tom, 'taking care' meant only one thing—the elimination of Rosemary White, who alone could identify him. He didn't tell his brother Bert about the warning. He wanted no argument. He decided to act himself.

CHAPTER 19

The next day dawned cold and dank. It had been raining ever since midnight in a steady downpour, which by nine in the morning had become a mournful drizzle. Greg White, calling goodbye to his wife and daughter, left his house. He said good morning to the uniformed constable who was trying to shelter under a tree that offered little protection, and told him to go and stand in the porch.

'You can guard us just as well from there,' he said. 'No one else will be going out this morning. So when you feel like it, ring the bell and tell my wife you could do with a hot drink.'

'Many thanks, sir.'

The police officer was grateful. He had been on duty since six, and it would be another three hours before he was relieved. He was not a young man and privately Greg wondered if he would be of much use in the event of an attempt to enter the house. But at least he was a symbol of the law. Smiling at the thought, Greg got into his car and started for the College.

Rosemary watched him from her bedroom window. She had needed to visit the bathroom but, having observed the weather, she was glad to get back into bed and snuggle under the duvet. She was feeling much better, and her temperature was normal. Later, she proposed to dress and spend most of the day up, as she had done yesterday. But this required an effort, and for the moment she lacked the energy.

Neither Greg as he drove down the street, nor Rosemary as she watched him go, noticed the blue Mercedes that was parked a couple of hundred yards along the road. The policeman had seen it, but it had not occurred to him to question its presence. Admittedly, Mercedes cars were not that frequent in these North Oxford residential streets mainly inhabited by dons with families and mortgages, but he had only been warned to look out for a white van or a motorbike. No one had mentioned a Mercedes, and no one had told him that such a car had been stolen during the night, or that the man sitting behind the wheel in a chauffeur's peaked cap which hid his sandy hair was other than what he seemed.

Tom Sarson had seen Greg leave the house, and had been relieved that he was alone. He had thought that on such a vile day her father might have driven Rosemary to school. Tom, of course, had no idea that Rosemary had been ill; his plan, such as it was, had been hastily formulated without thought of reconnaissance or discreet inquiry; reasoning and analysis were hardly part of Tom's impulsive nature. He waited, expecting the girl to appear at any minute, though he was beginning to worry. He couldn't understand why she was so late.

Jean White had washed up the breakfast dishes and was about to go upstairs to make the beds. She had decided that it was time for Rosemary to have a bath and get dressed; her routine must start to return to normal now that she had recovered from the bug. But as Jean passed through the hall she saw that the letters she had written the evening before were still lying on the table; Greg, who had promised to post them, had forgotten. She swore under her breath. One of the letters was important.

For Jean had made up her mind that as soon as Rosemary was well enough to travel, the girl must go to stay with Greg's parents, as had been planned. At the same time, she herself would pay a visit to her sister, who lived in Scotland. Greg would have to cope by himself, but she didn't care. He could always move into his rooms in his beloved St Xavier's. She needed to get away from Oxford and find some place where she was not an object of curiosity to friends and strangers, where she could try to relax. And she also knew that she must get away from Greg, if only for a short time. But the letter asking her sister, who had married late and had several small children, if a visit would be convenient, remained on the hall table. She would have to post it herself. For a moment she thought of the phone, but then dismissed the idea; it would be discourteous to confront Isobel with the need for an instant decision.

'Rosemary!' she called up the stairs. 'I'm just going out. Won't be five minutes. Your dad forgot the letters.'

'OK, Mum.'

Jean picked up the mail and went to the cupboard by the side door where the family kept raincoats, boots, Wellingtons and a miscellany of gardening clothes. The postbox was only at the end of the road, and on such a day she didn't care what she looked like. She put on some boots and took down the nearest raincoat. It was an old school mackintosh of Rosemary's which she had abandoned as too short, but it still fitted Jean who was not as tall as her daughter. What was more, it had a hood that would protect her hair. She slipped it on and let herself out of the house.

'Going to the post,' she said when she saw the police officer. 'I'll make us some coffee when I get back.'

'Thank you, ma'am. That would be most welcome.'

Shoulders hunched and head bent Jean hurried through the murky drizzle towards the postbox. She was unaware how very like she was to Rosemary, in the school raincoat and with her face hidden. And Tom Sarson had been waiting for Rosemary. He was expecting her to appear and when he saw the figure turn out of the Whites' driveway and come along the pavement towards him, it never occurred to him for a moment that it could be anyone but Rosemary.

He started his engine and jammed his foot hard on the accelerator. As the Mercedes surged forward he was fleetingly pleased with his foresight at having chosen to steal a big and powerful vehicle for the task he had in view.

Without hesitation he mounted the pavement and drove straight at Jean. She had no time even to scream. Nor was the watching police officer, dashing towards her and shouting into his walkie-talkie as he ran, in time to be of any help.

There was merely a dull thud as Jean's body was thrown up on to the car's bonnet and then the screech of brakes as the Mercedes scraped along the wall in front of a house. In a moment Tom had the car under control again. He bounced off the kerb, causing Jean's body to slide into the road, and deliberately drove over her, before speeding away.

He had no idea that he had killed the wrong woman.

Dick Tansey, alerted within minutes, faced a situation that was typical of so many cases; after a period of seeming inaction, a sudden spate of activity made it vital for him to make rapid decisions, determine his priorities and delegate.

The Chief Inspector wished that he could be in three places at once. He would have liked to have broken the news of Jean's death to Greg, and helped him cope with the formalities which were always shattering. He would have liked to have been with Rosemary, and so assure himself that she was in no danger. He would have liked to arrest

Bert and Tom Sarson, especially Tom, because he sensed that an attack of this kind—irrational and hazardous as it was—was more in keeping with Tom's character than Bert's. In addition, he judged that Tom was the kind of villain who, if cornered, wouldn't hesitate to kill again.

He gave the matter a few moments' consideration, spoke briefly to the Chief Constable, doubled the protection on the Whites' house and sent WPC Robertson there with instructions to stay close to Rosemary and get in touch with the Pulents who, he was sure, could be depended on to give the girl every support. He dispatched Inspector Carey to St Xavier's, knowing that he could trust Carey to be both tactful and sensible. The Sarsons he reserved for himself.

With Bill Abbot driving, Tansey set off for Colombury once more. He was followed by a small convoy of experts, including a van with a sniffer dog. Their purpose was to take Bert and Tom Sarson into custody and if necessary tear apart the Sarsons' house and outbuildings in search of any evidence of the presence of explosives or the means of making an explosive device. It took but a short time to swear out the necessary warrants, but even that delay meant that the Chief Inspector was out of luck.

His party missed both Bert and Tom. As soon as the police cars reached the house, Meg, hearing them, came out. Her eyes were wide with fear and she clutched the two children to her.

'Is something wrong, Mrs Sarson?' Tansey asked.

'You tell me,' she replied. 'You've come for Bert, haven't you? And Tom? Well, you're wasting your time. They've gone and it's no use asking me where because I don't know, and if I did I wouldn't tell you.'

'When did they go?'

'A while back.'

'That's not very helpful.'

'It's not meant to be. Bert's my hubby and if you think I'm going to shop him you've got another guess coming.'

'Mrs Sarson, around nine o'clock this morning Jean White, the wife of Gregory White, was deliberately run down by a car and killed. It was murder.'

'Jean White? And she's dead? Oh Christ!' There was no doubting Meg Sarson's distress.

'Jean White, yes. Is that what surprises you, Mrs Sarson? Were you hoping the victim would be her daughter, Rosemary?'

'I wasn't hoping it would be anyone. And I'm sure Bert wasn't. It wasn't him! He was here at nine o'clock. He's only just—'

'Just left? And Tom?

'He's left too.'

'OK.' Tansey paused, considering. 'We'll go into that in a moment.' He gestured to Abbot. 'Get all the wheels in motion, Sergeant. Circulate their descriptions and let's pull them in as soon as possible.'

'Yes, sir. The white van's here but the motorbike isn't.'

'Good.' Tansey turned back to Meg Sarson. 'Mrs Sarson, even if you had no prior knowledge of this crime, there's such a thing as being an accessory after the fact, so you'd be well advised to cooperate with us. I want to question you further, and I've a warrant for my men to search your premises. All right?'

'Yes,' she said grudgingly. 'You'd better come into the kitchen. The old man's there and I'm not having him frightened by your lot.'

They trooped into the house, and Tansey's men dispersed. The Chief Inspector found himself in a large pleasant kitchen, warm and comfortable and obviously the centre of family life. Mr Sarson was sitting in a wicker chair in front of an open fire, and the two children immediately ran to him. It had all the appearance of a happy scene until Meg Sarson ruined it.

'Here's that Chief Inspector Tansey again, Pa. And more trouble.'

'There's always trouble,' said the old man gloomily, 'always has been, ever since our Steve died.' He ignored Tansey. 'It's the young 'uns you must care for now, Meg. There's hope for them.'

'Sure, Pa.' Meg sat herself at the long scrubbed wooden table, and gestured to Tansey to sit opposite her. 'Go on,' she said. 'Ask your questions.'

Perhaps partly because of her father-in-law's admonition, and partly because she was resigned to what she feared was about to happen, Meg Sarson became reasonably co-operative. Tom had arrived home on his motorbike about ten o'clock that morning; she didn't know how long he had been out. He had filled his saddle-bags with plastic carriers that she guessed contained a few clothes and personal belongings. Then he had a brief talk with Bert, said a hasty goodbye to everyone and left. She had no idea where he planned to go.

Tansey believed her. 'And Bert?' he said.

Meg sighed. 'Bert came to me,' she said. 'He was upset. He told me that everything had gone wrong, Tom was crazy and had done for them both. He said he loved me, but he couldn't stand life in prison and he wished they'd never found Steve's diary.'

'What?' Tansey couldn't suppress his surprise.

'That's how we know about the lies that the Master of his College told about Steve,' old Sarson suddenly interrupted.

'Be quiet, Pa!' Meg was sharp. 'Yes, Chief Inspector, Steve kept a diary. He hid it under a loose floorboard in his bedroom. Bert discovered it two or three months ago when he started to redecorate the room.'

'And that's when they decided to blow up the Master in his Lodgings,' said Tansey, and thought that the Sarsons' delay in attempting to avenge their brother had at last been explained.

'I suppose so. They didn't tell me. I knew nothing about

it, I swear. If I had, I'd have tried to stop them. It was a mad thing to do.'

'You must have guessed afterwards, Mrs Sarson.'

'What if I did? What would you have had me do? Bert's my husband. I'd never have shopped him,' she repeated.

Tansey didn't press her. 'What else did Bert say before he left?' he asked.

'Nothing much. He was in a hurry. He knew after what Tom had told him that you'd soon be on your way here. He just kissed me and said, 'I love you. Take care of Pa and the kids.' Then he went. I didn't even see him go.' Her voice broke and tears filled her eyes. 'Little Alf had wet himself and I had to change him.' She pointed to the smaller of the two children.

'Bert didn't take the van?'

'No. He knew we'd need it and—and he's always been considerate.'

'Where's the diary now? I'll have to take it with me. I'll give you a receipt.'

'I'll fetch it. It's in my room,' Mr Sarson said, as he slowly got to his feet and shuffled from the kitchen, the two children playing around his legs and impeding him.

Meg Sarson looked at Tansey. 'What happens now, Chief Inspector? If you take me in, the kids'll have to go into a home, and so will Pa. He's too sick and old to care for them, and there's nobody else but me.'

Tansey nodded. He could have commented that the considerate Bert might have thought of the possible consequences for his family before reacting so violently against St Xavier's and its Master, even if he believed some such action was justified on his brother Steve's behalf. But Tansey kept his peace. He too could be considerate, and he accepted that no good would come from charging Meg Sarson. She was no danger to the Whites, and her children would be the main sufferers if she were sent to prison.

'You stay here, Mrs Sarson—at least for the time being.

We'll need you as a witness when Bert and Tom are brought in, but otherwise you should be all right, though I can't promise. You'll have to wait and see. I'll leave a police guard with you.'

'Ta!' Meg managed a crooked smile. 'Here's Pa,' she said.

Old Mr Sarson had returned with the diary, which was in fact a collection of exercise books held together with a thick elastic band. He handed the bundle over to the Chief Inspector.

'Thanks,' Tansey said. 'You'll get these back in due course. Now I must go and see how my men are getting on.'

Meg Sarson followed him to the front door, and they were standing together when they heard a dull report.

Immediately a police officer came running from one of the outbuildings. 'It's Bert Sarson, sir,' he shouted. 'He's blown the back of his head off with what looks like a service revolver.'

Tansey took the bundle of Steve Sarson's exercise books home with him, and started on them after a quick supper. His wife Hilary had gone early to bed and there was nothing to distract him, but he was tired and he had to force himself to concentrate. It had been a bad day, one of the worst he could remember. There had been two deaths, Jean White's and Bert Sarson's, both of them in his opinion avoidable, as he had had to admit to the Chief Constable in his oral report late that afternoon.

Because he wanted to get a clear picture of Steve Sarson, Tansey resisted the temptation to tackle the books in reverse order, though he was sure that the last of them would be the most relevant. Steve had been methodical and had devoted one book to each of the nine terms he had spent up at Oxford.

As Tansey had expected the books that covered Steve's

first two years were of little importance, though they were
touching in many ways. They revealed the wonderment
and awe of a young man of eighteen suddenly flung into an
environment that was alien to him. Reading between the
lines, it was clear that St Xavier's—small and new, and
therefore a little exclusive and self-defensive, and with few
fellow-undergraduates from similar backgrounds—had not
been the ideal choice for a boy like Steve.

Nevertheless, he had worked hard. He had enjoyed the
work and he had been determined to get a good degree. His
work had also provided him with a safe haven, where he
need have no fear of doing the wrong thing; he had been
lucky in having Greg White, whom he liked and admired,
as his tutor. But White, though he had probably tried, had
been unable to save the boy from various embarrassments,
such as Fairchild's amusement when he had mistaken the
head porter, Dobson, for a don, or Lady Pinel's obvious
disdain when he had upset a plate of cakes at one of her
tea parties for undergraduates.

He had joined several clubs, but by the end of a couple
of terms had more or less abandoned them. He wasn't interested in politics or religion or sport and, though he enjoyed
some meetings of an experimental theatre club he met no
kindred spirits there. He had never found it easy to make
friends and he had little spare money, which didn't help.
Nevertheless, it was clear from what he had written that he
was enormously proud of being up at Oxford, and that the
place lost none of its magic as time went on.

During this period his social life had been virtually nil,
but everything had changed at the beginning of his third
year, when he was allocated to a different staircase, and
found himself in a set of rooms opposite those of Peregrine
Courcey. Why Courcey should have befriended him was a
mystery, but one that no longer bothered Steve once he had
met Hugh Fremont and Amanda Hulton. From then on he
seemed to have lived in a dream world.

It was after midnight when Tansey reached Steve's last
exercise book, with its account of Steve's final term. Inevitably the dream had come to an abrupt end. Amanda had
merely laughed at his proposal of marriage. She had treated
it as a joke and told Fremont and Courcey about it. Courcey
had been kind but blunt: Steve would never be 'one of
them'.

Although Steve had been made miserable by this, there
was no suggestion that he considered taking his own life
because of it. He had found some consolation in a renewed
return to his work, which he knew he had been neglecting,
and in the kindness of Emma Watson whom he had got
to know earlier through a chance meeting in the College
library.

Then there had been the stress of his Final examinations,
though he had been pleased with the papers. The accusation of cheating had come as a tremendous blow. 'I did
NOT cheat,' he had written several times, and underlined
the words. 'How could I?' he asked.

Tansey read through these pages several times. He was
appalled. Steve Sarson's account of events was fundamen-
tally different from Sir Philip Pinel's. According to Steve,
he had been given no chance to defend himself, and no
notice had been taken of his denials. Pinel had simply said
that denial was useless; the senior members of the College
had decided that he should withdraw the suspect papers,
that he would not be awarded a degree and that he must
refuse the teaching post he had been offered at London
University—if London did not withdraw their offer first.
In return the authorities would be silent about the matter,
and would save him and his family from disgrace.

There was absolutely no indication in the diary that Steve
had ever admitted his guilt. In fact, he had refused to
cooperate with the College authorities. Yet it was clear that,
on reflection, though he knew he had *not* cheated, he also
realized that it would be difficult to convince anyone who

mattered that he had just been lucky in the topics he had
chosen to revise. He remembered the subjects Emma had
suggested, but of the three that had turned up he had himself already marked down two for special treatment, and
anyway Emma could not possibly have had any inside
knowledge. He was innocent, he repeated, and one day,
please God, someone would find the diary, and the truth
would become known. In the meantime he had no choice.
He couldn't face the disgrace with which the Master had
threatened him, and he wouldn't make an effective admission of guilt by doing what the Master demanded. There
was only one way out.

Tansey shut the last exercise book as the clock struck
two. It was lucky, he thought, that Steve Sarson would
never know the cost of his vindication.

CHAPTER 20

It was several months before Tom Sarson came to trial. He
had been recognized in a public house by an observant
off-duty police officer in Birmingham, some two weeks after
he had disappeared. Ironically, the day he was arrested was
the day of Jean White's funeral; his brother Bert had been
buried the day before.

Tom Sarson was brought back to Oxford, and formally
charged with the murder of Jean White and the attempted
murder of Sir Philip Pinel. The DPP had decided that
Dr Dawson's death, though probably indirectly related to
the case, would prove to be merely a complicating factor.
Sarson appeared before the magistrates, who remanded
him in custody at the request of the police for further
inquiries.

The trial, when it eventually took place, lasted for four
days, during which time the court was packed, and the

media did their best to satisfy the curiosity of viewers and readers, while respecting the fact that the case could not be fully reported until a verdict had been reached. An attempt to have the charges reduced to manslaughter failed, and Sarson pleaded not guilty to both.

Chief Inspector Tansey was convinced that Tom was guilty, but he wished he could be as certain about the verdicts that would be brought in. Unfortunately, in spite of the time the police had had at their disposal and the efforts they had made, very little further evidence had come to light. No positive proof had been found that Tom had been the driver of the Mercedes that had killed Jean. Tom had been lucky. The car, left with the keys in the ignition in a supermarket parking lot, had been driven away by a couple of teenagers, who had crashed it against the wall of a house, where it had burst into flames. The two boys, who had been lucky to escape with their lives, had been scared when they realized they had stolen a murder vehicle, but there was no question of their involvement in the major crime. Nevertheless, the Mercedes had been reduced to a half-burnt-out hulk, and any forensic or other evidence against Tom that might have existed had been destroyed.

It was on the second day of the trial that Tom Sarson, to the annoyance of the young barrister who was defending him at the taxpayer's expense, suddenly announced that, while he had wished no one to die, he was partly responsible for causing the explosions at St Xavier's College. Tansey was not impressed. He was sure that the admission was not the result of remorse, but due to a certain native cunning on Tom's part.

The motive for killing Jean White that the prosecution attributed to Tom—that he had mistaken her for Rosemary, who might identify him as one of the men who had held her family hostage and initiated the bombing of the Master's Lodgings—was admittedly not strong. And the fact that he was now prepared to admit to the bombing seemed, somewhat illogically, to make the denial of the more serious hit-and-run charge more plausible.

As far as the bomb outrage was concerned, Tansey thought that Tom had reasoned that his best hope was to play on the sympathy of the jury. It could be argued that though the explosion had been relatively large no one had been killed and damage to persons and property had been limited; the prosecution had been prepared to concede that the fatal heart attack suffered by the Senior Tutor could have been coincidental. What was more, the reason for the assault on the Master of St Xavier's and his senior colleagues—an attempt to avenge a younger brother who had committed suicide when falsely accused of cheating in his Final examinations—if not to be condoned, was at least understandable. And Tom could lay the major blame on his brother Bert, who had had the expertise to make the bomb.

It was also advantageous to the defence that Sir Philip Pinel, when he was called as a prosecution witness, did not appear as a sympathetic character. He toyed with the truth, he blustered, and he showed little regard for anyone except himself. He was not given an easy time by the defence, but he was not ill-prepared for the fact that he might well have to face a potentially damaging cross-examination. Tansey had at least seen to that.

The Chief Inspector had pulled no punches when he had insisted on another meeting with the Master. Backed by what he had learnt from Steve Sarson's diary, and supported by Professor Massey-King—who had been horrified by the relevant information that had been passed on to him—Tansey had been blunt.

Sir Philip, he had claimed, presumably out of a desire to avoid a scandal, had bullied Steve Sarson, had threatened his career and his family, and had given him a completely false impression of the situation. Steve had been *suspected* of cheating—no more than that; he had not been convicted

by the Master and the Senior Fellows of St Xavier's from
the evidence of his work, as Pinel had told him. He had
not admitted his guilt, as Pinel later maintained. On the
contrary, even after he had decided to kill himself, he
had sworn that he had not cheated. The law made
no mention of death-bed denials rather than death-bed
confessions, but the last entries in Steve's diary were the
nearest approach to such a denial as the jury were likely
to come across.

In his interview with Tansey, Pinel had blustered. He
had pointed out that it was Sarson's written words against
his personal testimony but, reminded that on the witness
stand he would be under oath, he had tempered his attitude. And what Professor Massey-King said to him, or what
influence he brought to bear Tansey was never to know,
but the Chief Inspector was delighted to read in the *Oxford
Mail* some time after the trial that Sir Philip Pinel was
resigning his post as Master of St Xavier's at the end of the
Trinity Term to become the head of a minor university in
Mid-West America.

But if Pinel's evidence and personality raised some sympathy for Steve's brother Tom among the jury, Greg White
and Rosemary cancelled it out. They were excellent witnesses, clear, composed, and they showed no sign of vindictiveness in spite of what they had suffered. Tansey was
delighted with the impression they made—especially
Rosemary.

'Wasn't she wonderful, Chief Inspector?' Tony Pulent
said.

'Absolutely splendid,' Tansey agreed.

He had met the Whites and their small party—Tony
Pulent and his mother and Ailsa Mackay with the Bursar,
Peter Lacque, who had attended the trial each day—as
they all left the court by a side door to avoid the media. He
was pleased to see that the Whites had plenty of support.

'How do you think it's going, Chief Inspector? Or is that

not a fair question?' Greg White asked; he was looking drawn but not unhappy.

'It's difficult to tell,' Tansey said. 'One never knows with a jury. Let's hope this is a sensible lot.'

'How much longer do you think the trial will last?'

'With any luck it should be all over tomorrow.'

Tansey was proved right. The judge's summing-up was damaging, and the jury were out for only three hours. Then, to the Chief Inspector's relief, they brought in a unanimous verdict of guilty on both counts. The next day Tom Sarson was sentenced to life imprisonment for the murder and fifteen years for the bombing, the sentences to run concurrently. An appeal was ultimately denied.

However, the long shadow cast by Steve Sarson's death was not altogether bleak and sombre. Some three months after the conclusion of the trial Chief Inspector Tansey went into an antique shop in Charlbury to buy his wife a birthday present. To his surprise he was met by Emma Watson. Yes, she explained, she had decided to go into business for herself, and had taken on Meg Sarson as an assistant. Meg lived above the shop with her two children and the old man. 'I was fed up with teaching,' Emma said. 'I've always been interested in antiques and Meg's got some knowledge of the second-hand furniture trade. And we're doing well.' She hesitated, then added, 'Besides, I felt I owed Steve something.'

'Good for you,' said Tansey.

Through his growing friendship with Greg and Rosemary, Dick Tansey maintained some contact with St Xavier's. He was pleased to be told later in the year that Peter Lacque was to marry Ailsa Mackay.

As far as the Whites themselves were concerned, though they both mourned Jean, and especially the manner of her death, neither—not even the seventeen-year-old Rosemary appeared to have suffered any lasting ill-effects from their traumatic experiences; Tony Pulent's continuing understanding and support were a great help. Greg's life returned gradually to normal, as he found that St Xavier's, having settled down under a newly-elected Master, was a much happier place where he could continue to enjoy his work; in the following year he completed his *magnum opus* on Milton.

'All in all, a satisfactory case,' concluded Tansey, and the Chief Constable concurred.